BURNING TO DIE!

"I have just set fire to the gambling hall," I told them, "and the quicker you answer some questions the sooner you can go put it out."

Keno Mora's chair crashed to the floor, Fancy Pace goggled at me with eyes as pretty as a woman's, and Calico's hand snaked toward his shotgun . . . then stopped when he saw a .45 looking at him.

"You're lying!" Mora rasped. He was in a crouch, his right hand an inch from the open middle button of his coat.

"You can look out that window," I said. He stepped carefully past me, opened a shutter and his face went pale.

"It's true!" he cried. And as though forgetting everything else, he ducked and ran, angling past me toward the door. I kicked him in the belly and he fell backward, rolling into a ball on the floor. The interval gave Calico time to grab his shotgun and he lurched upright bringing it around.

Somebody was going to die . . .

GREAT WESTERNS
by Dan Parkinson

THE SLANTED COLT   (1413, $2.25)

A tall, mysterious stranger named Kichener gave young Benjamin Franklin Blake a gift. It was a gun, a colt pistol, that had belonged to Ben's father. And when a cold-blooded killer vowed to put Ben six feet under, it was a sure thing that Ben would have to learn to use that gun—or die!

GUNPOWDER GLORY   (1448, $2.50)

Jeremy Burke, breaking a deathbed promise to his pa, killed the lowdown Sutton boy who was the cause of his pa's death. But when the bullets started flying, he found there was more at stake than his own life as innocent people were caught in the crossfire of *Gunpowder Glory*.

BLOOD ARROW   (1549, $2.50)

Randall Kerry returned to his camp to find his companion slaughtered and scalped. With a war cry as wild as the savages', the young scout raced forward with his pistol held high to meet them in battle.

BROTHER WOLF   (1728, $2.95)

Only two men could help Lattimer run down the sheriff's killers—a stranger named Stillwell and an Apache who was as deadly with a Colt as he was with a knife. One of them would see justice done—from the muzzle of a six-gun.

CALAMITY TRAIL   (1663, $2.95)

Charles Henry Clayton fled to the west to make his fortune, get married and settle down to a peaceful life. But the situation demanded that he strap on a six-gun and ride toward a showdown of gunpowder and blood that would send him galloping off to either death or glory on the . . . *Calamity Trail*.

Available wherever paperbacks are sold, or order direct from the Publisher. Send cover price plus 50¢ per copy for mailing and handling to Zebra Books, Dept. 1728, 475 Park Avenue South, New York, N.Y. 10016. DO NOT SEND CASH.

BROTHER WOLF

BY DAN PARKINSON

ZEBRA BOOKS
KENSINGTON PUBLISHING CORP.

ZEBRA BOOKS

are published by

Kensington Publishing Corp.
475 Park Avenue South
New York, NY 10016

First printing: December 1985

Printed in the United States of America

For Cleo and Jim,
and for Pearl and
the memory of Harry.
For parents.

1

In those dark hours before winter dawn sometimes the wind will lay for a minute or two, and when it does the sudden silence of the frozen prairie seems less chill, a fool's promise of warming.

Sam Dance knew better. In darkness below the rim he lifted tired eyes skyward, then hunched deeper into the feeble protection of his sheepskin coat. The sky was full of stars, more than a man could count. They blazed fierce and cold in the black of morning. There was no trace of cloud anywhere, not even mist on the horizons. It would get colder, not warmer.

His temples throbbed with the cold. His feet were numb and his breath froze in his mustache.

To his right and slightly above Ted Mason's voice shook with chill. "I don't think anybody's comin', Sam. This is a fool's errand if you ask me."

Nobody had asked Ted Mason, but Dance ignored the complaint. He was just as miserable as the rest of them, huddled out here half the night under the rim of Cross Canyon.

In his pocket Sam Dance carried a brass star. He

hadn't worn it since the election, probably had no right to wear it. Sim Guthrie had contested the election vote and the county had upheld him. It was still undecided, but Sam Dance was resigned to losing. Today, tomorrow at the latest, the district court would review the county's canvass and they probably would swear Sim Guthrie in as sheriff of Seward County.

It would not be easy to step down. One way and another, one place and another, Sam Dance had been a lawman for half of his fifty years. There had been times in those years—which looking back now seemed so brief—when the people who elected him or hired him knew just as he knew that there was more to wearing a star than getting votes. But times changed. The gray in a man's hair drew a lot more notice day to day than the things he had learned in earning it.

Sim Guthrie might make a good sheriff. He could learn, given time, and if he was lucky it might be a long time before he had to meet the test. Maybe he never would face that sort of test. Times changed.

Still, when trouble came, it was Sam Dance the judge had sent for. The judge would rule for Guthrie and not think twice about it, but when it was the judge's life that was threatened, he wanted a man who had tasted the water.

It was no surprise that someone had threatened to kill Judge Will Tomlin. About twelve miles west of where Dance now huddled below a canyon rim, with eight men who were his posse, was the Stevens County line. And beyond that line there were a lot of people with reason to hate Tomlin. For that matter, there were some in Seward County who might feel the same. And a few miles south in the Neutral Strip, that no-man's-land where no law held except the law of the gun, were men willing to come into Kansas to commit murder for the price of a meal or a bottle.

Dance had some questions of his own about this threat that Tomlin had received. There was much that was odd about it. But those were questions for later. Right now it was his job to be here, shivering under the little cliff that topped Cross Canyon. If someone intended to kill the judge here this morning, that someone would find a badge here, not a gavel.

Dance turned a little to look south across the Cimarron Valley, a black distance stretching away a mile or more to where the stars began. Squinting, he could make out one star below that horizon. That would be a lamp in the window of the judge's house. Or maybe—the light seemed to waver—maybe it was the judge himself, lighting his way across his yard with a coal oil lantern.

In the darkness just below, young Henry Lattimer was watching the same speck of light. "I know what he'll likely do," he said.

"Who?" Dance knew what the young man was thinking, but it would be interesting to hear it. Lattimer was just a pup, but he had grit and he had a mind that could add things up and find answers.

"The judge. That's him out there swinging that lamp. There'll be light pretty soon and he'll want to be where he can see. So he's on his way out to his windmill. He'll climb up there and watch us through a telescope."

"He won't see anything but a half-froze posse

sittin' in a canyon," Ted Mason rasped. "I don't think there's any sense to all this, Sam. Nobody's comin'."

"You're supposed to be watching, Ted. When's the last time you stuck your head over that rim to see if anybody's out there?"

"Few minutes ago. I'll look again in a little bit. That wind is cold and it's too dark to see, anyway."

The light across the valley had stopped its swaying. The judge was at his windmill, had set the lantern down and was getting ready to climb the short tower. Maybe he was already climbing. Henry was right about what the man would do. Tomlin was a complex man, in many ways an unpredictable man, but he would not be one to miss a chance to witness his own murder. "If that's what this is all about to begin with," Dance muttered.

"Did you say something, Mr. Dance?" Henry Lattimer shifted to look up at him. Dance noticed he could make out the young man's face now, a pale place in the darkness. Dim light had touched the cold sky. "Just my teeth chattering," he said.

From the left, a short distance away, Sim Guthrie called in a hushed voice, "What's that down there?"

"Where?" someone responded and there were whispers of clothing on cold stone. Gravel chittered as men shifted their positions under the rim to look behind them, into the valley.

"Down there, below us," Guthrie hissed over the sigh of wind, gusting again after the minutes of calm. "I thought I saw something move."

Dance squinted. His head ached from the cold and his eyes felt dry and raw. "How about it, Henry?

10

Your eyes are better than mine. See anything?"

"No, I don't think so, Mr. Dance. Might have been an antelope. I don't see anything now."

"There isn't anybody out here but us and we're a bunch of blame fools to be here," Mason grumbled.

"That might be the case, Ted." Dance held his irritation in check. "But as long as we're here why don't you take a look over the rim now and again, just to see if anybody is on the road."

"Well, I'll look," Mason conceded. Dance could vaguely see his movement as he raised his head above the canyon rim. "Lord, that wind cuts like knives. I don't see any . . ." Mason paused, then suddenly dropped down behind the rim as a gunshot ripped the frozen dawn. Flakes of sandstone showered over them as a bullet ricocheted from rock ledge. "My God," Mason almost screamed it, "they're up there, almost right on us!"

"Who? How many?"

"I don't know. I couldn't see. But there's a lot of men. That shot . . . they shot at me! One of them shot at me!" As he spoke, Mason was scrambling down the canyon slope, making for lower ground.

Dance was already in motion. With hands like ice he grabbed the half-cocked Winchester beside him, rolled and dug his heels into the steep bank. In an instant he was at the top and hesitated as another shot whistled over his head, then he peered over the flat rim, bringing his rifle up.

Some of the men on the road were on horseback. Others were on foot now, and they milled toward the canyon rim in a cluster of confused, vague motion, barely fifty yards away. Dance leveled a shot over the heads of the nearest group, worked the lever and fired again. He felt Henry Lattimer pushing up beside him. Someone else fired from the rim, to his right, and the mob halted, seeming confused. White flares erupted with the crash of two more shots from the road and there was answering fire from the men around him. Then Dance called, "Hold your fire!"

In the silence he raised his head a bit higher, trying to see the men out there. There wasn't enough light. He ducked back below the rim, then raised until just his eyes cleared the edge. "You men! Who are you? What's your business here?"

From the road came an answering shout, "You say who you are, then!" The mob on the road was spreading, men crouching, running both ways along the track. Dance caught his breath. There must have been twenty of them, maybe more. He could see their silhouettes, the gleam of weapons.

A voice that might have been the same voice shouted, "Come up where we can see you! We don't know who you are!"

Dance lowered himself and turned, working another shell into his Winchester. Across the valley Judge Tomlin's windmill was silhouetted now, tiny and distant. He imagined he could see the judge high in its rigging. He lowered his gaze as his eye caught movement in the valley, far out in the bottom. In the gloom he could not be sure, but there seemed to be a horseman down there, coming toward him. He blinked, wiped his cold sleeve over his eyes and squinted again. Yes, a man on a horse, running. Still distant. Angling up from the east, across dry river bottom toward the canyon. Vague in the darkness.

"Henry, can you make out who that is?"

Henry turned and stared, then shook his head. "I can't tell, Mr. Dance. Maybe Ted?"

"No, he went the other way. And where would he get a horse out here?"

The galloping figure came closer. "He isn't going to try to jump that bank down there, is he?" Henry hissed, and Dance tensed as the figure approached the river's high bank without slowing. That bank was eight feet high and almost vertical. The rider charged it, partially disappeared under it and then appeared at its top, head and shoulders of a struggling mount, its rider tight along its neck. It scrabbled at the bank for a moment, then disappeared. "He fell," Henry said. But then they could see him again, circling in the bottom below the bank, one arm waving. "He's trying to tell us something."

No sound came to them. The wind whistled and the rider's words were blown away. For a moment he sat down there, then bent low on his mount and spurred up-valley, to the west. He disappeared beyond a shoulder.

Another gunshot sounded above the rim and one of the posse answered it. Dance barked, "Hold your fire!" and turned. Henry Lattimer hoisted himself on the steep slope.

"Mr. Dance, they're coming!"

There was no more time. Sam Dance raised himself to the rim and called, "Stand your ground out there! I'm coming out to talk!" The dawn light was strengthening. He could make out shapes and bulks, shadows under hatbrims. He slid the brass star from his pocket, pinned it to the lapel of his coat. "Just stand steady now!"

Each word was a puff of frost in the lee of the rim, shredded by wind above it. He felt as if his jaws were frozen. "One hell of a way to finish being sheriff," he muttered. "Two days from now Sim could have had the honor all to himself."

Henry Lattimer's glance said he had heard the words, but he made no comment.

Dance stood, braced his hands atop the rim and hauled himself up to stand facing the mob on the road. They were all afoot now, some of them holding their horses over beyond the track. The rest were spread in a wide arc, the flanks fifty yards from him on either side, the nearest men in its center twenty yards away. Guns trained on him and breath-frost obscured their shadowed faces.

"Who are you?" one of them demanded.

"Sam Dance. I'm sheriff of Seward County. I want you men to . . . uh!" The screaming pain that blossomed in his right side bent him over, made everything go red before his eyes. The gunshot was a vague echo of the shock that exploded in his guts. He tried to speak, tried to straighten, dimly saw his Winchester lying on the ground beside his right foot. He raised his head, still trying to see the faces before him. He staggered. It was colder. The wind howled and it was cold and his mind felt soggy and dim. Something punched him in the ribs, lower left, and exploded inside him. He tried to breathe and choked on blood rising in his throat. He stepped back, felt his legs go dead and was aware of falling backward, slowly, infinitely falling as the dawn sky of morning rolled into view before dimming eyes. The whole sky went by, leisurely, so that he could see it one last time. And at the end of it was an upside-down silhouette of the far side of the Cimarron valley with a tiny windmill hanging there in the distance.

Henry Lattimer saw the sheriff fall, saw him slide head-down thirty feet down the slope. He saw him lying there then, spreadeagled and still, with the dark blood on him. Then Henry raised his .44 Winchester and opened up on the nearest clot of men, levering and firing as fast as his cold hands would move, twelve shots rolling like thunder echoing down the valley. Around him, up and down the canyon wall, others fired, and the mob of men on the road scattered. They ran, ducked, flopped to return fire. Guthrie was shooting, and Brister and Peterson and others, but they were too few. The fire slowed, and the men above regrouped and advanced, sweeping the rim with gunfire.

"Run!" someone shouted. "We can't stop them!"

Henry ducked down to reload, and heard men scrambling on the slope. All around him possemen broke from cover, stumbling and running, dropping guns and shedding heavy coats in their panic to get away. Eight men could not stand before twenty. Seven did not want to try.

A shot in the rim kicked rubble down on Henry Lattimer. He jerked back, dropping his .44. It skidded downhill and he followed it, sliding, trying to catch it. Just as he grasped it his knee hit a rock and he pitched forward, fell again and rolled over a low wash-bluff. He lay stunned and saw movement above him. A man stood on the lip in the strengthening dawn, just above where Henry had been a moment

15

before, and looked down thoughtfully at the body of Sam Dance. He stood a moment, just looking, then he drew a revolver from a belt holster, aimed carefully at the fallen sheriff and fired one shot. A moment more he stood there, then he holstered his gun, turned and walked out of Henry's sight.

Shaking his head to clear his vision, Henry got to his feet and climbed, using his free hand to grasp at rock and shrub, pulling him upward. He didn't stop at the rim, but climbed over it and stood, panting, staring around at the shadowed faces of men he did not know.

"Put it down!" one of them demanded. He stooped to lay his rifle on the ground.

"Who are you?" another asked.

"Henry Lattimer. You fellows have already killed one man today for sure. Is that enough?" He squared his shoulders and glared at them.

One of them, a husky man with dark whiskers, chuckled. "Go on home, Henry Lattimer. Hurry, and maybe you can catch up with all them other fighting men."

"Move, boy, move!" another snapped. Henry could not see his face, but he knew he was not laughing.

Stunned, still reeling from the shock of his fall, Henry walked through their line toward the road and heard laughter behind him. "Oh, By," someone said, "tell Henry to turn to the left and avoid the other wing of the party."

Dazed and stumbling, his head and knee throbbing, Henry did as he was told. He reached the road and looked back. They were watching him. He turned left and walked, expecting at any second to feel the first bullet in his back, wondering vaguely how it might feel . . . to be punctured and blown up inside and to die. Sam Dance had known in his last instant. He had known how it felt to be shot down. Tears froze on the young man's face as he stumbled on into the January wind. Tears of outrage became tears of grief, and the grief became an anger. Sam Dance had known. Someone had shown him.

A tumbleweed sailing on the wind hit him in the face and knocked his hat askew. He stopped and looked around. Bright morning lay around him, clear and cold and rustling to the sighing of the wind.

He had come more than half a mile. The road now angled downward from the rolling prairie, curving away into the Cimarron valley. East where the sun would rise, the way he had come, was only the wagon road where it topped out on the plain. He was beyond sight of the canyon where Sam Dance lay dead, beyond sight of the road there and those men.

Henry Lattimer wiped his face on his sleeves, pushed the hair out of his eyes and replaced his hat. Then he turned back. Where the road topped the valley rim open prairie spread before him, rolling upward to the north, spreading in swales and dips to the east. As far as he could see, the wagon road and the world around it were empty. A half mile away was the bend where the road passed the head of Cross Canyon.

With sunrise in his face and the chill wind quartering behind him, Henry Lattimer began to run.

2

I was in Seward County that Monday morning when the sheriff was killed. I had private business to attend to over by Fargo Springs, then I had to turn around and ride down to the new town of Liberal. Had I gone west from Fargo Springs to cross the river on the Springfield road, I probably would have met the men coming out from Springfield to bring in the body. But instead I followed the river down to Arkalon to use the wire, so I missed all that. Then from Liberal I went over into the Neutral Strip and it was a few days before I got back into Kansas.

But I heard about it. When a sheriff is shot down the talk goes around.

The sheriff's posse, they said, had been attacked by an armed mob two miles south of Springfield and they probably would have heard the gunfire in town except the wind was out of the northwest the way it generally is in January.

The posse was outnumbered and after some shooting they lit out, most of them. They scattered, but six of them made it to town a little after sunup and rounded up a few dozen men to go back out there. The word was at first that there were two men dead at Cross Canyon, the second being the new sheriff, Sim Guthrie. But they found Guthrie later that morning, lying up in a patch of soapweed. He had a twisted ankle.

Sam Dance, though, was dead. He had been shot twice while he stood on the canyon rim. Then after he fell and was lying on his back, head down and thirty feet below the rim, someone came up and shot him again. That last shot, because of the angle at which it was fired, took him in the right leg and went all the way through his body.

When the men from Springfield got to Cross Canyon they found a young deputy named Henry Lattimer still out there, waiting for them, standing over Sam Dance's body. He gave them a clear layout of what had happened. Then they wrapped the sheriff in a quilt and took him into town to the undertaker's shed. They found some guns and gear lying around, things dropped by possemen when they retreated, so they knew the murderers hadn't stayed around to clean up. That bunch had headed east along the river.

They said the trouble came when the sheriff went out to head off someone who had threatened to kill the local judge. Some said the murderers came over from Stevens County, and that made sense because that judge had made some bad enemies over there. First they had a county seat war, then there was an attempt to disenfranchise the county, and that judge got pretty thoroughly mixed up in the politics of it both times. The story was, that was why he was transferred over to Seward County. Nobody knew for sure.

At any rate it wasn't the judge that was killed, it was the sheriff, Sam Dance, who wouldn't have been sheriff any more if it had happened a day or so later because that same judge turned around and ruled that Sim Guthrie had won the election.

Of course there were some, as always, who laid the blame squarely on men from the Neutral Strip. That made a good case, too, because there were plenty of men down there who wouldn't shy from doing most anything.

The young deputy had some descriptions, but they were vague. About the only piece of hard evidence he could offer was that one of the murderers had called another one "By." So there were a lot of people searching for somebody who might go by that name.

And that was how I got tied into it. My name is Byron Stillwell and one of the things I have been called is "By."

The day of the shooting, as I said, I had some business in Seward County, and then I headed off down into the Neutral Strip to find Lloyd Harper and help him haul a load of bones up to railhead. Lloyd had his own wagon and mules and had made good money as a teamster while the boom was on. In those days new people had been moving into western Kansas by the hundreds and every man of them building a soddy so far from anyplace that hauling a supply route was good business.

But the boom had tailed off and towns had sprung up, so Lloyd was getting by hauling whatever he could. One of those was buffalo bones. The prairies were full of them and there was a market up east.

I had met Lloyd down on Beaver Creek and spent some time helping him load and haul bones. I worked on shares and it gave me a chance to move around and get to talk to people that I wouldn't have found otherwise. If you want casual conversation in No Man's Land you need a harmless reason for being there. Picking up old buffalo bones is pretty harmless.

When I got back to the territory and found Lloyd Harper he had been away from civilization about as long as he could stand and there wasn't anything going to keep him from stopping off at Beer City before we made the haul across the line.

Beer City never was much to look at, just sheds and some tents right at the edge of the territory, but the whole state of Kansas didn't have as much of certain kinds of attractions as Beer City could offer. Lloyd needed two days there to go on a tear and do it right.

While he was doing that I visited around with some of the soberer citizens. That was where I heard a lot about what had been going on over in Seward County. And naturally by the time I heard they were looking for someone named By, there were already a bunch who knew that was my name.

Beer City is strategically located. If you leave town and walk ten paces north, you are in Kansas. And that was about how far we drove that Thursday before a posse of citizens came up on both sides and arrested us for murder.

They arrested me because my name was By and I carried a handgun and looked like the kind of desperate individual they had decided they were after. They arrested Lloyd because he was with me and in no condition, sleeping it off in his bone wagon, to protest.

The "posse" wasn't really a posse. Nobody had anointed them to come and get us. Rather it was just one of those citizen committees that will crop up in places where there is a general desire to become civilized and the people need evidence of progress in that direction.

The three giving the orders were solid citizens. Frank Murdoch I knew by sight, though he didn't know me. He was one of the men putting together the new town of Liberal, where the railroad was heading, and making it grow. He was a sober, well-dressed man of about forty, a shrewd and thoughtful individual who saw his fortune ahead of him wrapped in the business of a village that would become a town of means if he could keep it directed that way. The others were also Liberal businessmen but I didn't recall their names. Then there were four cowboys, two with some age on them and two still just buttons, and several nondescript types that might have come down from Liberal or just as well might have come out from Beer City. One of these was a broad, beefy man of about thirty with bright red hair and a face like a sulking, aging child. I had seen him at Beer City and I was fairly certain he was the one who had spread the word that somebody named By was around. His name was Bassett and they called him Penny. I had good reason to notice him. When they hauled me up and had some guns pointed at me Frank Murdoch told me we were being arrested as suspects in a murder and told me to climb down from the wagon.

I wasn't inclined to argue. I tied off the reins and set the brake, then I stepped down onto the hub and was about to step to the ground when Penny heeled his horse alongside me and striped me from shoulder to midsection with a fancy quirt, so hard it drove the breath from me and made my eyes tear. "You heard the man!" he ordered. "Move!" Then while I was still gritting my teeth from the pain of it he grabbed my gun out of its holster and stuffed it behind his belt.

"There was no call for that," Murdoch snapped at him, and the two old cowboys glanced at each other and shook their heads.

"This one back here is drunk," someone said. "Lord, he smells like sheep dip."

I got my eyes cleared, wiping them with my coat sleeve. My right shoulder had that hot, numb feeling that said I'd have a purple bruise there before long. The two younger pokes had climbed into the wagon and were examining Lloyd Harper.

"That's not sheep dip. That's 'Parson' Jolly's best rot-gut. I ain't found a gun on him. Just a clasp knife."

"He doesn't have a handgun," I told them. "But his rifle is in the back, there. Wrapped in a blanket."

They looked at me, then they rolled Lloyd over and covered him up again. When they had pulled the quilts off him he had begun struggling and moaning. Now he started to snore again. One of them found the rifle and handed it out to another man. "Obliged," he told me.

Frank Murdoch had walked his horse around to

23

where he could get a better look at me. He turned to Penny Bassett. "Is this the one called 'By'?"

"That's him." Penny glared at me. "He calls himself that. I guess I didn't need you fellas after all. I could have took him myself. He ain't so much."

I worked my arm a little, easing the throb in my shoulder blade where he had caught me with that leaded quirt. It was sore.

Frank Murdoch pulled his coat collar tighter at his throat. The day was bright and clear, but the north wind had a bite to it. He looked at me curiously. "This man says you are one of those who killed Sheriff Dance Monday morning," he said.

I glanced at Penny, then back to Murdoch. "This man looks to me like he'd lie about what day it is," I told him. "Why would you believe him, Mr. Murdoch?"

Penny grunted an oath and lifted his quirt but Murdoch edged his mount between us. "You know me?"

"I know who you are, and I know you're a smart enough man not to take the word of an idiot like this without proof."

"He says your name is By. That was the name of one of the men in the mob."

"How does he know?" I looked at Penny again and this time held his gaze until his face reddened and he dropped his eyes. "Was he there?"

"There is a witness," Murdoch said.

"I've been called By. My name is Byron Stillwell. The man in the wagon back there is Lloyd Harper. We're coming up to railhead to sell these bones."

"Is this your rig, Mr. Stillwell?"

"It's his. I'm just helping him for shares."

"Were you in Seward County on Monday?"

"Yes, I was. As a matter of fact I was over around Fargo Springs Monday morning, and I used the telegraph at Arkalon later that same morning, and I was in Liberal that afternoon and had a meal at your restaurant there. I was in Seward County the whole day."

"You see?" Penny Bassett pointed at me. "He admits he was there."

"I don't admit a thing," I told Murdoch. "You asked me where I was Monday and I told you. Now can we get on about our business?"

"Fargo Springs ain't but a mile or two from Cross Canyon," one of the punchers pointed out. "I guess he could have been there."

Frank Murdoch looked puzzled. Nothing I had told him was any kind of alibi. It added up that I could very well have been at Cross Canyon when the sheriff was killed. But still I didn't act like a man who had anything to hide. He chewed on his lip and frowned, trying to see through me. "Did you know Sheriff Dance?"

"I never met him," I said.

"Then how about Will Tomlin?"

"The judge? I know who he is, but I've never met him, either. Look, Mr. Murdoch, I've heard about this whole thing, and I was in Seward County when it happened and I don't know of anything I can tell you that would prove I'm innocent, so I guess you have to take me to jail. And I don't fault you or the rest of these men for it. I'd do the same thing. You ought to let Lloyd off someplace, though. He was down in the

25

strip all the time, and there are plenty who can vouch for that."

"I say take 'em both," Penny cut in. "They're together. That's enough to make evidence."

Murdoch glanced at the red-haired man as though he wished he would go away. The more I talked, the less he liked what he was doing.

"One favor I would ask," I said. "That handgun Penny has stuck in his belt is mine and it cost me thirty dollars. When all this is settled I'll want it back. I'd appreciate it if one of you others would look after it." I looked straight at Penny then. "I don't want it stolen."

"I'll be damned!" Penny turned bright red and started to swing down from his horse.

Murdoch reined his mount around, heading him off. "Mr. Bassett! That will be enough! Hand Mr. Stillwell's gun to me, please."

The two other townsmen were at his flanks, rifles in their hands, and all four of the cowpunchers were watching him with hands to their guns. If Murdoch needed any help, he would have it.

Penny had it sized up, too. He looked from one to another, then drew my pistol and handed it across to Murdoch, his movements curt and angry. "I guess you'd just as soon take him in without my help, too. I'm the one that found him, but I guess I sure as hell ain't going to get the credit for it, am I?"

Murdoch looked pained. "Mr. Bassett, there is no question of credit here. If you don't care to go along with us," his glance around included the other stragglers in this, "then I'm sure the seven of us can manage things."

Instead of calming, Penny flared again. "Well by God if that's the way you want it, Mr. Murdoch, then that's the way it will be!" He spurred his horse viciously, wheeling around, then hauled on the reins and turned back to glare at me. "They'll probably hang you. But if they don't I'll be waiting. You have an account to settle with me."

"I'll look forward to that," I told him.

With another glare, Penny Bassett turned and spurred away, eastward.

"I believe I would have held my tongue if I were you," one of the younger townsmen told me. "That man is a ruffian."

"He had no call to hit me," I said.

Murdoch pulled a watch from his coat pocket and opened it. "Four-thirty. Joe, what time did Vince Cole leave for Arkalon this morning?"

The younger citizen who had advised me shrugged. "I don't know. It was early when I saw him, though. He was hitching his team."

"Well, he should be back soon. Cass, why don't you and Pearly ride on ahead and tell Vince we are bringing these fellows in. The five of us can manage from here."

The two young cowboys swung into their saddles. Pearly hesitated, gave me a searching look as though he should know me from somewhere, then they nodded at Murdoch and headed north at a lope.

Murdoch had me climb back onto the wagon, and he and the remaining four took up positions around me. The sun was quartering down in the west and the air was turning colder. Gusts of biting wind searched out loose tumbleweeds here and there and sent them sailing and bounding toward the Neutral Strip. As we moved out the last of the stragglers turned back toward Beer City and it seemed to me that my escorts relaxed somewhat when they saw them leave. They glanced back over their shoulders as we rolled north, and their eyes were as bleak as the January plains on which we moved.

Three miles ahead I could see the cluster of buildings that was Liberal.

Frank Murdoch edged his horse close to the wagon. "Mr. Stillwell, I'm glad you understand we are only doing what we must. I am inclined to believe your innocence, but the law will have to decide, of course."

"Of course." My shoulder had progressed past numbness, and was aching as though I had been kicked. "What do you know about that man Penny?"

He hunched his heavy coat up higher on his shoulders. "Not very much. He comes to town occasionally, and he's one that the merchants keep an eye on when he's around. I think he works for Adolph Cort, but I'm not sure. He came in earlier today and told some of us that two of the killers were in Beer City, and asked if there was a reward. Vince Cole—he's the deputy in Liberal—was gone, so we came out to see what was going on."

"Well?"

"Well, what?" he squinted at me.

"Is there a reward?"

"Not that I know of. Listen, I really hope you didn't have anything to do with that shooting. It's going to go pretty hard on anyone who did. Sam Dance was a respected man."

"Yes," I told him. "I know he was."

28

As we approached the town three men rode out to meet us. Cass and Pearly had found Vince Cole. Before they reached us Frank Murdoch reined over to the wagon again. "It isn't any of my business, but if there is anyone you want notified . . . I mean that you have been arrested . . . any family or anyone?"

"Thanks," I told him. "But no, there isn't anybody who needs to know."

"You said you stopped in Arkalon Monday to send a telegraph message," he prompted.

"Yes. To my mother. But she's had enough bad news for a while. Thanks all the same."

3

Whatever ideas I grew up with about what makes a woman beautiful, I guess I based them on my mother. Mattie Stillwell was always considered a rare beauty. And though the beauty I saw in her as I was growing up was not what the men saw who celebrated her, toasted her health, and sometimes courted her, I knew after a fashion that they saw her so and it added to the Mattie Stillwell I knew. Small and striking with her gleaming dark hair and large dark eyes, she could light up a room with her smile or dominate a hall just by her presence.

On stage, where most people knew her, she was a radiance and her songs were pure silk struck through with bubbles of warm laughter and sparkles of song-bird brilliance. But I heard her songs more and I knew them differently. I knew her lullabies that were part of a bright, special world we shared, and the little tunes she would hum, that were somehow stronger in their optimism than all the dark realities of life as a woman alone and tending a growing son.

Even as the years passed and streaks of gray became pronounced in her dark hair, she remained a beautiful woman . . . even more so as time reinforced the strength that was part of her beauty.

I knew from the time it mattered that I had no proper father, and that the name I bore was her name only. And I never found shame in that, because she never did. Shame is a form of regret. The only regret I ever felt from my mother was that the fine, gentle man who had loved her could not be with us. Never for a moment did she regret her time with him, nor the son she bore after he was gone.

Later on, when I had my growth—or most of it—I had the occasion once to sweep the floor with a large, loud man who had used the word "bastard" unkindly. I doubt if he ever used it again. But I did that because he was talking about her, not because he was talking about me. She never taught me shame.

Somehow, all those years when I was getting my growth, when there were just the two of us, traveling from one place to another, me being schooled while she performed concerts in bright halls, she made it seem as though there were three. I had never seen the man who was my father. But through her, all those years, it seemed he was always there with us. I knew that as beautiful as she was, he must have been just that handsome. And as gentle as she was, he must have been just that gentle, and as strong as she was he must have been ten times that strong. She spoke of him often, always as though he was nearby and thinking of us, and I always thought of him that way.

But she would never tell me his name. "You have reason enough to be proud, Byron," she would say.

"You don't need a name to add to it. He gave you life and I know he gives you his love. It's better to leave it at that."

There were people who whispered sometimes about her being part Indian, as though that were something shameful. But she was proud of her Creek grandmother, as much so as of the one who was Welsh and the grandfathers who had both been Scotsmen.

So the whispers meant nothing, and we traveled from place to place, and she smiled privately at the glamor and glitter and the adoring crowds that gathered for her. "It will pass soon enough," she told me, winking as though at a huge joke. "Few enough people have something to give, and those who can't give must receive. There would be no celebrities if people didn't crave another image of themselves that they can think is better than they have. Out there on those concert stages, Mattie Stillwell is a reflection in a magic mirror. What they are looking at isn't me. It's an image they have of themselves. I sing so they can pretend and that makes them happy. It will pass soon enough."

And pass it did. But she had been prudent through those years and we were provided for.

The image she gave me was an image of my father. I could imagine no finer thing than to grow up to be just like him.

Sitting in a jail cell in Springfield, Kansas, waiting to be tried for murder, was not like that image. The Springfield jail was a three-cager. Two of them were occupied on this cold morning, one by me and the other by a hardcase named Ira Fox. The end one was empty. I had got his name from the deputy jailer

32

when he locked me in. I hadn't gotten anything from Ira Fox himself.

I tried a couple of times to make conversation, but he wasn't having any. He just glared at me, twitched his mustache and went back to his own thoughts. I did notice, though, that when I got up now and then to pace the little cell, rolling my shoulder and working my right arm to ease the stiffness out of it, he would watch me covertly. It seemed to bother him that I was there.

It was nearly noon when I heard the street door open, followed by a draft of icy air down the hall and through the bar cages. There were voices out in the sheriff's office. Then the deputy jailer, a large and lumpy individual named Everett, came into the cell block followed by an even larger man who had to duck to pass the doorframe. Will Tomlin, district judge in Seward County, was at least three inches taller than either Everett or me, and would have outweighed either of us—Everett by a little or me by half. He wore a dark suit of conservative tailoring and carried a derby hat in his hand. Dark hair was slicked back around the gleaming baldness of his dome. His dark mustache was carefully waxed and curled at the ends. His face was the kind you expect to see a smile on . . . and are surprised when the eyes tell you that you never will.

He shouldered past Everett and came to stand in front of my cage, studying me in the gray light of the barred window. "Stand up," he said.

I stood.

"Your name is By," he said. It wasn't a question, so I didn't answer. "The officer who delivered you

33

here from Liberal reported that you were cooperative during your arrest and transportation to Springfield. He advises me that you made no effort to escape, even when you had the opportunity."

I grinned at him and shrugged. "You mean when all three of them decided to water their horses at the river at the same time, and all turned their backs on me? Why, your honor, I never even thought about it, I just watered my horse, too."

"A guilty man might have made a break for it."

"Not if he'd had a look at that rifle your man Sturdevant carries alongside his saddle. I've only seen one Alexander Henry rifle before. Sturdevant must be hell on jack rabbits and guilty parties."

"Sturdevant is an officer of the court," he said sternly, his eyes narrowing. "Levity hardly befits a man in your situation, Mr. Stillwell. You have been accused of murdering Sheriff Dance. You will be brought to trial for that unless you can produce evidence that exonerates you. Can you do that?"

"I don't know what it would be," I told him honestly.

"Witnesses can place you in the vicinity of the crime," he said. "Later that same morning you were seen near Fargo Springs, and after that you were at Arkalon."

"Yes," I admitted. "I was at those places, and later I was at Liberal, and I guess several people saw me at places in between."

"You are called By," he went on, and now I looked at him closely. He seemed to be insisting on something, but he wasn't making it clear just what. "A person by that name was involved in the murder."

"So I heard," I said. "I guess it isn't a real common nickname, either, is it?"

He had a way of tilting his head and squinting the nearest eye, looking past his nose with the other one. He did that again. "Mr. Stillwell, are you guilty or innocent?"

I took a deep breath and shoved my hands in my coat pockets. "If I were guilty I would say innocent, wouldn't I, Judge? At least you would assume I would. And if I were innocent and said so it would sound just the same. I don't know anything I can say that will decide the matter for you."

Again he looked puzzled. "You have the appearance of a drifter, Mr. Stillwell, yet your speech is that of an educated man. Do you know that man?" he pointed at the next cage.

"I was told his name is Ira Fox, but I don't know him."

"Do you know what he is accused of?"

I just shook my head, and Ira Fox spoke up for the first time, rolling to sit upright on his slab cot. "The same thing you are, Pard," he said. "You and me and some other guys killed Sam Dance."

"I would advise a plea of guilty," Judge Tomlin told me. "You could avoid the rope that way. You would only go to prison."

I thought about that, then tipped my head toward the next cell. "How does he plead?"

"Innocent," the judge said.

"Then I guess if he's innocent and I was with him, then I must be innocent too."

I thought a look passed between the judge and Ira Fox. The light in those cells was dim. Then the judge frowned, his dark eyes intense on me. "You will have one opportunity, Mr. Stillwell. Judge Kendall will convene his court Monday. You will be asked to plead. If you plead guilty you will be sentenced to a prison term. If you plead innocent you will be tried, found guilty and hanged. It will be your choice. I have no more to say."

With that the big man turned, shoved past Everett and slammed out of the jail.

"He doesn't seem very happy," I told Everett.

"You're making a big mistake, Stillwell. The judge was tryin' to help you."

"He said Judge Kendall would preside. Why not Tomlin?"

"The judge can't preside. He'll be a witness. Why don't you do like he says? Do you want to hang?"

"Kendall is a visiting judge, then?"

"Yeah. Judge Tomlin called him in. He's from Larned. Just got in today."

"He isn't wasting any time."

"No reason to. We got two of you." He shrugged, turned and went back into the sheriff's office, closing the cellblock door behind him.

From my little window I could see the sides of some of the buildings on the main street. The air by the window was cold, but I stayed there and kept watching until I saw a large figure walk past an opening and turn to cross the frozen street to enter an imposing building beyond. It was the largest building on the street.

"That big building over there," I looked through the bars at Ira Fox, "the one with the white railings. I guess that would be the hotel?"

He gazed at me and shrugged, but I held his gaze. Finally he nodded and looked away.

"I suppose that is where a visiting judge would stay, isn't it?"

"I don't know where judges stay," he said. "Shut up." He lay back at full length on the plank cot, his feet toward me. His boots didn't match the rest of his clothing, I noticed. He was dressed as a drifter . . . nondescript, worn clothing that might have seen some trail drives or some hiding in holes. But his boots were different. They were scuffed, but they were sound and well cared for. The left one sagged a little at the ankle the way soft leather does, but the right one sagged only on one side. The outside of the leg was stiff and straight. I had seen that before. In Chicago they called it a "Denver rig," and a boot so fitted was expensive.

When Frank Murdoch and his citizens' posse turned me over to the deputy in Liberal, he had searched me thoroughly. Then when another deputy and that hawk-nosed Sturdevant arrived to begin the trip up to Springfield they had done even a more thorough job. There wasn't anything I had that they didn't know about. They were good at their work. Sturdevant was the best.

"That sure is some rifle Sturdevant carries," I said. Fox just grunted.

"Sturdevant bring you in?" I tried again.

"Sturdevant brings everybody in," he snapped. "At least those that get here. Shut up."

I paced the two steps back to the window and looked across at the hotel again. There was no way Sturdevant would have overlooked a Denver rig in a man's boot. A regular deputy, maybe, but not Sturdevant.

I heard voices out in the office, then Everett came into the cellblock again. He was wearing his coat and hat, and he carried a shotgun. "Time for dinner," he announced. "Mr. Fox, you can go first." While Fox got to his feet and put on his hat Everett unlocked his cell and stepped back. Fox stepped out into the corridor ahead of him. At the door Everett said to someone, "That's Mr. Stillwell in there, Henry. I'll be back after a bit." The cold wind flowed through again and the front door slammed. A moment later a youngster with a badge stepped into the corridor.

He was a lanky kid, too young yet to have meat on his frame but with a sober, steady look about him that said he was a man or would be one soon. He had big hands, big feet and ears he might never grow into.

He came to the cage door and looked me over. "They say you're called By."

"Sometimes. Who are you?"

"Henry Lattimer. I was Mr. Dance's deputy."

"So now you work for the new sheriff."

"Just temporarily. Mr. Guthrie will put on his own people, I guess. The ones that supported his campaign." He kept staring at me, as though he were trying to make up his mind about something. Then he asked, "Are you going to plead guilty?"

"I don't think so, although Judge Tomlin makes a strong case for it. He says if I don't plead guilty I'll hang." I turned away, walked to the cold little window again and looked out. Ira Fox was just going into the hotel, followed by Everett with his shotgun. There wasn't much traffic on the streets. The day was gray and cold and the wind rattled around like old bones. People who could would stay by their fires on a day like this.

When I looked back at Henry Lattimer he was still staring at me, puzzling over something.

"Something bothering you, Deputy?"

"It seems like I ought to know you from somewhere."

"I don't think so . . . not unless you plan to tell them you saw me out there when the sheriff was killed. You've had a good enough look at me now you could sure point me out and say 'that's one of them.' "

He stiffened at that and his voice took on an edge. "You know I was there, do you?"

"Everybody knows that. I heard about it clear down in no man's land. Henry Lattimer actually saw the shooting. He was a witness. Nobody else actually saw it happen. They were too busy running away."

"Well I might have run too, except I fell."

"That's not the way I heard it. You could have run off but you climbed out of that canyon and confronted them."

"If you were there, you know that."

"Everybody knows it, Henry. Word gets around. You must have thought a lot of Sheriff Dance."

He bit his lip and looked away. "Everybody thought a lot of him. He was a good sheriff and a good man." When he looked back there was a hard glint in his eyes. "No, I can't say I saw you out there. I didn't see anybody clear enough to identify. But I heard one of them call another one By, and I sure will testify to that."

I decided I liked Henry Lattimer. "How did Ira Fox come to be arrested? Did somebody see him?"

"Judge Tomlin named him. He said one of the men was riding an Appaloosa, and he knew Ira Fox from sometime back and knew he had an Appaloosa. So Sturdevant and a couple of the deputies went over to Stevens County and brought him back."

"That's a little out of the deputies' jurisdiction, isn't it?"

"Sturdevant's an officer of the court. He has jurisdiction anywhere the judge sends him." He was staring at me again. "Mr. Stillwell . . . were you there? Were you with that mob that killed Mr. Dance?"

I sat down on the cot. "Would it make any difference what I said?"

He paused, then shook his head. "No, I guess it wouldn't."

When Everett brought Ira Fox back he put him in his cell and opened mine and we walked to the hotel for my dinner. The wind had died and it was starting to snow, little hard midwinter flakes that wouldn't make much powder but would drive the stock to bunch and huddle and make a lot of hard work for the drovers tending them out there on their winter graze. I thought about those punchers who had helped Frank Murdoch arrest me—Cass and Pearly and the two older ones, Smith and May. They would be out on the range now, earning their keep.

With the Texas herds cut off from Kansas railheads now by quarantine against Texas tick, and the eastern markets clamoring for beef, a lot of folks were building prime stock herds here, grazing them on the high plains to wait for the spring markets to break in

Kansas City and Chicago. No place ever looked more bleak and barren than those Kansas prairies in the winter, but buffalo grass is deceptive. Even in the dead of winter, when it looks brittle and bleached-out, a herd can fatten on it and be prime for spring. But it takes raw hard work to make that happen. The cattle have to be tended and moved from place to place. They have to be bunched one day and spread another. They have to be pushed into the draws or under rimrock when the blizzards blow, and if it snows heavy they have to be pushed up onto the flats where the drifts won't bury them, then moved around to find graze they can reach.

I knew what Cass and Pearly and Smith and May were doing. I had done it too, from time to time.

There were some people in the hotel's big dining room, and they all looked at me when Everett brought me in. Accused murderers are always worth seeing. The one I looked back at the most had long, honey-brown hair and big blue eyes that were direct and unashamed.

Everett pointed me to a table in the corner and had me sit with my back to the room. He sat himself on a bench a few feet away.

"Aren't you going to eat?" I asked him.

"I already did. When I brought Mr. Fox over."

"Did Mr. Fox and the judge have a nice visit?"

"I don't . . . how did you know that?"

"I just guessed. Who is that over there?"

He glanced. "That's Si Rutledge. He has the newspaper over at Arkalon. The lady in the bonnet, that's Mrs. Rutledge. The other one is his sister, Mrs. Mills. She's from east someplace."

Rutledge was still looking at me so I looked back. He was a lean, sharp-eyed man a little older than me, maybe thirty-five.

"He'll probably stay over for the trial," Everett surmised. "He's partial to swift justice so he'll be wanting them to hang you and Mr. Fox. Of course if a fellow pleads guilty they usually don't hang him, just put him in prison."

"What does a fellow do if he's innocent?"

Everett looked at me sadly and shook his head. "Prove it, I guess. Can you prove it, Mr. Stillwell?"

As my meal arrived, so did two more people. One was the new sheriff, Sim Guthrie, supporting himself with a cane. The other carried a sheaf of papers. He was a young fellow, dressed in a shabby suit that should have belonged to someone larger. He was pale and nervous, and he squinted.

"It's all right, Everett," Guthrie said. Then, "Mr. Stillwell, this is Max Bernheim, attorney at law. He has come forward and offered to represent you if you want a lawyer." He glanced at the little man and shrugged. "Of course that is up to you."

I looked at the lawyer and he squinted at me. "You should at least talk to me," he said.

I asked Guthrie, "Can we talk?"

"You have that right." Guthrie motioned to Everett and the two of them moved away. Everett sat at another table, just out of earshot, his shotgun in his lap. The sheriff walked across to remove his hat and greet Si Rutledge and the two ladies. Max Bernheim sat down.

"I guess somebody sent you," I said.

He nodded. "I'm starting a practice in Liberal.

42

Frank Murdoch sent me to see you. He doesn't think you are guilty. Do you have any idea why he would feel that way, Mr. Stillwell?"

"Not the slightest. He knows I can't prove I wasn't with that bunch. He's the one who arrested me."

"Well, he asked me to see what I can do. Now as I understand it, the only evidence the prosecution can bring against you is the testimony of a deputy named Henry Lattimer. Can he identify you, Mr. Stillwell?"

"He's seen me since I was brought in, but he didn't see me out there. As I understand it, he heard someone use the name 'By.' Is that enough to make a case? I've been told by Judge Tomlin that if I am tried I will be found guilty."

The squint widened. "He told you that? When?"

"This morning. He suggested I plead guilty to avoid hanging."

He blinked at me solemnly. "Not very judicious of him. Or I should say judicial, I suppose. But then, he must be very upset. The sheriff's murder came during an attempt on Judge Tomlin's life."

"So I hear."

"Mr. Stillwell, before coming over here I had a look at your revolver. It is a very fine weapon."

"It should be. I paid thirty dollars for it second hand."

"I also talked with some people about you. The impression I receive is of a very . . . contained person. Your attire and your occupation when arrested indicate one type of person, while your manner and your speech indicates another entirely. And your words don't seem to indicate anything at all, yet I don't have the feeling you are really hiding anything.

Exactly who are you, Mr. Stillwell? Where are you from?"

"My name is Byron Stillwell. And I've been a lot of places. What does this have to do with getting me out of jail?"

"Maybe quite a lot. Do you know the other prisoner?"

"Ira Fox? He's in the next cell. He's not very talkative."

"Well, if you were like Mr. Fox—that is, if you were the type of person he seems to be—then slim evidence would be enough to convict you in the eyes of a jury. This is a new land, sir. The structures of the law are very flimsy. On frontiers, men have been hanged on less evidence than a chance of name. But I think a jury might have misgivings about you, Mr. Stillwell. If your clothing matched your manner, I doubt you would even have been arrested."

"That doesn't say much for the court system."

"No, it doesn't. But, as I said, this is still a very primitive country." He squinted at me, hard. "It would be best if there were no trial at all. Tell me, honestly. Is there any other evidence that can be brought against you? Anything at all?"

"Not that I know of."

"Very well, let me see what I can do. Judge Kendall is a jurist of high repute. He might waive an indictment in a case like this after seeing the evidence."

"What you were saying about my appearance and manner . . . does that mean that if someone really wanted a quick trial and conviction to put the sheriff's murder to rest, and had hoped someone could be caught and tried, that I would be a disappointment to them?"

For a moment the squint deepened, then his eyes twinkled. "Ah. Exactly. Very perceptive. And that may be the situation we have here. Sheriff Dance was a respected man, Mr. Stillwell. It is natural that people would like to see justice done."

"Even at the expense of an innocent man?"

He shook his head. "People are people. If a court says a man is guilty, no matter how it arrives at that conclusion, then he is guilty. People aren't interested in law. They are interested in retribution."

When Everett took me back to jail I lay on my cot for a while until everything was still and I was sure Everett was asleep beside his stove in the outer office. Then I said, "Ira? You awake?"

He grunted.

"Ira, are you still going to plead innocent Monday?"

"Yeah," he said, irritated.

"That's good. So am I. Because if I went to trial then I'd have to tell them how you and I were both involved in it and how it was you that actually fired the killing shot."

He came off his cot, his eyes round and his mouth open. "You're crazy! I never saw you before in my life! What are you talking about?"

"Well, I've been thinking about all this. Now if you were to plead innocent, and that judge was to decide he couldn't identify you after all, then there wouldn't be any other evidence to convict you so you'd go free . . . and that would be a shame if you were turned loose and I wasn't. So I decided that no matter what happens, we're in this together. If we hang, pard, we'll hang together. Because you see, no matter how I plead, if I'm tried I'm taking you with me."

4

Snow continued to fall fitfully as the pallid light of gray skies dimmed toward dusk. Henry Lattimer crossed the frozen ruts of State Street and stepped into the frigid calm of the doorway of Taft's Drug Store. He leaned his rifle against the wall, cupped his freezing hands and blew into them, his breath rising like steam around his hatbrim. He rubbed his hands vigorously, then tested the lock on Taft's door. It was firm. He picked up his rifle and moved on, testing the last three doors on the round. The third, on Saul Bingham's hardware store, was open and he leaned in. "Mr. Bingham? Everything all right?"

Bingham looked up from the clutter of a lamplit desk. "Eh? Oh, hello, Henry. Yes, I'm fine. Forgot to set the lock, didn't I? Getting old, son. Getting forgetful. Come in. Warm yourself."

"Well, just for a minute. I'm supposed to be finishing up." He entered and closed the door behind him. It was warm inside and he rubbed his hands by the stove. "Cold out there. Getting colder, too." He glanced up as he said it, at the little stack of pine coffins in the shadowed rear of the store, and was sorry he had mentioned the cold. It reminded him of the shed out back where other coffins waited sometimes, cold and dark, one or two now and then in the winter, waiting for someone to break a hole in the frozen ground to receive them and their burdens. There was only one coffin out there now, that he knew of. Sam Dance's frozen body lay there, awaiting Sunday services. He turned away quickly, and Bingham noticed the abrupt movement.

"He's all right, Henry," the old man said softly. "Nothing makes any difference to him now."

Henry nodded.

"I reckon we'll go ahead and have the service here Sunday," Bingham said. "A memorial service. Then I'll seal the casket and get the Miller boys to drive it to Arkalon for the train."

"The train?" Henry looked up. "What do you mean?"

"Why, the body's been claimed, Henry. Hadn't you heard? We got a telegram Wednesday. I never knew Sam Dance had family, but someone claims him. Instructed me to ship the remains to Independence for burial. Seems to me I do remember Sam saying one time he came here from Independence. I never knew he had family, though."

"He didn't come here from Independence," Henry said. "He came here from Joplin, Missouri. But he did live in Independence one time. That was where he started as a lawman. It was a long time ago."

"If that's where he started law, it must have been a long time. Sam said before the election he had more than twenty-five years of experience as a lawman.

That means he started out pretty soon after the war, maybe 1866 or '67. But did you know he had any relatives?"

"No, I don't think so . . . well, yes, maybe he did say something one time . . . It was like he'd had a son once, but didn't any more. Who sent the telegram, Mr. Bingham?" Henry had backed close to the glowing stove. Now he stepped away and rubbed his hands down the backs of his legs, enjoying the tingle of returning warmth.

Bingham wiped his glasses, returned them to his nose and searched through a stack of yellow papers, peering at some of them. "Here it is. Sent on behalf of his family. Says to please ship the remains of Samuel Raymond Dance, deceased, to a funeral parlor at Independence . . . it gives the name and instructions . . . says all arrangements will be made there, and I should wire charges and shipping to them and they'll take care of it. It's from a lawyer. Funny, though. It wasn't sent from Independence. It was sent from Mobeetie, Texas."

"Did Sheriff Guthrie see that?"

"Of course he did. He had to approve it or I couldn't ship out the body."

"He didn't say anything about it."

"He didn't . . ." Bingham looked up at him. "What was there to say? You know how busy he's been the past few days, just taking office and all this about Sam's murder and the ruckus over the judge."

"He might have said something."

Bingham tilted his head, studying the young man. Henry was hardly more than a boy . . . and a lonely one, at that. The old man smiled, gently. He got up, took a pot from the stove and poured coffee into two cups. "Here," he said. "Cold can give a man the bleaks if he lets it. Just like age. You don't think too much of Sim Guthrie, do you, Henry?"

Henry glanced down at him, across the rim of his cup. He hadn't thought too much about it. "Why, I guess he's all right, Mr. Bingham. He seems like a decent man . . . but how can he be sheriff? He isn't a lawman. Sam Dance was a lawman. Sim Guthrie doesn't know anything about keeping the law. All he's ever done is develop land and grow some crops and run a business. Mr. Dance was a sheriff!"

"But Sim beat him in a fair election, Henry. The people voted that way."

"Just barely. It took the commissioners and the court to say they did."

"But they did. You see, that's how it works."

"But all those people, Mr. Bingham. Half the voters in the county . . . how could they just throw out a man like Mr. Dance? Don't they know what they did? They broke his heart. I know they did. They just used him up and threw him out. I don't see how they could do that."

"Times change," Bingham shrugged. "New people come in, they don't know what's gone before. Sim Guthrie ran a good campaign. He won it fair."

"He didn't need the job. He just wanted it."

Bingham sipped his coffee. "You thought a lot of Sam Dance, didn't you, boy?"

"Yes, I did. He was a friend, I guess. I miss him. I want to see the men who killed him pay for that."

"Well, you go on wanting that. But don't be bitter against the whole world, son. Sunday morning, when the preacher says those good words over your friend and you walk by the casket to pay your last respects, you look at what he's wearing. Right there on his lapel, high up, you'll see a shiny new badge. It's the one Sim Guthrie bought for himself. But he came around Tuesday and told me to put it on Sam. He wanted him to have it."

Henry lowered his head and sipped at his coffee. "I guess maybe I ought to apologize . . ." he looked up quickly. "Mobeetie? Isn't that where the Double-D headquarters is? Mr. Dance said one time that some Stevens County men had gone to work there . . . that was after the Stevens County war."

"Could be. I don't recollect much about that. I was just moving my store from Garden City about that time. I know there was some kind of set-to about Texas drovers trying to get the county disenfranchised so they could bring summer herds in without quarantines. I guess that's what the fighting was all about. You might ask Judge Tomlin. He was over there then, he'd know."

"Some say that's why he left Stevens County," Henry said quietly.

"Probably just talk," Bingham set his cup down. "You can't go too much by what folks say. You know how stories grow. I never could see what the judge would have stood to gain by backing that anti-county faction over there. Besides, that was two years ago. It's all in the past. We need to think about the future."

Something in the old man's tone caught Henry's ear. "Some of the businessmen are talking about moving to Liberal next summer, when the railroad gets there. I heard Sid Gaffe say Springfield has lost its market. He was talking about setting up shop in Liberal."

Bingham sat down at his desk, frowning behind his glasses. "I'd want better counsel than Sid Gaffe's, I believe. A railroad through here would have been a great thing, Henry. But Springfield is strong even without it. We're the county seat. The market will be here."

"Sid says Frank Murdoch has a petition to call a county seat election, to move the seat to Liberal."

"That's foolishness, Henry. Springfield will always be the best place for a county seat. Right in the middle. Liberal is just barely in the county. For that matter it's just barely in Kansas. Nobody is going to vote to make it the county seat."

Henry emptied his cup, rinsed it at Bingham's basin and turned it up to dry. Nobody should have voted to trade Sam Dance for Sim Guthrie, either. But they had. "Times change," he muttered, too low for Bingham to hear.

There was an inch of powder snow on Springfield now. Henry completed his rounds and went back to the jail. "I'm done," he told Everett. "Everything is quiet. Just getting colder. You need any help with the prisoners?"

"Naw. I fed them a while ago. They're asleep now. That Fox was all riled up, said he wanted to talk to Judge Tomlin about the trial. But the judge had already gone home. If you see him in the morning, tell him Fox wants to talk to him."

"Okay. I guess he'll be in tomorrow. What about the other one, Stillwell?"

"No trouble with him at all. Real gentleman. You notice how he talks, Henry? That's an educated man. I sure can't see why he'd be running with a bunch of drovers and drifters."

"You don't think he did it, do you?"

"I don't know. It's mostly your testimony they got him on. Because of his name and all . . . and then he *was* around here Monday morning. He admits that."

Henry shook his head. "Pretty hard to prove anything on that. Does he look familiar to you, Everett?"

Everett pursed his lips, his fleshy face wrinkling in thought. "I kind of thought a couple of times that I might have seen him before, but then I look at him and I sure don't remember where. I guess maybe he's somebody I saw some time but never noticed."

"Well, I'm the same way. But you know, I can't make sense of that. Tall as he is, and the kind of face he has, he's the sort of man you'd notice, isn't he? I think I would. But I sure don't remember ever seeing him, even though he looks familiar." He walked to the front window. The light was gone, winter night had come, and the yellow lamplight in windows across the way looked vague and blurry. The snow was falling heavier now, larger flakes floating downward, blanketing the town. For the first time in weeks there was no wind, and the silence seemed strange. It was as though the world had gone to sleep and the snow was its dreams. Henry shook his head. "I better get home, Everett. I've got chores to do. Have you seen Rounder?"

"Probably over at the livery, sleeping behind the stove. He's kind of lost without Sam to follow around. Poor old dog."

"I picked up some meat scraps for him at the hotel. I'll see he gets fed."

The snow was ankle deep as Henry Lattimer walked to the livery barn beyond the hotel. Muffled sounds of winter broke the stillness, a door slamming, creaking of a gate somewhere, muted voices from the hotel, crunch of his own footsteps in the snow. Someone came toward him, a movement in the darkness that entered the light from a window and became Sheriff Sim Guthrie.

Guthrie stopped, peered at him, then came on, limping, using his cane. "Hello, Henry. Going home?"

"Yes, sir. I finished the rounds and checked in with Everett. Everything's quiet."

Guthrie removed his hat, knocked snow from it and replaced it. "Night like this, what else would it be?" He chuckled. "The wicked are thin-blooded people, Henry. They flourish in summer, not in winter."

Henry felt like pointing out that it had been cold last Monday, too, and the wicked had been out in force at Cross Canyon. But he saw no point to it. "Mr. Bingham said they're sending Sheriff Dance's body to Independence."

"Yes. I gather he had family there. Henry, we haven't discussed your position as deputy. I've been meaning all week to talk to you, but there just hasn't been time. Do you want to stay on? To work for me?"

Henry hesitated. The question caught him by surprise. "I hadn't thought about that. I just assumed I'd turn in my badge after the trial, that you'd want your own people."

"I want good people, Henry, whoever they are.

We're bordering on civilization here in Seward County, but this is still pretty raw country and there is a lot that can happen, that I don't know about. Sam Dance was a good frontier lawman . . . one of the best, and I never thought otherwise. You've worked with him, learned from him. And that was a brave thing you did out there. That took grit. I'll tell you what. Sometime next week, when things quiet down, we'll talk. Maybe we can see eye to eye on some things."

"All right. Good night, Sheriff."

He started away, then turned. "Sheriff, have you gone through all of Mr. Dance's papers and things?"

"As much as I've had time for. Why?"

"Well, a couple of months ago . . . maybe it was in November . . . he went over to Stevens County on business and when he came back he brought a box of papers that he was going to read. Some newspapers and notes on court records, things like that. He kept saying when he had time he was going to study them, but I doubt if he ever did. I looked for them at the office and couldn't find them. Have you seen them?"

Guthrie scratched his chin. "No, nothing like that. They might have been personal effects. If so they'd be stored in Bingham's barn. Is it important?"

"I don't know. I just keep wondering why he was killed."

Guthrie stepped closer, peering closely at him in the near darkness. "Henry, the reason Sam Dance died is because he was at Cross Canyon. Those men weren't there to kill him, they were after Judge Tomlin. That's why we were all out there. Because they had threatened the judge. Sam just happened to be the one they shot, that's all. You know that."

"I saw them kill him, Sheriff. I saw *how* they killed him. I don't think it was an accident."

Guthrie was silent for a time. Then he leaned on his cane. "Henry, when those two prisoners go to trial, the only evidence we have against them is your testimony about hearing Stillwell's nickname and the judge's about seeing an Appaloosa horse. That is damned slim evidence. The whole thrust of the prosecution has to be that Sam was murdered by a mob and we can place those two with the mob. The threat against the judge is what the mob was all about. If we don't have that case, we don't have a case at all. I hope you aren't going to compromise our case. You don't want to see those men go free, do you?"

"I don't know. I . . ."

"Henry, some people are very upset about what happened to Sam Dance. You're young. Maybe you don't see how important it is that we be able to show the citizens a swift trial and a conviction. Things fester if they aren't resolved. We have to show this county that the law here is in force and is effective. Just look at Stevens County and you'll see what happens when people don't believe that. They had a war over there."

"When I testify, Sheriff, I'll say exactly what I saw and what I heard. That's all I can do."

"Well, that's fine. But I want you to think about what I've said. If the law doesn't punish someone for what happened, these people . . ." he waved an arm, indicating a whole county, ". . . these people will make their own law. We can't have that. Civilization is a fragile thing. Order has to be enforced. Even

56

more important, it must be *seen* as being enforced. That's what has been wrong with the sheriff's office these past years, Henry. Not enough show, not enough visibility. But we're going to change that . . ."

While the man was talking Henry Lattimer turned away. He didn't want to hear any more. Another minute and the sheriff would be telling him to make a positive identification whether he had seen anyone or not. He didn't want to hear that. He started to walk away in the falling snow.

The night silence was shattered. Abrupt and hard, echoing among the buildings and along the street, gunfire erupted. One shot, then others, crashing in ragged volley. Henry spun, saw flashes of orange dim through the snow. He sprinted from the boardwalk, almost fell as his foot turned in a frozen rut hidden by new snow, recovered his balance and danced across the street, angling toward the flare he had seen. Another shot echoed, then there was silence, broken now by the slamming of doors, the babble of voices.

Henry reached the far walk, veered around the corner of a dark building and angled into the vacant lot next to it. The footing was treacherous here, heaps of rubbish and building debris scattered everywhere, blanketed by snow and hidden by darkness. It slowed him. Ahead and to the left he saw another flare, heard the crack of a rifle and then a larger flare backed up by the roar of a shotgun. The jail! Some-one was firing on the jail. Two more shots, then he heard the muffled drumming of horses, voices calling, and fast hooves going away. He ran.

Twenty yards from the back of the jail he saw by dim light where horses had milled, the trampled snow

57

scattered and dark earth churned beneath it. He heard a moan and ran to the jail. Everett lay there, propped against the wall near the east corner, his shotgun in the snow beside him. He was groaning, pressing a hand to his breast where dark blood flowed and steamed. Henry started to kneel, but Everett pushed him away with a bloody hand. "The prisoners, Henry. They were after the prisoners. Go see."

Henry paused, then nodded. "I'll be right back. Hold on." He ran along the side of the jail, skidded around the corner and stooped to peer into the open front door. No one was in the office. He entered, looked around, picked up the lamp and opened the door to the cell block. Lamplight flooded the darkness beyond. Ira Fox crouched in the far corner of his cell, his eyes huge. As Henry entered he cowered away, holding out a hand in protest. "No, Pony!" he shouted. "No! Not me!"

Henry shifted the light to the near cell. Its little window was shattered. Bullet holes pocked the wall opposite. A tattered hat lay in a near corner, and Byron Stillwell lay on the floor. There was blood on his head.

Carrying the lamp, Henry ran back through the office and into the cold night. Voices shouted, lights appeared. People were coming. "The jail!" he shouted. "Get the sheriff!" Then he ran around the building again to kneel beside Everett. The big man was pale in the lantern light, and blood covered his chest and stomach. "They shot me, Henry," he gritted through clenched teeth. "Oh, God, it hurts. I tried to stop them."

"Hold still, Everett." He turned and shouted,

"Someone get the doctor! Back here! A man is shot!"

"They didn't do for me, Henry," Everett said. "I'm shot clear across, but I don't think it . . . Oh, God, that hurts so bad! Help me, Henry." He pushed himself up with one hand, turned and got his knees under him.

"Everett!" Henry snapped, "Just lie still. The doctor's coming."

"No. I'm all right." With an effort Everett got to his feet, still pressing a hand to his bleeding chest. "You pick up my shotgun."

As Henry stooped to retrieve the gun, Everett walked on wobbling legs toward the street. There was light there now as people arrived, carrying lamps. Henry saw Sim Guthrie limp through the crowd, hurrying as fast as his injured ankle would allow. Everett reached the front corner of the building and sagged there. People gathered around him, supporting him.

Henry ran past them, into the office, dropped Everett's shotgun on a desk and reentered the cell block. He held the lamp high. Then he stopped still, his eyes widening in confusion. In the second cell Ira Fox rolled on the floor, moaning and cursing, his groans rising in pitch with each gasping breath.

Byron Stillwell stood at the cell bars in cage one, a sardonic grin on his bloody face, his dark eyes dancing in the lantern light. "Glad you came along, Deputy," he drawled. "It seems like Ira there got his arm caught in the bars and broke it." He reached through the bars, holding something out toward Henry. It was a long, thin knife, offered butt-first.

59

"Here," Byron Stillwell said. "This belongs to Ira, but I don't think he wants it any more."

Henry stared at him, then quickly took the knife and backed away. "You were . . . I mean, a minute ago . . . when I came in . . . I thought you were dead."

5

I could understand how the deputy had thought I was dead. I very nearly had been.

After I had told Ira Fox we were in this thing together I just eased back and let him carry it from there. I was pretty sure Ira wasn't in danger of being hanged, but I didn't know how he was going to manage to get cleared. All I could do was make it important to him to get me out too.

By that afternoon I had put some little pieces together, but they weren't enough to make much of a blend. Judge Will Tomlin wanted me to plead guilty to being part of the crowd that killed Sam Dance. He wanted that enough to threaten me with hanging if I didn't. Still, it didn't seem to bother him that Ira Fox was going to plead innocent, and it was the judge's own evidence they had arrested Fox on. I knew from what the judge said that it was important to someone that someone be arrested and convicted, and that for some reason he had settled on me as a particularly good candidate. And I suspected from what the lawyer from Liberal said that I had turned out to be not such a good candidate after all. I took the notion that maybe Penny Bassett wasn't too popular right then with whoever he had hoped to impress by coming up with a drifter named By.

So I stirred the pot and dumped Ira Fox into it and let him stew. And it wasn't two minutes before he was standing at his cell door hollering for Everett. Everett came with his shotgun and took Ira into the front office, and I could hear voices in there for a few minutes, then Everett brought him back and put him in his cell again and told him to shut up and go to sleep.

Ira did a funny thing then. He took off the bandana he wore around his neck, pushed open his cell window, working through the bars, and hung the bright cloth outside. I looked out my own window. It was a gray afternoon, beginning to dim toward evening, and powder snow was falling. The wind had stopped so the snow just sifted down, dead white.

I stood looking at Ira in the next cage and when he saw me looking he glared at me. "Smart-ass," he spat, "been better if you'd just done what you were told."

"I don't play people's games unless I know the rules," I told him. "And nobody has told me what this one is about."

"Well, you just dealt yourself out," he said, and turned away.

It was nearly half an hour before I heard a rapping sound, and saw Ira get up and reach through the bars to open his window. I tried to look out mine, but because of the bars I couldn't get close enough to see who was there. But he was talking to someone in a hushed voice, and he kept glancing my way to be sure I couldn't overhear.

The snow was coming heavier, the flakes larger, and still no wind. Those high plains can be silent sometimes, and when it comes it is surprising. A man gets so used to the constant wind that he doesn't hear it at all until it stops.

Ira closed his window, hunched his coat around his shoulders and went over to rattle his cell door. "Everett! Hey, Everett!"

When the jailer poked his head in Ira said, "Hey, get us a lamp in here. It's getting dark."

The big man sounded cranky. "What do you want a lamp for? Why don't you just go to sleep?"

"Aw, come on, Everett. It's dark in here. A lamp won't hurt anything."

Everett shrugged his shoulders, disappeared and returned with a coal oil lamp that he set carefully on a bench across from the cells, out of reach. He lit the wick, replaced the mantle and turned it just high enough to provide a soft light. "You can have it for an hour or so," he said. "But we can't burn oil all night just to keep you happy."

When he was gone Ira Fox sat down on his cot and stared at me. When I stared back he looked away. The whole thing began to bother me, the signal at the window, Ira's visitor, and now the sudden craving for a lamp. I looked out my window, but it was so near dark that there wasn't much to see, especially with the light behind me. After a time I thought I saw movement out there in the snow, but I couldn't be sure. I glanced at Ira and there was something about his intent gaze that I didn't like at all. On impulse I took off my hat, set it in the little window with the bars bracing it, and then backed away to squat on my heels next to the cot with my back to the wall.

Ira started to stand up, said, "What the hell are you . . . ," and all hell broke loose. Several gunshots sounded, almost together, and the window pane exploded. My hat sailed across the cell and bullets whanged off the iron bars and thudded into the far wall. There was a howling in the cells as bits of lead whined and ricocheted. An arm snaked through the window above me and fired three rapid shots downward, two going into the cot and one just missing my feet. The arm withdrew and there were more shots, chipping the window casement, whining off bars. The oil lamp shattered and went out, leaving darkness ablaze with gunfire. I stood, hugging the wall, and something slammed into the side of my head, something that burned like fire. The darkness turned red and swam inward. Distantly I heard shouts, the roar of a shotgun and more shots in volley. The floor seemed to rise up and smack me.

Strange light washed around, throwing dancing shadows, and I heard Ira screaming something, then the light was gone and I lay trying to get my senses back. My head hurt. I got to my knees, held a hand to my head and it came away wet. There was a ragged crease across my temple, and I felt blood flowing down my cheek and dripping from my nose and chin. For a moment I couldn't get my eyes focused, then I did. There was light from the open office door and dancing light from the shattered window, enough to see Ira standing big-eyed in the next cell.

I got to my feet and walked to the intervening bars,

leaning against them. "They missed me, Ira. All I got was a ricochet crease. You could have walked out of this the same way you walked in, Ira. All you had to do was take me out with you. But now the game is over for you. You lose."

I saw him crouch, watching from the corner of my eye. From the crouch he lunged, and I ducked aside as his arm came through the bars right where my belly had been. I caught it with both hands, bent it up against the bars and his knife clattered to the floor. He gasped.

"I have a message, Ira," I said softly. "I guess you know who it's for." Then I turned his arm so it was clamped diagonally between cell bars, rolled and hit it hard with my shoulder. "You deliver that message, Ira. Tell them it starts here."

I turned him loose, his arm flopping, and he sank to the floor and rolled there in pain.

When the kid deputy came in waving a lantern I turned Ira's knife over to him. There was a lot of commotion outside, and I heard someone say Everett had been shot. I remembered then the roar of the shotgun behind the jailhouse, a roar that had been followed by other shots.

After a while they brought a doctor. He took one look at Ira and had some men come in and take him away. Then he looked me over, got my face cleaned up, had them bring in hot water, and got out his sewing tools.

There were seven bullet holes in the cellblock wall, all opposite my cell. There were two holes in the cot, two in the floor and a dozen dents all over the cellblock where shards of ricocheting bullets had gouged the walls. It was a clear wonder that both of us in there hadn't been cut to pieces, the way those bullets had bounced around among the cage bars.

My hat might have made a gravel sieve, but nothing else worthwhile. It had taken the whole first volley.

Through half of that night and all of the next morning, while snow continued to fall on Springfield, people came and went, worried people trying to sort out what had happened. I learned that Ira Fox was resting under guard at the hotel, and that Everett would recover. He had been shot only once, but the bullet had entered his chest beside the left breast, almost at the shoulder, had splintered a rib there then traveled clear across his chest to exit at his right armpit. They shot him while he was pointing his shotgun.

When the sheriff came to see me Max Bernheim was with him. I told him all I could, about Ira Fox talking to someone at the window, about the shooting and about Ira trying for me with his knife. It was Max who put forth the suggestion that the same men who had killed Sam Dance had done this. He developed his argument skillfully, basing it on the idea that whoever had killed the old sheriff had me mixed up with someone else, just like the law did, and were afraid I might identify them.

He did a job of work, that lawyer. Within minutes he had the sheriff's sour agreement, though he didn't like it a bit. Max winked at me in encouragement.

Henry Lattimer was in and out. He looked at the broken window, the bullet holes everywhere, my shredded hat, and at me. "Somebody wanted you dead," he said.

"Seems like it."

"Ira Fox was one of them. Your story makes sense."

"Yes."

"And if he is one of them, it's pretty obvious that you aren't." He leaned his rifle against the far wall and brushed snow off his coat. "I just came from the hotel. The judge is over there with your lawyer and the prosecutor."

"Judge Tomlin?"

"No. Kendall. Judge Tomlin is probably snowed in out at his place. But Judge Kendall and the lawyers are reviewing evidence. They wanted to know if I had any more identification than the name By."

"What did you tell them?"

"The truth. That I don't have anything else. Mr. Stillwell, there's something I want to know and I don't know how to find out but I need to know anyway. Were you there when Sheriff Dance was killed?"

I hadn't seen that one coming, and the tone of his voice caught me up short. It wasn't a lawman's question, not even a very young and naive lawman's question. It was a personal question, from him to me, and he needed an answer and I looked at him there, young and strong and straightforward in the gray light of winter's day and I wanted to help him out. But there was nothing I could say that would help him and we both knew it.

I knew something else then, too, that I really hadn't realized before. "Sheriff Dance was special to you, wasn't he, Henry?"

The youngster nodded, his eyes clouding with resignation. "Yes, he was."

"Kind of like a father?"

"I guess so." He thought it over. "I don't remember my father very well, he died when I was ten. I have family, up around Hays and Garden City, but I've been pretty much on my own for a while now, and after I homesteaded down here, when I needed cash work and Sheriff Dance took me on, it was like he sort of taught me things . . . like he knew how things were and why they were that way, and he shared."

"I'd like to know more about him." I leaned against the bars and rolled my shoulder, flexing the muscles in my back. Most of the ache was gone, but the bruise was still there. "He sounds like a pretty good man."

"He was."

"And now you aren't going to rest until you find out who killed him."

"I want to know more than that, Mr. Stillwell." He picked up his rifle and there was a look about him that was too hard for his years. "I want to know why."

In mid-afternoon Max Bernheim showed up with a grin on his face and the sheriff in tow. "You're free to go, Mr. Stillwell," he said. "Judge Kendall has dismissed the charges for lack of substantive evidence."

Sheriff Guthrie unlocked the cell, looked at me sternly and hobbled out to the front office. We followed him.

The sheriff got out my saddlebags, wallet and pocket belongings and laid them on his desk, then handed me a piece of paper. "Your horse and saddle are at the hotel stable," he said. "Sign here, and you can go."

"I want my gun," I told him.

He shot me a hard look, then unlocked a cabinet and got out my holster rig. I buckled it on, drew my Colt and checked it over. "This was loaded before," I pointed out.

He opened a drawer, counted out six .45 cartridges and handed them to me. I loaded five of them and gave one back, then dropped the Colt home in its holster.

"You act like you've been naked and just got dressed," Guthrie said, his stern look taking on an element of worry. "I hope you will move on, Mr. Stillwell. Things are pretty upset around here."

I looked out the front window. Snow was still falling, the town rested under a thick blanket of white, and the wind was kicking up again. If it continued there would be drifts. "This doesn't look like traveling weather. Besides, I'm a free man now."

"The court dropping charges doesn't prove you innocent," he said. "It just means there wasn't enough of a case to prove you guilty."

Henry Lattimer had come in while I was signing the release. He stood by the door, taking the conversation in.

"Which puts me on equal footing with everybody else in Seward County," I told Guthrie. "Except that I was very thoroughly shot at last night. I gather you would like for me to go get shot at in some other county and leave yours alone."

"There's been enough trouble here."

"There was trouble when I got here, Sheriff. I

didn't bring it with me. You campaigned for it, now you have it. Good luck." I picked up my belongings and walked out into biting cold wind. The snow was a foot and a half deep, powder-dry and was shifting as the wind played on its surfaces. The sky was heavily overcast.

Max Bernheim was at my elbow. I hadn't thanked him, so I did now and he accepted the handshake with solemn propriety, squinting at me over the steam of his breath. I arranged to meet him at the hotel later for supper, and pay his fee there. I appreciated Frank Murdoch sending him to me, but the fee was mine to pay. I didn't want to be beholden to Murdoch or anyone else.

He walked away into the blowing snow and I set out for the stables to check on my horse. Henry Lattimer caught up with me at the outer corral. "You've had some practice with that six-gun," he said.

"A man should be competent with any tool he uses," I told him.

"Are you going to leave?"

"You know, this could make into a real blizzard. Feel the air. Thing about this part of the country, if you don't like the weather just wait a few minutes . . . it'll change."

"You don't tell anybody anything, do you?"

"Not much reason to. People usually don't listen, anyway."

He latched the corral gate behind us. Snow was dusting around our knees and beginning to pile in the lee of walls and posts. "Are you part Indian?" he asked. "You look like you might be."

"One-eighth Creek. My great-grandmother's name in English was Sarah Little Horse."

"That reminds me," he tossed the question casually. "Do you know anybody named Pony?"

I stopped right where I was and turned. The mind can be a funny thing. All sorts of puzzle pieces may be in there and none of them fit, then suddenly a word . . . or a name . . . can bring some of them together. And sometimes when that happens it makes whole new puzzles. "Where did you hear that name?"

"I guess you *do* know somebody called that. I heard it last night from Ira Fox. Now you tell me what it means."

That was fair. "Well," I said, "the only 'Pony' I know is a troubleshooter for a big spread down in Texas. The Double-D. His name is Pony Bidell. He works for Davy Dawes."

Now it was his turn to gawk. "The Double-D? You mean down by Mobeetie?"

"That's the one." I had the feeling that just as he had helped me with a puzzle of mine, now I had helped him with one of his. Snow sifted into my coat collar. I was going to have to find a new hat. I headed for the shelter of the stable.

Inside there was a warm stove, and a few men sat on crates next to it, playing dominoes on a plank table. They looked at us curiously, and one of them showed me where my horse was stalled. My saddle and gear were all there, and the horse had been tended.

I was just finishing my inspection when I felt a nudge at my knee and looked down. It was a dog, an old red hound with big sad eyes and some white on its muzzle, and it looked up at me like a long-lost friend, its tail wagging so hard it wagged the whole dog. I squatted to scratch its ears, and it wagged and whimpered and tried to talk, and nuzzled close against me in trembling happiness.

One of the men at the domino table said, "Well, would you all look at that! Look at old Rounder!"

"Never seen that dog take on so with anybody," another allowed.

Rounder. A good name. "Hello, Rounder," I told the dog, and he pushed against me and tried to burrow into my coat. I looked up then, and Henry Lattimer was standing there, staring at me like he had seen a ghost. As I looked up he turned away and went to the far end of the stable barn, then he turned and looked at me again. I didn't know what to make of it. I stood, then followed him. Rounder tagged at my heel, his breath fast and happy.

I reached Henry and stopped.

"Now I know," he said, barely above a whisper. "I thought you looked familiar . . . something about the way you move, the way your shoulders slope. Everett noticed it too. But it took the dog to make me see. Mister, old Rounder never made up to anybody like that, except Sam Dance. This was his dog."

6

He was a soldier, my mother said. He was tall and strong, young and handsome, and the ribbons on his blue coat matched one for one the hurts and angers that his slow smile tried to hide. He was one who should never have gone to war, because the senseless violence he had seen would never be forgotten. Somehow, she had felt, his life would be marked by his anger against such things.

He had been three years afield when his regiment encamped that summer in the valley of the James below Chapel Hill, and for eight months his letters home to Darke County had gone unanswered. He was twenty-two years old. My mother was eighteen. She saw him first at the little church where a few of the soldiers came on Sunday to sit stiff and silent among those who were their enemies, to hear for an hour the words of the gospel instead of the words of war.

He had no hymnbook, so when a hymn was selected she handed hers across the back of the pew to him. He sang with a rich, deep voice and she sang behind him in the voice that made her famous in later years, and she felt they were singing together, just the two of them.

Another Sunday they sat and talked beneath a willow tree, and then there were evenings when he would climb to the top of Sentry Point and she would slip away and meet him there. They would watch the stars come out over the James.

Those were the times she always remembered.

The blue soldiers camped on the James for nearly three months, then they were gone. I was born the following spring on a farm outside Brandywine where my mother was sent to be with an aunt, to be away from the war . . . and away from the bitter mouthings of people hurt by war.

She never saw him again, but she never stopped loving him and as I grew she taught me to love him too. We traveled a lot. Her early performances in Washington led to concerts in the finer cities: Philadelphia, Baltimore, then Hartford, Scranton and New York, then for a time with an opera company touring the great theaters. I had tutors and I learned from them, but I learned more from the people I met in the places we went. The theatrical world is a complex world, harboring always the best and the worst of people. They all had things to teach.

Before I was fifteen I knew both the rules of parlor etiquette and the tricks of the streets. And in the summers in Virginia I learned the way of the land and the ways of field and forest.

Mattie Stillwell always knew her son was learning and she encouraged all of it . . . even the parts I hoped she would never know. She had a way of looking at me now and then, as though inspecting her efforts, and when she approved what she saw a smile would creep into her face and she would say, "You are more like him every day."

I had her features, people said. Yet she said I was like him. I was twenty-seven and a long way from home when I learned my father's name was Samuel Dance.

"I didn't know it until just a few months ago," I told Henry Lattimer now as we ate beef and potatoes in a corner of the hotel dining room. "I guess I started trying to trace him five years ago, but I didn't learn anything for a long time. I didn't try very hard, mostly I had other things to do, but now and then I'd take a try at it."

"I don't understand why she wouldn't tell you," he said, shaking his head.

"It's just her way. She feels like the past is better remembered than recovered. Maybe she's right. I never really meant to find him, not to get to know him. I just wondered about him . . . like maybe if I could see him once, and learn a little about what kind of man he was, then it wouldn't bother me any more. Besides, he never knew about me. And I'll tell you for sure, there are some things it wouldn't have prided him to know."

He studied me while he chewed his food, and his gaze was wise for an eighteen-year-old kid. This one had seen some things in his time, too. "Does that have anything to do with the way you carry that gun so easy?"

"Maybe," I told him.

"You could have cleared yourself two days ago if you had let on you were his son."

"That's isn't anybody's business." I folded my arms on the table. "Including yours, except I told you about it anyway. What do you intend to do about it?"

The situation seemed to amuse him. He swallowed another bite of meat, then looked around the room as though in deep thought. When he looked at me again there was a devilish twinkle in his eyes. "What do you intend to do about Mr. Dance being killed?"

"Exactly what I have been doing. Find out everything there is to know about it."

"And if you do? Then what?"

"Whatever needs doing. Answer my question."

"What question?"

"Are you going to tell anybody about me?"

"Tell anybody what?" he was total innocence. "I don't know anything to tell about you, Mr. Stillwell, except that you sure have a way with dogs."

Under the table, Rounder thumped his tail in agreement and gnawed on a beef bone.

"I'm going to turn in this badge Monday," Henry stated. "I was proud of it while Mr. Dance was alive. I'm not, now."

The dining room was beginning to fill with people. It was nearly dark outside and the wind was rattling the windows, and people were coming for their dinner. From where I sat, with my back to the corner, I could see them all as they came in. Townspeople, coming from their shops and their houses. The hotel guests would arrive later. They would not be in a hurry to eat and get home.

"You'd better head for home," I told Henry. "This will be a blizzard before long." Henry's house was a homestead shack two miles northwest. He had built it himself to prove up on his claim. I knew where it was. "And don't be too quick to get rid of that badge. It might come in handy."

"Do you know that Sheriff Guthrie wanted me to build up my evidence, just to bring you to trial? He wanted me to say I saw you out there."

"He's new. He wants to establish himself. Unsolved murders don't set well with people."

"Well, he's not going to solve anything by politicking."

"And without a badge you won't either."

"You don't have a badge."

"I don't need one. You have one. Are you with me?"

The scowl disappeared from his face and suddenly he was an eighteen-year-old kid again. "Do you mean it? We'll work together?"

"We can learn twice as much that way. You've told me some things I didn't know, like the papers Sam Dance had, and the name 'Pony'."

"Pony Bidell, you said. What about him?"

"Well, if it's him Ira was talking about, then there is more going on here than I thought. Look, I've got to get myself a hat and you have to get home. Are any shops still open?"

He looked around. "I don't see Mr. Farley yet, so I guess he's still at his store. It's just around the corner from Bingham's."

Outside, the wind muttered and whipped, occasionally rising to a howl. Henry headed for the stable to get his sorrel, and was out of sight before he reached the street corner. The falling snow had slacked, but the wind was whipping what was on the

77

ground into scudding frenzy. It would be like this for a time, then the snow would come again, this time blinding in its density and driven by gale winds straight down from the north pole with no more than a barbwire fence to slow them.

People die in high plains blizzards. They get lost and freeze, sometimes within feet of their own back door.

Farley's shop was still open. I found a hat that fit, and bought it. I also bought a heavy wool blanket with a stitched center slit, the kind the Texans call a poncho and the Californios call serape. I bought some other things, too, including two boxes of .45 cartridges. Everything I bought fit into the pockets of my heavy coat. I put on the serape and immediately felt its warmth.

Farley closed as soon as I left, and from Bingham's dark doorway I saw him plod off down the street, his collar around his ears and the wind whipping his coat tail. There was no one else around.

The undertaker's shed and Bingham's barn were the same building, one roof covering two spaces with a pair of doorways between. The shed was dark and cold, the back half of it open to the freezing air, its windows wide. It didn't matter here if snow drifted in. It was only storage.

Three closed caskets lay on sawhorses. Two of them were empty. The third was draped with dark cloth. I went and stood by it for a moment. I had candles in my pocket, and got one out. Then I put it back. I had always wanted to see him, just once. But I didn't want to see him now. There were others I wanted to see instead . . . the ones who killed him. I would remember him better from the bright images Mattie Stillwell had woven than from the face of a dead old man. Much better.

In silence I moved on, to the door leading to Bingham's barn. I started to push it open, then stopped. I heard faint sounds beyond it. I hesitated, then pushed it open just a crack as a gust of wind rattled the shutters.

The man in there had his back to me. By dim lamplight he was moving boxes and crates, methodically, rearranging as he inspected tags or labels on each one. I slipped into the barn and closed the door behind me. He glanced around. I was in shadows.

"I thought you were going to wait," he said, and went back to studying boxes. Then he lifted one with both hands. "Here it is."

"Set it on that table, Key," I told him.

He jerked around, peering at me. "Who are you? Do I know you?"

"I said set the box on that table. Easy."

"Look, I thought you were somebody else. I'm just getting some personal things. I don't . . ."

"Just set the box down and let me see it."

Staring at me, he stepped to the table and set the box there.

"Now the lamp," I said. "So I can see the label."

"Look, I don't know what this is all about. Who are you, anyway?"

I threw back the serape so he could see the gun at my side. He brought the lamp and set it by the box. I edged around to where I could read: "Sam'l Dance—Effects."

"I must have picked up the wrong box," the man

79

said. He was wary and sharp-eyed. He had nervous hands.

"Who sent you for this?" I asked.

"Look, I said I picked up the wrong box, that's all. Over there, that's mine."

I glanced away where he had pointed, and his movement was a blur in the corner of my eye. He dodged aside, swept back his coat and came up with a pistol, a fast, professional movement. He left me no choice. The .45's roar was muffled by a howling gust of wind that whistled in the rafters.

I found an appropriate place to deposit him, then spent a half hour going through the personal effects of a man I had never met. There were some old letters—a commendation from the town council of Independence, Missouri, another from a town in Texas, a letter from a man in Virginia—dated nineteen years ago—saying the information Mr. Dance requested was not available and suggesting the state archives . . . and there was a folded and faded theater poster announcing the appearance of Miss Mattie Stillwell for a matinee performance at the Denver Grand National. The date was in 1878. That was fourteen years ago. I put the poster in my pocket.

There was a tied package of newspapers bound with a file of carefully-written copies of court documents. These I set aside.

The rest was the sad legacy of a man who spent his life enforcing the law. There was a gold watch, two Colt revolvers, a little Smith & Wesson .22, a latched wood box containing a finger ring and six badges of various kinds from various places, an old tintype of a blonde woman holding a baby, and a little collection of books. One of them, wrapped in oilcloth, was an old hymnbook with brown-edged pages. A tortoise-shell place marker was inserted at Selection 17: *Shall We Gather At The River*. I took that, too.

The remnants of 50 years of living.

I replaced most of it, resealed the box and put it back where the gunman had found it. Then I had other things to do.

Most of the way to the hotel stables I traveled blind, guiding by walls and hitchrails and by the feel of frozen ruts deep beneath the heavy snow.

Only a single attendant was there, an aging man asleep beside the glowing stove. I didn't bother him. Old Rounder came from behind the stove to wag his rear and look up at me. I scratched his ears, fed him, then shucked down to the waist, poured water in a basin and got cleaned up. I shaved, put on my good shirt and coat, and combed my hair.

Serape, greatcoat and most of my purchases I stowed with my gear. I patted Rounder again and headed for the hotel.

Beyond the stable door was a wall of dark snow. The wind howled now without letup, and the snow was a million little bullets that burned where they hit skin. Bending into the wind I got a hand on the corral fence and followed it to the gate. From there, someone had strung double ropes to the hotel's back porch. I was numb with cold and puffing from exertion by the time I reached shelter. I hoped Henry Lattimer was snug in his claim shack by now. It was no time for anyone to be out.

Yet inside, the hotel was snug with that special coziness that comes of a stormy night. As the wind sang dirges in the eaves and sills and battered at the walls with shuddering force, chandeliers and lamp-light brightened the lobby and dining room. It was a different crowd now. The townsfolk had gone, and the guests had the place mostly to themselves.

Max Bernheim and several other gentlemen sat in easy chairs before a roaring fire, and I saw Si Rutledge and his two ladies at a lighted table. I went to the fire. The men there looked at me as I approached, and for a moment there was no recognition. Then Bernheim jumped up. "Ah, Mr. Stillwell! Good evening. I hardly knew you, sir."

"When we met earlier I was dressed for hauling bones . . . and for being in jail. I'd like to repay you for your services, if I may."

"All in good time. I'll draw up a bill. May I introduce you to these gentlemen?"

I had already met Sheriff Guthrie. Judge Kendall was a middle-aged man with a mild face, eyes like flint rock and a shock of graying hair. He stood to shake hands, and those eyes didn't miss a thing, including the gun under my coat.

"May I congratulate you on the turn of events that led to your freedom," he said drily. "The lack of evidence has saved many a man from justice."

Bernheim sucked in a hard breath but I waved him off. I smiled at the judge. "And brought justice to many a man who might otherwise have been sacrificed for show. It appears you made a trip to Springfield for nothing, your honor . . . unless you have an opportunity to try Ira Fox for complicity and attempted murder at the jail."

"No charges have been brought in that matter," he

said, and sat down.

"I don't suppose Judge Tomlin made it into town today?" I asked Bernheim. He shook his head. "Well, he won't make it now. I was hoping to visit with him."

That caught their attention, but I didn't say any more. I was introduced to the others there—two lawyers and a cattleman—then excused myself.

At Ira Rutledge's table I took off my hat and held out my hand. "Mr. Rutledge? My name is Byron Stillwell. I would like to persuade you not to be too distraught if I am not hanged."

He stared at me blankly for a moment, then frowned in puzzlement and took my hand. "I was advised," I said, "that you might be disappointed if I didn't hang for murder. I hope that won't stop you from introducing me to these lovely ladies."

Rutledge's wife giggled and his sister, Mrs. Mills, looked at me appraisingly.

"You see," I told Rutledge, "I really was innocent."

"Damned direct manner, I must say," he said. Then he grinned, a rueful turn of his cheeks. "Mr. Stillwell, recently of Springfield's county jail, may I present my wife, Barbara, and my sister, Patty Mills." I took their hands in turn, then joined them at their table. "You surprise me," Rutledge said. "Is it bravado or gall that brings you to me?"

"Simple innocence, sir. And a desire not to be thought otherwise . . ." I met Patty Mills' direct gaze, ". . . by anyone."

A look passed between Rutledge and his wife. He said, "I should have guessed."

Patty Mills was still staring at me, slight puzzlement in her blue eyes. She looked to be about twenty, but I guessed twenty-five or so. Her hair was drawn back from the temples to cascade behind her from an onyx comb. She had lovely ears.

"Are you trying to read my mind?" I asked her. "I imagine you could."

She blinked, and a sly smile pulled her lips. "Oh, yes. I can. You are congratulating yourself on a successful direct attack that has confused my brother. You are wondering whether there is a Mr. Mills, and you are wondering whether any of us believe your innocence."

"You are a wonder," I assured her. "Could you possibly enlighten me on just one of my wonderings?"

"There is no Mr. Mills," she said. "I have been a widow for almost five years. Is that the one?"

"The very one. Thank you. And when you aren't visiting your brother on the frontier, where might you be found?"

"Philadelphia. I have a house there."

"Anywhere near the Cornwell district?"

"At Camden, actually. Just across the river. But I have visited the square many times. I have seen plays at the Rouge and the Independence."

"And had a sherbet afterward at the China Sea, I imagine. Everyone should."

"Fascinating," Rutledge put in. "A bone hauler who knows the best places in Philadelphia."

"I was a bone hauler Thursday," I told him. "Not today."

"And what are you today, Mr. Stillwell?" Mrs.

Rutledge asked pleasantly.

"In love, I think, though such a conclusion should be fortified with extensive research."

Barbara Rutledge blushed and giggled. Mr. Rutledge coughed. Patty Mills laughed aloud and there was music in it. "You do have audacity, sir," she said. "Are you as quick with that gun as you are with your tongue?"

She hadn't missed a thing. I eased around so my coat covered it better. "A habit of long standing, Ma'm. In the west there are places where a handgun is a comforting thing to have."

"We see so few in Philadelphia."

"Of course. In Philadelphia weapons are seldom seen. Derringers and stilettos are much more elegant than a .45 at the hip. Will you be in Kansas long, Mrs. Mills?"

"For a few months, at least. I'm helping Si with the newspaper."

I turned to Rutledge. "Are you a good reporter? Are you fair and impartial?"

"I try to be," he said. "Why?"

"Do you care about the murder of Sam Dance?"

"Do I care?" he flared. "Of course I care. Sam Dance was more than a good sheriff and a decent man. He was a friend. What are you driving at?"

I studied him. It is hard, making decisions about people. You never know what is inside. But the man had a directness about him that I liked. "I'd like to leave a package with you, in trust. You may look at it and think about it, and possibly you might find it interesting. But I would appreciate it if you'd keep it strictly confidential. And that means no one but us here must even know about it. After you have looked through it, I want you to share it with that young deputy, Henry Lattimer. He has a right to it. But *no one else*. Is it a bargain?"

His eyes went shrewd. "What is in the package?"

"I don't know. I haven't had a chance to study it, and I won't for a time. But it is something Sam Dance was interested in. Is it a bargain?"

He looked at his sister and his wife, then at me. "Bargain," he said. "Though I may regret it."

"Yes. So may we all. I'll leave it at the desk for you." I turned back to Patty Mills. "I understand they performed Rimsky-Korsakov's *Scheherazade* in Philadelphia last summer. Did you attend?"

7

Through the evening I listened to that slamming wind that was the blizzard's teeth. From inside the hotel it was a potent force, barely at bay, howling and whining like an insane thing. It rocked the walls and wailed in the doorwells. It chittered and sang at the windows and drove little drifts of sparkle through them where the caulking was loose.

I listened because it was important to me to catch the first of those momentary silences that would mean the blue norther had vented itself and was about to subside, at least temporarily. And I listened because it reminded me of Chako. This storm was moving due south, and it wouldn't stop for a thousand miles yet. It would rage across the prairies south of the strip in a few hours—or maybe was already there—and its bite there would be the worst of all.

It would flail around the mesas, scream its cold anguish through the canyons, dump running drifts into the valleys and drive the stock upward through the high breaks, right into the teeth of the killing wind. Unless someone were there to turn them, someone who knew the land very well.

Chako was there, and he knew the land like no white man could. Chako was a Kwahadi. He was older than me, but not much, and until he was eleven years old he had never seen a white man. His first experience were the pony soldiers of the eagle chief Mackenzie who exploded into his village one September evening, killing twenty-seven people, kidnapped more than a hundred women and children and burned all the lodges. Chako's father was one of the dead. His mother and two sisters were taken, and he escaped on a soldier's horse with the soldier's blood on his hands. By the time he was twelve he was following the buffalo with Quanah Parker.

During the year that I was learning mathematics and elocution at Bryant Academy while Mattie directed the Baltimore Opera Society, Chako was learning English on the Kiowa reservation near Fort Sill. While I was learning various high arts and low skills in New Orleans, Chako was surviving alone in the Palo Duro breaks, learning to use the Colt revolver that a white drifter had tried to use on him. And while I was on the run in the Sangre de Christos because of a shootout in a canyon below Red River Pass, Chako was growing corn and raising a few horses down in the Canadian valley.

He did all right there until the Double-D moved in and Davy Dawes celebrated his twenty-first birthday by sending out riders and gunhands to clear out every pothole outfit in two days' ride so he could have room for his cattle.

With the Dawes fortune behind him, and fielding men like Morgan Hayes and Pony Bidell to do his work, young Davy hit the Texas panhandle like a plague and even the old barons like Charles Adair pulled in their boundaries to accommodate him.

Chako never had a chance.

They came upon him by a little stream where he was watering his stock, Pony Bidell and three others. They rode him down, hazed and mocked him, then broke both his arms and left him there while they went upstream to trample his field, burn his shack and drive off his horses.

There was a man dead in Fort Worth just then, whose friends were looking for me, so I was abroad and traveling. I saw the smoke of the burning shack from a mesa-top, and went to see. When I found Chako he tried to fight me, even though his arms were broken.

I got him pacified finally, rigged splints and slings on his arms and built a lean-to over him to keep the rain off when it came. Then, since I had nowhere else to be, I stayed around there for a while. A man without arms needs a lot of help. And since we had to eat, I fed us Double-D beef and vegetables out of Key Begley's pantry. That seemed poetic justice. Key Begley was one of the men who had been with Pony Bidell when they hazed Chako. Also, his line camp was the furthest from Double-D headquarters, and the nearest to us. I located it, then I watched for a day or two until the supply wagon came and left and from that day on when Key was out on the range I just helped myself to what we needed.

Sometimes after a run I would ride up on a mesa, let my horse feed on the high grass and I would sit there with a telescope and watch that gunslick try to work out my trail.

Within three weeks Chako was doing for himself, though his arms still were bound and splinted, so I rode down to Mobeetie to send some telegrams and get caught up on things.

That was where I first saw Davy Dawes. He walked right by me in front of the telegraph office, with his two best gunslicks flanking him, Pony Bidell and Morgan Hayes. They were in town on business. The telegraph operator told me who they were.

Dawes was a strapping young fellow, as tall as me and beefier through the shoulders. He had brown hair and pale eyes that glowed with the love of power. At twenty-one he was already a legend. His grandfather was Peter Llewellyn Dawes, who hailed from Ohio and now owned as much of south Texas as anyone would want to reckon. Davy had been raised by his grandparents, and when he was of age the old man turned a fortune over to him and suggested the Panhandle. It would be a second Dawes empire.

Pony Bidell I knew by reputation. He was the only one who had walked away from the Stanton Ranch shootout in New Mexico a few years before. He had done it by killing six men—two of them his friends. He was sheet lightning with a revolver, and deadly, and always looking for another chance to prove it. Morgan Hayes was older, an ex-lawman gone sour, and nobody crossed his path. These and their ilk were the tribe Davy Dawes had bought to establish the Double-D. I was impressed.

I sent a telegram to Mattie, just to let her know I was safe and doing well. And as I had been doing fairly regularly for nearly three years, I sent a new batch of messages off to the War Department, the Archives of the Commonwealth of Virginia and a couple of new leads I had, one of them an old retired preacher in Georgetown who had agreed to help me. I never said anything about all this to my mother. It just didn't seem appropriate or necessary.

I stayed around Mobeetie long enough for the responses to come back. Mother was having a fine time organizing hospital volunteers and giving singing lessons. The War Department still had nothing for me, and the Virginia Archives were getting a little tired of my inquiries. But the preacher had something. In the spring of 1864, a few months before Sheridan's forces arrived on the James River, a makeup company of survivors and stragglers from three volunteer outfits had been assigned to the brigade commanded by Coleman. The company came from remnants of the Fourth Ohio, First Pennsylvania and the Second Illinois.

I stayed another day, wording and sending out inquiries to those states, hoping someone would look into it for me and be ready to respond next time I had a chance to send a wire.

Moving north then, I went right up through the heart of Double-D and what I saw there was awesome. Dawes was bringing in cattle from the south, as fast as his drovers could push them. They were mostly longhorns fresh out of the South Texas brush, wild and spooky, and the Double-D was packing them in. Good pasture in that llano country will graze a beef for every two acres and remain stable. Dawes had pretty nearly filled the range for several miles around Double-D headquarters north of Mobeetie, and I saw two big trail herds coming from the south.

It was high summer and the grass was crisp and yellow, and Davy Dawes was filling the range with cattle at a feverish rate. Unless he expanded his range or began moving them to market by the thousands, and did one or the other soon, there would be no range left.

I had seen some shaking of heads in town. Other ranchers around Double-D saw what was happening and they were nervous. But nobody, not even Charlie Adair, was going to go up against Dawes' crew. The word was that he paid gun wages to every man on his range.

And he had carved a big swath. Double-D had spread out to occupy more than a million acres—an octopus of first-class graze reaching as far as the Salt Fork of the Red on the south and well past the Canadian on the north, bounded by the reservations on the east and shoving up against the old Adair spread on the west.

The only place Dawes was cautious about spreading out was eastward, because there he would have run into federal problems. Times had changed in a decade or so. Reservation boundaries were more to keep encroachment out than to keep the Indians in.

Every line camp and range house had its remuda, but the big horse herds were kept on a three-or-four section spread in the hills above Clear Creek, a natural corral miles wide where bluffs and good grass did the work of keeping the horses in. There was fine stock there, a lot of it blooded stock.

I was across the Sweetwater and heading north when three horsemen came up from a draw to confront me. They were lean, tough customers with ready sixguns and were out to earn their pay.

"Mister, you're on Double-D range," the lead one told me flatly.

"Just traveling through," I assured him. "It's pretty hard to miss Double-D if a body is traveling in this country."

He looked me over while the other two held back, their hands near their guns. "You lookin' for work?"

"Are you offering?"

"The boss could use more men. Can you use that iron?"

I looked at him sadly and shook my head. "The kind of work I might look for, the first question would be, 'Can you swing a rope,' or 'Can you set a brand first stab.' This gun is for snakes. I don't look for fighting."

He grinned sourly. "Just a poor, driftin' poke, huh?"

"I guess so."

"Well, Mister, you just keep driftin' then, the way you're goin'. Don't change direction, don't turn back and don't let any grass grow under you. And don't stop until you're off the Double-D. This ain't no excursion route."

To make his point, he drew his gun and rapid-fired three shots around my horse's feet, spraying gravel. I leaned into the animal's motion as it reared and bolted, and just let it run. They were laughing back there like it was the best joke of the week.

When I got back to Chako he was doing pretty well, taking care of himself, and I brought in another Double-D beef with me.

"That was Johnny Saxon," he told me. "I know him. Big man with a gun, little inside. You should have killed him." The way he said it there was no doubt in his mind that I could have . . . all three of them.

I tipped my head at him. "What makes you think I could take those three?"

He grinned. "I have eyes, Brother Wolf."

A couple of weeks passed, and we took the splints off his arms. The bones had healed straight, but his arms were weak. He began exercising them, and his exercises always included an hour or two at a time of drawing his gun.

Then he taught me some things I had not learned before—a way to roll your hand so the heel of the thumb catches the hammer as the gun is drawn, shaving a blink off firing time, how to wear a belt so the butt of the gun is just above the wrist, where the fingers will catch it rising—I thought I was pretty good, but Chako showed me how to be better. And we had become friends during those weeks.

I told him about the Double-D spread, about the horse herd I had seen, and his dark eyes narrowed and glowed like a cat on a rock. They had taken his horses. Now he decided he would take some of theirs.

"We can get a bunch out of there, all right," I told him. "But we'd never get them away. It's just too far to get off Double-D. They'd be all over us."

"You think white too much," he sneered. "We take horses and run away, sure they catch us. Problem is run away. How about we run toward?"

"Toward what? Double-D?"

"Sure. We take horses, they come out to get us.

They come out, we go in. You want to help?"

Of course I wanted to help. Whatever he had in mind, it sounded more interesting than any plans I had.

He needed a horse, so I went and got him one. It was a second-hand horse. One of Johnny Saxon's friends was using it when I found it, but he didn't need it any more.

Late one afternoon we lay atop a bluff looking out across the bounded flats where Double-D's riding stock grazed. Chako didn't miss a thing. He studied movement of the horses, terrain, distances and options like a general planning a campaign.

"We can take most of them," he told me. There were hundreds of horses out there.

"Where can you go with that many that they can't find you?"

"I only want twenty. They took nine, I take twenty. Fair trade."

"Then what are the rest for?"

"Satisfaction."

At moonrise we were mounted and quartering the flats. Within two hours we had the stock bunched quietly on a stream in the west end of the pocket pasture which was the highest part of the sections. Then we moved them out, slow and easy, westward through a wide draw with water in it. We went about four miles, angling north of west, before Chako eased to the head of the herd and began turning them into a cross draw. He cut two fences to make way for them.

It was past midnight when we brought the herd up onto open range, and only two miles from the central headquarters of Double-D. Chako's teeth glistened in the moonlight as a devilish grin spread across his dark face. Between us we were moving nearly four hundred horses, and we pointed them right at the ranch headquarters.

"They'll have night guards," I told Chako.

"No," he said. "Too big. Guards are out there, not here. Nobody would bother the home place." He grinned again.

For another mile and a half we drifted the herd, then we bunched them and put ourselves on the flanks. "Okay?" Chako called.

"Okay." I drew my gun and fired when he did, and I yelled when he did, only his was in Comanche. The herd bolted, lined out and thundered down on the ranch headquarters.

Horses don't stampede the way cattle do. Cattle go only one direction and if they are contained they pack and mill. Horses will turn and keep running. And in a closed compound this means they will go around and around, stomping everything they can stomp, until very little is left. They won't shatter buildings, which cattle might, but they can play hell with garden plots and low fences, and they are death on tents.

A lot of the crew on the new Double-D was still sleeping in tents.

We drove them on and we drove them in and we backed them up with gunfire. Then we cut off the last twenty or so and headed straight east at a run. A half-mile away, we could still hear the pandemonium behind us.

We ran them another mile, then eased off and lined them out southeast.

"Probably some broken arms back there," Chako said happily.

"At the very least," I agreed.

Moving fast and light, staying to the draws and out of sight, we came at evening to a place Chako knew, a broad, lush valley just above where the Sweetwater joins the north fork of the Red. It was scrub land, full of mottes of low oak and wild grape, and the soil was the color of sunset. But there was good grass and water to be had. "I know a place," Chako pointed. "Haystack Mountain. Not far. Cheyenne-Arapaho reservation land but they don't need it. I can use it."

"This is awfully close to Double-D," I pointed out.

He turned in his saddle. "We left Texas three miles back. This is Indian land. They won't come here."

"They will if they can prove you stole horses."

He gazed proudly around at the twenty-three head of prime stock starting to spread across his claimed property. "Thing about whites and blooded horses," he said. "Whites take pride in what they can buy. Not a mark on any of these. Who can say they aren't mine?"

He was right about that, at least for the time being. He stayed there and tended his horses and nobody bothered him.

That was two years ago, and the horse I rode now was the one he had selected for me from his little herd, the best of the bunch. We had clasped forearms in the Indian manner, and he said, "You ever need a friend, Byron, you let me know."

I thought of him now as I waited out a blizzard that was heading his way. In a way, Chako was a man at peace . . . because he knew who his war was with.

I wasn't that sure of mine.

I visited for a pleasant time with Patty Mills, and we hardly noticed when Si Rutledge and his wife left us and went off to their room. The hotel was cozy, a warm place bounded by howling wind, and most of the guests had turned in.

"Will I see you in the morning?" she asked.

"When this storm blows over, I have some things to do. I may be busy for a while. But you can be sure I'll see you around."

She looked at me with those direct blue eyes, and frowned. "I have enjoyed this . . . talking with you like this, I mean. I don't think I have felt really close to someone in a very long time. But you worry me, Byron Stillwell. I don't know who you are."

"I thought you could read my mind."

"I can read parts of it very well." She blushed then, and I grinned. There was no pretense between us, at least on certain points. "But I can't make you out. I have no idea who you are or what you are doing . . . except I know you are doing something."

"I'm looking for the answers to some questions," I said. "It's a puzzle I've stumbled across, and maybe it's the first thing in my life that has been important enough to me to keep me searching until I solve it."

"But what is it?"

"Maybe you'll know more when you and your brother look at the package I have for you. Maybe then you can help me get some answers. I want to know why Sam Dance died."

"You mean, who killed him?"

I turned away. "I want to know why."

In my room, I slept for a few hours, always aware

98

of the keening and shuddering of the wind. It was nearly morning when the song of it began to rise and fall in pitch, to become erratic. I got up and dressed, took my saddlebags and went down through the silent lobby. Between the hotel and the stables, snow was drifted head-high along the fence but was only about knee deep behind the drift. It was dark and gusty and snow was still falling. And it was bone-chilling cold. The wind was confused: short, howling gales followed by silence, then moments of swirling, tumbling powder washing about in turbulence.

Someone had built up the fire in the stable stove, but no one was around. I left some meat by the stove for Rounder, then got my horse out and saddled him. I tied on saddlebags, draped a large wool blanket over the whole rig with tie-ups for the stirrups and a draw to keep the wool high on the horse's neck, and put on my heavy serape. It would be a hostile world out there this morning.

There was barely enough light to see as I left Springfield, heading south. But the wind had calmed and the still-falling snow would leave no trail behind me.

8

Henry Lattimer awoke shivering. The coal fire in his cast-iron stove was down to mottled ashes and the little house was intensely cold. Gray light filtered through his two windows, and seep snow was drifted on the floor beneath them. A gust of wind rattled the chimney pipe, then whined into silence. His teeth chattered as he wrapped his blankets around him and sat up, cross-legged, dreading to touch his bare feet to the cold floor.

But it was late, and he had to get moving. With a sigh of resignation he threw off the blankets and danced across to the stove, where he squatted freezing in his red flannels to get a fire going again. The few ounces of coal oil he used to start it made a pretty blaze and he held his hands inside the firebox, relishing the warmth. Then he sat in his chair, pulled on stockings and boots, shrugged into his coat and pushed the back door open. It plowed snow, cutting an arc in tail-drift nearly three feet deep. Leaving the door open he jumped over the crest of the drift, which rose toward the south side of the house, and landed in soft powder that sifted over the tops of his boots. Puffing and whistling, he ran for the outhouse. The little upright shed was half buried in its own drift.

Another gust flapped his coat as he gained the icy safety of the outhouse.

Returning up the path a few minutes later, trying to dance tip-toed around the deep places, he noticed that the snow had almost stopped and the gray light was brighter. The clouds were thinning. From the north he saw another gust moving in, sweeping powder before it in a swirling mist. He ran for his open door, slammed it behind him, and sighed. There were things to be said for homesteading on the plains, but winter wasn't one of them.

The stove was hot to the touch and he huddled before it, his arms wrapped around its iron belly, until the heat became too much. He didn't want to scorch his coat. It was the only one he had.

By the time he was dressed in shirt, pants and wool pullover, the stove was glowing and the room was beginning to warm. He swept up the little snowdrift under the north window, then wiped the floor with a cloth. Henry was proud of his plank floor. He had labored to install it.

His house, his snug little barn and the small crop he had harvested the past summer were Henry Lattimer's claim to a future which opened wide and bright before him. One more year, and he would prove up on his claim. Then this land would be his—all 160 acres of it, a quarter section. From his house he could see all four of its corners, carefully staked, and could visualize fences and cornfields, a few cows grazing on a good pasture, a garden plot close in and a dooryard with flowers to be picked.

But at the moment, as he peered through the steaming glass pane of one of his two windows, there was nothing out there but white. Dead snow white under a leaden sky and nothing moving anywhere.

He set a pot on the stove top, scooped in a handful of milled oats and added water. He would make coffee when the oats were hot. There was space on the little stovetop for only one vessel at a time.

He scuffed a path out to the barn, tended and fed his horse, used an axe to chop a slab from a frozen ham, and went back to the house. A line of blue showed on the north horizon. Soon the clouds would begin to break and drift.

He hoped the sun would shine when they held services for Sam Dance. Few people were likely to be there, and he would tell himself it was because of the snow though he would suspect it was indifference. That would be all right if the sun would shine. People didn't matter to Sam Dance now. But he had liked the winter sun.

After breakfast Henry Lattimer did his chores, closed his house, saddled his horse and headed for Springfield. His scuffed trail wandered among great wind-peaked drifts, keeping to the shallow places between where sometimes the snow was only inches deep.

A dark-eared jackrabbit broke from snow-muffled sage ahead of him and bounded away, leaving a line of craters behind it eight feet apart. Henry shifted his rifle instinctively, then grinned. "Go on, scat!" he shouted as the jack veered out of sight beyond a tall drift. "Man could starve to death on the likes of you, anyway."

In town he put his mount away, then walked to the jail, plowing through drifts at the building corners he passed. Sim Guthrie was already there. "Good morning, Sheriff," Henry told him. "How is Everett this morning?"

"I haven't checked," Guthrie said, glancing up from the papers on his desk. "Henry, did you check out Bingham's warehouse yesterday? Bingham says he thinks somebody has been in there. Some boxes have been moved."

"I looked in about dark, just a while before I went home. Everything looked all right then." He turned from the stove. "What boxes? Did he say?"

"No. Just that somebody had moved things around. Why?"

"Sheriff, Mr. Bingham said Sheriff Dance's personal effects are in the barn there. Would it be all right if I looked through them?"

Guthrie glanced up. "I'm afraid not, Henry. Now that the body has been claimed, personal effects go with it. I've already signed the waiver. None of that is in my custody now. What did you want to see?"

"Oh, nothing." Henry turned away. "I just thought I'd like to see what he left. Ah, Sheriff?"

"Yes?"

"The other day you asked me if I wanted to stay on. I guess I will, for a while, anyway . . . if you want me to."

Guthrie tapped a pencil on the desk, "I'm not Sam Dance," he said. "You know I'll run this office my way. Can you go along with that?"

"I guess so. But you know that what I know about

103

lawing I learned from Mr. Dance. I can't be different than I've been taught to be."

"You can keep learning. There's more to being the law than Sam Dance . . . I'm sorry, than *any* one man . . . puts into it. Will you try to see my side if I do things differently?"

"I'll try."

"Then it's done. And I'm proud to have you with me, Henry. We'll go on from here."

There was a rattling from the street. A wide moldboard drawn by a double-hitch team worked its way along the street, plowing snow into a high comb in the center. The driver walked behind, working the reins. A milkwagon crept along behind the plow, and muffled people were out and about. As Henry watched from the window, morning sun broke through the thinning clouds and struck the snow-laden town with radiance that made his eyes burn. He stepped out onto the fluff-covered walk and turned his face upward, his eyes watering with the brilliance. "Thank you," he whispered.

Carrying his rifle, wading through snow sometimes hip-deep and in other places swept clean, Henry made the morning rounds. He routed himself to end at the hotel. When he arrived there his cheeks shone red and his toes were numb. He went straight to the fire and opened his coat to soak in the warmth. Someone set a mug of hot coffee on the mantel before him and he turned. Si Rutledge's sister, Mrs. Mills, smiled up at him. "You look as though you need that."

"I sure do. Thank you."

She glanced around. No one else was near. "Deputy . . . ah, Henry, my brother and I would like to visit with you when there is time. Privately."

"Yes, Ma'm. What about?"

"We have some . . . rather interesting documents that you should see. Mr. Stillwell left them with us. He wanted us to look them over and discuss them with you. I believe they are papers Sheriff Dance had collected."

Henry was puzzled. He knew of some papers, but how could . . . the moved boxes! By Stillwell had found the papers. His law-abiding soul twinged at the thought, but he found himself grinning at the pretty woman. "Yes, Ma'm. I would like to see those." Then he cocked his head. "You said he left them? Has he gone somewhere?"

"Apparently. He isn't here this morning. He did tell me he would be back, though."

At 10 o'clock a small group gathered in the brilliant snow before the lot that fronted Bingham's storage barn and the undertaker's shed. There were only a few people. Sid Mason was there with Si Rutledge and his wife and Mrs. Mills, and Sim Guthrie and Mr. Bingham, and Bob Rice who now was night deputy. A few others. No one had come from out of town except Frank Murdoch and one of his friends whom Henry didn't know. He bit his lip, bleak thoughts bothering him. Where was Will Tomlin? Where were the people from Fargo Springs who had called on Sam Dance when they needed help? Where were all the people who had elected him and needed him and used him and then elected someone else? Henry's eyes watered and stung and he blamed the glare of the sun on snow.

He was not surprised that Byron Stillwell was not here. Byron had never met the man he had discovered was his father. And not having him to remember alive, he would not want to remember him dead. But where were all of Mr. Dance's friends? Henry looked around at the little group and had his answer. They were here.

The Miller boys came with their wagon double-hitched and draped in black, and shoveled a path to the shed to back in and then drive out with the coffin. They stopped in the street, and Pastor Bell and Mr. Farley came from Farley's store to join the group. All the men removed their hats.

Henry heard the preacher's words, but they made no impression. The preacher was doing a ritual thing. It had no meaning. Henry gazed at the casket on the wagon and remembered the big, easy-going man who had been sheriff of Seward County . . . who had worked so hard and worried so much for people who cared so little. Mr. Dance had been a lonely man, always keeping his personal thoughts to himself, reluctant to burden those he served with his personal life. And that reluctance, Henry understood, had cost him the crowd his funeral deserved. Only those who knew him were here, and few had ever really known him. The thought reminded him sharply, suddenly, of Byron Stillwell. They were so different . . . yet some ways so alike.

The preacher finished his words and Mr. Bingham clambered onto the wagon bed to open the casket. Those present filed by, glanced inside, then turned away. Henry chose not to look. He simply walked past, head averted.

When the casket was closed Ted Miller switched his reins and the wagon rolled away to the east, leaving crisp hub-deep ruts where the street had not yet been cleared.

Henry looked after it for a time, watched it leave town and begin its slow journey across snow-layered plains to the railhead at Arkalon. Goodbye, he thought. Goodbye, Mr. Dance.

The others went their ways, and Henry had started toward the hotel when Mr. Bingham burst from his door, white-faced, and grabbed him by the arm. "Come quickly," he said, and led Henry through the store, out the back and to the casket shed. Two caskets rested there on planks, two caskets that should have been empty. But one was not empty.

The man inside, staring upward with frozen eyes, was very dead. He was lean, wiry-looking and unshaven. He wore a dark coat and a dark hat lay beside his head.

"I started to move this," Bingham babbled. "It was very heavy, so I lifted the lid. Who is it, Henry? Do you know him?"

Henry shook his head. The dead man's arms were crossed on his chest. There was a pistol in his frozen right hand. Just beneath was a dark stain. The bullet hole was hidden by the hands. No other wounds were visible. "I've seen him around here a time or two," the deputy said. "But I don't know him."

He kept a fact to himself, at least for the time. Henry knew where he had seen the man. Twice that he knew of he had seen him, and maybe a third time. Once, a month or two ago, he had noticed this man mounting a horse in front of the blacksmith shop.

That was all. The man had simply mounted his horse and ridden away. But Henry remembered clearly. It had been mid-morning, the air crisp with coming winter, and there had been people on the street going about their business. Sturdevant, the judge's court officer, had been here. He remembered the grim, taciturn officer lounging at a corner of the blacksmith shop, watching the same man mount and leave.

Then two days ago, the afternoon before the shooting at the jail, Henry had noticed the man again. He had ridden past the jail, glancing around as Henry stepped out the door.

And maybe a third time. Poor light, confusion and shock make for poor memory. But now Henry looked at the dead face and a presence once-noted built in his mind. Without clearly remembering a face—only a confused impression of outline in the dark of morning—he remembered a voice. "Move, boy, move!" it said.

It was Frank Murdoch who identified the body, later in the day. The man was one of several who had taken rooms at Murdoch's hotel in Liberal a week or so before. He was not quite sure when. "They seemed to have plenty of money," he told Guthrie and his deputy. "I had the impression they came from the south, but I really don't know that. I remember this one, though, because he had a peculiar name. Begley. 'Key,' they called him. Key Begley."

"You said there were others," Guthrie said. "Are they still there?"

Murdoch shook his head. "I don't know. I think they were yesterday, but I came up here last evening. It looked like it would storm and I didn't want to miss the services for Sam."

Guthrie shrugged. Henry knew he was wishing for a telegraph line. But the nearest telegraph right now was at Arkalon, the railhead. Neither Springfield nor Liberal had wires so far. He turned to Henry. "I guess I need somebody to go down there. Henry, do you want to go? It'll be a little rough, but not too bad now that the sun is out."

"Sure," Henry said. "I'll go. What do you want me to do?"

"Find those men who were with Begley. Find Vince Cole, get him to go with you, and the two of you find them if they're still there. See if you can get them to come up here . . . voluntarily, of course. But whatever, I want to know who they are and where they're from and why their partner's body is in a box in Springfield."

Henry headed out a half-hour later, provisioned for a hard trip. On the plains a rider could avoid most of the drifts. But the Cimarron valley was between, and it was wide and deep and rugged, and would be heavy with snow.

The bright sun lay at noon-point, south of overhead, and cast blue shadows in the sweeps and dunes of snow. The snow was unmarred. No one had yet used the south road today. Only rabbit trails marked the purity of the landscape. Not even a wolf had been this way since the snow stopped. But then, watching the soft contours of blue-shadowed brilliance, he got the impression someone else may have passed this way, but earlier, while it was still snowing. Gentle dips at close intervals ahead of him could have been tracks of a horse.

Two miles south he turned to angle right at the head of Cross Canyon, gauging the location of the road from memory. He stopped there and sat for a few minutes, his eyes on the lip of Cross Canyon less than a hundred feet away. Beyond the lip blue shadows showed the sweep of the canyon down toward the bottom of the Cimarron Valley. Far away down there, nearly a mile from where he sat, a tiny frozen stream threaded its way along the sand flats of the river's channel. Where he sat men had assembled a week before, assembled to commit murder. Beyond that lip he and Sam Dance and others had waited. And down in that canyon the sheriff had died. Now the snow covered it all.

He angled west, following the invisible road, and noticed the faint impressions he had seen before were no longer visible. Whoever had come along earlier must have turned . . . or come from . . . the other way.

The road dipped down and he leaned in the saddle as his horse fought through the first of the high drifts of the valley. Henry Lattimer took a deep breath. The trip would get tough now. And it would get tougher and tougher before it got better.

He remembered, then. He had promised Mrs. Mills he would look at the papers Sam Dance had left. But it was too late now. He hoped they would be in Springfield when he returned.

9

Chako had chosen well when he selected a horse for me. The gray gelding was well suited to take a man where he wanted to go. Sturdy and long of limb, he had that compactness that comes of good structure and fine muscles, a mix of racing stock and cowpony with the best features of both. We traveled nearly blind for several miles, in morning dark and whipping snow, and his sure-footed breeding was the best thing I had going for me.

Even in greatcoat and heavy wool serape, it was fiercely cold out there where the plains fell away into the Cimarron bottoms. But the killing edge of the winter storm had gone on past, howling away into the south, and I rode east now through the trailing gusts of it.

Old Fargo Springs, what was left of it, was drifted, buried and silent in the gray of dawn. I skirted around it to take the trail south, down the rim of the Cimarron cut and into the river valley. The rimrock here was steep on both sides of the trail, and for a space beyond it the sloping ground was almost free of snow. Blizzard winds had hurtled above it and thrown the snow far out, to settle into the lower places. Even with first morning light the valley was vague, its floor a shifting puzzle of moving dry drifts and its far side lost in the dancing mists of still-falling snow.

The going was easy for a quarter of a mile, then we came to the blizzard's first deposit. Deepening powder rose to the gray's belly, then curved up before us in a knife-combed drift that was higher than my head on horseback. The shifting, erratic winds were just now beginning to erode its crest. It was a wall of snow, and the gray wanted to balk at it, but I backed him away, circled on the slope above it, then touched spurs to him that he felt through his draping blanket. "Hit it, Sport," I yelled, and he leaped into the belly-down run of his cowpony ancestors. Loose snow crunched beneath his hooves and showered away in his wake. Almost beneath the standing drift I leaned, put heels to him and lifted his head. Powerful hind legs thrust, and we sailed into an arcing jump, straight into the face of the towering drift. It was like hitting a mountain of talc. We thudded into it, seemed to hang for an instant, buried in fluff, then exploded from the trailing side and landed in cushioning snow beyond, still running. I reined him in quickly. There was a graded trail here somewhere, under the snow, but to each side of it the terrain was treacherous, a stairstep sweep of erratic banks and rock rims. I let him move by instinct, testing the ground beneath the snow.

Twice more we battered through high drifts, but the gray was used to it now. He seemed to enjoy charging the blind white walls, leaping into them and bursting through into open air beyond. I was glad Chako was not there to see how I was using his horse.

By the time we reached the bottom there was good light. We fought drifts for three quarters of a mile then, wending among stands of cottonwood bare in the winter morning, avoiding towering peaks of snow, thrashing through belly-deep fall for hundreds of yards at a time. The gray went down once, where snow hid the bank of the river's sandy bed. He fell and rolled, and I rolled further, but neither of us was hurt. Across the frozen, snow-laden sands we started up the south side of the valley. It was easier here. The blizzard winds had scoured the slopes, and in most places the snow was only inches deep.

A line of blue showed on the north horizon, and looking back I could see the far rim of the Cimarron Valley and the snow-laden jumble that was Fargo Springs. Springfield was beyond sight, miles away to the northwest on the high prairie. The wind was dying now, fitful gusts directionless in the valley, with silence between. I dismounted below the rim, removed the gray's covering blanket, unsaddled him and rubbed him down, then saddled him again. He steamed and pranced in the chill. I rolled the blanket and tied it behind the saddle.

"Let's move, Sport," I patted the gray's neck. "We still have a way to go, but from here it's only snow." We went over the rim and into climbing hills where the grass prairie was scoured clean on the high spots, a crazy-quilt of winter ground, wide patches of bright snow and occasional standing drifts where the terrain had fought the wind and stolen its white burden. As we topped out on the plains the sun broke through high clouds to dazzle the eyes with blinding distance all around.

Six miles ahead was the end of track of the railroad, a construction job abandoned until spring. With summer there would be track to lay and grades to extend, and it would reach Liberal by fall of the year. Changes would come then, and I wondered if anyone—even those bringing them about—knew what changes they would be.

We set out then at an easy lope, and by the time the sun was high I could see the shacks and sheds of the rail project. I reined in to get my bearings, and snow exploded from a brushed ravine nearby. A prairie wolf which had been watching me streaked from its shelter and sped on strong legs for the protection of a duned rise further away. The mist of fine snow that trailed him drifted a few feet and settled again, wide of his track.

I made a sign Chako had taught me and murmured, "Go, brother wolf. The rabbits are fat and you know their burrows.".

From a distance I found the shack I was looking for, and circled around to approach it from the west where tall drifts in the lee of a tie-pile hid my coming. I left the gray on a patch of wind-scoured ground where he could paw through to graze, and walked the rest of the way.

"Parson" Jolly was seldom far from the rails, and having no home and wanting none, he would go to ground wherever was available in winter. The parson was a whiskey peddler, one of those who supplied the railhead camps and the cowtown saloons, and out in this new land he was a cautious man. He wanted no chance of anyone following him to his caches. He also had a weakness for his own product.

The shanty was still, with no smoke coming from its stovepipe, but I knew he was there. I crouched beside a thin wall and in the stillness between breezes I could hear groans and snores from inside.

I kicked the door open and went in. The shack was dim inside and freezing cold, and the snores came from under a heap of bedding in one corner. There were bottles strewn around on the floor and the place smelled like a distillery. Business would be slow now in Beer City, with the snow, so Parson had holed up to wait for better times.

I left the door open to air the place out while I got a fire going in the iron stove. Then I found a pot, heaped it with fresh snow and put it on to make coffee. From the heap in the corner came groans, snores and occasional babbling.

When the coffee was boiled I walked over and kicked the heap. Nothing particular happened, so I kicked it again. This time the blankets flew and Parson Jolly came up bleary-eyed and stinking, trying to focus on me. "Wuzzat? Whayawant?"

"Get up," I told him. "It's morning and the coffee's on."

"Go 'way," he groaned.

I kicked him again, and this time he howled. "Get up," I told him.

He was awake now, on his knees, and he glared at me. He turned, got his feet under him, then spun around, drawing a pistol from somewhere in the layers of filthy clothing he wore. I knocked it spinning from his hand, grasped his lapels and slapped him soundly, open hand and backhand. Then I shoved him backward to rebound off a wall. He backed into a corner. "Who th' hell are you?" he snarled. "What do you want?"

"Good morning," I told him. "The storm is past and the sun is shining. You can have some hot coffee, and then we'll talk. I need some answers from you."

The coffee was good for Parson. It brought color to his face and a glint to his eyes and I told him, "Don't try me, Parson. I'll hurt you."

I saw the intent dissolve. "Who are you?" he grunted.

"My name is Stillwell." I leaned on the doorframe and studied him. "Next you are going to ask how I found you and the answer to that is I am very good at finding people. You might want to remember that. Any more questions?"

"What do you want?"

"Good question. About ten days ago, down in the Strip, a man told me that somebody was going to kill the sheriff of Seward County. He said he heard it from you when you brought supplies to Beer City. Tell me about that, Parson."

He swallowed some more coffee, then frowned at me. "Whoever it was got it wrong," he said. "What I'd heard was that somebody was plannin' to kill the judge. I guess I probably mentioned that, but it was the judge I heard about, not the sheriff."

"That's funny," I told him, "because the man who told me about it distinctly said *sheriff*. He said, 'that sheriff up there has been nosing into things that aren't any of his concern and they're going to kill him

116

for it.' "

"Well I don't know anything about that. All I heard was maybe somebody was gunnin' for Judge Tomlin. It's no secret a lot of people don't like him much. Hell, everybody knows he got a threat. That's why the damned sheriff was out there. That's why he got killed. Why don't you just leave me alone?"

"I'm looking forward to leaving you alone, Parson. Just as soon as I get a straight answer. Who told you they were going to kill the sheriff? You heard it someplace, and you told it when you were drunk. Now tell me."

"Maybe I got mixed up. I guess I *was* drunk. Maybe I said sheriff. That's probably what happened. But I meant judge." His hands had begun to shake.

"You're lying to me, Parson." I folded the serape back over my shoulder and flexed my fingers an inch from the butt of the .45. "Nobody knows you're out here. They won't find you until spring."

His face went white and he began to sweat in the cold room. "I . . . I'm tellin' you, mister. That's all I heard, so that's all I could have said. Maybe I was mixed up, but I know what I heard. Look, I'll say anything you want, but I heard they was after the judge."

"Who?"

"I don't know. Somebody that doesn't like him. I never heard."

"Who did you hear all that from, Parson?"

"I don't know . . ." He picked up the coffee cup and I drew and put a bullet through it. Coffee exploded over him and the tin cup clanged away to

117

bounce off a wall. The blast was deafening in the shack. Parson Jolly went over backward and rolled to stare at me. "Holy Christ, mister! Don't shoot me! Penny . . . I heard it from Penny Bassett!"

"And what did Penny Bassett tell you?"

His teeth were chattering, his eyes wild, but he hesitated. Then, "Just what I told you. That the judge was going to be killed. Not the sheriff. The judge."

I put the Colt away. I wouldn't get any more. Even staring into the muzzle of a Colt .45, the man was more afraid of someone else than he was of me.

His gun was lying on the floor, near his hand. His fingers wanted it but his eyes were afraid. "Let well enough alone, Parson," I told him. Then I turned and walked out.

The clean, cold air, after the stink of Parson Jolly's hidey-hole, was a blessing. I sucked it in and watched its bright mist as I exhaled. Even though the air was chill, the bright sun's rays were warm. I folded the serape and tied it with my blanket.

The Cimarron dominates Seward County. It enters from the northwest and leaves to the southeast, and its course is a series of arcs and miles of straight valley that divides the county into two triangles. Sometimes in the spring, the old hunters said, the river would go on a tear and overflow its banks and fill half its miles-wide valley with moving water. But this was rare. Usually the visible river was just a stream winding through the bottom of the valley, sometimes just a ribbon of water atop yellow sand. Whatever else it may be, though, the valley is the dominant landmark in these plains. I followed it southeastward, staying three or four miles away on high prairie above the rolling hills. Here and there in the distance were the chimney smokes of lonely soddies and claim shacks. I chose the nearest one.

Approaching, I knew this was a place that had been established for several years. Three quarter-sections showed signs of being worked. One half-mile square was bounded by rows of tough little hedge-apple shrubs thrusting through the snow, some of them horse high. The field within showed fingers of stubble between drifts. Another quarter was fenced with three-strand barbwire, and a third contained a windmill and frozen tank. The house was only a dugout, its roof starting three feet above the ground and mostly buried now in snow. But the barn and outbuildings were neat and sturdy. People were in the dooryard. A man in a heavy coat and pulled-down hat was hitching a mixed team to a wagon while two women and two younger men carried blankets and containers from the dugout.

I rode to the gate in front of the house and the man looked up and saw me. Carefully, keeping his eyes on me, he lifted a shotgun from the wagonseat and cradled it under his arm. "Good morning," he said cautiously.

"Good morning. Whose place is this?"

"Abel Selman's. That's me. What can I do for you?"

"My name is Stillwell and I guess I'm lost. I'm looking for a place owned by an Adolph Cort."

He looked at me curiously. He was a strapping man of forty or forty-five, short-bearded and sun-hardened. The rest were obviously his family. The two grown boys, who had approached and stood near their father, were maybe twenty and fifteen in years and looked like him. Behind them were a pretty woman with gray in her hair where it escaped her bonnet and a girl of maybe seventeen with her mother's dark eyes and her father's firm chin. She was striking. More than striking, she was a beauty.

"Adolph's place is about five miles southeast," Selman pointed. "Third house you'll see in that direction. But I doubt if he's there. He took his wife over to Liberal a few days ago to visit, and they probably stayed out the storm. You come far?"

"Just down from Springfield. Would there be anybody at Cort's place?"

His brow lowered slightly. "The hired man, I guess, if you want to see him."

"If his name is Bassett, I do."

"That's his name." Selman's gaze was stern now. "Are you a friend of his?" He didn't think much of Bassett.

"Not so you'd notice. But I owe him a favor, you might say."

He glanced at the sun, then back at me. "That was quite a storm we had. Guess you stayed over in Springfield until it passed." He looked suspicious. He knew what time it was, he knew how far Springfield was and he knew about the Cimarron Valley.

"I left early."

"I see. Any word on those murderers they have up there? The ones that killed Sam Dance?"

"Not much. One of them has been turned loose and the other has a broken arm. That's about it. I appreciate the directions. You folks on your way to

120

town?"

"To Liberal," the man nodded.

"Well, if you see Adolph Cort, you might tell him his hired man needs a doctor."

The girl's eyes widened at this. "Penny? How do you know? What happened?"

Oddly, her parents both looked pleased at the news.

"Oh, nothing yet," I told her. "But it's about to." I touched my hatbrim and wheeled the gray.

The man called after me, "What did you say your name is?"

"Stillwell," I waved to them. "Byron Stillwell."

I found Cort's place an hour later—a well-appointed place with a good house, a bunkhouse and three big barns. Cort's main venture, it seemed, was a dairy herd.

I rode past the main house, pulled up to the bunkhouse to reach down and bang on the door, then walked the gray across to the first barn, where I tied his reins to a corral bar. I removed his saddle, tossed it on the corral fence and rubbed him down quickly with a blanket.

Across the yard a door creaked on leather hinges and a cranky voice called, "Who is that? What do you want?"

I finished wiping the horse, then took off my heavy coat and hung it on the fence. Behind me I heard the door slam and then the crunch of his boots in the snow. "Can't you hear?" he rasped. "I said, what do you want?"

I hung up my good coat and hung my hat atop it. In shirtsleeves, the air was like ice. It was exhilarating. He was right behind me then, and glancing down

121

and aside I saw the leaded quirt dangling in his hand. I turned and grinned at him. "Hello, Penny. Remember me?"

10

Well, I had to let him have his chance. What I needed right then was Penny Bassett's undivided attention. I'd have to earn it.

"You!" he choked. "You're supposed to be in jail."

"Well, I got out and came to see you. Hit anybody from behind lately, Penny?"

His expression went from sour to mean. But he glanced at my hip and held his temper. "Big talker with that iron on your belt, ain't you, drifter? A lot bigger than you was without it."

"Oh, does this bother you, Penny? Well, then, I'll just put it away." I unbuckled my gunbelt and reached behind me to join the ends of it and he did exactly what I knew he would do. He charged.

For a big man Penny was quick. I dodged the quirt but took a left to the belly that almost doubled me over.

He spun, lashed out with the leaded quirt again, this time at my head, and I went in under it to clip him on the chin. It was a poor shot. It only made him mad. While he was shaking his head I did it again, then stepped aside and hung up the gunbelt I was still holding in my left hand.

He roared and charged again, pummeling. I dropped to my hands in the snow, took a solid blow from the quirt on my back and came up under him, digging in my heels. I heaved. He went over and thudded into the trampled snow, flat on his back. I jumped, trying to get a boot heel on his quirt hand, but he pulled away and caught my ankle, twisting as he rolled. I fell backward against the corral fence and slammed a knee to his face, then slid away and turned. He got to his feet and came for me again, but his foot slipped on the packed snow and he fell on his face.

"Woops," I told him happily.

It seemed as though everything I did just made him mad. He lashed out with that quirt and caught me across the shin. It hurt like fire. I hobbled off, my eyes watering, then turned as he got to his feet again. "I wish you hadn't done that, Penny," I said, and sidled in to bury my fist in his breadbasket. "First it was my shoulder, now it's my leg." As he doubled over I took his right arm at wrist and elbow and twisted it up behind his back, shoving him face-down in foot-deep snow. I heaved and heard him moan, his voice muffled by snow. His fingers opened and I took the quirt from him, then backed off and let him up. "Your turn now, Penny," I said.

He raised a big arm to club at me and I slashed him under the armpit with the quirt. As he turned I brought it down across his other wrist, then drove it hard against a kneecap. He howled and toppled, and I slashed him across the shoulders. He tried to get up and I hit him again, the heavy quirt thudding into his shortribs. He tried to crawl away and I whacked him on the tailbone. He went flat in the snow.

"Did you ever play questions and answers, Penny? It isn't difficult. Even an idiot like you should get the hang of it." He started to roll and I whipped him again for effect. "Now I'll ask the questions and you give the answers. Who first told you that Sheriff Dance was going to be killed?"

There was silence for a moment, then he raised his head to look at me. "You're crazy! You're plain crazy!"

"That isn't the answer." I striped his shoulder with the quirt. "Try again."

"Ow!" he sang, and flopped into the snow again. I waited.

"I don't know what you're talking about," he said finally, his breath ragged.

"Oh? Well, sometime recently . . . maybe a couple of weeks ago, you told Parson Jolly that Sheriff Dance was going to be killed. Old Parson told someone else about it and someone else told me. Now what I need to know is, where did you hear it?"

"All I know is I heard he'd been shot. I didn't know about it before . . . ahh!" I gave him a deep bruise along the thigh.

"Come on, Penny," I suggested. "Do you think I'm enjoying this?" I punctuated it with a hard blow across his back, where blood was seeping through his coat. That quirt was wicked.

"Oh, God!" he screamed. "Stop!"

"Where did you hear about it?"

"B-Beer City. Bunch of boys there. But they didn't

125

say the sheriff. They said the judge."

"Then how come you told Parson it was the sheriff?"

"I didn't! I . . ." I raised the quirt again and he cringed. "All right! Maybe I said the sheriff. Hell, they were talkin' about the sheriff too, that's all."

"About killing the sheriff?"

"Maybe. I don't know for sure. I just heard some words passed."

"Who passed them?"

"I don't know . . . for God's sake, I really don't know! He was a fellow I used to see around a couple of years ago . . . big heavy-built man with a dark beard . . . used to work over in Stevens County . . . Damn it, I don't know his name! Maybe they called him Morton, somethin' like that. I don't know! I hadn't even seen him around since the Stevens County wars!"

"But he's back?"

"He was at Beer City. Once. I saw him once."

"Come on, Penny. I really want more than that."

He rolled onto his side, curling up like a baby, and there were tears of pain and rage on his face. "I'll kill you," he promised. "Hell, I'll shoot you down like a wolf. You're crazy!"

"That may be so." I knelt beside him, holding the quirt where he could see it. "What did he say, Penny?"

"He said . . . he said the old man would be waiting at Cross Canyon, and they'd kill him. That's all. Sure, I thought they meant the sheriff. Everybody knows he was diggin' around in things best left alone. But then when I heard about that note the judge got, well I knew that wasn't right. It was the judge they were talkin' about. God damn it, leave me alone!'"

I had been tapping his temple, gently, with the quirt. When he raised a hand I whacked him across the fingers and backed off. I stood and stepped away from him. I shook my head. Penny Bassett. Local bully. Lying there curled up in the snow he looked like a big, red-haired, blubbering baby. I got out my pocket knife and sliced around the braided leather of the quirt. Then I pulled out the lead bar inside and dropped it in the snow. "Don't ever hit a man with one of these things again, Penny. It makes people angry."

I glanced up and Penny wasn't on the ground anymore. He was at the fence, pulling my gun from its holster. I sprinted two steps, dived and hit him in the middle of the back with my shoulder. The force of it slammed him against the rails and he hung there for a moment, then crumpled.

I put on my belt, coat, hat and overcoat and straightened my collar. Then I dragged Penny across to the bunkhouse and dumped him in his bed. I stoked up the fire and put water and a dipper beside him. He was breathing.

"Tell them," I said, not knowing whether he was conscious or not, "that Byron Stillwell is looking for them."

I made a cold meal from food I found there, then borrowed some of Mr. Cort's oats for the gray. We still had a long way to go.

The old man would be waiting, the man had said. The old man would be waiting at Cross Canyon and they would kill him there. What old man? The sheriff? Would "old man" mean Judge Will Tomlin? It could. He wasn't so old, but "old man" can mean many things.

And yet, who had been waiting at Cross Canyon? Who had indeed died there?

I had first seen the name on a telegraph message, written there in a telegrapher's neat hand: *Samuel Raymond Dance, Lieutenant of Volunteers, Fourth Ohio Regiment, attached brevet Captain Seventh Infantry Division, Grand Army of the Republic, at Chapel Hill, Virginia, 11 May 1864.*

Twenty-eight years ago. One year longer than the years of my life. And in that year he had loved Mattie Stillwell. And in all the years since she had loved him. She had made him as much a part of me as she was. Did I want to have known him—as the person he really was, not just the fantasy my mother had built for me? How could I know? People with guns had taken that choice away from me.

There had been other messages, too, from that same retired preacher and war historian. Samuel Raymond Dance was honorably discharged on March 15, 1865, at Fort Brighton, Ohio, and had returned to his birthplace, Darke County, Ohio. March 15. A week before I was born.

On May 12 of that year Samuel Raymond Dance was indicted for murder in the shooting of three men in Darke County. He was tried in June and acquitted. What were the circumstances? Maybe I would know one day.

And then just months ago, in the fall, I had

received a new message by agency telegraph at Fort Sill, Oklahoma: *S.R. Dance presently sheriff of Seward County, Kansas.*

Where had he been those intervening years? More than ever, I wanted to know. 1865 to 1891. A man can do a lot of living in twenty-six years. I had.

I was just saddling the gray when a rider appeared at the dooryard gate, looked around and then came toward the barns. It was the older Selman boy. He pulled up and looked around. "I guess you didn't find Penny," he said.

"I found him. He's over in the bunkhouse."

He stared at me for a minute, then got down and walked rapidly to the bunkhouse, opened the door and went in. In a minute he was back, running. "What did you do to him?"

"I beat him up." I tightened the cinch, gave the gray a pat and swung into the saddle. "I thought you folks were on your way to Liberal."

"We were . . . I mean they are, but Pa thought maybe I better look in down here. Penny can get pretty mean sometimes. He looks terrible!" he gazed at me suspiciously. "Did you pistol-whip him?"

"No. I used his quirt. Don't worry about him. He'll come around. Want to ride with me?"

"You mean you're just going to go off and leave him like that?"

"Sure. Come along, if you're coming." I touched heels to the gray.

He caught up with me before I reached the *bois d'arc* at the corner of the pasture. I headed the gray west across snow-muffled prairie and he tagged along. The slanting sun sheened across crusting snow, struck splinters of glare from drift-tops, blazoned the wide country with a brilliance all diamond and shadow-blue. With afternoon a cold breeze had risen, but the snow lay still beneath it. The high sun had sealed its surface. Footfalls of horses crackled as they broke the crust.

Winter sun on prairie snow can blind a man if he looks into its rays. It can burn the sight from his eyes. We rode west but kept our eyes averted, only squint-tight glances to see the path ahead.

"Nobody's ever whipped Penny Bassett before," young Selman said. "At least, not that I heard about. You told Pa your name is Byron Stillwell. Mine's Matthew. Matthew Selman."

"You folks have a nice place. How long have you been here?"

"We came in '83. Pa filed first on the quarter where the house is. He proved up on that, and since then he's proved up two more quarters and filed on a fourth one." He spoke proudly. "Now I have a quarter of my own ready to prove up this spring, and Joe . . . that's my little brother . . . he will file on the one next to it this summer and I'll file on the one on the other side. Peggy was going to file on the quarter alongside the hedgeapple lot but Ma doesn't want her to because of Penny Bassett. He's been payin' attention to her and ma's afraid to have her livin' out there by herself."

I could understand his mother's concern. A man like Penny could be a problem. "Has Penny Bassett been around for quite a while?"

"I don't know," he said. "Four or five years, I guess. I never saw him much 'til he got to looking at

Peggy all the time. The folks don't like that much. He used to work for the Davidson's but old man Davidson ran him off so he went down to work for Mr. Cort. But he spends a lot of time over in the Strip. I guess he has friends down there."

"Do you know who they are, Matthew?"

"No." He glanced at me and there was a stubborn pride there. "We have a place to build. Pa says Seward County has promise. But he says we're just on the edge of civilization here and down there . . . the Strip . . . that's the wilderness. He says no good will come from there." He glanced at me again, concerned. "I guess that's where you came from, isn't it? I recognized you when you came to our place, Mr. Stillwell. I was in Liberal last week when they brought you through there. Some of them said you killed the sheriff."

"People will say most anything. You don't seem to mind riding with me."

"You don't seem like you did anything wrong. But then you don't seem like you could whip Penny Bassett, either."

When I glanced at him he was grinning.

The cold miles slid by, the sun sank lower and the wind became colder. I untied the serape and slipped it on. Matthew got a blanket from behind his saddle and wrapped it around him. Another mile and we found wagon tracks and fell in with them. In the distance, hazed by the blinding snow-shine, was a town.

"He'll be looking for you when he comes around," Matthew said. "People around here are afraid of Penny Bassett. He'll have to get even with you for beating him."

Ahead in the blaze was a wagon and we came up with it after a while. I touched my hat to the ladies, and Matthew reined over to talk to his family. After a moment they all turned their heads to look at me, and I noticed again what a striking young woman Peggy Selman was. Her eyes were large and unreadable. Abel Selman looked curious, more than anything else. "Will he need a doctor?" he asked.

"He won't die from what I did," I told him. "He's just going to hurt for a while."

"Well, we'll tell Mr. Cort. He may want to send a doctor out, anyway."

"Why did you have to beat him?" Peggy accused.

Her father turned to her. "Somebody had to, sooner or later."

"I didn't have to, Miss," I said, marveling at those eyes. "But I did need to." I touched my hat to them again, and kneed the gray. He was fidgety. He wanted to move out, to run. I gave him his head.

Near Liberal there was more traffic. The storm was over and people were moving in and out of the new town, going about their business. A good small herd of solid-looking shorthorn cattle had been brought in from somewhere, and men drove haywagons out to them. I recognized a couple of them. The old puncher who had helped arrest me . . . the one named May . . . drove the haywagon and the youngster called Pearly rode beside. I turned to intercept them.

"Looks like they weathered all right," I commented to May, indicating the herd. "Those are good stock."

"Breed stock," he nodded. "We lost a couple, but

132

not bad. That was a hard storm. What are you doin'
out of jail? Let loose or broke out?" He didn't seem
too concerned either way.

"Let loose," I assured him. "Whose are these?"

"Most of them are Mr. Murdoch's. Some of Blasingame's and Simpson's mixed in. We held them in a
canyon til' the blizzard blew out, then brought them in
to feed. You know cattle, Mr. Stillwell?"

"A little."

"Then you know these are top stock. When the
markets open in the spring we'll take them to rail.
There'll be good money in prime beef up east."

"I guess the market's grown since the Texas trail
herds are stopped," I nodded.

"Grown like a man wouldn't believe." There was
pride in his voice, but a little melancholy too. "Them
was the times, all right, bringin' the big herds north.
Longhorns and open range stock. Head price at the
rail was for some meat and a lot of bone and gristle,
but Lordy didn't we bring them up! These ranchers
up here, though, they're a different breed, just like
their cows are. Here it's managed pasture and haulin'
hay and movin' them as a herd from feed to feed.
Times change."

"Hard work," Pearly chipped in. "These critters
may be better beef, but they scatter just like the
longhorns do an' they ain't even got the brains that
those has."

"Civilization, boy," May shrugged in his heavy
coat. "Folks up here raise cattle and grow crops all in
the same territory. Fences everywhere you look nowadays. Things change."

"I guess there are some," I said, "that would like to

go back to how it was."

"Oh, sure. There's folks down in Texas that don't hold with herd law at all, and some that would give a lot to bring their range beef up here where the rails go to Chicago. Man could do that, nowadays, he could glut the market and make a fortune. Course, he'd ruin it for everybody else, but there's some don't care about that. You be around for a spell?"

"I don't know," I told them. "I have things to do. Do either of you know someone named Morton—something like that—big fellow with a beard? I hear he used to be over in Stevens County, then was gone for a while."

Pearly just shook his head, but May rubbed his stubbled chin. "There's a Morton over at Tyrone, but that doesn't sound like him. You sure the name's Morton?"

"No. Why?"

"Well, when you describe him, it sounds a little like that marshal they had at Hugoton a couple of years back, the one that killed some folks and left town. But his name wasn't Morton. It was Hayes. Probably not the same fella, but I think of him because one of the boys said he'd seen him around Beer City a while back."

"Hayes?"

"Hayes was the name. Big, tough cuss. Morgan Hayes."

11

It was high noon when Henry Lattimer led a lame horse up the south slope of the Cimarron Valley, panting with exhaustion from two hours of fighting drifts, and turned left to trudge the mile to Judge Will Tomlin's house.

From the dooryard gate he hailed the house and saw blinds move at a front window. Then the door opened and Will Tomlin ducked through it, pulling on a heavy coat. He waded through foot-deep snow to the gate, following other tracks that had been made earlier. There was no cracked crust around their edges.

Lattimer touched his hat and pointed at the horse standing three-legged in the snow. "Sorry to bother you Judge, but Sheriff Guthrie sent me to Liberal and my mount is lamed. Could I borrow a horse from you?"

Tomlin finished buttoning his coat and pulled his hat tighter on his head. He squinted in the glare and his round cheeks were pink with cold. "It must be important, for him to send you across the valley today," he said.

"Yes, sir it is. There's been a murder at Springfield. They found a dead man in one of Mr. Bingham's caskets."

"Appropriate," the judged noted without humor. "Who was it?"

"A stranger. Mr. Murdoch said the man's name was Key Begley. He had been at the hotel in Liberal. Things have been pretty busy since you were in town, your honor. Do you suppose you could spare me a horse? I need to be on my way."

Glancing past the tall judge Henry thought he saw the window blinds move again and wondered vaguely who might be visiting. Tomlin's wife had died some years before. The judge lived here alone. Beyond the house stood the windmill tower and Henry recalled with a shiver the winking light that had been over here the morning of Sheriff Dance's death.

Tomlin stared at him as though he would say something, then changed his mind. "Take your horse to the barn," he pointed. "I'll be there in a minute." He turned back to the house.

Trudging around the house, skirting deep drifts, Henry noted broken paths to the outhouse and barn but no tracks coming or going from the place. He led his horse into the barn, past several occupied stalls— the judge was noted for his fine riding and draft stock—and found an empty near the back wall. He had his horse unsaddled and was rubbing it down when the judge came in.

"You can take that sorrel mare over there," Tomlin said. "Zeke Chaster is supposed to be around today. I'll have him look at yours. What happened?"

"A stone bruise, I think," Henry said. "It's tough crossing that valley. Some of the drifts are head-high."

"I mean what happened in town? You said things have been busy."

"Oh. Well, somebody shot up the jail the night before last. It looked like they were after the prisoners. Everett is shot through the chest, but the doctor says the bullet hit a rib and went across under the skin."

"What about the prisoners?" Tomlin stared at him intently.

"Ira Fox has a broken arm. They've got him under guard at the hotel."

"And the other? Stillwell?"

"Oh, Judge Kendall released him for lack of evidence. The sheriff wasn't too happy about that, but a lot of people figure he didn't have anything to do with the shooting." He turned away to pick up his saddle and gear, not comfortable under the tall man's scrutiny. He had the feeling that Will Tomlin might look right through him if he wanted to.

"Released him," Tomlin breathed, and Henry barely heard it and pretended he hadn't.

The mare was a good animal, strong and long-legged, and he got his blanket and saddle aboard her and bent to the cinches. Tomlin stood apart and watched him. Glancing around, Henry thought the man's face wore a haunted look.

"Ah . . . this Stillwell . . . is he still in Springfield?"

"I don't know, sir. The sheriff had me leave right after they identified that body at Bingham's."

"Where are you going?"

"To Liberal, to talk to Vince Cole about him." Henry kept his head down. He didn't want to say more until he had to.

"Did anyone leave Springfield ahead of you, Deputy?"

Henry hesitated only an instant. Then he said, "I didn't see anybody, sir. And there weren't any tracks through the valley where I crossed. I was the first one through."

He had the sorrel saddled. He strapped his gear on and checked the bit, then took the reins. "I appreciate the horse, sir. I'll take good care of her."

Judge Tomlin followed him from the barn, watched him mount and was still standing there when he rode away, following his own lonely tracks back toward the main road. At the road he turned left and touched the sorrel's ribs. The horse was fresh and willing, and the snow was shallow on the scoured faces of upward-rolling hills. She loped a mile, then settled into an easy trot. It was nearly three miles from the judge's house to the highest rises where the hills gave way to flat prairie. As Henry topped out there he reined up, giving the sorrel a chance to blow, and looked around at the endless miles of snow dazzle beneath bright winter sky. He was puzzled, in a way, at the conversation with Judge Tomlin. It was purest happenstance that he had gone there at all. Except for a lame mount he would have pushed straight on toward Liberal, still twelve miles away from where he now sat his saddle.

But he had gone there, and he had seen the judge, and a vague uneasiness rested on him now. Something in what the judge had asked him—the questions or their tone, he wasn't sure—or something in what he himself had responded, bothered him.

Maybe, he thought, it was both. The judge's attitude had seemed . . . remote. Yet the questions had been pointed, the voice strained. And to the extent that the judge had seemed distressed, so had Henry been evasive in his answers. There was no reason he could think of now not to have just told the judge everything that had happened in Springfield, but he had skirted it. Instinct had driven him to stay to the bare bones of it, to let it seem simple and let himself seem uninformed.

The judge had not seemed disturbed about a man being found dead, but he had seemed startled by the name, Key Begley. As though he recognized the name but didn't want to appear to.

He had not, however, seemed particularly startled that there had been a shooting at the jail, though he didn't seem to have known about it. His questions about the prisoners had seemed real enough. And again, he was disturbed at By Stillwell's release, yet seemed not to be concerned with the whereabouts or condition of Ira Fox.

Henry Lattimer was eighteen years old, and felt strongly now his lack of experience. He wanted to understand what his senses told him, but there was nothing to relate it to.

A hint of far-off movement caught his eye and he looked around, shaded eyes peering into the bright distance. Almost due east—he guessed at least three miles easy—a horseman rode the prairie, a tiny shimmer of dark movement across the dazzling, mirage-bent miles of snow. Out there someone rode a fast horse, heading south or east of south. He watched for a minute, then the rider was gone in glare and distance. Henry rubbed his watering eyes. He touched heels to the pawing mare and pointed her south toward Liberal.

In the monotony of distance and glare, with no answers presenting themselves to any of his puzzles, with sun crusting the new snow and a breeze like ice whispering through the seams in his coat, Henry watched the slow miles pass and dreamed of things remote yet urgent.

In his mind he added a room to his claim shack, laying the boards himself, one by one with careful craftsmanship, building it snug and weather-tight, a place to cherish and hold treasures one day. He imagined good furniture, a soft chair to comfort him at day's end, a sun porch for the hot days, a circulating stove for the cold—he had seen such a stove in a Sears & Roebuck catalog, and was saving toward it. He thought of a sturdy bedstead with coil springs and a real mattress, of featherbeds and quilts, and of the warmth of another body near his own on winter nights, a body that would turn to him in the darkness . . . always in the darkness, because he had never been able to picture a face to go with it. Sometimes in dreams a face would be there, but it would be a face in constant change—the face of the dairyman's second daughter that he had seen near Arkalon one day, shifting then to become the face of Mack Lane's daughter who worked at the hotel when traffic was good, then changing somehow into the face of Abby Hutton whose parents had a claim four miles west of

140

his and who teased him sometimes at town socials. The faces teased him, too, because each would appear before him, pert and beautiful, then be gone. There were other faces, too, from earlier times, but they didn't fit the warm body because he didn't recall them as having bodies. The faces had become vague.

He shivered in the biting cold, pulled his coat more closely about him and gritted his teeth to keep them from chattering. Even in the cold, his thoughts left him uncomfortably warm in his lower regions. With an effort of will he shifted back to the house he would build. There would be white curtains at the windows, a large, oval rag rug on the waxed plank floor with colors to catch the sunlight coming in. And there would be a piano.

He wondered which face might play the piano. Probably he would have to learn it himself, the way he had learned to strum and pick his old banjo.

A homestead claim on the prairie can be lonely. Henry Lattimer had come to love his banjo. One day he would play it for someone else to hear.

He shook himself again and concentrated on the living, frozen land. Rabbit trails stitched the snow here and there, and a white-tipped hawk circled above him, waiting for him to pass before it returned to its hunt or to its cooling kill. He crossed the trail of a pair of coyotes, and sometime later the larger prints of a prairie wolf fresh in the snow. Shading his eyes, peering into distance, he saw the wolf, loping along, misty-seeming in the glare yet powerful and intent upon its hunt.

He wondered where Byron Stillwell had gone, what he was doing.

Nearing town he crossed the mulled trace of a herd of cattle that had been driven southwestward. The drovers would be gathering their stock, hauling hay for them. They might feed them for days before the ground was clear enough to graze them again.

Liberal was a cluster of buildings in a broad, shallow swale on the prairie. Most of the buildings were new, though many were made from materials brought from Fargo Springs and Bethel when those towns began to decline. There were soddies and dugouts, and among them and more prevalent were the new houses, the commercial buildings, the barns and liveries, and the three-story hotel owned by Frank Murdoch.

Kansas Avenue had been drag-plowed, the snow piled in a long heap down its center, and there was traffic on the street. Henry found Vince Cole, heavily bundled and apple-cheeked, on the swept walk in front of Dahl's Emporium and they walked the block to Smith's Pharmacy to find hot coffee and a place to talk. Cole had drawn deputy pay for nearly five years in Seward County. He was a careful, observant man, a family man with a place at the edge of town and three proved-up claims a few miles out where he raised sheep, broomcorn and watermelons, and he did a competent job for the badge and stayed out of politics.

"I know the bunch you're talking about," he told Henry. "A couple of them used to live over in Stevens County, but I hadn't seen them around for a couple of years I guess. Slim Cavanaugh and Jack Little. Seems like they got caught up in that mess over there and just left the country. Heard they went to work for some ranch in Texas. Some of the others might have been over there, too, but I didn't know them. At any rate there were five or six that showed up here about a week and a half ago, checked in at the hotel. I saw them around for a while, kept an eye on them, but they didn't cause any trouble."

"Why did you keep an eye on them?" Henry held his coffee mug in both hands, drawing its warmth from it.

"Oh, they seemed like they could be a bunch of hardcases. I know Cavanaugh and Little used to have that kind of reputation, and the rest looked like they could match them for tough. But they didn't do anything. They were just around for a while."

"You mean they're gone now."

"Some of them are, at least. Two of them checked out a week ago and headed south. Names of Johnson and Smith, by the register. And I don't remember seeing any of the others since before the storm. Let's check the hotel."

"Let me finish this coffee. I'm about half froze. The one Mr. Bingham found in his box, Key Begley, did you know him?"

"No. I remember him with them but I didn't know him. I kind of thought he might have been from over in Stevens County, too, but that's just an impression. But you know, the whole bunch came here from down in Texas, not from Stevens County."

"Anybody have any idea why they were here?"

"Not really. You know how it is, with new people in and out all the time. Nobody pays much attention. Kenny Barber thought they might have been horse traders, but they didn't look like wranglers to me. To tell you the truth, what they looked like was a bunch of gunslicks. But they minded their manners while they were here."

Henry took a long breath, pursed his lips and made a decision. He glanced around. They were alone. "I want to tell you something, Vince, but I don't want anybody else to hear it right now because . . . well, because I want to follow it along a little more."

"Fair enough," Cole said.

"Vince, Key Begley was one of the men who killed Sam Dance."

Cole's mouth opened, then closed again and he stared at the younger deputy. Finally he crossed his arms on the little table between them, leaning close. "Are you sure, Henry?"

"As sure as I can be without being able to prove it. I was out there. I heard them. I sort of saw them, even though it was dark. Begley was the one standing right next to the bearded man. He was the one who said, 'Move, boy, move,' when they sent me away. I'm just as sure as I can be."

"Then that would mean the rest of them—the bunch that were around here—were in it, too."

"That's right. Vince, keep this under your hat, too, but is there any reason why Will Tomlin would have known Key Begley?"

Cole blinked. "You aren't startin' to bark up trees, are you, Henry? Who do you ask that?"

"I stopped at the judge's place to trade horses today. When I mentioned the name to him, I'd have sworn he recognized it."

"What did he say about it?"

"Nothing. That's what was puzzling. If he knew

the man, why not say so?"

"Well, if Begley was one of the old Stevens County bunch, like Cavanaugh and Little, it's pretty likely the judge did know him. He was over there, remember? How would you feel if a bunch of people were out to kill you—had already killed a sheriff trying to get at you—and you didn't know who they were? Hell, Henry, I imagine Will Tomlin is jumping at his shadow these days."

"You said two of them checked out a week ago and headed south. If they hadn't got the man they were after, Vince, why would they have left? Wouldn't they have tried again?"

"Tried again how? They tried once, had it all set up, and somebody tipped the judge to it so they missed. They killed Sam instead. What more could they do? Tomlin has had guards around him every minute since then. Sturdevant is even staying out at his house. You think they'd tackle Sturdevant and that rifle of his?"

Henry remembered the blinds moving at Tomlin's house. That was Sturdevant, then. He nodded. What Vince said made sense.

"You said they shot up the jail," Cole said. "I guess that could be the same bunch. But why were they after the prisoners?"

"They weren't after them both. Just Stillwell. I saw that."

"Then maybe Stillwell was in on it with them and they didn't want him to talk."

"No," Henry set down his cup. "Stillwell wasn't in on it. You'll just have to take my word on that, Vince, but he wasn't one of the killers."

"Appears you know a little more than you're talking about, Henry. Are you sure?"

"Yes. I'm sure."

"Well, at any rate we have some names now. Cavanaugh, Little, Johnson, Smith, Begley—who is dead now," he ticked them off on his fingers, "and I think the other one's name was Doyle. That's the six. Let's go to the hotel."

"There were more than twenty men out there."

"Well, six names is a start. And maybe add Ira Fox to that list, if the judge can make a positive identification."

"Fox still lives in Stevens County. He didn't leave."

"Maybe some others didn't either. Henry, I don't think any of this is over yet. I think that was just a first try, and they'll be after him again."

As they walked across the hard packed street, detouring to go around a plowed mound of snow, Henry asked, "Vince, what do you think of Will Tomlin?"

The older deputy looked at him quizzically, then shrugged. "Just between us, I think the judge is a devious son of a bitch and I think it's a damn shame that Sam had to die protecting him. But at the same time, I don't want him murdered."

The names in the hotel roster were easy to find. L. Doyle, T. Smith, E. Johnson, M. Cavanaugh, J. Little, L. H. Begley. "Well, will you look at this," Cole pointed at a scrawl beside one name. "Cavanaugh even wrote where he is from. But I can't make it out."

Henry turned the book, getting better light on the dim pencil marks. "I thought you said he was from

Stevens County."

"That was a couple of years ago. He left, I think."

"Well, this says he's from Mobeetie, Texas."

The two deputies spent the next few hours asking questions, but came up empty. No one recalled seeing any of the six men since Thursday or Friday, two or three days before the storm.

"I have to ride over to Arkalon tomorrow, to see if the train made it in today—damned thing's probably snowbound somewhere—but while I'm there I can get a wire off to the sheriff at Hugoton to check out these names. Maybe he can tell us something. You can report back to Sheriff Guthrie and see what he wants us to do from there." He glanced at the lowering sun. "You aren't going back today, though, are you?"

"Not if I don't have to. That valley was tough enough in daylight. I wouldn't want to cross it in the dark."

They turned the corner at Second and Kansas, heading for Cole's little office. Across the way a wagon pulled up in front of the mercantile and a farm family began unloading from it. Henry glanced at them, looked away and then looked back, his chin dropping in astonishment. He pointed. "Vince, who is that?"

Cole looked across. "Them? That's Abel Selman and his tribe. Have a good place over east. Been there for years. Why?"

Years? Henry thought. "You mean she's been around all this time and I haven't . . ."

"Ah," Cole smiled. "That's what the interest is all about. Well, Deputy Lattimer, what you're gaping at is Abel Selman's daughter Peggy. Pretty thing, isn't she?"

Henry's face flushed red in the cold and he glanced aside to see Cole studying him. "I . . . I just wondered, that's all. I hadn't seen them around."

"Your problem is you stay home too much, Henry."

Henry ignored him. He stood in wonder, gazing at a face to match his dreams. He hardly noticed when Abel Selman turned toward them then hurried across the street.

"Vince!"

"Afternoon, Mr. Selman. Have a good trip in?"

"Fine. Colder than blazes, but fine. Have you seen Adolph Cort in town?"

"Yeah. He's around somewhere. Check the hotel. Any problem?"

"Well, his hired man is beat up pretty bad. He might want to send a doctor out."

"Penny?" It was Cole's turn to gape. "Somebody beat up Penny Bassett? Who was it?"

Selman glanced around. A rider was dismounting a few feet away. "Him," he pointed.

The deputies turned. Byron Stillwell looked up from tying his reins and grinned. Henry thought again of the prairie wolf he had seen.

"I had to," Stillwell said. "He needed it."

12

With evening the wind stilled. As the last blue light of day winked out an oval moon rose over silver plains and the stars hung crisp and near at hand. Southeast of Liberal fires burned bright where drovers tended their mixed herd of shorthorns and hereford breeds, cattle gathered from ranches all around for hay-feeding until the snow had cleared.

Here and there on the bright prairie lights shone in windows, visible for miles across a land asleep in moonfrost. From the east a high-wheeled buggy rolled toward Liberal. Its two-horse team pranced in the traces and its wheels crunched knife-sharp tracks in the frozen crust.

Henry Lattimer and Byron Stillwell stepped out of the hotel's main entrance to stand at the rail of the wide, deserted porch and watch the night. They had talked for hours, first in the office of Deputy Vince Cole, then over dinner at the hotel where Henry's attention wandered repeatedly from comparison of information to the bewitching sight of Peggy Selman seated with her family at a table nearby, and finally, privately, in the little cubicle they would share that night with two other men. The hotel was full to overflowing. If all the guests paid their bills Frank Murdoch stood to make a killing this night.

"So he did have family," Byron Stillwell said, more to himself than to Henry.

"A lawyer wired Mr. Bingham," Henry said. "From Mobeetie. They sent the body and effects to Springfield. That was the instruction."

"Mobeetie," Byron said. His breath was a flag of drifting mist that hung in the air and then dissipated.

"The more I try to make the pieces fit the more they slip away from me," Henry mused. "I can't seem to get the picture of it. The ones who killed him . . . the ones we know about . . . were Stevens County men, but that was two years ago. Some of them went to Texas. Mr. Dance told me that, and Vince said the same thing. Then they came here from Texas, and that was when Mr. Dance died, and I know at least one of them was there. But it wasn't him they were after. They were after the judge, and he tracks back to Stevens County, too. But not to Texas. Why would they come up from Texas to kill a man over something that happened in Stevens County two years ago?"

"You're talking in circles again."

"I can't help it. I'm thinking in circles and I go 'round and 'round and come up with nothing."

"Did you ever hear of Morgan Hayes?"

"Yeah. You told me. He used to be a town marshal in Stevens County. Where? Woodville?"

"Hugoton. But he joined up with the Woodville bunch and they pulled his badge. Did I tell you he's one of Davy Dawes' ramrods now?"

150

"Yeah. At Mobeetie. We're back to Texas again."

"I didn't describe him to you, though. He's a big man, thick through the chest, and he wears a full beard. Ring any bells for you?"

Henry looked at him, his eyes large in the moon-shadow. "The man at Cross Canyon? The bearded man?"

"Could be. Penny Bassett described him pretty well when he told me who he heard about the killing from."

"He said his name was Morton."

"He said Morton or something like that. Morton-Morgan. Penny Bassett isn't long on brains."

"If I could see him I'd know. If I could hear him. I heard him out there. I think he—the bearded one—was the one that joked about turning left . . . the one that called the name By."

They stood in silence for a time, then Henry turned to Stillwell. "You know, I would never have believed you were innocent . . . not known for sure . . . if it hadn't been for old Rounder. That dog knew you."

"Yes."

"But I know something else, By. You were out there that morning."

Stillwell's breath caught. He dipped his head slowly toward the younger man, his dark eyes flinty in the shadow light. "What makes you say that?"

"What you told me, about finding Parson Jolly and then Penny Bassett. You were tracking back from something you had heard before it ever happened. You heard about it and you tried to stop it."

"Keep talking."

"That night . . . that morning . . . there was a

151

rider in the valley. He came across and tried to jump a shoulder down there and almost made it. I thought he had fallen, but then I saw him again and he was waving. That was you, wasn't it, By?"

"Not bad." His teeth glinted in a sardonic grin. "Chalk one up for the young deputy. Yeah, I heard it and tried to stop it. But I was too late. I was too late all the way around."

There was ice in his tone colder than the ice of winter and Henry shivered. Then he squared his shoulders and looked away. "You killed Key Begley, didn't you?"

Stillwell's silence was answer enough. Henry nodded. "Are you as handy with that sixgun as I suspect you are?"

Again there was no answer. He had expected none. "Can I ask you something, By?"

"As long as it's not another dumb question."

"I know why I want the men who killed Mr. Dance. You told me. He was like a father to me. But what I want is to bring them to justice. I get the feeling that isn't just what you have in mind."

"You wear the badge, Henry. I don't."

"That's what I thought. But why, By? I know he was your father, but you never knew him. You had never even seen him. You didn't know anything about him."

Stillwell's eyes were unreadable in the shadow of his hatbrim, and Henry thought again of the wolf out on the prairie. "That's why," the dark man said. "That is exactly why."

Movement down the street caught their attention. A buggy with two horses made the turn at Second and Kansas, veered around heaped snow and rolled to a stop before the deputy sheriff's dark office. A man in long coat and wide hat stepped down, went to the door there and knocked.

"Over here, Doctor Price!" Henry called, and walked down the wooden steps, snow crunching beneath his feet as he reached the boardwalk. "Vince has gone home. Can I help you?" Stillwell tailed along behind the youngster.

The doctor adjusted his spectacles, peered at them, then came to meet them. "I have a dead man in the buggy," he said.

"Dead man? Who?"

"Penny Bassett. They told me he had been beaten. But when I got out there I found him dead. He was lying on his bunk. One shot killed him. It was fired from directly above him, point-blank. The bullet went through his heart, through the bunk and into the floor underneath."

Henry swung around, his rifle coming up. "By, you said you beat him up."

Stillwell shrugged. "Ask young Selman. He saw him alive after I'd finished with him. Besides, what do you think this is . . ." he indicated the gun at his hip, "a cannon?"

Lattimer lowered his rifle. Chill premonition tightened his scalp. "I saw a rider today, after I left the judge's house . . ."

"East of you?" Stillwell's voice was eager now, his eyes aglow in the silver light. "A few miles off and going south?"

"Yes."

"Keep adding the pieces, Henry. I think the ball

has opened."

"What are you talking about?"

"There is a shack at end of line, this side of Arkalon. I'll bet you a steak there's more dead meat there. I'll bet Beer City's best supplier has a hole in him tonight just like the one in Penny Bassett. I've been issuing invitations ever since I landed in jail, Henry. Maybe somebody has decided to accept."

They followed Doctor Price around to the hooded box-bed of his rig. The doctor lifted the tarp and Henry looked inside. Moonlight was adequate to show the still form there. Henry turned away. Another dead man in Seward County. Maybe two, if By Stillwell was right. The young deputy wondered how Sim Guthrie was going to handle this.

Stillwell was standing a few feet away, spreadlegged in the snow, hands at his hips, slowly turning to study the night-quiet town. "He should be here by now," he said.

"Who?"

"Whoever killed Penny. If he's following me he's here."

Henry stared at him. "You think someone is out to kill you?"

"Well, if not, I've wasted a lot of valuable time. I've left pretty plain track since the storm blew out this morning."

"Then what are you standing out in the street for? Are you crazy?"

Stillwell continued his careful study of buildings, shadows, and confusing, moon-washed terrain. "I certainly hope not." He glanced at the wagon. "You and the doctor have things to do. Remember what we talked about, Henry. I'll see you around." He touched his hat and walked away, toward the hotel.

Henry looked after him, then turned back to the tired doctor. "Let's find someplace to put him. You'll need to give Vince Cole a report, but that can wait 'till morning."

"I'll put him in my shed. He'll keep."

Within the hour Henry Lattimer returned to the hotel, brooding thoughts chasing one another around in his head. It was after 10 o'clock and the town slept in still, cold moonglow.

He climbed the steps, started to open the main door, then stopped and turned. A small, muffled figure stood at the porch rail.

"Hello," he touched his hat.

She turned to him. "You're the deputy, aren't you? Henry Lattimer?"

"Yes, Ma'm."

"I saw you earlier. In the dining room. I heard people talking inside. They said Penny Bassett is dead."

"Yes, Ma'm. The doctor just brought him in. Someone shot him."

"Was it that man . . . that Stillwell? Matthew told us how he beat him."

"No, I don't see how it could have been him." He stepped closer to her, looking down at her large, dark eyes. "Did you know Penny Bassett, Miss?"

"He came to our place sometimes. Pa told us one time he was afraid he'd have to horsewhip him if he didn't mind his manners."

"Well, I guess you won't have to worry about that. Ah, do you and your folks come into Liberal often? I

155

mean, I don't think I've ever seen you before, and I
. . . well, I sure would have remembered." He felt
himself flush and was glad of moonlight and shadow.

"Sometimes we do. Who is that man? Matthew
said they thought he had murdered the sheriff, then
let him go."

"Yes, Miss, they did. He didn't do it."

"He came by our place this morning. He was
looking for Penny, and he said he'd need a doctor.
What kind of man is he? They way he said that . . .
well, it was scary. But he smiled."

Henry felt a sudden and unexpected tightness in
his chest, a mixture of irritation and something else
unpleasant. He didn't want to talk about Byron
Stillwell and he didn't want Peggy Selman dwelling
on him. He wished fervently for a way to turn the
girl's attention to Henry Lattimer instead. He felt
hopelessly outclassed and it bothered him. "You
don't need to worry about him," he said, too
abruptly. "He won't bother you. I won't let him."
Then he blushed again in the darkness, realizing how
silly that must sound. Vividly he pictured Byron
Stillwell—tall, dark, enigmatic and handsome with
an air of mystery about him—and he pictured himself
as he must look to others—a gawky eighteen-year-old
kid wearing a badge too big for him.

"That was a stupid thing for me to say," he muttered. He started to turn away in his embarrassment,
but felt a small hand on his arm. He looked at her
again and found no trace of ridicule in her shadow
smile.

"I've heard a lot about you," she said. "You were
the one who stood up to those outlaws out there,

when they murdered the sheriff . . . when everyone else ran off. Pa said those other men should be ashamed of themselves, that they should take a page from Henry Lattimer's book."

A warm glow washed over him and he grinned at her. "You're liable to freeze standing out here like this."

"I couldn't sleep. It's pretty out here. It's still and bright and sort of secret. I like it."

"And cold. Do you like tea?"

"Yes."

"I don't guess there is anybody in the kitchen now, but we could probably find some tea. If the stoves are out we could heat water at the fireplace in the parlor. Would you like some?"

"Yes," she said. "I believe I would."

In the dark of morning, before anyone had begun to stir, Byron Stillwell descended the stairs on soft bootsoles and glanced into the dim-lit parlor. At first glance the big room was deserted. The remains of a fire glowed in the fireplace, and an oil lamp was turned to low-wick on a side table. Then he looked again, cocked his head and walked in. Dimly, on a couch by the fire, he made out two huddled figures. Henry Lattimer's head rested on the high back of the couch. His mouth was open slightly and his eyes were closed. Close beside him, her head on his shoulder, Peggy Selman was curled beneath a down comforter. Empty cups sat on the end table and Henry's hat and rifle lay on the floor at his feet.

They were both sound asleep.

Stillwell stood over them for a moment, a slow smile tugging at his cheeks. "Kids," he muttered. Then he leaned to touch Henry's shoulder.

The deputy's head came up, his eyes popped open and he blinked. The girl stirred beside him.

"If anybody comes down and finds you," Stillwell said, "It isn't going to do this young lady's reputation a bit of good."

"Huh?" Henry blinked again, stretched and rubbed sleepy eyes. "Oh." He looked at the girl, then back at Stillwell. "We were just talking," he whispered. "I guess we went to sleep."

"I guess you did. Now you probably ought to do the honorable thing and help this girl slip back to her room without anybody knowing she's been with you all night."

"All night?" Henry came more awake. "What time is it?"

"Around five. Still dark, but the roosters'll crow in an hour or so."

Henry shifted cautiously, freeing his arm from the sleeping girl. "I found her on the porch," he said. "I mean, she was out on the porch and we made some tea and came in here to . . . damn it, By, we were just talking! That's all!"

"I didn't ask any questions, did I?"

"Well, you can quit that darn grinning!" Henry noticed then that Stillwell wore his serape and had wide saddlebags hung at his shoulder. "Where are you going?"

"I may be gone for a while. You look into that Stevens County thing, will you?"

"I'll get Vince Cole to help me."

"And Si Rutledge. Find him and talk to him."

Henry got to his feet, combing his hair back with his fingers. "Yeah, you told me. Mr. Dance's papers. But where are you going?"

"It shapes up to be a long hunt, Henry. I'll be in touch."

Henry shrugged. He wouldn't learn anything more. He glanced down at Peggy, still asleep in her comforter, and his face softened. "What should I do with her, By?"

"That depends on whether you mean right now or eventually. I could give you some dandy ideas for eventually, but I think you'll come up with them all by yourself. Take care, Deputy."

Then he was gone into the darkness and Henry rubbed his bristled chin and considered various means of awakening a beautiful girl.

13

Was it Ira Fox who had passed the message? That didn't seem likely. He had plenty of opportunity in Springfield, but the blizzard had come and had cut off traffic for a time. I had made it across the Cimarron Valley, and Henry Lattimer had a little later, but not many would be crossing yet. And with no wires nearer than Arkalon, how would the message have gotten south except by personal delivery?

It could have been Parson Jolly or Penny Bassett, but the timing was wrong. Whoever killed Penny had probably been on his way there while I was teaching Penny about quirts. I didn't know about Parson, but I suspected he was dead.

My hunch was that whoever killed Penny had followed my tracks from the Cimarron southward to find him. I had told Penny, "Tell them I'm looking for them." Maybe whoever came to Cort's and found him heard that from him. And maybe that person didn't want to leave any messages behind to be repeated.

The bullet had gone through Penny's chest, exploding the heart, then had gone through a good fiber mattress—and probably through a slat—and into the floor beneath. What kind of gun did that? Probably a rifle. Few handguns produced ballistics like that.

Sturdevant kept coming to mind. Silent, flint-hard, hawk-nosed Sturdevant with his flat hat, dark deacon's coat and an Alexander Henry rifle. Sturdevant who calmly turned his back on prisoners in case they would like to try making a run for it. Sturdevant, the judge's man, the officer of the court.

The Alexander Henry could have done what was done to Penny Bassett.

But why?

Did Judge Will Tomlin believe I was one of a gang that meant to kill him? If so, he might have sent Sturdevant to finish the job the law had failed to do. But why kill Bassett if that was the case?

If there had been a threat against the judge at all . . . and I had serious doubts about that. Still, I couldn't point a finger at Tomlin. I had studied him when he talked to me in jail. I took him for a smart, devious, unscrupulous bastard, but there is no law against being any of those. If there were, who would be left to hold public office? He had seemed intense . . . determined. And puzzled. He had seemed to be everything a man might be who is afraid somebody is trying to kill him and doesn't know who.

Did he care that Sam Dance had died? Probably not. Unless he had a hand in it. But that led off into lines of thought both vague and bizarre, and far too complex to fit any circumstances I could imagine.

All I had were questions. Why did Sam Dance die? What did it have to do with Stevens County? What did it have to do with Mobeetie? What did those places have to do with each other?

Snow-covered prairie on a still cold night is a fantasy world. The white captures moonlight and throws it back in dancing glitter. The shadows are black holes in the earth's surface where distant stars peep through as bright as the stars in the sky overhead. And when the wind is still there is no sound except the crunch of hooves in frozen crust and the faint, forlorn wintersong of a coyote out on the edge of the world.

A couple of miles out of town there was an abandoned soddy. The blizzard had used it as the anchor for a ridge drift that started roof-high and stretched out more than a hundred yards. I rode past the soddy, parallel to the drift, and a little way further when it tailed out. Then I turned the gray hard around and doubled back along the other side. Back at the soddy I pulled in close to its wall and waited for a time. My back trail was clear and sharp in the snow.

Long minutes passed but I saw nothing back there, though I had the feeling someone was watching me. The night can play such tricks.

Finally I headed south again.

Beer City was almost invisible until I was there. The blizzard had torn down what was flimsy and buried the rest. It was a miserable sprawl of humps and drifts, with angles of shack roof showing here and there and plumes of smoke seeking the dark sky from three or four chimney pipes. There wouldn't be many folks around. Most of the denizens would have gone to cover, to return later to rebuild for the thaw.

The State of Kansas enacted prohibition in 1880.

Several things happened then. Drinking men became serious about their drinking, a lot of non-drinkers became drinkers and every county in the state was faced with how to enforce—or get around—the ban on alcoholic beverages. Along the border it was easy. The powers that be took a stern and righteous stand and were applauded by their upstanding constituencies who had only to ride a few miles to keep their appointments with John Barleycorn.

Later, when the federal law stepped in and closed down the Cherokee Strip, those Kansas towns over there chose up sides and alternated between dry-and-legal and wet-and-who-cares.

But out here where the state bordered no man's land, nothing changed. Borders were surveyed casually by the surveyors and carefully by the bootleggers, and a whole string of little paradises blossomed just south of the line. Beer City was one of them.

Ace Pruitt and Keno Mora were the current kingpins of Beer City, by virtue of having a monopoly on the commerce of liquor and women. They had acquired their status by jointly employing a wadcutter named Calico to vacate the management positions previously held by a Missourian named Darcy Fellen and his associates. Calico's negotiations were direct and brief. He preferred a shotgun and had an uncanny knack for arranging back shots. Darcy Fellen and his associates all were buried in the Beaver Creek flats. All the Beer City entrepreneurs now paid off the top to Ace Pruitt and Keno Mora, with Calico taking a nice cut of the action.

The biggest building in Beer City was a barn, and I went there first and counted the stock by lantern light. The place was big enough for maybe thirty horses, but I only found six. I left the gray there and borrowed a good helping of sorghum grain for him out of somebody's feed bin. Then I found a ladder, climbed to the top of the place and squatted there for a while counting trails by waning moonlight. I had hoped to find a lot of men at Beer City—specifically those who had been running with Key Begley. But from everything I could see the place was almost deserted.

There were two frame buildings facing each other and several paths through the snow between them, and there was a tight little cabin off to one side with smoke above its pipe and tracks leading back and forth between it and the larger buildings. These, and tracks leading to and from the barn, were all I could see.

Three people—maybe four. Everyone else had pulled out ahead of the storm.

From that roof I could see the lights of Liberal, three miles off, and my backtrail was clear in the snow. I saw no one else out there.

I had been up on that barn for more than half an hour, and there was light in the eastern sky when a door slammed below and two men stepped out into the clear, stretched, then walked across to the building with the false front and entered. The chimney smoke from there carried the odor of frying meat. I waited.

Several minutes later a man stepped from the little cabin, trudged around to the outhouse and disappeared inside. When he came out he hoisted his shotgun across his arm and walked toward the false-front building. I sat very still and he passed within fifty feet of me. He was a big man with a paunch that even his heavy coat couldn't hide, and long hair fell from beneath his hat. Calico. I had seen him before, stalking the alleys of Beer City when the crowds were in, his shotgun always ready.

Day was breaking in the east, fading the stars on that side of the sky. I climbed down from the barn, rolled and rubbed my right shoulder to get the stiffness out of it, rubbed warmth into my fingers, flipped up the serape to clear my right arm and went hunting.

The building the two men had left was Keno Mora's gambling house. I went there first.

It was a square, fairly secure building, fifty feet on a side. No one was inside but a fire burned in the stove and a lamp was lit on one side of the tables. Beside it were a stack of ledgers and an assortment of loose papers.

I had heard that Keno Mora once worked for a bank over in Colorado, before he got in trouble there. I looked over his paperwork. It was neat and precise, income and expense accounts showing a surprising profit for the winter months. I remembered how the trade had been a week or so before when I was here, before the snow. It had been cold then, but a lot of people had been in Beer City, parting with their money.

Tables and chairs littered the open room. One massive table was covered with a sheet. I looked under it. It was Keno's prized, ornate roulette wheel. Out of curiosity I looked beneath it. The thing must have cost a fortune. What was on top—elaborate ivory and silver inlays in polished wood bordering a raised rim and a fine-balanced wheel two and a half feet in diameter—was nothing compared to what was hidden below.

Tiny pins rested on a circular cam beneath the rolling slot, ready to raise invisible points a hair above the slot's surface anywhere around its perimeter. The whole thing was controlled by a foot pedal operating a gimbal.

Good eyes and a trained toe could make that ball drop into any cup the operator wanted it to. Keno—or one of his deceased predecessors—must have spent three years' worth of ill-gotten gains on that machine . . . and it probably paid for itself every couple of months.

In a little back room were a pair of rumpled cots and shelves of supplies.

It didn't take a minute to find Keno's hidey-hole. I had spotted it on my prior visit. People operating border pleasure palaces rarely use safes. They are heavy and hard to transfer in a hurry. Keno's bank was an iron box under the stove's heat-shield. It looked like part of the shield, except that a gentleman in Richmond had taught me a lot about looking for things like that.

The box contained a little over four thousand dollars and some change. I left the change.

From there I went to the little cabin and looked in. It was a single room with a bed, bureau and wash-stand and some open cabinets. It wasn't deserted. A woman lay asleep in the bed, rolled in quilts. She was one of the saloon girls, and Calico had obviously kept her over as a playmate. The place stank. She had a dark bruise under one eye and a cut on her lip. I let her sleep.

In the side shed I found a can of kerosene. I took it and went back to Keno's place. The sky was lighter. It would be morning soon.

I doused one end of Keno's place pretty thoroughly and set a match to it, then walked across to Ace Pruitt's saloon and invited myself in.

There were five people there. Keno Mora, a dealer named Fancy Pace, Ace Pruitt and the killer Calico sat at a plank table eating slab meat and fried potatoes while a tired-looking woman served them from a cookstove.

They looked around when I walked in, and Calico reached for his shotgun standing against the table beside him.

"Don't touch it, friend," I told him. "It isn't worth the price."

Of them all, Ace Pruitt was quickest on the uptake.

He blinked away his surprise and swallowed his mouthful of breakfast. "We didn't expect any customers this soon after the storm," he said. "But I guess we can accommodate. What's your pleasure?"

"My pleasure is information," I told them. "I have just set fire to the gambling hall over there and the quicker you answer some questions the sooner you can go put it out."

Mora's chair crashed to the floor, Fancy Pace goggled at me with eyes as pretty as a woman's and Calico's hand snaked toward his shotgun again . . . then stopped when he saw a .45 Colt looking at him.

"You what?" Pruitt was half out of his chair.

"You heard me," I told them. "Where is Morgan

Hayes?"

"You're lying!" Mora rasped, wide-eyed. He was in a crouch, his right hand an inch from the open middle button of his coat.

"Bring out what you have there, very slowly, and throw it away."

I waggled the Colt in his direction and he backed a step, bumping against Calico. He hesitated, then, carefully, reached inside his coat and brought out a little derringer. He tossed it aside.

"You can look out that window," I said. He stepped carefully past me, opened a shutter and his face went pale.

"It's true!" he said. "My place is on fire!" As though forgetting everything else, he ducked and ran, angling past me toward the door. I kicked him in the belly and he fell backward, rolling into a ball on the floor. The interval gave Calico time to grab his shotgun and he lurched upright, bringing it around.

I had already told him twice about that. My shot should have been dead center but it was high and shattered the butt of his shotgun. He staggered back, triggered his gun and a load of buckshot went through the front wall over my head. Its recoil drove splinters into his shoulder and sent him tumbling back against the stove. The heavy implement slid on its hearth, sections of stovepipe clattered down in a cloud of soot and smoke, and a fuel well spilled and began to blaze on the floor. The woman screamed and dove under a table.

Ace Pruitt tried to pull a gun from beneath his coat and Fancy Pace echoed the woman's scream and toppled over backward in his chair. I took two strides and knocked the gun out of Pruitt's hand, mashing some of his fingers in the process. Then I backed off. Keno Mora was on hands and knees, gagging, and I put a boot to his rump and shoved him toward the rest of them.

"Get Calico out of that mess before he fries," I told them. Pruitt looked at me a moment with hatred blazing in his eyes, then bent to pull Calico away from the fire. He turned back. "What do you want?"

"Morgan Hayes," I repeated. "Also Slim Cavanaugh, Larry Doyle, Jack Little . . . you know the bunch. Where are they?"

"I don't know who you're talking about!"

"Ace!" Mora gasped, trying to get to his feet. "My place is burning down!" He turned a pale face to me. "They ain't here. We don't know where they are. Let me go!"

"When did you see them?"

"M-maybe they was here . . . a while back. But not since."

Pruitt glared at him, nursing his mashed hand. "Keno, you know what'll happen if . . ."

"What, Ace?" I trained the Colt on him. "What will happen?"

"Nothing," he subsided. "But he's right. None of them have been back since they went through here."

"That's a lie, Ace. I know two of them came back through. They gave their names as Smith and Johnson."

"Well, they didn't stay. They were heading south."

"To where?"

Mora was having apoplexy, watching the flames build up across the way. Suddenly something changed in his face, and I saw it and dodged aside as a gun roared behind me. I turned and fired and the man who folded up and fell there looked vaguely familiar. I had forgotten about one other smoking chimney, the one at the little shed beyond the barn. Ace Pruitt was going after his gun, but he stopped when I turned. Calico was getting to his feet, a hand over his bleeding shoulder, and I knew if he lived through this I would see him again.

I pointed the smoking Colt at Ace. "You have one chance, friend. Everybody has a place to go to, to wait it out if trouble comes calling. Where is it?"

"You can go to hell," he snarled.

"Ace, for God's sake, do something!" Keno was wild now.

"All right." Pruitt sagged a little. "Down on the Beaver, there's a place. Nothing much, but it's shelter. That's where they go. South of here. At the fork bend. That's all we know."

"Smith and Johnson, who are they?"

"They're Texans. Hell, I don't know who they are. They came through here, a few days ago. Had a drink and moved on. That's all."

"And Hayes and the rest?"

"We told you. They haven't been back. That's the God's truth."

The fire was spreading behind them. Firelight from the gambling hall flickered at the open window. I indicated the dead man in the doorway. Who is he?"

"Dobbins," Pruitt said. "Wiley Dobbins. He keeps . . . kept . . . a string of girls."

If hatred were a tangible thing I would have been suffocating right then. "I'll see you again, Stillwell,"

Pruitt rasped. "When I do I'll kill you."

Mora would break, but Mora didn't know my answers. Calico didn't know anything but what he was told. Fancy Pace was a hireling and a fool. And I might kill Pruitt but I wouldn't learn any more.

"Sorry I can't stay for breakfast," I told them. "But I've got places to go and you all have fires to fight. Don't do anything foolish."

I stepped over Wiley Dobbins, backed out the door and hightailed for the barn.

Aboard the gray I gathered in five of the six other horses and drove them out ahead of me. I leaned low and kept on their far side until we were clear of Beer City, then I turned east, circled the town and angled south toward the Beaver. I could still see them, running between buildings, as I passed the outskirts, and I was sure they saw me, too. I rode south a mile or more as the sun rimmed the clear horizon in the east. The land became broken out here, and I headed straight into the breaks then doubled back until I was just within sight of Beer City. I had left them one horse. I wanted to see what they did with it. If the hidey-hole was on the Beaver, someone should be riding south very soon.

It didn't take long. I saw the rider as he cleared the barn, tiny in the white distance.

But he didn't come south. He set out at a lope, going west, leaving me a long way behind him.

14

I always knew Mattie Stillwell worried about me sometimes during those growing-up years when we moved around so much, from city to city.

She was doing her best to raise and educate me, and to provide for us the best way she knew how. She sang and we never lacked for the comforts. But she was aware, as a mother is, of those other aspects her son was developing as time went by.

"You have a fierceness in you, By," she would say, "and I don't know where it comes from. Sometimes it seems to me that people are afraid of you. We need to talk about that."

She knew I fought sometimes. Early on, it was the "new kid in town" problem. But after the first couple of times that happened I learned ways of handling it. When we moved to Atlanta, for example, I spent almost a week locating the predominant bully in town and then went after him. I was eleven years old and he was fifteen or sixteen, but I jumped him and kept hitting him until he broke and ran. I had a broken rib and a dozen bruises and could hardly move for several days, but there was never a question of being established in that neighborhood.

"I might have had to fight a lot of them," I explained to her. "This way I only had to fight one."

It troubled her, and there was a revulsion in her eyes. And yet, in her way, my mother was always aware of the ways of the world. I knew she was asking herself, "what would *he* do now? What would *he* say to our son if he were here?" She worked it out and then she talked to me about it.

"There are people who don't understand any other way," she said. "Only force will sway them, because that's all they know. That's why there are wars, I suppose. That's why your father had to pick up a rifle and go out and hurt people, even though the one he hurt worst was himself. He couldn't let them have the upper hand, and I suppose you can't either. You are like him. But By, always remember, your father is a gentle man. That's why it hurts him when he must do such things.

"I'm glad you did what you had to do, By. But I'm glad you got hurt doing it. You're still a boy, and your hurts will heal, but I want you to remember them. Otherwise you could be like those others. Think about your father, always. He is strong, By. No one will ever doubt his strength. But a strong man can cry when he's hurt, just like anybody else. If he couldn't he would be only half a man."

That was in the early years. I grew, and I learned— from people she would have approved and from some she would not. We lived in New Orleans for a time, and in Chicago and Kansas City and Denver, and we were in San Francisco the day I came home with a bullet hole in my side and blood running down my leg and told her I would have to go away.

She cried. Then she stopped crying and helped a doctor patch me up, and when he was gone she looked at me for a long time.

"Whatever has happened, your father would understand and approve. I believe that, By. Do you?"

I thought about it. "Could he be blind angry, Mother? Could he be angry enough to take a sledge and crush a man's skull with it . . . and not regret it? That's what has happened."

She was quiet for a time, and when she spoke her voice was shy. "Do you regret it, By?"

"No. Not at all. It needed to be done. He shot me first."

"Then," she said, "I guess you had to. The way your father had to fight in that war."

"Was he angry in the war?"

"No . . . well, yes. He was angry. So angry it knotted him up inside and would never go away. But he wasn't angry at the soldiers, By. He was angry at the war."

"Does it make any difference?"

"Oh, By, it makes all the difference in the world!"

All the difference in the world. My father, whom I always felt was with us but had never known, was the answer to a lot of puzzles in my young head and sometimes I wished I could see him. If I could see the tangible reality of him, it seemed, then I would understand it all. Somewhere out there was the man I must be, and sometimes the need for him was desperate because I was fast becoming what I would be and

I could never be sure how like him that was.

I turned eighteen in Arizona, learning to tend cattle. And learning some other things as well, that I would never tell Mattie Stillwell about. Some skills came so easily that I suspected he—whose name she never told me—must have them too.

I bought my Colt Peacemaker on the outskirts of Tucson. Its owner was a kid no older than me. I lay on the hard ground with a bullet in my leg and he lay ten yards away with a knife in his lungs. His face was painted with pink froth. I dragged myself over to him and he turned dying eyes to me. "You're quick," he said. "Too damned quick."

"Why were you after me? Why did you shoot me?"

He tried to grin at that, and coughed up blood. "I reckon you can worry over that," he said. "Maybe there'll be others."

"Is there someone to bury you?" I asked.

"No. Nobody. No money, either. I would have had some, but it don't matter now."

"Sell me your gun."

Pain and puzzlement filled his eyes. "What?" He coughed again.

"I have thirty dollars. I'll buy your gun. Thirty dollars will pay for your burying."

People had come running from town to gather around us.

"I guess," he said. "All right." He tried to lift his hand, but couldn't. I took the Colt from it, then got out the money and put it there instead. His fingers were cold.

"You won't be good enough," he whispered. "You'll never be as good as me."

"You weren't good enough," I told him. But he didn't hear it. He was dead.

By the time Mattie Stillwell had gone back to Baltimore and I went there to join her and enter the academy, I knew how to use the Peacemaker. There had been others, just as he said. And I had learned again the lesson I first learned in Atlanta. I had learned to hunt.

I hunted now. Somewhere were men who had killed Sam Dance, and where they were I would find the reason why.

I stayed to the breaks a few miles into No Man's Land, angling westward as the sun climbed, until I came into an area of wide, hayfield valleys where the broken land edged north flanking a frozen stream. I guessed I was ten or twelve miles west of Beer City. I turned due north then, up through diminishing breaks toward the prairie, and came up into a great, bright stillness broken only by a gentle wind out of the southwest.

Farther west they call them Chinook, those winds that come warm in winter to thaw the frozen land and bring a touch of spring before the final snows. On the plains they have no name, but sometimes they can come right on the heels of blizzard.

By the time I cut the rider's trail, several miles into Kansas, the snow was slush in the shallow places and it was warm enough to remove my serape and spread my coat to the breeze.

I judged from the trail that whoever was ahead of me was either an idiot who would be afoot soon, or didn't have much further to go. The prints had the erratic look of a played-out mount, but still he held it to a lope. I got out my telescope and took a long look. At first I didn't see anything, then there was a hint of smoke in the distance. It came and went and came again, and was two or three miles away.

The land here was more rolling than those lands around Liberal or north of Springfield, the kind of terrain that looks totally flat but can surprise a man unwary. While I had the scope out I took a look back where I had come from. The only way to tell that there were rises and dips out there was the way my track in the distance would disappear and then start again at a different point, off to one side. Distances can be confusing when they run into miles and the snow hides contours.

There was a movement. Just for an instant, far back, there was a dark speck. Then it was gone. I watched for a time, until my eye hurt from the glare, but it didn't come again.

I was a dozen or more miles west of Liberal, and a little north, which put me somewhere in the near corner of Stevens County. I put away the telescope and headed for that vanishing plume of smoke.

The place was a ramshackle farmstead between low hills, hidden from view but for its chimney smoke. I located it, then backed off and began a circle, wide around the place. I had only gone a little way when I found tracks outbound. People had been here but had left, heading east. The tracks were of a half-dozen horses, and there was crust melt in their packed depressions.

I didn't wast any more time. I touched heels to the gray and headed for the house.

One horse stood at a hitching post out front, head-down and beginning to shiver. The poor damned thing had been ridden half to death and then left standing wet. I angled in from the side, stepped down and ran to the near corner of the shack. I edged toward the open front door, gun drawn.

I could hear sounds from inside—sizzle of water on coals, the clang of a stove hatch, someone bumping against furniture. I waited. It was only a minute or two before he came out, carrying a bundle wrapped in a blanket. I put the muzzle of the Colt behind his ear and drew the hammer. The double click was loud in the bright, empty day.

"Hello, Fancy," I said. "Now we can have a long talk."

I guess twice of me in one day was too much for Fancy. He took one look, his eyes bugged out and he began telling me everything he knew.

Ace Pruitt had sent him, to tell the men here about me, about what I had done at Beer City, about what I had said. As I had thought, this was Ira Fox's place. He didn't know the names of any of the men who had holed up here, except one. That one was Morgan Hayes. There had been five others, one of them an occasional customer at Beer City and maybe a friend of Ace Pruitt's, but Fancy didn't know his name, just that he was thin and bucktoothed and ran with a bunch down in No Man's Land. The only one of that bunch Fancy could put a name to was Goldie Locke.

My hackles raised at that name. Timothy Locke, better known as Goldie, was one of those dark, half-legendary figures who had surfaced over in the Cherokee Strip in the old days when that territory was even wilder than No Man's Land. Locke was no fast-draw artist, no daring outlaw, not even a cardsharp or bountyman. The way I had heard it, Locke was quiet, low-key and a little reclusive. He went to church, he minded his manners and on occasion he would be gone for a while from wherever he was hanging his hat. He would be gone, and return with enough money to keep him for a time.

They said Locke's price was a straight $2,000, and that he worked in his own way.

I doubted whether Locke had anything to do with the murder of Sam Dance. Locke always worked alone, without witnesses. He killed and collected and went his way.

"You know some nasty people, Fancy." I put the Colt away. Fancy sat hunched in a corner of the shack, and his nose was running. But he wouldn't quit talking now until he was done. I found some canned goods and stale bread and wolfed down a snack while I listened.

When Fancy had come to Ira Fox's place with the news from Beer City they had listened, then kicked him out while they talked. He might have listened at the door, but he didn't. He was afraid. So he stood out in the snow, wishing he was somewhere else, until they came out carrying their gear, saddled their horses and left.

"I don't believe you, Fancy," I said. He winced. "You hear a lot more than you ever let on. You deal and you listen and sometimes people pay you money to keep you quiet. You're a good listener. I'll bet you even know who killed Sheriff Dance."

"No! I don't know anything about that! Nobody

does."

"Nobody? There was enough talk around the hovels down there that I heard it before it ever happened, and I was just passing through."

"I told you, I don't know!"

"Let me give you some names, Fancy. How about Morgan Hayes? How about Key Begley? How about Jack Little?"

He just stared at me, quivering.

"Give me another name, Fancy. One I don't know." I got out the Colt again, leveled it arm's length at the center of his head and cocked it. I thought he was going to scream.

"C-Calico! I don't know but Calico knows! Ask him!"

Calico. I knew he was telling the truth.

"Why did they kill the sheriff, Fancy?"

"He wouldn't let the past alone. That's all I ever heard. That's all I know."

"The sheriff? The sheriff wouldn't let the past alone? Are you sure it was the sheriff, not the judge?"

Suddenly his eyes took on that hooded look that said I had pushed too far. "M-Maybe it was the judge. I don't know."

He knew. But nothing I could do would get the truth now, because I'd never know when he was lying.

The bundle he had been carrying was a blanket full of odds and ends. Even as scared as he was, when he was left alone he had stayed around to pilfer everything of value he could lay his hands on. I went through it, but there was nothing of interest except to a thief.

I dumped the stuff out and threw the blanket at

him. "You'll need this before you get home, Fancy. Get on your feet and start walking."

"You're letting me go?"

"Afoot. You've done enough damage to that horse."

"Christ, it's twenty miles from here, at least."

I nodded. "And when it's dark it will get very cold. You'd better get a move on. Go!"

He went. By the time I had finished unsaddling his horse, rubbing it down and putting out feed for it in the barn, along with the saddled gray, he was just a dark dot in the blinding distance.

When the gray had finished a hatful of grain I mounted again, and headed east.

A few miles out from Ira's the trail of the riders split. Two of them had turned northeast. Three more had angled a little south of east and one had turned straight south.

I sat there on a much-ridden horse and rubbed my shoulder beneath my coat. Names ran through my head, names of people I was certain had been at Cross Canyon the morning Sam Dance died. Morgan Hayes. Slim Cavanaugh. Larry Doyle. Hobie Moore. Jack Little, five names, six horses, and the sixth was a skinny, bucktoothed type who associated somehow with Goldie Locke.

Key Begley was dead. A pair named Smith and Johnson had gone south. That made nine. Maybe Calico was ten, I didn't know. Maybe Ira Fox was in it too. They had holed at his place. That made eleven . . . maybe.

But there had been more than that out there, at least twenty in all.

Twenty men to kill one man. Twenty men, to put three bullets into a fifty-year-old sheriff who might once have been a soldier angry at the war, angry at the manipulations and greeds that set men against men and made blood flow.

That war was over twenty-seven years ago. Can anger last that long? If so, what does it become as time passes? I had always known the phantom father my mother painted for me. But I had never known Sam Dance.

Two riders northeast. That could be toward Springfield. Henry Lattimer would be heading back there and he would tell Sim Guthrie what he had learned. Lattimer was young, but not dumb. They would be alerted.

Three riders southeast. Toward Liberal. Vince Cole would be there. Vince Cole didn't miss much.

The six riders were on fresh mounts and had chosen three directions. I was on a tiring gray and could choose only one. I had told Henry this shaped up to be a long hunt.

I almost missed the sound when it came. I would have missed it if I had been moving. It was faint and far off, somewhere west or southwest and carried on the wind, the thin, distant crack of a rifle. It was just a suggestion, the echo of an echo. But I remembered the hint of motion far back on my trail. I remembered Penny Bassett with a hole in his heart. And I thought about Fancy Pace.

I turned south, following the single track that led that way. It was as good a choice as any.

By sundown I was miles into No Man's Land and the tracks stretched out ahead, still south, until they disappeared into the Beaver breaks. Twenty-five miles of No Man's Land lay ahead, and beyond that an awful lot of Texas.

15

In the mesa lands above the north fork of the Red, chill winds mourned across the flats and plucked at new snow on brushy slopes. Gray-white devils of frost and dust whirled giddy paths down hillsides and the sky was like close slate.

Three horsemen walked their mounts around the shoulder of a flat-top butte, their eyes tight slits, their faces shielded from the driven grit. The lead rider leaned from his saddle, hard eyes studying the ground. The trail he followed had, for some miles, been no trail at all, but in the past mile it had become more pronounced. He paused, held up a hand, then stepped from his saddle and crouched, studying the ground. He looked up at the others, sitting their mounts. "I thought you said you missed him, Roy."

"I shot his horse, but he lit and dodged and I missed him. You saw it."

"Well, you may have winged him. Here's blood."

"Why wasn't there any before now?" The other rider, a square-faced man with a shock of dark hair whipping beneath his hat, looked around, taking in the rough gray-white land with suspicious eyes.

"I dunno, Johnny." The tracker stood, scratched his chin and swung back into his saddle. "Maybe Roy just clipped him. But that's blood there, and it's his."

"All right. Go on. He can't get far afoot."

They moved on, the tracker reading the ground ahead, the other two scanning the land through slit eyes. The tracks, barely visible, led straight ahead now, angling up the incline of a squat mesa.

From a crack in the limestone caprock Chako watched them come. Hidden from them, he crouched in shadow and his hard shoulders moved rhythmically as he worked to enlarge a horizontal fault in the soft stone before him. Using his heavy knife as chisel and prybar he labored to drive the hairline crack deeper and deeper into the standing slab of stone. His breath was hoarse but deep and steady in the chill. Muscles rippled on dark forearms below rolled sleeves as he inserted the knife point in the crack, drove it deeper with a blow of his hand, then twisted and lifted to pry at the stone. Nothing perceptible happened. Without pausing he pulled the blade free, moved it an inch, reinserted its tip and began again. Despite the chilling cold his brow was beaded with sweat.

Chako had come into Double-D range seeking game. There was not enough beef at Fort Sill this month to feed the reservation people, and no more coming until the winter weather eased. And he was tired of reservation beef, anyway. A man could still find game up on the scarp if he could get there. Mule deer ranged here sometimes, and now and then a wandering buffalo that had escaped the white men's guns.

The only thing between Chako's camp beneath Haystack Mountain in the treaty lands and the scarp was Double-D. Since the coming of Davy Dawes, the people on the reservations had stopped looking west. The Texas border was a barricade of riders with ready guns. They shot Indians as readily as they shot wolves. But by territorial instinct far older than Double-D, this was Chako's land and he ventured here riding proud and careful. He had come a long way.

He was more than fifty miles into Texas, two days of travel, riding a good paint mare and leading a packhorse, when the three riders cut his trail and found him. The paint mare was dead now and Chako's rifle lay still in its sheath on its saddle. Afoot, he had led them six miles into the flat-top breaks that climbed toward the scarp.

As he worked now he watched them, coming closer. One of them he knew from old times. Johnny Saxon hadn't changed in the years of working Double-D. He had just become meaner.

Pacing himself, measuring his deep breaths, Chako labored at the base of the hiding slab as the horsemen angled up the mesa's climbing slopes, coming almost directly at him.

The stone was soft, chalky and yellow-white, old rotting limestone of the kind called *caleche*. He drove his knife deep again, twisted and pried, and thought he sensed give . . . just slightly, but the stone had seemed to respond. He stopped. He sheathed his knife.

On the slope the three riders were fifty yards away,

walking their mounts, Saxon, and another one flanking the tracker closely, their eyes surveying the slope ahead of them. Saxon's head turned slightly and Chako froze in position and looked away. He knew the danger of eye contact, even unseen. A man sometimes could sense presence when eye met eye. He held his breath and waited.

The cloth wrapping his left forearm had soaked bright red on a patch of its surface, but the blood had stopped spreading. He had cut himself just enough to spill a few drops of blood. He had seen them find it, had seen then pick up their pace just slightly as they came on then. The sight of blood had called them to him.

Saxon had peered at the narrow cleft, then looked away. Chako shifted his position. The crack where he hid was barely two feet wide at its bottom, spreading to about three feet at the top, twelve feet above him. Cautiously he stood, listening now to the rhythmic fall of their horses' hooves. They were beyond his view now, approaching the slab of limestone.

Bracing himself against the rock behind him, levering upward with strong legs, finding finger grips where he could, Chako climbed. Halfway up the cleft he anchored himself with spread fingers, his shoulders against the rock behind him, and walked his feet up the slabrock until they were level with his chin.

In silence he hung there, curled almost double, while his ears read the position of the riders. Then he took a deep breath, hard muscles bulged in his shoulders and legs, and he pushed.

The slab was immensely heavy, a huge dead weight perched on a striated base, but narrower at the bottom where wind erosion had hollowed it through the ages, and now freed by the hairline crack Chako had expanded. For a long moment inertia fought him, and he increased his pressure. Muscles cracked and rippled, tight as whipcord on a war axe. Then, hesitantly, the huge stone shifted an inch and he thrust with every ounce of his strength. It teetered, shifted again on its base, then tipped and fell outward. Chako plunged down, landing on his shoulders at its sheering base, and the world went dark for a moment. On the slope below the great slab thundered down, exploding into bounding shards and boulders. A stone the size of a wagonbed broke free, bounced and slammed into one of the riders, grinding man and horse beneath its weight. Exploding rubble cascaded around the pawing hooves of the other horses. One went down and its rider leapt free only to be buried beneath tons of rock rolling downslope.

At the base of the limestone bluff Chako rolled over, shook his head to clear the shades of concussion and got to his feet. Below him was dust and turmoil. Just beyond the path of the rock a horse pitched and plunged, stirrups and gear flapping crazily. Gusting wind whipped the dust into a vortex and flung it back at the limestone face, then away across the receding slopes. Far below now, the last ripples of rockslide fanned onto the flats and rested there.

Chako crouched behind a stub of rock and looked around. The remaining horse, a muscular black with silver-trimmed saddlery, had stopped its pitching and stood aquiver, head up, staring wild-eyed at the strewn slope. It was the only living thing he could see.

With instincts born to the Comanche, Chako began

working his way down toward the black horse, approaching quietly, always at a diagonal, letting it see him and know him, never seeming to close in on it but always nearer with each silent step. It had been thoroughly spooked and he took his time approaching. It danced and shied, watching him, but held its ground. When he was near enough, almost within reach of its bridle and trailing reins, he stood still and looked at it for a moment then turned his back and began walking slowly away. He heard its steps behind him. Curiosity had overcome its fear. He took another step and stopped. When its soft nose nudged him from behind he turned slowly, took its bridle in a strong, gentle hand and breathed into its nostrils. Then he patted its head and scratched its ears.

Something moved in the field of rubble and Chako squinted into the whipping wind, then ran toward it. He stepped up on a slab of rock, jumped across to another and looked down on a man just getting to his feet. His hat was gone, his shirt torn and he was covered with bone-white dust. Dark hair blew wild in the wind. He stood, staring around him, his back to Chako on the rock. The Indian noticed the man's hand went to his hip, fingers touching the holstered revolver there, making sure of its presence. The gunfighter's first reflex.

Chako's voice was soft and as cold as the winter wind. "Johnny Saxon," he said. "Up here."

Saxon whirled around, clawed fingers an inch from his gun. His eyes widened as he saw the Indian standing casually on the rock, ten feet away. He had not known who they were tracking, only that it was a stray Indian alone on Double-D. Now he knew. The thick red band with long hair tossing below it, the tattered wool coat, high soft boots . . . and the worn Colt revolver slung low at the right—this was the one on whose head Davy Dawes had put a price, the one who had cost Double-D stock, supplies and riders, the one some of them called Wolf. He saw him, knew him and a slow grin spread across his smudged face. Johnny Saxon was quick with a gun, and deadly with it. Though there were some he would not brace, they were few. They called this one Wolf, but he was only an Indian. Johnny saw the sixgun there, but only an Indian wore it.

"Red bastard," he rasped. His fingers closed on the butt of his gun.

He barely saw the flicker of movement as the Indian's hand fanned across his holster and up, but even as his gun cleared leather Johnny Saxon was staring into hellfire flowering at the muzzle of a .45 Colt. Shock numbed him, tearing pain erupted in his chest and he was thrown backward. His gun triggered into empty air.

Chako looked down at the body of Johnny Saxon and dropped his gun back into its holster. "Stupid," he muttered. The Kwahadi had seen that look before, the look that had come into Saxon's face and remained there in death. It was an expression of profound surprise.

He left Johnny Saxon where he fell, the gun still in his hand, and climbed again to the limestone bluff that capped the mesa. Finding finger-and-toe holds in the soft rock face he climbed to the flat top of the hill and squatted there, studying the land around. Up here, he could see for miles. The wind moaned and tumbled, but it did not carry the grit of the lower lands.

A few miles to the west, the escarpment began beyond which lay the high *llano estacado*. There in the hollows and valleys rimming the high plains he would find game—deer, possibly elk—meat to fill his belly. Everywhere he looked, in the distances, were the cattle of Double-D. Too many for the range. If he found no game he would take beef. But elk would be better . . . or buffalo.

His good rifle still lay in its sheath on his dead horse, several miles back. And somewhere near he would find his pack animal. The white men had interrupted Chako's hunt. Now they were dead and he would continue.

He turned to climb down, then paused. Far to the northeast, almost beyond sight, there was movement. When it came again he squinted and crouched, waiting for a moment of clearer view. It came. They were two riders, miles away, plodding southward through the lonely land. He could not make out their path, except that it was south. More Double-D riders, he guessed, but they were far afield if so. They moved with the rhythm of far travel behind, and were north of the Sweetwater, just below the Canadian.

Leaving the mesa top Chako mounted the black horse and skirted east around the field of rubble on the killing slope. He backtrailed, pushing the black along at a mile-eating pace, and found his packhorse still rigged, nibbling grass in a shouldered gully. He took it in tow. Three miles beyond he found where he had been ambushed. He removed his gear from the dead paint mare, then stripped saddle and tackle and carried them some distance away to hide them in a frostblown wash. He would pick them up on the way back home. His rifle was unharmed. He laced its boot to the black's saddle.

The wind had diminished and lost some of its chill, quartering now from the southwest and driving the icy edge of storm weather before it. Chako hurried to complete his packing, aware of the increasing visibility as dust settled from the air and the lowering sun sought breaks in the clouds to the west. He was exposed here, more so than he would be back in the hills.

Astride the black again, leading his pack animal, the Indian turned west but angled slightly north toward a lone mesa on the plain. Curiosity drove him to see a high place and look again at the two riders he had seen. They had the look of travelers, rather than range riders. For two years Chako had taken an active interest in the comings and goings of those who rode for Double-D. Many things about the Dawes operation piqued his curiosity, and that was tempered by an abiding hatred of everything associated with the spreading Dawes empire. Chako had not forgotten what Pony Bidell and his riders had done to him.

Angling up the rise of the lone mesa Chako reached its cap, found an old trail and rode to the top of it. While the horses pawed snow crust and cropped at the yellow grass beneath, Chako chewed on a strip of jerky and studied the lands afar.

From the mesa to the bend of the Sweetwater was only a few miles, and when the sun shafted through breaking clouds low in the west, the visibility took on that sudden startling clarity that sometimes follows storms on the high plains.

After a few minutes he saw them, closer now but angling eastward along the Sweetwater. Thirty miles beyond, as they now headed, lay Mobeetie and the Double-D.

Chako squatted at the lip of the mesa and studied them, tiny in the distance, as patterns of evening sunlight washed across the broad land. He watched their movements, how they sat their mounts, how they chose their paths, and a scowl creased his dark face. He knew them. One was Ed Johnson, who had come up with Davy Dawes from south Texas. The other was Pony Bidell.

For a long time the Indian watched the distant riders, and a temptation gnawed at him. He had killed three of Dawes' men this day. He was tempted to add two more. But he looked at the distances, and knew he could not reach them before dark. And by dark he wanted to be within the sheltering wings of some cove below the escarpment. He had come to hunt game this time, not men.

Finally Chako remounted the black, took the pack horse's lead and rode down from the lone mesa, heading west. But he remained puzzled.

Bidell and Johnson had been gone from Double-D for a time. Now they were returning. He wondered where they had been.

16

Henry Lattimer stayed over in Liberal that Monday. He had no orders to the contrary, and Vince Cole had asked him to stay around long enough for Vince to ride to Arkalon and back.

With the storm blown over and a warming wind out of the west, there were people on the roads—such as they were—coming and going about their business. But there was no traffic yet across the Cimarron Valley. It would be a day or two before the road there was really passable.

After making Vince's rounds for him, Henry secluded himself in the deputy's little office and started reading files. Vince had collected accounts of the Stevens County War two years earlier. "Sheriff Dance wanted to know everything about it," Vince had told him. "We have accounts here from newspapers all over Kansas, court records from Topeka and Larned, a copy of the state militia report submitted by Colonel Phelps . . . Land, Henry, we have a box full of stuff. The sheriff was really interested in what happened over there. He kept me after stuff like this half the time, the past few months."

"He didn't collect this when the whole thing was going on?"

"No. He didn't get interested in it until later. Sometime last year, I guess. But when he got interested he got real interested."

"Why?" Henry had asked, puzzled. He recalled the sheriff talking about the Stevens County troubles, too. The affair seemed to haunt the old man.

"I don't know," Vince had said. "Just something set him off, I guess. Anyhow we collected a lot of paper in the past season or two."

Henry dug into the records.

It had started, apparently, over a county seat battle between Hugoton and Woodsdale. Hugoton had been the stronger town, with more population, and had been declared county seat. But then Samuel Woods and his friends had contested it. The matter had been in and out of court, Woods raising challenge after challenge, and things had become nasty. Hard words were said and repeated. There had been fighting . . . an occasional brawl, but just making matters worse.

Finally it had seemed to be resolved. Hugoton was the county seat.

Then Samuel Woods had brought out his big guns. With affidavits and petitions he challenged the elections . . . and went further than that. He challenged the legality of Stevens County. The census, he said, had been fraudulent. Under Kansas law Stevens did not qualify for organization as a county and must be disenfranchised.

The war had started then. A Woods supporter had been gunned down in the street at Hugoton. Armed men from Woodsdale had retaliated, marching on Hugoton with their guns loaded and fire in their eyes. The Hugoton town marshal, Morgan Hayes, had met them at the outskirts of town and—in what some felt to be a masterpiece of diplomacy—had turned them away with no shots fired. But they had returned, and Morgan Hayes was strangely absent this time. Gone into the Neutral Strip, some said. The Woodsdalians killed two men in Hugoton and set fire to a building before retreating.

Henry found names that were familiar. Hayes, Larry Doyle, Slim Cavanaugh; B. J. Cavanaugh and Jack Little had bragged in Hugoton that they could raise fifty men to ride upon the town, that they would burn the place to the ground. Shots had been fired at a claim shack north of Hugoton. Men had been found dead. Hugoton men riding south to harvest hay in No Man's Land had been ambushed and killed. Henry found more names, among those suspected but never brought to trial . . . Begley . . . Key Begley? L. Doyle, H. P. Moore . . . that could be Hobie Moore.

Morgan Hayes had returned to Hugoton, but there was a cloud over him by that time. He resigned as marshal and joined the Woodsdale forces.

Then, as abruptly as it began, it was over. Henry scratched his head and frowned at the sparcity of the reports. What ended it? It just . . . ended, apparently. Several people had left Stevens County. Some went to Colorado, others disappeared into the Neutral Strip. Henry wondered what those men had been doing in Stevens County to begin with. Most of them weren't farmers. They weren't family men, nor settlers. Most of them were troublemakers, and he began to understand some of Sheriff Dance's puzzlement over the affair. Here it was, all laid out, just as it happened.

The only problem was, it didn't make any sense. At least a dozen men—and maybe three times that many—had died in a war that seemed to have no point. Old Samuel Woods was assumed by most to have been insane. The courts that heard his testimony had left the dissolution issue undecided.

And yet, men had followed him and died.

Henry put the materials away, a question puzzling him. Had the men followed Woods? Men like Hayes and Begley, Little and Cavanaugh—they didn't follow a zealot to war. What they did was done for money or power, and what could Woods have offered them? He wondered if Woods' troublemaking had ever been the cause of anything, or whether the old lawyer might just have been a handy excuse for somebody else to get away with something. But if so, what? As far as he could see, the war in the next county had accomplished nothing for anybody. Or had it?

Sam Dance had wondered about all that, and his concern had not been simple curiosity. Henry had known the old sheriff, had worked with him, and knew when he was truly worried about something. A year or more after the Stevens County War ended, the sheriff of Seward County had begun investigating it. And he had been serious.

Henry had an odd thought then. It was as though the Stevens County troubles had been turned on and then turned off—like pulling the valve chain on a windmill's flow spout—by someone remote from the whole thing. Maybe even by someone outside of

Stevens County.

He had the distinct impression, for a moment, of reading the reports of something that had been no more than a test. But a test of what?

An aging cowhand whom Henry knew only as May stuck his head in the door as Henry was putting the boxes of records away. "Vince around?"

"He went over to Arkalon," Henry said. "Something I can do for you?"

The puncher came in, closed the door behind him and stamped his boots on the straw mat. "Slush," he said. "Wind's above freezin' an' the whole shebang is turnin' into slush. Ain't one thing it's another. We come in to get hay while ago, heard somebody had shot a hole in Penny Bassett."

"That's right. Doc brought him in."

"Well, now, what do you know about that?" May shrugged, then glanced at the coffee pot on the stove.

"Help yourself," Henry told him.

"Believe I will, thankee." He found a tin cup, poured thick coffee and pulled up a chair to straddle, his arms folded across the back. "Any notion who it was?"

"Not so far."

"No surprise. Old Penny, he's been askin' for it ever since he come to Seward. Pure-dee trouble." Sharp eyes squinted from a monkey-mask of weathered wrinkles. "Also heard tell that Stillwell fella took him down a few notches before that happened."

"I heard that, too. Stillwell didn't shoot him, though."

"Wouldn't reckon," the puncher muttered, sipping coffee "Regular prairie wolf, that'n. Puts me in mind of Sam Dance when he was younger."

Henry had his back to the man, sorting through warrants in a wall cupboard. Now he stiffened, turned slowly. "The sheriff?"

"You've noticed it, too, ain't you? I ain't sure just what it is . . . same sort of build, I guess . . . walks like him . . . but that ain't it so much. He's got a edge about him, that one. Maybe that's it. Like he's got a coil spring inside him just a-fixin' to let go. Sam Dance was the same way when he was younger."

"You knew him, Mr. May? The sheriff?"

"Oh, sure. Though he weren't a sheriff then. He was hired on as town marshal down at Tulia. I guess that must have been fifteen years ago. Yep, the big herds was still comin' up from San Antone and down there, an' Charlie Goodnight was cuttin' a wide swath right where the old trails come through, and old Sam, there he was right in the middle. Yeah, I got to know him some. Me and Smitty, we rode for Goodnight then, and that whole country down there was a powderkeg. But not Tulia. Land, everybody knew . . . or soon found out . . . that if you wanted trouble you better keep it out of Sam Dance's town. Quiet young fella he was, always good manners and straight as a rod, but sudden! Mercy, could he be sudden!" The old puncher's face clouded, his eyes averted now in reminiscence. "I reckon the years must have just caught up with Sam. No bunch of sidewinders would have boxed him in back then, no sir. Guess times do come around, though."

Henry had perched himself on the edge of Vince Cole's desk, and he found himself almost holding his breath. "I never knew Mr. Dance had been a lawman in Texas," he said.

May glanced up at him. "Why, Boy, you couldn't have been more'n a baby then. Sam moved to Tulia in seventy-five. I know that because it was the year it never rained and we had locusts. Casper Johanssen lost more'n half his herd in two months. That was when it was. Tulia was a rip-roarin' place an' when times got so hard the good folks there decided they'd had enough. They hired Sam and told him to keep the peace. Land, didn't he ever keep the peace! By the time he was there a month that town was quiet as a Monday mornin' church. Then he moved his family in an' rented a nice little house an' I guess he was there two year at the least."

"He never mentioned it," Henry said. "Not once."

May looked at the young deputy quizzically. "Thought a heap of him, didn't you, son? That's all right. You sure could have picked worse to look up to. Some folks didn't hold with Sam, but I always got a fair shake from him. Not surprised he didn't talk much about Tulia, though. That town was hard on him. That's where he buried his wife. Pretty little thing, she was. Hair the color of cornshucks at harvest. But she was sickly. I guess it must have been seventy-seven when she took the fever and died. Left Sam with that hellion kid of his that he didn't have no earthly idea what to do with, broke up like he was."

"He did have a son, then."

"Sure did. Regular handful of a kid, maybe eight or nine year old. Way I heard it, there was family somewhere an' Sam sent the boy off to them. Then he turned in his badge and just . . . left. I hadn't set eyes on him 'til he showed up here a few years ago an' hired on, then run for sheriff. Never seen a man had aged any more. But he still had that edge about him. He still did."

"Yes." Henry gazed out the window at the traffic on Kansas Avenue, the scraped snow turning mushy and chocolate brown under the wheels, hooves and boots of the people out there. "Yes, he had an edge to him."

"Heard you was out there when he died. You saw it."

"I saw it. They murdered him."

"I reckon." May's eyes were steady on the young deputy. "I tell you, I never did think that Stillwell fella done it, even if I did bring him in . . . leastways helped to."

"Just curious, Mr. May, but why did you think he hadn't?"

"Oh, lots of reasons. Like, they say there was twenty men out there that killed the sheriff. You'd know that. You was there. But that Stillwell, well sir, I seen lone wolves afore an' he's one if ever I seen one. Now he might send a fella to his reward . . . be surprised if he hasn't, for a fact. But he's no pack wolf, that one. Not him. Then, I never seen a fella so obligin' about bein' took to jail. Land, it was almost like that was just what he had in mind. It just didn't hold water to me. Who is he, anyhow? Where's he from? I seen some drifters, and maybe he looks like one but he ain't. And that's a fact."

"I don't know where he's from," Henry answered truthfully. "He doesn't talk a whole lot. What did you want to see Vince about, Mr. May?"

"Oh. I wanted to tell him a fella came out our way

201

and said there'd been a doin's at Beer City, early this mornin.' Keno Mora's place got burned about half down and that fella Wiley Dobbins—Pruitt's bodyguard—he's shot dead. There's another one, big sidewinder named Calico, that's banged up some. I thought Vince might want to look into it, that's all."

"That's outside our jurisdiction," Henry pointed out. "But he'll probably want to ask around. Any idea what it was all about?"

"Not much. Ain't likely anybody's gonna get a straight answer from that Pruitt or Mora. But the word is Ace Pruitt's put out the word in No Man's Land, lookin' for men to ride gun. If I's Vince I'd keep a sharp eye. Some of them hoorahs would just as leave shoot up Liberal as they would anyplace else if they find who they're after."

"Do you know who they're after?"

"Sure. Didn't I tell you? They're after Byron Stillwell."

Henry's jaw dropped. "Byron? They're after Byron? What for?"

May squinted at him. "That's what I just told you, son. They're after him because he killed Wiley Dobbins an' busted up Calico an' burned Keno Mora's gambling house an' took all of Mora's money."

Henry sat dazed. He tried to think of a good question to ask and could not come up with one. Confused thoughts raced through his mind . . . dark of morning and the sardonic face of Byron Stillwell grinning in the hotel sitting room, the soft voice suggesting he get Peggy back to her room before anyone was up; the hard humor in Stillwell's eyes up in the Springfield jail as he calmly explained that Ira

202

Fox had broken his arm; the body of Key Begley in a mortician's box . . . and he thought of Penny Bassett, brutally beaten with his own leaded quirt, and of a ghostly rider on a pale horse flying in cold darkness across the Cimarron bottoms, leaping at a ridge, almost making it and then falling back to reappear a moment later, waving at them, trying to warn Sam Dance, then disappearing again. Byron Stillwell always seemed to disappear . . . and reappear.

"Fella sure reminds me of Sam Dance," May mused. "Me, I never put much stock in spirits an' ha'nts. But was I one of them that done the old sheriff in, I guess I'd be shakin' in my boots about now."

Henry gazed at the old cowhand. He wondered how much he knew . . . how much he guessed. "He's out to find them," he said slowly.

May's expression didn't change. "Figured as much," he said. "What's Sim Guthrie think about that?"

"Sim Guthrie doesn't know it."

"But you do. Well, now. I guess that don't surprise me any. Old Sam, he put a heap of store in you, son. Knew from the way he talked. Vince an' Everett, too . . . he thought a lot of both of them, but mainly of you. I reckon if you had a chance to draw bead on them that done him, you'd do 'er, wouldn't you, son?"

"I would have then." Henry chewed his lip, wondering about the older man's question. "I guess if I had to . . . I'd give a lot to know who they are, Mr. May. I'd like to see them go to trial, and I'd like to see them hang."

May snorted. "Just like ol' Sam. Law an' order all the way. I tell you for sure, hangin' ain't what Stillwell's got in mind for that bunch."

"No." Henry thought of Key Begley, dead in a wooden box. "But he doesn't wear a badge. I do."

He was uncomfortable under the puncher's stare, but then the man snorted again and shifted his gaze. "You be all right, son. Sam wasn't wrong about you. Me and Smitty, we been listenin' and talkin' things over. I was goin' to tell Vince, but I'll tell you. They is somethin' shapin' up around here that ain't good, an' killin' Sam Dance weren't the end of it. Lot of folks doin' a lot of funny things the past few months. You an' Vince keep your eyes open, son. And if you get in a pinch, you holler for me and Smitty. We may be old an' slow, but Sam Dance was our friend too. And Pearly an' Cass, they're good buttons. An' there's some more around that wouldn't mind pitchin' in if you need us. You just keep us in mind."

Henry felt warm and glad at the offer, but he held up his hand. "Don't you think you ought to be telling the sheriff all this, Mr. May?"

"Sim Guthrie?" the wrinkled face dissolved in a scowl. "Hell, I might as well tell a fence post. You an' Vince, son. You keep us in mind."

17

May walked with him for a time as Henry made rounds of the little town. Since coming to Seward County to homestead, Henry had confined himself mostly to the area north of the Cimarron. Between building up his claim and working for Sam Dance, he had found little time to get to the south area. It was different from the north, just as Liberal was different from Springfield.

The new town bustled. It was growing, building and seemed to have a vitality that Springfield lacked. That could have been because of the railroad coming this way. Two years earlier, it had been thought the rails would go to Springfield. And since the decision had been made to come south, the larger town's attitude had changed. There was a defensiveness there, almost a bitterness, that Henry had not really noticed until he compared it to Liberal.

Twice in an hour he saw copies of the petition being circulated to call a county seat election, and there was open talk of a deal being made among businessmen of Liberal and Arkalon for Arkalon's support of Liberal as the new seat. In return, they said, the Arkalon people would be provided free lots and sites in Liberal and assistance in moving there.

He thought of Saul Bingham, who said it would never happen. He wondered.

"The Stevens County thing was a big hoorah," May chatted as they strolled along Front Street, avoiding the piles of seeping, crusting swept snow. "Might have started over a railroad election. They was tryin' to vote bonds to get the line to build to Woodsdale with a spur to Voorhees, an' the Hugoton people was dead set against that. Fella got knocked in the head at a town meeting, and somebody else swore out a warrant against the town marshal—that was Morgan Hayes—an' then Hayes an' his friends went after the fella that filed the complaint. Everybody chose up sides an' there was some killin' over it. Samuel Woods was eggin' them on all the way, too. Never knowed a man could make so much trouble."

"Woods," Henry said. "That's the one that was killed last summer over at Hugoton. Shot down in the street."

"The same. That's one reason Judge Tomlin moved hisself over here to Seward County. Lot of folks over there think he had a hand in killin' Woods. But there's others think he was in it with Woods up to his eyeballs."

Henry touched his hat to a trio of ladies on the Boardwalk, their skirts held above laced shoes to keep the hems out of the slush where the walk had not been cleaned. "In what?" he asked May.

"Why, in whatever it was ol' Woods was tryin' to pull off. Nobody makes that much trouble for that many folks without a reason."

"I thought Woods just wanted his town to be the county seat."

"Naw. That was just part of it. Lot of folks about decided what he was tryin' to do was get this whole country chopped out of Kansas for its own territory. You know the state militia was called out four times?"

"No, I didn't know it was that many."

"Well, it was. Lot of folks back east at Topeka about ready to toss in the rope an' disenfranchise the whole place. It costs a bunch of money to send out the militia."

They turned north on Lincoln toward First Street where a steam mill wheezed and thumped busily, baling sheds of hay that had been brought in from No Man's Land before the snow. Wagons waited in line to haul the bales out to the tending grounds where several nearby ranchers had bunched their small herds.

"If Pete Waverly hadn't been drunk for a month he'd have had all that baled by now," May declared. Then he pointed. "Them two buttons there with the humpback wagon, them is Pearly an' Cass, that I told you about. Good boys, both of 'em. Got their heads screwed on straight. Them and Smitty and me, we worked together a lot the past year or two. Me and Smitty, we're too old to have good sense. Had it all stomped out of us years ago. But Cass and Pearly, they ain't workin' for drinkin' wages. They're buildin' themselves a stake."

Both of the younger cowboys turned as they approached, and one of them waved. "This is our second load, Mr. May," the other grinned. "You got all our possibles?"

"Over at the Emporium, just waitin' for you slow-pokes to bring a wagon. Boys, this here is Henry Lattimer. Deputy sheriff up at Springfield. Henry, this yayhoo is Pearly an' that one is Cass."

"Howdy," Pearly grinned again. "Aren't you the one that faced down those men that killed the sheriff?"

Henry shook his head. "I didn't face down anybody. I was just there."

"But you didn't run off," Cass said.

"I fell down."

"You workin' with Vince Cole?" Pearly asked. "We helped him bring in that Stillwell fellow."

Cass glanced at his partner. "We didn't exactly help him. What we did was went along with Mr. Murdoch and some others to pick him up. He's loose again, now, though."

"Yes," Henry admitted. "I know."

"By the way," Pearly thumbed back his hat and looked around. "Where's Vince?"

"He went to Arkalon this morning. Why?"

"Well, one of the boys said Vince was askin' yesterday about some people. One of 'em was Slim Cavanaugh. You know anything about that?"

Henry nodded.

"Well, I was over to the hotel just a little bit ago . . ."

"I thought you went to the tackle shop," Cass glared at him. "What were you doin' at the hotel?"

Pearly grinned at his partner. "Some things that is a body's own business ain't nobody else's business."

Cass snorted. "Shoot, you think I don't know the Selmans come to town, Pearly?" He looked at Henry apologetically. "Pearly here, he's got his heart set on courtin' Peggy Selman but didn't have the nerve to while that Bassett was around. But now he's gone, you can just bet there won't be anything hold this'n back. Randiest stud bull you ever seen, Deputy . . . what's the matter?"

"Nothing!" Henry snapped, his voice too loud. He glared at Pearly. "What did you start to say before you started getting coarse?"

Pearly stared back at him, then reddened. "Coarse! What do you mean, coarse? Look, Deputy, all I said was . . ."

"I don't care what you said," Henry thrust a belligerent chin at the young cowhand. "All I want to know from you is, what did you start to say?"

Cass and May looked at each other in confusion.

"Look, if you want to make somethin' out of it," Pearly hunched his shoulders, crouching slightly.

May's brows lifted then and he caught the deputy's sleeve. "Henry, I don't suppose you know Peggy Selman, do you?"

Henry's gaze held the hostile Pearly. "We've met."

"Oh," May shrugged and turned to Cass. "That explains it."

Cass still looked confused.

"Pearly," May suggested, "why don't you just ease off an' tell the deputy what he wants to know?"

"He started it!" Pearly barked.

"I didn't start anything," Henry said. "It was you that began insulting the young lady."

Pearly reddened even more. "I never insulted a

lady in my life!'"

"Yes, you did, Pearly," Cass pointed out. "You remember when we took that load of watermelons up to the Crocker place and . . ."

"Shut up, Cass!"

"You want to apologize now?" Henry suggested.

"Apologize for what? I didn't say anything!"

"All that business about a stud bull and paying court to Miss Selman. That was uncalled for."

"I didn't say that. Cass said that."

As one, the cowhand and the deputy turned to glare at the offending Cass.

"Godalmighty," May muttered. "Buttons."

"You're both crazy," Cass said, looking from Henry to Pearly.

May stepped into the space among the three. "Cass and Pearly," he ordered, "you all get that hay loaded an' get about your business." Then to Henry, "Come on, Deputy. Let's walk some more an' I'll tell you about how it was in the old days." He tugged the deputy's sleeve and turned him away, still fuming. They had gone several steps before Henry remembered what had started the conversation, and turned back. "You still didn't tell me what you started to tell me," he accused.

Pearly glared at him. "About what?"

"About Slim Cavanaugh!"

"Oh. Well, I saw him just a few minutes ago over at the hotel. Him and two other hardcases come in from the west an' went to the hotel. Cavanaugh went in. The others stayed out front."

Henry's face went pale, then he spun on his heel. May caught his arm with surprising strength, stopping him. "Son," he said, "you might need some help."

With Cass and Pearly at his heels and May limping along behind, Henry Lattimer ran the half-block north to First, then another block to second and skidded half way across the street as he made the turn there, his feet throwing muddy slush. He heard Cass grunt as he fell, then picked himself up and came on. Townspeople hurried to get out of their way.

At the corner of Kansas Avenue Henry pulled up and surveyed the scene diagonally across. There were several horses at the hitchrail, people walking along the boardwalk, and a pair of hard-looking men lounged at the bottom of the hotel steps.

The three bunched there at the corner, staring across. "That's the other two," Pearly said. "What do you aim to do with them?"

"I'm going to arrest them for murder and take them to Springfield."

They were joined by the gimpy May, grumbling at the unaccustomed footrace. May was a cowboy of the old school. If a thing couldn't be done on horseback it wasn't worth doing . . . with maybe two exceptions.

"Son," he stared across at the two men, "you sure don't tackle anything easy, do you? Those are gunmen over there."

"We have guns."

May glanced at the young punchers, eager hands on their weapons. "With one possible exception . . . and maybe two if you know how to use that rifle . . . the guns in this outfit are mostly decorative."

Cass and Pearly shot hard glances at the older man but held their tongues. They were working cowhands, not gunmen. And they knew it.

"Those men helped kill Sam Dance," Henry said.

May's monkey face turned hard. "Are you sure, Henry? Real sure?"

"I'm real sure. And even if I wasn't, the sheriff sent me here to find them and I'm not going back without them."

"Well, then, I guess we got it to do."

"Lot of people on the street," Cass pointed out.

May thought it over. "Good," he said.

In the cold air and warm sun of winter afternoon Jack Little and Larry Doyle loitered in front of the hotel, sharp eyes on the busy street. There was no mistaking the warning Fancy Pace had brought them. Someone was looking for them, and that someone had names. That meant maybe the law had names, too. They knew Vince Cole was out of town. They had checked on that. But they were taking no chances. Cavanaugh had gone in to collect Key Begley if he was here, and to get some food packed for them.

A pair of cowhands, neither of them much over twenty in age, sauntered toward them on the board-walk, embroiled in an argument. Without looking up, the two turned between the gunmen and walked toward the hotel porch. One of them had been there a short time earlier.

As the two passed, a weather-beaten old cowpuncher came from diagonally across the street and followed the first pair up the steps. Doyle and Little looked after them, glanced at each other and shrugged. They looked back toward the street and caught their breaths. A tall boy with a deputy's badge on his coat stood there, a .44 Winchester in his hands.

"You two men are under arrest," Henry said loudly, stopping the traffic along the walk. People turned to stare.

Doyle gawked at the youngster. Little was quicker. His hand went to his gun, then hesitated as the rifle's muzzle trained on him.

"What's this all about, Boy?" he asked.

"Just what I said. You are under arrest."

Little glanced at Doyle. "They're makin' them young these days, ain't they, Larry?" He looked back at Henry. "What do you want to arrest us for, Boy?"

"For the murder of Sheriff Dance. Pull out those guns easy, and drop them on the ground."

Doyle started to grin, as at a huge joke, and his fingers twitched beside his gunbutt. Then he froze as a muzzle was jammed into his back and a hand pulled his gun from its holster. Out of the corner of his eye he saw Jack Little being disarmed and a voice drawled, "Just stand real still fellers. Me an' Cass never did miss anything at this range."

At that moment Slim Cavanaugh came out of the hotel and his mouth dropped open at the sight below the porch. His arms were laden with bags, and he hesitated before dropping them to draw his gun. The hesitation was enough. A gunsnout was thrust against his side and a deft hand relieved him of his weapon. "Come on down and join your pards, Slim," a voice said. "And don't do anything stupid. Sam Dance was a friend of mine."

When Vince Cole returned to Liberal he found three angry gunmen sitting in the middle of the floor, back to back, their arms tied to each other's at elbow and wrist. Henry Lattimer sat with his back to the stove, rifle across his lap, watching them.

"Mr. May helped me take them," he told Cole. "And Cass. And Pearly, I guess he helped too."

Cole walked around the three, identifying them. "Nice work," he said to Henry.

They walked outside, where they could talk privately and still keep an eye on the prisoners.

"We'll have to get them to Springfield," Cole said. "But that makes a problem." He pointed at the wagon he had driven to Arkalon and back. Blankets covered a still figure in its bed. "Your friend Stillwell was right. That's Parson Jolly. I'm going to be busy for a while. Maybe you could get those cowboys to help take your prisoners to jail."

"They've gone back out to the herd. Let me have your wagon, Vince. I can take them in."

Cole glanced at the sun. "Not much time, Henry. Maybe we better find a place to keep them here tonight, get some help in the morning."

"No. These three killed Mr. Dance. I want them behind bars. They're my prisoners, Vince."

Cole hesitated, not liking the idea but finding himself torn. He was senior deputy here, but he saw the determined set of the youngster's jaw, the strength of purpose in the way he held himself, and he did not want to pull rank on him. Henry Lattimer was on his way toward being an exceptional lawman one day, and Cole hesitated to deflate what he saw there. Besides, even if Henry was wrong, he was right.

Among the people who had begun to gather around the wagon, Pete Waverly had sidled close enough to

214

eavesdrop. "Let him alone, Vince," he said. "The boy knows what he's doin'. He can stop off at the judge's place an' get Sturdevant to help him. Nobody's gonna argue with Sturdevant."

"I don't think . . . ," Henry started, then hesitated. He didn't want to give Vince Cole a chance to overrule him. "Yeah, I can do that. Sturdevant's brought in a lot of prisoners. He can help me get them across the valley."

Cole paused, then nodded, still dubious. "Well, you be sure you get him, then." To the men gathered around he called, "One of you go fetch Doctor Price. Hurry, now." Then to Henry, "All right. Let's get the Parson on ice and get your prisoners loaded and I'll get a fresh team hitched for you . . ."

"One horse," Henry said.

"One?"

"I'm going to let them drive, and I'll ride along. I wouldn't want them trying to make a race of it."

With the three gunmen securely attached to the wagon with lock cuffs, ringbolts and chains, Henry mounted the judge's sorrel mare and checked the loads in his rifle. There were long hours between here and Springfield, and they would be difficult hours.

Vince Cole handed a pouch to him. "Give these to the sheriff," he said. "My reports and the messages from Arkalon. There's one I think is real interesting. From Topeka. Somebody has filed a protest, jointly and severally, against four counties, and Seward is one of them."

Henry looked down at him, blankly. "What kind of a protest?"

"It's a claim that all four were illegally organized.

215

Meade, Seward, Stevens and Morton. Somebody is asking the court to dissolve all four of them as counties."

"But, if they do that, there'd be no law. They can't do that!"

Cole shrugged. "Who knows what courts will do? I just thought the sheriff ought to see it right away."

Henry started to turn away, then a cold chill stopped him. He turned back to Vince. "I went through all that stuff Mr. Dance and you collected . . . about Stevens County. Does all that remind you of anything, Vince?"

Cole hesitated, then his eyes went hard. "Yeah, come to think of it, it does. What came of all that was that the county almost got itself dissolved."

"But not quite. Like somebody turned it all on, and pushed it that far, then turned it all off."

Cole stared at him. "That is exactly what Sam said. Just exactly."

"What's going on, Vince?"

"I don't know, Henry. I really don't know. But I'm beginning to think maybe Sam did."

18

When Henry Lattimer didn't return, Sheriff Sim Guthrie sent Ted Mason to find him. He had expected the young deputy to stay over one night in Liberal, but to return the next morning. Mason rode as far as Cross Canyon and a mile down the south road, then turned back. An hour and a half after leaving the courthouse in Springfield, he was back.

"Hell, Sim, that road isn't passable yet," he argued. "There's drifts in the Cimarron higher than a man's head."

"Well, where is Henry, then?" Guthrie stared at him in annoyance. Mason had filled in as deputy since the day of the shooting at the jail, but Guthrie was beginning to learn a difference among his deputies. Mason was basically lazy.

"Oh, I guess he got across all right. From down on the rim I could see where he punched through. The trail led all the way across. But I bet he lamed a horse doing it. Another day or two won't matter that much, will it?"

Guthrie glared at him. Short of a horsewhip, there

was no way he was going to get Mason to cross that valley. It was cold and hard to move and Mason just didn't want to go. He wondered for the thousandth time how Sam Dance had gotten people to do what he wanted them to do. He frowned at the stubborn man standing in front of his desk, then shrugged. "Go away, Ted. Just go put your feet up someplace and stay out of the way. I'm busy."

"You don't have to act like that about it," Mason complained. "It ain't like I didn't go and look. If it had been halfway clear down there I'd be half way to Liberal by now."

"Of course you would." Guthrie busied himself with the stacks of paperwork on his desk. Maybe Henry would show up soon. If not, he'd just have to go himself.

As Mason went out the door, muttering to himself, Otis Kramer stuck his head in. "Sheriff, you done anything about finding my cows yet?"

Guthrie glanced up. "I haven't had time to even think about your cows, Otis. Why don't you find them yourself?"

"Well, because I think somebody stole 'em, is why. That's what I told you. Look, I pay taxes, Sheriff. I think I deserve some help from the sheriff's office."

"Otis, nobody stole your cows! People don't go out in a blizzard and steal cows. They just drifted off somewhere, and if I was you I'd be out looking for them instead of waiting for somebody else to do it. I have other things to do."

"If Sam Dance was here he'd find my cows."

"Otis, I'm busy!"

"Look, Sim, I voted for you. I'm going to be

218

awfully disappointed if I don't get some service."

Guthrie sighed. "All right, Otis. You go find Ted Mason and tell him I want him to help you find your cows. Tell him I said so."

"Well, all right!" Otis slammed the door.

Guthrie went back to his papers. There were court warrants to be issued, delinquent taxes to be collected, a jury to be impaneled, summonses to be served, and the county attorney had notified him peremptorily that it was up to the sheriff to compile evidence in larceny cases, not the prosecution.

O.P. Grimes alleged that T.L. Raney had stolen his plow horse. Raney insisted he had bought the horse, and said Grimes had tried to cheat him in the deal. The Zimmer twins were accused of looking in the window at the widow Farrell's house. Jack Simms' moldboard had skidded while he was plowing snow on State, and knocked down a hitchrail in front of Halliburton's Dry Goods. Halliburton had filed for restitution, and he wanted the county to force the city to paint his front door while they were at it.

Homer Potter was accused of being drunk in public. Harold Blessing demanded police protection because his brother had threatened to kill him, and the city council refused to pay its bill for law enforcement by sheriff's officers within city limits. Their reasoning was that there was no trouble in Springfield except what came from outside and that was county jurisdiction.

Saul Bingham was raising a fuss because he still had an unidentified body in his shed and was afraid it would thaw. And where in blazes was Henry Lattimer?

"God!" Guthrie swore. He looked angrily at the rows of files from past years, everything neat and orderly, most cases solved, disputes settled and the peace—mostly—kept.

Since his election, Sim Guthrie had not had time to tend his store, and business was falling off. His plans for development of the haymeadows property were gathering dust. And with the valley plugged by snow he didn't know when the commissioners would get together to approve a budget so he and his deputies could be paid.

Guthrie had held no hard feelings for Sam Dance. It was just politics. The office of sheriff had been up for election, and everybody told him he could handle the job, so he had filed. He had campaigned and won. That was all well and good. Now he surveyed the work involved and cursed the friends who had swayed him. He had promised a businesslike, no-nonsense sheriff's office, with prominent, visible law enforcement. That was the line that had gotten him elected. Now the whole operation was a shambles.

He needed to go around to the hotel to look in on Everett. The big guard was heavily bandaged and would be in pain for weeks, but his wounds were healing. Guthrie didn't have a line on who had done the shooting. Ira Fox, his arm in a sling, was back in jail, and probably knew all about it, but the sullen homesteader refused to talk and there was nothing Guthrie could do to change that. He had an uneasy feeling that Judge Tomlin was going to turn the man loose, anyway. There was almost no evidence to connect him with anything.

The thing that haunted the new sheriff most was

Sam Dance's death. The more he thought about that, the more puzzling it became. Someone had threatened to kill the judge. They had killed the sheriff instead. Two men had been arrested, but one was free now and the other was about to be and—most puzzling of all—nobody seemed to care. His fear had been that the county would be up in arms. There had been protest, but it was minor and had died out. People had other things to occupy their time besides worrying about who killed the sheriff.

Sim Guthrie began to realize that there was more to being sheriff than getting elected and wearing a badge. And he pondered more and more on that puzzling word, "lawman." He had never really considered it before. "Sheriff" he understood. It was an elected office, open to anyone who could get the votes. "Lawman" was something else. Guthrie had no answers for the puzzle.

An irate Ted Mason entered the office, trailed by Otis Kramer. "Sheriff, I just got my horse put away. You don't want me to go lookin' for cows now, do you? It's gonna be suppertime before long."

Guthrie sighed again. "Go find the man's cows, Ted."

"Tomorrow morning, I've got to take some potatoes over to Pattersons'. How about I look then, along the way?"

Guthrie's temper boiled over. "Ted, you either go find this man's damn cows or you turn in that badge. Right now."

"Sheriff, I need the money . . ."

"Then, dammit, work for it!"

Two men on horseback hauled rein in front of the

office, and tied at the rail. Through his window, Guthrie could see that their mounts were steaming and stamping. They had come a distance. One of them peered through the window, then entered. He held out a piece of paper to the sheriff. "We've come for Ira Fox," he said. "This is a release order from Judge Tomlin."

Guthrie frowned at the paper. Release without bond or constraint. Lack of evidence to hold.

"Tomlin was the one who identified him," Guthrie said.

"Well, I guess he's changed his mind." The man was a lean, crusty-looking individual with several days' growth of whiskers on his cheeks. He looked like a hardcase, and the sixgun visible beneath his open coat added to the impression. Prominent buck teeth added a rodent-like cast to his face, but there was nothing furtive in his manner.

"Do I know you?" Guthrie asked.

"I don't reckon. I don't live around here."

"This order isn't dated. The judge should have dated it."

"I don't know anything about that. Where's Ira?"

"You'll have to give me a name," Guthrie shrugged.

"Byers. Horace Byers."

Guthrie wrote it on the judge's order. "And your place of residence?"

"Stevens County. Same place Ira lives. He and I share the claim."

"Then you'll be returning Mr. Fox to Stevens County?"

"I don't think that's any of your business, sheriff,"

222

the man rasped. "You got your order. Just turn him over."

"I'll bring him out, sheriff," Ted Mason volunteered.

Otis Kramer glared. "How 'bout my cows?" But Mason had already gone through the cellblock door.

"How did you get across the valley, Mr. Byers? My deputy says it isn't passable."

"We just rode across. It ain't so bad up by Willow Ford."

"Oh, then you didn't come directly from the judge's house?" If they had, Guthrie thought, they had certainly chosen a long way around. Willow Ford was nearly ten miles west.

Mason came out of the cellblock with Ira Fox in tow.

"This man has come with a release for you, Mr. Fox," Guthrie said. "Lack of evidence, no charges. Sorry about the inconvenience."

Ira glared at the newcomer, then glared at Guthrie. "Inconvenience! How'd you like *your* arm broke?" Then he subsided. "Aw, crap. Just gimme my stuff and let me out of here."

"Hobie's gone down to the stable to get your horse, Ira," Byers said.

"Anybody else . . ." Fox began, then glanced at Guthrie and stopped. Byers didn't respond. Instead he stared at the sling on Ira's arm.

"Broke?"

"Yeah. I'll tell you about it later."

Guthrie retrieved Fox's belongings, had him sign for them, awkwardly with his left hand, and turned them over. Fox had trouble getting his gunbelt on, but

223

managed with Byers' help, then hauled it around so the holster was on the left side, the gun butt-forward. "I'll get that son of a bitch," he muttered.

Out front, the second newcomer appeared with Fox's Appaloosa, saddled and packed.

"Come on," Byers said. "We still have to find Key and . . ."

Fox hushed him with a frown, but Guthrie turned at the name.

"Key? What Key is that, Mr. Byers? Who do you mean?"

"Nobody," Fox said. "He don't mean nobody." With another frown he pulled Byers to the door, wrestled it open and hustled him outside.

"Now wait a minute," Guthrie began, but Otis Kramer was in his way.

"Are you gonna make him find my cows or not?"

By the time Guthrie reached the door, the three had mounted and were going away, south along State. Guthrie stepped out, watched them for a moment, then shook his head and walked back into the office. "Ted," he ordered, "you get this . . . taxpayer out of here, and you find his damned cows for him, and don't come back until you do!"

Key. Even in a place and time where nicknames were common, that was an unusual one. Guthrie could only remember hearing the name once, and that was when Frank Murdoch said it. Key was the name of the man in the box at Bingham's, the man with a gun in his hand and a hole in his heart, the man Henry was supposed to bring people to identify.

Key Begley. Nicknames. What, he wondered, would be the nickname of a man named Byers? A chill ran through him then, and he paced the little room. He had a feeling that something else had just gone wrong.

South of Springfield, three riders made good time toward Cross Canyon Road and the Cimarron Valley. And as they rode, they talked.

"No," Ira Fox growled, "you didn't kill him! You came as close to killin' me as you did to killin' him, the way that lead was flyin' around them cells."

"Well, we didn't do that, did we?" Byers indicated the man's broken arm.

"No. He did this. Afterward. You missed him so I tried for him and he got me caught in the bars. The son of a bitch broke it intentionally."

"That ain't all he did, either," Hobie Moore said. "You know Wiley Dobbins, down at Beer City? He's dead. Stillwell killed him. And he burned Keno's place and shot Calico in the shoulder. Hell, Ira, who is this yayhoo, anyway? What did you find out about him?"

"Not much. Except he's no drifter. I don't know what he is. But I'll kill him if I get the chance. Crap, I never seen a man could give me the willies that way. Just bein' there in the next cell . . . it was like bein' in a cage with a curly wolf. You know what I think? I think he killed Key, too. I don't know anybody else that would have, that I wouldn't have heard who it was."

"I didn't know Key was dead!" Byers said.

"Hell yes, he's dead. Stiffer'n a board in the undertaker's shed. Somebody shot him and put him

225

in a casket, the night of the storm. I'd be willin' to bet it was that Stillwell."

"But who the hell is he? What's he got to do with any of this? He ain't law, is he?"

"I don't know. I don't think so. They don't act like that."

Turning right at Cross Canyon Road the three angled down toward the valley, almost to the rim, and pulled up. The wide valley was a landscape of whipped and tumbled snow, tall drifts shadowing other drifts in the late sunlight.

"That sheriff said his deputy couldn't get through here," Byers said.

Hobie squinted. "Well, somebody's been through. There's a trail. Come on, we better try it. The others'll be lookin' for us."

"God," Fox muttered. "There must be two miles of that stuff."

"It ain't that much. Come on."

Hobie tipped his head to shade his eyes with his hat brim. "There's somebody over there on the other rim." They watched for a long minute, then Hobie nodded. "Somebody startin' down, comin' this way."

"I can't make 'em out," Byers said. "Is that a wagon?"

"Looks like it. A wagon and maybe somebody ridin' along behind."

"It's gettin' late," Byers said. "We got a long way to go."

19

By the time Henry came within sight of the Cimarron Valley the sun was low in the west and he was thoroughly tired of escorting prisoners, Slim Cavanaugh, at the wagon's reins, had done everything in his power to make the trip unpleasant—running into drifts, angling off the trail, alternately going too fast and too slow—until Henry had offered finally to lay his scalp open with a rifle barrel. And what Cavanaugh had not managed, the other two had. For miles they had sat in the wagonbed, keeping up a running commentary in Henry's direction. First they were sullen, then provocative, then threatening, then sullen again.

After five miles of that he had ordered them out of the wagon and made them walk beside it, still cuffed to it, until they had no further interest in abusing his patience.

Finally they rimmed the valley, and Henry turned them right on the track toward Judge Tomlin's house. Doyle and Little had gotten their second wind and now began cursing him again, but he paid no attention. They followed his own earlier tracks, and he saw no sign that any others had been along here.

At the house Henry ordered Cavanaugh to pull up at the fence gate, and he rode forward, took the reins and secured them to the fence. Dismounting then, he walked through the dooryard and banged on the door.

When the door opened a rush of warm air and cooking odors met Henry and he realized how hungry he was. But the judge made no sign of inviting him in. Instead he pulled on a coat, slapped a hat over his bald head and came outside, closing the door behind him.

"Are you returning my horse?" he asked, then looked at the wagon with its chained and cuffed inhabitants. "What have we here, Deputy?"

"Prisoners, sir. Sheriff Guthrie sent me to Liberal after these people."

"Yes, I remember," Tomlin said. "But why are they chained?"

"I have arrested them, sir. For murder."

Tomlin turned sharply, looking down at the deputy. "Murder? Whose murder?"

"The murder of Sheriff Dance, sir. I believe they were part of that mob."

"Ah." Tomlin stared at the men again, looking vaguely puzzled. "I gather more evidence has surfaced, then."

"Well, yes, sir, after a fashion. I'll make a full report to Sheriff Guthrie, sir."

Tomlin's gaze was lofty and cold. "Do you believe you can make a case against these men?"

"Yes, sir, I do."

"What evidence will it be based on?"

"My own testimony, your honor. That, and some supporting testimony from Vince Cole . . . and possibly others."

"Vince Cole wasn't out there that morning. As to your evidence, as I recall you had nothing to offer except an overheard name. Isn't that correct?"

"Yes, sir. I mean, well, that *was* correct. I think I can do a little better now. You see, I know who one of the men was who spoke out there."

Tomlin eyed him, waiting, but Henry didn't elaborate. Tomlin shook his head. "Sketchy, Deputy. Extremely sketchy. I believe the best thing for you to do would be to apologize to those three men and release them. I strongly recommend that you do so."

Henry gaped at him. "Sir? I couldn't do that. I have a case against these three, and I intend to lock them up for trial."

The judge's stare turned authoritative. "You are very young, Deputy, and I applaud your enthusiasm. But you may not have understood me. I said to release those men."

For a moment Henry stood with his mouth open, literally speechless. This was the same man who had sent officers to the next county to arrest a suspect merely because he thought he might have seen an Appaloosa horse . . . in the dark, from more than a mile away! This was the same man who had been willing to push capital charges against Byron Stillwell just because his nickname was By.

Henry squared his shoulders. "No, sir. I'm sorry, but I can't do that. These are my prisoners, in my custody, and I'm taking them to jail. I came by here to see if my horse is sound again, and to see if you might have Mr. Sturdevant ride with me the rest of the way. It will be hard, getting through the valley with prisoners and a wagon. I could use some help."

Tomlin stared at him for long moments, his eyes like dark ice. Then he turned away. "Your horse is sound. You can switch off your saddle at the barn. And I want my mare rubbed down before you leave her, is that clear?"

"Yes, sir. What about Mr. Sturdevant?"

"Mr. Sturdevant is not here, Deputy."

"Oh." Henry was sharply disappointed. He dreaded the trek across the valley with the three desperate men. "I see. I thought he might be, since he was here when I came by yesterday morning."

Tomlin's flat eyes turned to him again. "Here? Mr. Sturdevant wasn't here yesterday. No one has been here but me."

Again Henry's mouth opened and no words came out. He clearly remembered the curtain moving in the window. Someone had been there. He clamped his jaws shut. "Yes, sir," he muttered. "I'll trade horses with you then. I've taken care of your mare."

He unsaddled the mare in front of the barn where he could keep an eye on his prisoners. He rubbed her down, then hurried to put her in a stall and bring out his own chestnut gelding. He saddled, still watching his charges. The chestnut was hale and fresh, its limp gone.

The judge had returned to his house, and did not come out again as the wagon was turned and trundled away along the track to the road, Henry riding behind it, rifle across his saddle.

At the rim of the valley Henry ordered the wagon

230

forward, down the angling slope. He paused for a moment to look across, and thought he saw riders on the far side. He hoped someone was coming. He could use some help.

For a time, the going was easy. The south grade of the valley was freer of drift than the north grade. The wagon rolled through crunching crust seldom hub-deep, angling downward into evening shadow where the tops of drifts were blue and the hollows deep purple, catching a trace of red from the sunset sky.

For a quarter mile the trek went smoothly enough, then they veered around a high drift and suddenly the wagon skewed sideways into deep snow. Henry swore and spurred his horse forward, starting to berate Cavanaugh, who was on his feet in the wagonbox, sawing at the reins. Too late he realized Cavanaugh couldn't be upright . . . not with his chain in place. The man dropped his reins, whirled and leapt from the wagon, taking Henry with full tackle force, driving him from his saddle.

He lit on his shoulders in heavy snow, Cavanaugh on top of him, and tried to roll away, but the man clung like a cat, kicking and pummeling, and Henry felt the wind driven from him. He fought back desperately. He still had his grip on his rifle, and managed to get it free and bring it down across Cavanaugh's back. The man howled and rolled away, but bounded back at him before he could get off the ground. Distantly, he heard the other two shouting and wondered where they were. He tried to swing the rifle again, but Cavanaugh got a strong hand on it. Henry twisted his left hand free of the other's grip and swung a short, hard blow to the side of Cavanaugh's head. The man arched back, and Henry got a knee into his belly and shoved. The pair flipped over, Henry on top for a moment, then rolled again and ice-crust relented before them as they half-buried themselves in a drift.

Cavanaugh had shifted his grip on the rifle. Now he brought its muzzle down hard against Henry's face. The sharp sight tore skin along his cheek. With a desperate twist Henry rolled under the older man, rolled over onto his rifle, bringing Cavanaugh's hand under his own body. Then he rolled again, hard, and felt Cavanaugh slide across his back, flailing. He was finding it hard to breathe, and could barely hear the shouts of the others now. He felt numb. He tried to roll again, but couldn't move. With his left hand reaching back over his right shoulder he found Cavanaugh's face, stabbed curled fingers into the man's mouth, thumb under his jaw, braced himself and pulled. He felt something give, and a knee took him in the side but he held on. He saw only darkness. Suddenly Cavanaugh arched his body, pushed off with his legs and flipped entirely over Henry, responding to the excruciating pressure on his jaw. Darkness exploded into light, there was air to breath and Henry clambered to his knees, then to his feet, still holding the underjaw of the screaming, flailing man. Crouched, he kicked Cavanaugh in the belly as hard as he could, then yanked his hand loose and swung his rifle around to rap him soundly above the ear.

He stood then, panting and gasping, bleeding from the cut on his cheek and from toothmarks on his knuckles. For a moment he was disoriented, then he realized they had fought all the way through the base of a heavy drift. On the other side of it was the wagon, and Doyle and Little stood there, half-crouched in its bed, each with an arm still secured by chain.

Henry looked down at Cavanaugh. The man's face was all out of proportion, and Henry realized he had unhinged his jaw. Kneeling beside him, he braced the man's head in packed snow, grasped the protruding jaw with one hand and hit it with the heel of the other. The pop of returning connection echoed from snowdrifts. Cavanaugh groaned, but his eyes remained closed.

Weary and battered, Henry Lattimer dragged his prisoner back to the wagon, hoisted him over the sideboard and dumped him in the bed. He pointed his rifle at Doyle. "You drive," he said.

Climbing back aboard the chestnut, his bleeding hand slipped on the saddle horn and he swore again. "Probably come down with hydrophoby," he muttered.

His clothing was full of snow, crusted with snow, and he was sweating beneath it. To make things worse, the sun was down and the wind was turning cold again.

Doyle worked the reins and freed the wagon from the drift. Then he headed on down into the valley. Jack Little huddled in the bed, against the seat brace, and glared at the deputy riding behind.

"If I have any more trouble," Henry told him, "I'll shoot all three of you and come get you after the thaw."

It was nearly dark by the time they reached the

bottoms. Here the going was hard, the pulling slow. By following his own track of the morning before, Henry was able to keep them on the graded road. Crossing the bottoms, the wagon plowing snow with its hubs even in the shallow places, Henry saw riders coming from the other way. They seemed to hesitate, then stopped, peering at him.

"Come on over," he hailed them. "I'm a deputy sheriff and I need some help."

Still they hesitated, peering in the uncertain light. Then one of them called, "Who's that you get there, Deputy?"

"Prisoners . . ." he started, then Doyle sprang partially upright in the box.

"Ira!" he shouted. "Ira, is that you?"

"It's me!" the voice came back. "Larry? What happened?"

"We been arrested! Me an' Slim an' Jack! Help us!"

"We're comin'," another voice called, and Henry could see the motions of guns being drawn.

Jack Little was on his knees. "It's By! Come on, By! There ain't but one kid deputy!"

Henry's rifle was coming level, but he froze at the name. By.

Henry brought up his rifle.

Across an intervening hundred yards, the three riders' horses were plunging through snow, leaping and hesitating and hopping, coming at him. He sidestepped the chestnut to get clear of the wagon and a gunshot flamed. He heard a bullet "thunk" into a snowbank beside him, spraying shards of ice.

Willing the chestnut to stand, he brought up his

234

rifle, sighted on the nearest rider and fired. The man went down, his mount pirouetting away. The other two charged, firing. Henry felt a bullet nip at his sleeve, another sting as it grazed along his ribs. He fired again, then heard rebel yells behind him, closing in.

He tried to turn, but felt woozy. He focused on the approaching riders, shaking his head to clear his vision. From behind, two riders leapt past him, one on either side, drawn guns blazing, and charged down on the approaching gunmen. They swerved, backtracked, and Henry heeled the chestnut to fall in with the dark pair that had come from behind him.

Rifle blazing into blue-dark, seeking shadows, he ran with them and then there was no opposition. A rider sat a pawing horse, one hand in the air, and Henry grabbed the gun out of it. He heard a thump and saw another rider slide to the ground.

"This'n is going to have a headache directly," said the bantering voice of Pearly.

"There's one on the ground back here," Cass said from a distance. "Henry nailed him, I guess. He's hit hard." Henry looked around, dazed and squinting in the deepening dusk.

"Vince Cole got worried about you, Deputy," Pearly said beside him. "He rode out an' asked us if we'd like to look out after you. Good thing we did, ain't it?"

"I didn't need any help," Henry snapped, and felt foolish at the words.

"Sure, an' hens don't lay eggs, either. What's the matter with you, anyway?"

"I'm sorry." Henry shook his head, still trying to

235

clear its fog. "Thanks, Pearly."

It was full dark when they pulled into Springfield . . . a wagon loaded with six prisoners, a young deputy and two young cowhands, and three extra horses. They pulled up in front of the sheriff's office and Sim Guthrie came out, his limp less noticeable now.

Henry confronted him. "Sheriff, I got Ira Fox here. How come he's out of jail?"

"He was released," Guthrie gaped at them. "Lack of evidence."

"Well, I've got some more evidence and I want him put back in again. And there's five more. Two of them need a doctor. Oh . . ." he remembered his manners then. "Sheriff Guthrie, this is Cass and that's Pearly. They helped."

Over a meal at the hotel an hour later, Henry stopped pushing steak into his face long enough to ask Guthrie, "Sheriff, if you were a judge and somebody stopped by your house with prisoners, and they might have been people who wanted to kill you, what's the first thing you'd want to know?"

"What do you mean?"

"I mean if somebody had threatened your life and somebody else said he had some of them, what would you ask first?"

"Uh, I guess I'd wonder who they are."

"Yeah, I would too. But you know something? Judge Tomlin told me to turn these men loose, and he lied to me about nobody being at his house yesterday, and . . ."

"That would be his own business," Guthrie interjected.

"Yeah, I imagine. But I had three of those men right there in that wagon, and he came out and looked at them, and he never once asked me who they were."

20

A historic maze of obscure treaties, state politics, federal shenanigans and some left over bitterness from the war between the states—all these things added up to No Man's Land.

Bounded on the south by Texas, on the north by Kansas and Colorado, on the west by New Mexico and on the east by what had been the Cherokee Strip, the Indian territories now being parceled out to homesteaders in a series of land runs and being called Oklahoma in anticipation of one day becoming a state, the rectangle of land called the Neutral Strip was a left-over, forgotten piece of the world.

Thirty-five miles wide and nearly two hundred miles long, it was a land without law. No court had jurisdiction here and no badge had prestige. Throughout the nearly seven thousand square miles of what had become known as No Man's Land, no law held except that of the gun. I had heard it estimated that as many as two thousand people lived—one way or another—in No Man's Land, and every one of them on the run from something, someplace else.

I had been in the strip before. The first time was four years earlier, after the Lambert thing at Pueblo. I had been minding my own business up there, but Brad Lambert didn't choose to see it that way. Lambert owned a big chunk of Pueblo and a bigger chunk of the land around it, and ran things pretty much as he pleased. He had a son who fancied himself as a fast gun from reading too many dime novels, and a covey of thugs who amused themselves with people passing through when they weren't busy helping old Brad expand his empire. One of them was an ex-prizefighter named Boston Charlie Magill.

Magill stood six-four and weighed two hundred and sixty pounds when he was in the ring. He had gained a few pounds since going to work for Lambert.

Mattie was on her last tour then and I had gone to Denver to see her perform. I was on my way from there to Trinidad and had stopped off in Pueblo for a drink, a meal and a night's sleep. Nobody had told me that the rule around Pueblo was to give space at the bar to Lambert hands.

So when I was having my drink and this big man with the mashed nose decided he wanted to stand where I was standing, I pushed back. The next thing I knew he nearly took my head off with a left cross that would have done a kicking mule proud, and I wound up sitting on the floor, shaking my head and watching little sparks whirl in front on my eyes.

While I was so occupied, somebody relieved me of my pistol and somebody else kicked me in the ribs. The way everybody was laughing then, I must have been a comical sight.

"Thing about Charlie," someone choked out, "is he just don't care for dudes." And that set them to laughing even more. It might have been the pinstripe pants I was wearing that day, or the swallowtail coat, or maybe the silk shirt with agate studs, but whatever, I was a comic scene to them.

I was a little unsteady on my feet when I got to them, but I brushed myself off and glanced around to make sure who it was who had my gun, and who had kicked me. They were a pair of range toughs, the kind you find around a little pond that has a big frog in it.

"Be careful with that," I told the one with my gun. "It cost me thirty dollars." Then I walked away from them.

"They makin' 'em big in the fancy-pants league these days," someone suggested, and the laughter started all over again. But I wasn't leaving yet.

The big man at the bar hadn't even looked around. He stood with his back to me, ignoring all of it. I walked to within three feet of him, hesitated for just an instant, then planted my boot in his tailbone just as hard as I could kick. He howled, his hands went to his butt, and turned on tiptoe. And that gave me plenty of time to swing from the knee and plant my right fist in his breadbasket, still rising. His face went fiery, his cheeks puffed out and I stepped back as he went to his knees, then snapped a hard left to the point of his chin.

That, I assumed, should hold him. I whirled around, picked up a chair and broke it over the head of the fellow with the kicking habit, then caught the other range tough by the wrist, twisted him around

240

and retrieved my gun from him.

I noticed there wasn't anybody laughing. There are some things a man can learn in the French Quarter and Hell's Kitchen and the bad side of State Street that aren't common knowledge at Pueblo. One of them is to not waste time with fancy fighting.

I had just put my gun away and tossed the second tough aside when I heard a bellow like a bull loose at breeding time.

The big man should still have been on the floor. He wasn't. He was on his feet, fit and fast, and he knocked me clear across a card table and came over it after me. I rolled away and got some space between us, and recognized him then. Boston Charlie Magill, the Bay Mauler. I had seen him fight.

I wouldn't have lasted a round in the ring with Boston Charlie. But this wasn't the ring. As he got his knees under him I kicked him in the face, then jumped and slammed both heels into his kidneys.

It flattened him, and he moaned and rolled over and I said, "Stay down for the count, Charlie. It isn't worth it."

We were even and I had nothing against him and it could have ended right there. He wasn't getting up. But then a man yelled, "Kill him, Mack," and I turned. There was a bright-eyed young fellow just inside the door, already crouched and waiting, and as I turned he drew his gun.

Mack Lambert had practiced. He was fast . . . too fast for me to pick my shot. I had to kill him.

I didn't know he was Lambert's son when I fired. But I knew it by the time I was out the door. And I had heard enough about the Lamberts to know that I had to run.

They must have picked up my trace in the breaks of the South Charles River, and from there they dogged me southward into the high Cimarron country. Old Brad Lambert had a lot of connections, and the word was out, and I never knew during those long days and nights who was coming at me, or from where.

The chase ended in a nameless box canyon. The man they killed there—the man they thought was me—was a shooter from Kansas who had come to join the fun and got there at the wrong time. The blood money Brad Lambert paid out was for one of his own hardcases.

I spent that fall and part of a winter around Black Mesa, a few miles into No Man's Land, then I just faded into the Strip. It was a time I needed to rest.

I was tired now, four years later, following a lonely track through crusted snow over ground I had seen before. As the day dwindled I put on the serape and walked, leading the gray, breaking the crust ahead of him so it would not cut his legs.

We moved through a vast, rolling snowfield of deep blues and hazes that seemed to go on forever, where only the skeletal tops of winter trees and the green mist of cedar motts gave evidence of the curls and folds of the terrain. By last light I left the trail to seek a hollow, a place to hide.

Shelter was a rocky bluff overlooking the little valley of a creek that led to the Beaver a few miles down. In a pocket there I rubbed down the gray and loose-rigged a blanket over his back while he foraged. It was a wind-scoured meadow and there was an acre of fairly clear pasture for him to crop.

Cattle had been there, and the droppings were fresh. I found where they had wandered through patch snow, moving west and up the valley, but I found no sign of horses or men. I was alert then, because cattle are fair game in lawless country and a herd that moves far attracts attention. Either someone has them or someone will take them, but where there are cattle there are men. Yet, I saw no human sign.

It was almost full dark when I gathered enough cedar fall to make a little fire in a pocket under the bluff. In the distance, out on the snowfield, wolves were barking and I thought again of Chako—lonely, intense, deadly Chako, a man out of time, a warrior too late for the era of warriors but still fighting his own war against those who had savaged his people. Chako had tried to adapt to changing times, had tried to mind his own business and stay out of the way, and men had broken his arms for it.

That, I knew, would not happen again. Somewhere south Chako was tending his horses, keeping to himself, but they would not again catch him off his guard.

The wolves were out there somewhere. I could hear their barking, distant in a night that was dark crystal. "Go, Brother Wolf," I thought. "The rabbits are fat and you know their burrows."

Somewhere south of me was a man I wanted. I wanted to see him, to know his face, because he had been there when Mattie Stillwell's soldier died . . . or an old man who had been that soldier once and she had loved him. Times change. Would she have known the old sheriff who died at Cross Canyon? Would he have been, to her, as she remembered? Mattie's hair was gray now, her waist fuller and the face that had charmed so many men had begun to show the years, but I thought there was still the young girl there, inside, the girl who had gone to Sentry Point to meet a lonely blue soldier far from home in a war that tore at his guts.

Would they have known each other if they could have met again? Would the changes have mattered?

Times change. So many things would never be known because it had been convenient for someone to kill Sam Dance. I wondered what Si Rutledge would make of the bundle of papers I had left for him. And what would his sister make of them? Behind the bright eyes of Patty Mills was a quick, intuitive intelligence that I admired. She would see things I might miss, make connections I might not see. In those papers were clues to all the missing years, the life of the aging lawman who had stepped up before gunmen at the rim of the Cimarron and been cut down there.

I was tired. I made a simple meal over a handful of fire, then rolled in and slept as a huge moon poked above the eastern hills to hue the tops of No Man's Land with lemon.

It was a night for wolves.

I didn't know then what sound woke me, but it was out of keeping with the night.

Hours had passed. The light was soft silver from low in the west, near moonset and dark of morning. I listened for a time, then raised my head to look around. I was in shadow under the bluff. Some distance away, at the low end of the wind-cleared meadow, the gray horse stood with his head up, listening.

A curling breeze, chill from the west, poked around the rims and shoulders of the little valley, muttering to itself. Again, carried in the wind, came the pack-talk of hunting wolves.

What sound I had heard did not repeat itself, so I sat up, pulling serape and blanket roll around me, then stood. I stepped away from the bluff, peering up and down the valley, then turned.

He was right on top of the bluff, had been right above me, and he chuckled as I turned to see him there. The gun in his hand didn't waver.

"Good thing I decided to double back, wasn't it?" he said. "Otherwise I might never have known you were on my trail, much less found you."

He was a big man, heavy-set and bulky in his thick coat. His face was shadowed, but I could see the dark beard that molded it.

"Let me tell you who you are," he said, with a cold humor in his voice. "You're the one they picked up after the sheriff died. You're the one that showed up at Beer City asking questions about me and the boys. You're the one that busted up Ace Pruitt's breakfast and burned down Keno Mora's place . . . and scared that pansy Fancy Pace so bad he ruined a horse getting to us. You're Byron Stillwell."

I stood still, wondering how I could get my Colt up before he dropped the hammer on his.

"They say you're hell in a handbasket," he said. "But all I see is a fellow who should have stayed home. What do you want, Stillwell? Why are you after me?"

"Because I know you, Hayes. Because you and your pards killed Sam Dance and if I don't get you for it someone else will, and your best chance might be with me because some won't listen and I might."

He chuckled again. "Slick. Here you are, cold meat, and you're tryin' to deal. Sorry, friend, but I've heard it all before. Too many times. No, don't move. You don't have a chance. Are you going to tell me about it?"

I just stared at him.

"Well," he said, "it doesn't make any difference. Before long none of it will make any difference." And he fired.

The slug knocked me reeling, my chest seemed to explode and bright fire echoed in my ears, diminishing slowly. I was on the ground, face down, and I tried to move but I couldn't. I burned. I seemed to be melting, and the melt burned in me. A darkness blacker than the sky closed down and I felt another bullet strike me but it didn't seem to matter. Far away I heard laughter, and a voice said, "Goodbye, Byron Stillwell."

Black. Deep black nothing. Faces in the black. Mattie Stillwell wiping dirt from a little kid's face and saying that everybody gets knocked down sometimes, it's whether they get up again that matters. Face that was no face at all because I'd never seen it, a smiling, strong face with a soldier's kepi atop it, winking at me in encouragement. Blood-flecked face of a kid with a knife in his lungs telling me there would be others when he was gone. Face of a man, almost forgotten, in a room somewhere with bright chandeliers, telling me, hour after hour, things about staying alive . . . that he had nothing Miss Mattie needed, but he could give something to her son. Pretty face of Patty Mills, reading my mind while I read hers . . .

Light. Blinding light subduing slowly, becoming light and cold and numbing pain.

Sound. Scuffling sounds, crunching, muted sounds, crackle of grass being cropped by flat teeth, snort of breath intaken, hesitation and the soft padding of hooves on hard ground. Hot breath behind my ear, another snort, scuffing of grass, then something hard and sharp hooked into my side and lifted me, flipping me over, and I screamed.

It was a longhorn cow, almost on top of me, and as I howled the sound and the scent of blood threw it into a frenzy. Its head went up, eyes wide, and it snorted and backed away, then turned tail and ran, spooking the others around it. They milled, then ran toward me and past me, breaking to either side, one going directly over me, its rank, hot smell strong in my nostrils.

With a clarity focused on one observation, I saw markings on some of them. They were Double D cattle. Then I blacked out again.

When I came to again the sun was high and I was aware of a wider world and there were wolves in it. They had come around me, curious and sniffing, and one had hold of my bootheel and was pulling on it. When I moved they backed off, a ring of yellow eyes watching me, ears perked high on intelligent heads, muzzles flecked with guard hairs, tongues red across strong teeth as they grinned at me, laughing in the winter chill, wondering what they had found.

I tried to sit up and they bristled and backed away, but not far. The blood smell was strong about me, and attracted them. Pain almost knocked me out again, but I couldn't let it. If they saw me fall it would be all over. I braced myself with both hands and kept my head upright.

There was a seep of dark blood where I had lain, and the serape and blankets around me were matted and stiff. It hurt like hell to breathe. It hurt like hell to move. The pain seemed to come from my right side, deep, and from a point high on my back. For a time I didn't remember anything, just that I was here and there were wolves and I must keep going, upward.

Somehow I got to my knees, teetering there, afraid I would fall and afraid to try for more because then I would fall for sure. The wolves were sleek and fat, and their eyes bored through me and they yipped and laughed among themselves. They weren't hungry. They were enjoying a fine sport.

Slowly, fighting awful jolts of pain, I found my gun and got it out, then scuffled on my knees to the little bluff and clawed at its face, getting my feet under me. My legs felt like rubber, but they held me. I leaned there and the wolves circled further away, one old patriarch pausing to sniff the blood where I had fallen.

A gnarled cedar staff lay there, propped against the bluff. I had cut it in case I needed a lean-to during the night. It was almost six feet long, and sturdy.

Using it as a cane, I tried walking a few steps and almost collapsed, but by bracing it against my shoulder, spreading my legs and leaning on the wood, I stayed upright while the dizziness receded. I was thirsty . . . terribly thirsty. I scraped snow crust from the top of the bluff and ate it, wanting more.

My gray horse was gone. So were my saddle and gear. The man had taken what he wanted. The man . . . Morgan Hayes.

When I started walking, eastward, the wolves followed along for an hour or more. But I was slow and tedious and they had better things to do. One of them crossed the trail of the cattle and told the others and they went loping off, ahead of me, interested now in other subjects. One turned, hesitated, and looked back at me. I was still moving. He turned away. It was the patriarch. Go, Brother Wolf, my mind told him. Long after they were gone I concentrated on taking a step at a time, moving in a tight little world with no horizons, no universe around it, just a world of steps taken one at a time, always with the creek bank to my left.

Then there was a place where the bank receded, sloped gently away, and I angled toward it, sweating and trembling as the ground edged upward. An eternity passed, like those before it, and I raised my head and looked around. I was up on the flats, again moving east, pausing now and then to brace tripodwise against my stick. I noticed that the Colt was still in my hand, so I put it away and used both hands to stay upright, leaning on the stick.

When I could no longer stand the thirst I dropped to my knees, pain reeling me like a smashing club, and scrabbled handfuls of snow. Then I went on.

A shadow grew in front of me, stretching out longer and longer, and it was the shadow of a man walking with a stick, dragging himself against a white world that went nowhere but went on and on and on.

Once I thought the wolves had come again, but it was just shadows on the snow, circling shadows of a pair of buzzards wheeling overhead in the cold, bright sky.

I talked to the faces that came and went. I told Mattie Stillwell I was all right and in good health and she needn't ever worry, but she worried anyway. I told Patty Mills about the Victor Hugo concert at Fort Worth and asked her if she would attend with me. I told Henry Lattimer about the Double-D cattle in No Man's Land. That's important, I told him. Those cattle shouldn't be up here. They couldn't have drifted so far.

And I rode across a freezing valley, on and on, endlessly in the night, trying to reach the man with no face, trying to tell him . . . what? I couldn't remember. But it was terribly important to reach him. And yet no matter how far I rode he was always just beyond, just out of reach.

And he died just out of reach.

I could hear myself babbling, and it helped remind me to keep moving, to follow the shadow of the man with the stick.

Then there were two shadows, and one grew to a team of mules, pulling alongside, and there was a wheel there and I tried to lean on it but I fell. I rolled over and looked up at the man climbing down from the wagon.

He looked at me and his weathered face paled. I tried to laugh because he was Lloyd Harper and I was glad to see him.

"By?" he said. Then he was kneeling over me, looking back the way I had come. "My God," he whispered. "Oh, my God."

21

Fires roared in the hearths at both ends of the main room at Double-D headquarters. The room was hot, but the old man who sat beside the main fireplace was wrapped in a heavy shawl and seemed barely able to absorb enough of the fire's heat to satisfy himself.

He watched the men moving about the room, and those who lounged in various parts of it, and his eyes missed nothing and expressed nothing about what they saw. They were ancient and cold, those eyes. They were the hard eyes of winter.

Peter Llewellyn Dawes was seventy-one years old. He had made fortunes in those years and built them into larger fortunes. He had bought and sold men with the same objective disinterest with which he had bought and sold mines, cattle herds, railroads and shipping lines. He had made men powerful when their power served his purposes, and he had as often brought the powerful to ruin. There was little he had not done in his time, and even less he had not had others do for him.

For a time his cold eyes rested on two men who sat

in low hide-back chairs at the far end of the room. Ed Johnson sprawled there, oblivious to the activity around him, his teeth clenched on a cigar and his hands clasped behind his head. He had the look of satisfaction on his brutish face. That kind, Dawes thought, came easy. Put a meal under his belt, a drink in his hand and a female in his bed and he would do anything for you.

A few feet from him, Pony Bidell seemed asleep in his chair. One leg was crossed over the other knee, his hands rested idly on his slim belly—pale hands, Dawes noticed again, like a woman's hands, slim and delicate and uncallused, the hands of a man who lives by his gun. Bidell's flat hat was over his eyes and his mouth sagged open. Feed him regularly, Dawes thought, and give him a kill now and then. Bidell lived only for that. Give him a kill upon occasion and he was content.

In the center of the room Davy Dawes strode from one group to another, talking, hearing reports, issuing orders. The old man considered his grandson sourly. Twenty-three years old, strutting and blustering, bullying his men because his payroll gave him the right to bully them. Tall and big-boned, yet fair and almost pretty of face, like his mother, young Davy was a ladies' man and a rounder, but the old man was not interested in any of that.

He won't hold it long, he thought. What I build for him will be gone in a few years. But then, I'm not really building it for him. I build for myself. He happens to be the one I build around because there is no one else.

He considered the kingdom he would hand to Davy

Dawes, and he knew that once he was gone the kingdom would begin to dissolve around the youngster's ears. But it would be a kingdom, for all of that, and maybe when Davy folded someone strong would be there to hold it and rule it. A bleak humor took the old man. I can't even choose my successor, he thought, because I don't know who will be so strong. I can only build around young Davy, and build solidly enough that the man who takes it from him will have to deserve its keep.

He pulled the shawl tighter around him, immune to the heat from the roaring fire. He was always cold these days. Always. It was as though his body had begun to reject the energies within him, to ignore the heat of ideas, the flame of ambition, the searing energy of ruthless conquest. But reject it or not, it was there, and the brain that generated it had lost none of its power.

Peter Llewellyn Dawes had been at Double-D since the end of December. He had endured the hardship of a train ride to Fort Worth, then the rough ride along a spur to Mobeetie, and the jolting passage from Mobeetie to Double-D by surrey, to be at the point of action when it came. For nearly seven years he had manipulated people and events from afar, testing situations, creating issues, maneuvering forces into play. But now the time was at hand when he must direct from the field, as a general when the campaign begins. And he was prepared to travel again, this time north to the battleground, when the time was right. It would be soon.

At the moment, Davy was hearing a report from a heavy-coated rangehand who had just come in, and the old man listened with vague curiosity. Someone had been killed.

". . . still had his gun in his hand," the man said. "The other two, well, they was mashed under a rockfall. Looked to us like somebody brought it down on them, then outgunned Johnny."

A short distance away Pony Bidell showed signs of life. He thumbed back his hat, revealing cold blue eyes. "That Johnny Saxon you're talkin' about?"

"Yeah, Pony," the man said, talking past Davy Dawes. "He's dead."

"So who got him?"

"We don't know, but some of the boys said that Indian was seen out there, not too far from there."

"What Indian?" Bidell and Johnson had returned only a day ago from Kansas.

"The same one that's give us trouble before. You know."

"Tell it to me," Davy blustered. "Not him."

"Yes, sir. Well, some of 'em over on the perimeter said that redskin is back on Double-D. The same one, they said. We thought maybe Johnny and them run into him. We found a shot horse a few miles back that's ear-notched like an Indian would do."

Davy swore, explosively. "How many times is that, now? How many of you hardcases does it take to put one Indian in the ground?"

"He's slippery, Mr. Dawes," the man said, fidgeting with his hat. "He comes and goes, and the boys can't seem to catch him. The word's out, though. We'll find him."

"The word's out," Davy sneered. "The word's out! Hell, the word has been out for two years now!" He looked around the room. "All right, raise the price on him. Five hundred dollars to the man who brings back his head . . . with or without the rest of him. Tell the men."

He turned to a pair of rough-dressed punchers near the door. "How's the drifting coming?"

"East and middle sections are moving," one of them said. "The west section should be moving soon. That's harder land out there. The storm held everything back at least a week."

"Well, keep at it," Davy said. "Don't drive them, just drift them. I don't want cattle in the Strip until we're ready to move, but I want them all where they can be put there soon, when we're ready."

"Yes, sir. But you know, there's an awful lot of cattle out there, Mr. Dawes. It's pretty hard to control every one of 'em that tight . . ."

Davy had started to turn away. Now he swung around to face the man. "What are you saying, Willie?"

"Well, it's just that when the storm come up, the east section was already on the move, and they think they may have lost a few head up there. They don't know, but it could be a few of them drifted over into the Strip."

"It could be? What do you mean, it could be? Did they or didn't they?"

The man glanced around him, embarrassed. "That's just it, Mr. Dawes. They don't know for sure. But they said even if they did, it wasn't more than a few."

Davy swore again, and the old man under the shawl frowned. Too much attention to trivia, he thought. Not enough delegation. Davy seemed intent on being in charge of the details. He should simply lay down the rules, and expect them to be followed . . . and enforce it severely if they weren't. Instead he let his men argue with him.

"You get back out there," Davy pointed at the pair, "and get the word up and down the line. Drift them north—all of them! But nothing goes beyond Wolf Creek until they hear it from me. Nothing! Not so much as a mossback or a calf! Is that understood?"

"Yes, sir," one said, and they both turned and left the house, straight-backed like men who had been humiliated. Davy Dawes had never worked cattle in his life. What did he know of the difficulty of starting a drift . . . or of stopping one, particularly when the head of the drift was a hundred miles wide? Double-D had a lot of men, but not that many.

Lupita, the dumpy halfbreed woman who was the main-house cook, flustered about her serving-table corner setting out china and silver, then came to the fire to remove a boiling pot from its trammel. She studiously ignored the men in the room, and she walked wide around the old man by the fire, her eyes downcast. Carrying the hot water, she passed around him again, returning to her corner to pour water into a porcelain pot. She dumped dark, cured tea leaves in, closed the pot and draped a cozy over it to steep. She set out a strainer.

Lupita had been a good choice, the old man thought. He had chosen her himself, from among his servants at Port Lavaca, and sent her to Davy as cook and housekeeper when he built Double-D. Lupita was a woman without spirit. The years of being used by Dawes' rangehands and vaqueros in South Texas had broken her of that. Now at thirty-three she was fat and silent and docile. She was the spawn of a Mexican whore raped by plains Indians. She was illiterate, barely conversant in Spanish and spoke no English. She was perfect.

While the tea rested Lupita went to the woodbin, selected an armload of firewood and built up the fire. The old man frowned. The stupid bitch was using green wood again, and he thought about chastising her for it, but changed his mind. She would not learn. He looked away, shifting his attention to his grandson conducting the business of the ranch. Behind him Lupita fingered the chain that closed the flue.

"Seven thousand head," Davy Dawes said, turning to his grandfather for approval. "That's what we have on Wolf Creek now. When the central and west sections drift them up we'll have eighteen thousand head there. And the men to line them out and push them in one big herd right through No Man's Land and into Kansas. Those squatters won't know what hit 'em."

"Never be too certain, Davy," the old man said quietly. "One does not succeed by taking anything for granted."

"Nothing is taken for granted," the young man said. "You heard Pony. There's no opposition up there. That's all been taken care of. We'll hit the rails with more cattle than they've ever seen before, and there won't be anybody shutting us out because they don't even know we're coming."

"They'll know," the old man said. "That isn't the point. The trick is to make sure there is no *organized* opposition."

"Well, there won't be. Pony says that sheriff up there was the only one who was nosing around, and that's been taken care of."

Lupita set a small table beside the old man and set a cup of tea on it. There were pots of coffee in both hearths for the others.

A shielded wagon had pulled up outside, and now two more men came into the room. Troy Wilson hung up his coat and hat. He was an imposing man, tall and genial of feature, with a mane of iron-gray hair to show for his sixty years of living and several comfortable investments to show for his thirty-five years of service to Peter Llewellyn Dawes. Troy Wilson was the perfect politician. He was handsome, he attracted confidence, he had no scruples and once bought he stayed bought.

He crossed to the main hearth and handed a packet to the old man. Davy scowled at his back. He was supposed to be in charge at Double-D, but it seemed that every bastard around still answered directly to his grandfather.

"Messages," Wilson said. "Court has accepted the suits on four of the five counties up there. That's really better than I'd hoped. Three would have been enough—Seward, Stevens and Morton."

"They accepted suit on Meade, too?"

"Yes, sir. All four of the counties above the Strip. They threw out the second-tier counties, but we didn't need those, anyway. It was only a negotiating position."

Dawes was reading through one of the messages. "I see you have filed different cause of action clauses on all four."

"Yes, sir. We're contesting population on Morton County, and that's one I think we can win on the face of it. They'd have to count the jackrabbits to come up with 2,000 residents. Then in Stevens, we have disruption and a proven breakdown in law enforcement." His eyes crinkled. "That was the prettiest piece of work I ever saw, how you got old Woods to mess things up like that. He always thought it was his own idea, didn't he, sir?"

Dawes glanced at him. "Save the flattery, Troy. Just report."

"Yes, sir. We had to dig for a cause in Seward County, but that judge up there—Tomlin—he's handing it to us on a platter. By spring that county will be split right down the middle, and there'll be militia law. That's grounds for disenfranchising."

"I ain't sure of that," Pony Bidell spoke up from his chair. He had only seemed to be asleep. "We done like you said up there, but I didn't see no 'split down the middle' happening."

Dawes glanced at the gunman. "You did very well, but these things take time. I expect Morgan Hayes will have further reports for us when he arrives."

"Maybe so." Bidell dropped his hat back over his eyes. "He ought to be here soon. He didn't have that much left to do. We nailed that Stillwell drifter for him, at the jail."

Wilson pulled a chair around. "I guess I've missed something," he said. "I knew you had sent some of the men to Kansas, but what was that for?"

Dawes glanced at him, his eyes cold. "Troubleshooting, Troy. Not everything can be done through the courts. To make crops, you have to break some ground."

Wilson just looked at him, waiting.

"Mr. Hayes and Mr. Bidell had several things to do up there. Some of our people needed visits—to assure their continued compliance—and there were some loose ends to be wrapped up."

Wilson glanced at Bidell and Johnson. He knew the sort of "loose ends" these men were used for. "I heard there was a sheriff killed in Seward County."

"Yes," Dawes said. "Very unfortunate." He paused, looked at Wilson and then at his grandson, and a gleam of hard humor came into his eyes. "I gather neither of you has yet heard the name of the sheriff."

Davy shook his head, listening curiously. What difference did that make? Wilson said, "No, I don't think so." Under his hat, Bidell grinned.

"I thought not," the old man said. Sharp eyes studied the two of them. "His name was Samuel Dance."

Wilson's mouth dropped open. He looked as though he were going to choke. Davy Dawes shuddered and turned pale. They looked at the old man as though they had never seen him before.

"Sam Dance?" Wilson rasped. "He's dead? You had him killed?"

"Did you think I wouldn't, Troy? Eventually, when the time was right? You are so naive, Troy. Really, you are."

Davy Dawes just stared at his grandfather, and his lower lip began trembling. He was speechless.

The old man turned hard eyes on his grandson. "I

wondered how you might take that, Davy. I have raised you to be strong. Now I think we'll see how strong you are."

Davy tried to speak, found he couldn't, and turned away, trembling violently. Without a word he hurried from the room, Pony Bidell grinned and Ed Johnson puffed his cigar. Others, further across the big room, glanced around curiously and then resumed what they were doing. Then one of them looked back and pointed. "Look at that!"

They turned. Heavy smoke was pouring from the fireplace, coiling up around the mantel, rising in a roiling cloud to the ceiling. Lupita came running, veering around the men, to flutter helplessly about the hearth.

"Open the goddamned flue!" someone shouted, and she turned, not understanding, seeking instruction. "The flue!" someone pointed, gesturing. "Pull the chain!"

At the gesture she turned back, fumbled with chains and pulled one. The roiling smoke dissipated at the hearth, flames blazed brightly and the draught roared. She bumped the boiling pot and water cascaded onto the flames, belching a huge cloud of steam. In a panic, she pulled another chain, and coughed as smoke and steam pushed out at her.

Troy Wilson shoved her aside, found the flue chain and opened it again. "Get her out of here," he said. "Damn squaw hasn't got a brain in her head!"

Someone slapped Lupita hard across the face and shouted at her in English. She reeled away, tears in her eyes, then hurried toward the servants' door. As she went through she glanced back, her moist eyes cryptic and Indian. She had done all she could.

In the evening, when all the men had been fed, Lupita put on her coat and carried buckets of refuse from the kitchen out to the midden pit. When she was finished, she walked on, her passage ignored by those who saw her. Lupita was a fixture, nothing more.

A mile from the compound she stopped at the narrow head of a deep gully, pulled her coat about her and sat on a rock, waiting. She would wait here every evening now, for as long as necessary. If Chako had seen her signal he would come, and she would tell him what she had heard.

22

The arrest of six men, charged with the murder of Sam Dance and other crimes, caused a flurry of interest in Seward County. Between the affidavits of Henry Lattimer and the corroborating evidence furnished by Vince Cole, Frank Murdoch, Pearly and Cass, and others, a dozen charges were prepared against the six and it was obvious they would pay . . . if not for Sam Dance, then at least for *something*.

Public opinion, seeking neat answers, also tried to tie the six to the unexplained murders of Penny Bassett, the whiskey-runner Parson Jolly and a Beer City dealer found dead in a pasture across the line in Stevens County. But this was just talk. There was no evidence to connect the six with any of those shootings.

Sheriff Sim Guthrie, troubled at first by the unexpected arrests, was ecstatic when he found himself being touted as a hero by his political cronies and complimented guardedly by former Dance faction supporters. Whatever else Henry Lattimer had accomplished, he had made the new sheriff look good.

A brooding Judge Will Tomlin, holding court in Springfield again now that the road was open across the Cimarron Valley, visited the jail to interview the prisoners and then removed himself as judge in any cases concerning them. "It was my life that was threatened," he told the members of his court. "Therefore I cannot adjudge myself as impartial." The result was that the prisoners were bound over for trial and Tomlin referred the matter to Circuit Justice Hanlon of Wichita, despite the fact it might take months to bring Hanlon in.

A change of venue was argued, however, and defeated by Tomlin, as was a suggestion that he recall Judge Kendall again. "The honorable Judge Kendall," Tomlin declared portentously, "has not indicated an understanding of the weight of these matters in this county."

Si Rutledge, sitting in the court as an observer and making notes on the proceedings for his newspaper, leaned toward Patty Mills and whispered, "That's because Kendall turned Byron Stillwell loose."

Patty Mills did not respond to her brother's ironic smile. She was worried about Byron Stillwell. Long days had passed without word of him. It was common knowledge that, a little more than a week past, Stillwell had launched a one-man raid on Beer City. A hired gunman had died, a gambling hall had burned, and the word was out in the Neutral Strip that Ace Pruitt would pay for Stillwell's death.

But he had simply disappeared.

After the storm the Rutledges and Patty had returned for a few days to Arkalon, where Rutledge published his two-page newspaper. Now Rutledge and Patty were back for the opening of court, while Barbara Rutledge and their printer handled the details of distribution of the news.

The docket was heavy. It was almost four weeks now since there had been a regular session of court in Springfield, and much had accumulated in that time. Strayed cattle, damage to a barn, a dispute between brothers that had led to a shooting, a divorce case brought in from Meade County because no one in Meade County was impartial on the matter—these and like items fairly buried the Monday docket and carried over through most of Tuesday before the judge allowed hearing on some major matters that began to pack the courtroom with interested citizens.

"As is generally known," Tomlin told the court, "this bench has been presented with a petition signed by certain citizens of Springfield seeking to block—for cause not yet elucidated—the acceptance of another petition proposing an election to determine whether Springfield or Liberal should henceforth be the seat of Seward County."

The room was packed now, and the Springfield townsfolk who made up most of the crowd glanced with unveiled hostility at the smaller contingent from Liberal headed by Frank Murdoch and Jim Henson. These, in turn, kept their attention focused on the bench. It was, after all, primarily a business matter—being county seat could mean fortunes to a town's developers.

"Why is Tomlin messing around in this?" Patty whispered to her brother.

"I don't know. Somebody got it put on the docket."

266

Tomlin rapped his gavel and continued. "Since this matter has come to the attention of this court, I have studied it and find the court has three options in the matter. One, the original petition could be held valid and the second denied as not being pertinent to the question at hand, which is, simply, the calling of an election . . ." There were growls and shuffling among the Springfield contingent. Tomlin rapped his gavel again. "Two, the court could find the second petition valid on the grounds of established jurisdiction of county offices and hardship worked on county officials in the conduct of their business . . ." This time the muttered protests were from the Liberal group.

"Or, third," the judge went on, "this court is empowered to view both petitions with regard to their possible effect on the safety and welfare of the citizens of this district and the possibility of a threat to the sovereignty of the State of Kansas . . ."

"What is he talking about?" Patty whispered. Si didn't answer. Cold premonition was raising the hair on his neck.

". . . and in view of these considerations can choose to refer the entire matter to the attorney general of Kansas, as well as to the office of the governor with a recommendation of military intervention . . ."

Throughout the crowd now, people gawked at the tall jurist, unable to believe what they were hearing.

Jim Henson jumped up. "Your honor, nobody is making a war over this matter. We just want to put it to a vote . . ."

Tomlin pounded his gavel. "Silence! I'll have order in this court!" He glared at the assembled public and dabbed at his gleaming forehead with a kerchief. Although it was not hot in the room, he was sweating. But he turned hooded dark eyes on the crowd and continued, "In view of this," he raised a telegram, then put it back in its sheaf, ". . . a message from the State Court in Topeka that suit has been filed to dissolve this and three other counties . . ."

"Oh, Lord," Rutledge muttered and began furiously making notes on a pad.

"To do what?" someone shouted.

"Judge, where'd you get that?" someone in the back called, raising his voice over the rising babble in the room.

Frank Murdoch of Liberal turned to Saul Bingham of Springfield, across the center aisle. "That's ridiculous. Had you heard of that?" Bingham ignored him.

Tomlin pounded his gavel. Sturdevant appeared from somewhere to stand beside the judge, cold eyes sweeping the crowd, his big rifle at the ready. The court bailiff shouted, "Order! Order!" and drew his gun. In the front row of seats Sim Guthrie looked back at the crowd, perplexed. Beside him a heavily-bandaged Everett nudged him. "Sheriff, I thought you was going to give that to the county commissioners. Why'd you give it to him?"

Slowly, the pandemonium in the courtroom subsided. Tomlin waited until there was silence.

"In view of this," he said finally, "this court hereby remands to the attorney general the question of the petitions, and will await his ruling on the matter before further action is considered. Further, I wish to advise that a message was sent yesterday to the governor, requesting state militia presence in Seward

County for so long as it may take to resolve these issues."

"What issues?" Patty whispered. "He isn't making any sense. He makes it sound like there's a war going on here."

Si Rutledge turned a pale face to his sister. "For whatever it's worth, there is now. Judge Tomlin just started it."

"But why?"

"Lord only knows."

"Is this going to be Stevens County all over again?"

"No." Rutledge pulled at his lip and his eyes shifted as ominous, cloudy possibilities raced through his mind. "No, not like Stevens County. I have a feeling that may have been a dress rehearsal."

"But for what? What's going to happen?"

Whatever his muttered reply, it was drowned by the shouting in the courtroom. At the bench, Judge Will Tomlin rapped his gavel and his mouth moved, uttering words no one could hear. Then, with Sturdevant backing him and the bailiff and two deputies flanking him, the judge retired from the courtroom.

"I didn't give that to him," Guthrie told Everett, wide-eyed with confusion. "He must have got his own message. The one I got is still in my desk drawer. I forgot about it." He got to his feet and hurried off after the deputies, who had covered Tomlin's exit and now were working their way through the crowd toward the front door. Everett stared after him. He mouthed the words, trying to cope with the enormity of them. Forgot about it. He forgot about it.

"My God," Everett muttered. "He forgot about it."

* * *

On that day Henry Lattimer turned nineteen and celebrated his birthday by rescuing County Commissioner Joseph Bennett from a shed where he was being held by four armed citizens of Springfield. The captors included a pharmacist, a pair of teamsters and the postmaster.

"You are going to have to let him go," the young deputy pointed out, peering around the edge of a barn door thirty feet from the kidnappers. He could see only two of them, crouched behind an upturned wagonbox, but he knew there were two more, probably inside the shed with their prisoner. "At least a dozen people saw you kidnap him. You can't get away with it."

"We're not tryin' to get away with anything," the postmaster answered. "But we won't let him go until they adjourn their meeting. He's got the petition."

"Mister Pratt," Henry said, trying to be calm and patient, "it's against the law to seize and detain a legal petition. That's in the statutes of the State of Kansas."

"We ain't seized and detained the petition," Pratt assured him. "We ain't touched it. It's still in Commissioner Bennett's pocket."

"But you're detaining Commissioner Bennett!"

"You show us where the law says anything about that," Pratt argued. "Why don't you go over to the courthouse and tell Commissioners Brown and Masters to adjourn their meeting, then we'll let him go."

Henry shook his head and raised his eyes skyward. "Mister Pratt, they can't adjourn their meeting. They haven't called it to order yet. They're waiting for Commissioner Bennett. We only have three commissioners. Come on, now, just let him walk out of there and I'll take him and we'll go on our way and forget all this."

"Masters is the chairman. He can call the meeting to order any time he wants."

"Yes," Henry sighed, "I know. But every time he does Commissioner Brown demands a quorum call and then they're right back where they started."

Pratt shifted behind the wagonbox and Henry could hear him in murmured conference with the pharmacist, Abel Long. Moments passed, then Long's head appeared over the wagonbox. "It only takes two of them to be a quorum, Henry."

"Not if Commissioner Brown won't answer the quorum call," Henry shot back at him. "That's why the meeting hasn't been called to order."

"You said it was Brown who demanded a quorum call."

"Yes, but when it's called he refuses to answer it."

"Who the hell's side is Brown on, anyway?"

"That's a little hard to tell, Abel," the postmaster pointed out. "I mean, him bein' from Arkalon, he might have throwed in with Bennett on this thing."

"He can't!" Long declared. "My brother voted for him."

"Gentlemen," Henry reasoned, "you're just wasting your time, anyway. The petition has been referred to Judge Tomlin. That's where everybody is right now, over at the courtroom waiting to see what will happen."

"We got Bennett and he's got the petition."

"That's just one copy of it. There are two more."

"Well, what's Tomlin got to do with county seat matters, then?"

"I don't know," Henry said, "because instead of being over at the court I'm out here talking to you gentlemen. Come on, now. Turn him loose. Please."

He could see their heads, turned to each other. Then Abel Long arose, went to the barred shed door and peered inside. He closed the door and turned. "Deputy, are you going to arrest us?"

"I probably am, but you don't have to make things any worse for yourselves. Just turn him loose."

Long set his shotgun down and rubbed his cold hands. "Supposin' they had been playin' three-hand stud in there and Commissioner Bennett had won a dollar-ten off Mack and thirty-five cents off Louie, and me and Mister Pratt was witness to that? You gonna arrest Commissioner Bennett for gambling?"

Henry stepped into the open, shrugged helplessly and shook his head. "Just turn him loose, Mr. Long. It's getting late."

"Can we keep his petition here?"

"No, you can't. That's against the law!"

The meeting of county commissioners that day lasted only minutes. Chairman Masters, scowling at the deputy who escorted Bennett into the room, called the meeting to order and Commissioner Brown demanded a quorum call. Masters and Bennett answered "aye," Brown abstaining on principle. Reading of the minutes of the previous meeting was dispensed with on a vote of three to none, and the bills and claims were approved by vote of two to one. Then Bennett presented the petition from Liberal, calling for a county seat election, Masters tried to refer the matter to a committee of the whole and was overruled two to one, and the petition was accepted by vote of two to one. Masters then requested a motion to table the matter, received none, and gleefully read to the others a court order holding any such petition in abeyance pending action by the district court.

Brown slammed a fist on the table. "Why didn't you say you had that?"

"You didn't ask," Masters advised him smoothly.

"When is court in session?" Bennett inquired.

Masters pulled out a pocket watch. "It has been in session since ten o'clock this morning."

"Move we adjourn," Brown erupted.

"Second," Bennett chimed in. "Let's get over there."

"Byron Stillwell left us these things before he left Springfield," Patty Mills told Henry Lattimer that evening in Si Rutledge's room at the hotel. The rooms were small in Springfield's best lodging, but Patty had brought chairs from her own room so the three had places to sit. The bed with its crazy-quilt cover was almost filled with small stacks of paper, laid out in order.

"He told us to share it with you," Si Rutledge added. "He felt we might learn something from it about who killed Sam Dance."

"He didn't say 'who'," Patty corrected her brother. "He said 'why.'"

"Well, then, about why Sam was killed. He said

these things were from Sam's personal effects. I don't know how he got them."

"I do," Henry said, then shut up on that subject. "What have you found out?"

"We're really not sure," Si told him. "We've gone through them. There are a variety of things here: old letters, copies of what seem to be court records, newspaper clippings, handbills . . . a lot of things, as you can see, and most of them don't seem related to one another, but they were bundled together and I have the impression Sam had kept them that way."

Patty stepped to the bed. "I have them arranged here in chronological order." She pointed. "There is a letter dated in 1866—twenty-six years ago, almost—from a man named Troy Wilson. It's addressed to Mr. Dance at Independence, and it urges him to come to Port Lavaca, Texas. It says there is a promise of employment there, if he will come."

"Port Lavaca?" Henry shrugged. "Where is that?"

"Place down on the Gulf Coast," Si said. "Beef and shipping town with a couple of big ranches spreading out from it."

"Then there is a wedding picture," Patty said. "It looks like an old tintype, but there is no question it is a wedding picture. And it is dated: June 20, 1868, Port Lavaca, Texas. But there are no names." She handed the pale old print to Henry. He held it close to the light.

"This could be Mr. Dance," he said finally. "When he was a lot younger. It might be." The woman in the picture, a young woman with light hair and barely discernible features, stood at the side of the seated, dark-haired young man who might have been Sam

274

Dance a quarter-century before.

"And then we come up with a name," Patty said, lifting a yellowed and flimsy clipping protected in tissue. "Sarah Dawes Dance."

It was a brief obituary, almost no detail except that the beloved wife of Marshal Samuel Dance of Tulia had died, leaving behind her a grieving husband and a son, whose name was Samuel David Dance and who was eight years old. The date was November 20, 1877.

"Mr. May told me about that," Henry said. "He said Mr. Dance had been married and had a son, but that his wife died at Tulia when he was the marshal there." He pulled at his lip, puzzling over . . . something. It didn't come to him.

"I wonder what happened to the boy," Patty mused.

"Mr. May said he remembered Mr. Dance sending him away to live with relatives." Still he puzzled.

"Well, anyway," she said, "the next stack is more recent. It is all sorts of material about the troubles in Stevens County, starting as early as 1886."

"I don't think Sam was even here in 1886," Si said. "He was somewhere in Missouri then."

"Joplin," Henry said. "He was sheriff there. He came here early in 1888."

Patty Mills straightened a stack of papers. "I didn't see anything about Joplin anywhere, but there is some old stuff here about Stevens County."

"He must have dug back for it," Si suggested.

"We did find something interesting here, though. Where is it? Ah. It's a letter to the county clerk of Stevens County—if it has a date we can't make it out—asking for a list of taxable holdings of one J. William Tomlin. Our judge!"

"Tell him who it's from," Si said.

"It's from that same man who wrote to Mr. Dance back in 1866. Troy Wilson. The man wrote on behalf of a P. L. Dawes, and the letter is from Port Lavaca. There is no evidence of a reply."

"I wonder how he came up with that," Si said.

Henry Lattimer stared at the stacks of documentation and felt as though there were answers there, just beyond his reach.

"The rest of this, the big stack," Patty said, "Is a lot of material about federal rulings, court cases, legal background . . . mostly on the designation of territories and the requirements and steps for organizing territories. It's all recent research, but there's some pretty old stuff here, going back fifty years or more. Oh, and the next stack, that's related, but it is all details about annexation of adjacent lands by designated territories of the United States."

"I didn't ever know before that a territory could annex from a state," Si said. "But apparently under certain conditions it can. It depends upon where the lands are in contiguity, and when there there is organized government . . . also there are some population requirements and the like."

Patty Mills looked at Henry. "So! Does all this tell you something that it hasn't told us? Byron Stillwell seemed to think it was awfully important. He swore us to secrecy, except for you."

Henry bit his lip, then his jaw sagged and he sat back in the hard chair, his eyes fixing on distances beyond the little room. "Dawes," he muttered.

Si looked at him. "What?"

"Dawes! P. L. Dawes . . . the name on that letter from Wilson. And the obituary, Sarah Dawes Dance. And the little boy, his middle name was David. P. L. Dawes could be Peter Llewellyn Dawes. That fits the Port Lavaca thing. And Mr. Dance's wife was a Dawes. From Port Lavaca. And Peter Llewellyn Dawes is the grandfather of . . . of Davy Dawes. The Double-D."

For a long time the room was silent. Patty Mills looked from one to the other of them in puzzlement, but Si Rutledge sagged in his chair, and his face went gray. "The boy," he said. "Sam's son."

23

From a high place, Chako the Kwahadi watched coated riders scouring the breaks, crisscrossing miles of flats in precision drill as they "drifted" tens of thousands of cattle northward, across the Sweetwater and into the valley of the Canadian, moving them slowly toward Wolf Creek and the No Man's Land that lay beyond.

Chill vagrant winds blustered on the caps of the escarpment, whipping chalk-mist from mesa tops and quarreling through the breaks. They were the winds of early spring, west winds from the Llano Estacado which could blow cold at night but lose their edge at daylight to free the streams that flowed now in their canyons. Chako breathed the cold winds and knew the time of new grass would come early this year.

Lupita had told him all she knew, and now Chako watched Double-D with the fascination of one who has been bitten and now watches snakes.

He knew of the old man who had come to Double-D, and of the evil that seemed to center there with his arrival. Lupita, who used no English among the white men and seemed to them a dumb creature, listened always and told him everything that was said. He knew of the massing of cattle to the north, and of the men who had gone into Kansas to kill those who were in their way. He knew of the price on his own head and he knew that Byron Stillwell, the strange white-Indian man who seemed always Brother Wolf to him, was the enemy of these people.

Chako had no plan, but he had a clear purpose. His horses, his hut and his little field under Haystack Mountain were in good hands. A young Cheyenne named Jimmy Blue was there, and he owed the Kwahadi his life and his honor. Jimmy Blue would take care of Chako's holdings until he returned. Chako watched and waited for his chance to hurt the snake. He would not be done until he had.

Haunting Double-D had cost him two more horses. Davy Dawes had put out a reward for the Indian and his gunhands were eager to collect it. The horse he had taken from Johnny Saxon was shot from under him on the bluffs above the Sweetwater, and seven riders had ridden over him as he lay hidden in a draw too small to seem a hiding place. From the trailing seventh he had taken another horse. Then two days ago he had ridden that animal to exhaustion when range hands chased him across the Canadian valley. When the horse could no longer run, Chako had gone ahead on foot. Now he crouched below the rim of a caleche-topped mesa and watched the Texas cattle moved north. The herd he watched was one of three, all being grouped just below the Neutral Strip. The dried beef he chewed on was from a pack taken from a rider who had become separated from his group with a lame mount.

Low clouds brought by the warming winds formed a deepening layer of gray above the broken prairies, and fitful cold rains moved across the land, obscuring vision here and there. Chako wished for a storm. Alone, in open country, he could do little to harm the riders of Double-D. But with a storm to assist him, there were many things he might do. A man who knew the land might turn cattle in such conditions . . . might even turn entire herds back upon the men who drove them. But there was no storm-scent, only the squabbling winds and the occasional cold drizzle they brought with them.

Where he crouched now, watching, was thirty miles north and a little west of Double-D headquarters. Twenty miles further north, the three great drifts of longhorns and brush cattle arrowed toward a common point, the flats between Wolf Creek and the Beaver. From there, in three days, a concentrated drive could take a herd east of the Beaver breaks and north in Kansas, across No Man's Land with only one river valley to cross short of the Cimarron railhead. Some of what Chako had learned from Lupita was vague— the references to territory law and dissolution of counties. But Chako knew where cattle went when they were moved north and though he had never seen herds so big he knew where they were going.

It was late afternoon and most of the loosely-gathered, drifting cattle had moved beyond his view into the Canadian breaks. Chako had about decided to move, to watch them again further north, when riders came into view far out on the flats, moving south, and something about them caught his attention. For an hour he watched them, coming slowly closer, before he recognized what he saw. There were four of them. Three he had seen before, moving cattle northward. The fourth, a bulky, bearded man, rode a gray horse. Chako studied the gait and movements of the animal and knew even before it was near enough to see mane and markings that it was a horse he had seen. It was the fine gray he had chosen from his own herd for Byron Stillwell.

When they passed below his hole in the caleche cap of the mesa, the four were near enough that he could see their features. One he knew was Pony Bidell. He and the bearded man rode ahead of the other two, talking. They were beyond range of Chako's pistol, and some of them carried saddle-guns. He hid and watched them pass. When they were beyond him, angling southeastward toward Mobeetie, the Kwahadi stood to stretch his cramped legs and looked again to the north. Beneath his blanket he rubbed bare arms that sometimes ached to remind him of his purpose. Then he ate the rest of the food from the pack and threw the pack away. Miles to the north, just at the edge of the Canadian's far rim, riders appeared as specks in the distance and grouped below the windy flats. The remuda would be held there, and they would make camp, letting their cattle graze in the Canadian bottoms through the night.

The cloud cover had lowered and the spitting rains were colder. Distances dimmed in gray mist. Chako eased himself down, below the caleche bluff, then paused atop the open slope of the mesa. He rolled his blanket and tied its tails around his waist, freeing his legs. His moccasins were worn, but still sound. The coat he had taken off a Double-D gunhand was heavy and encumbering, and he cast it aside. Muscles rippled under the bare, brown skin of his arms. With a last look back toward the south, where the four riders had gone—where Byron Stillwell's gray horse had gone—Chako strode down the mesa, heading due north. By the time he reached the open flats he was running, strong legs taking the distances in long, easy strides. He ran as a wolf runs, easy and intent, brown legs rippling as he floated over the land. It was a pace the Kwahadi knew from long before the time of horses. It was a pace learned from Apache and Mountain Ute, a pace ghostlike and efficient, that would cover miles until the miles were gone.

Dark evening dimmed the escarpment lands. Gray clouds rested on the mesas and brooded over the flats, and chill sullen winds brought freezing rain. Chako blended with the mists, became one with the shadows and ran toward the Canadian five miles away.

Somber dusk pervaded the wide valley when the Indian crept to its edge at a place where shallow canyon walls hid him. Here the high plains sheared away, injured by the miles-wide gash that rent their sameness. Far below in the bottoms, where cottonwoods stood barren along a freezing stream, the land was dark with cattle. As far as he could see, east and west along the monument-rimmed valley, the herds of Double-D spread grazing. Riders walked their mounts beyond them, keeping them to the flats.

Chako breathed deeply, steadily, letting the sheen of sweat chill on his skin. The nearest dark clusters of cattle were still a mile away, and the far side of the gather was three miles. Beyond that, high on the north rim of the valley, firelight twinkled where the cooks were making their camp.

Nostrils flaring, all his senses keened, Chako read the wind. He knew there might be men on the south rim, but none were near where he lay. He waited until the dusk had deepened to eye-deceiving grays, then slid and clambered down the facing bluffs, dropping nearly a hundred feet in a series of abrupt descents, to the sloping shoulders of the valley. From here there was no cover, not even clumps of sage or stands of cedar. He unrolled his dark blanket, wrapped it around his shoulders and back under his arms to tie behind him. Then at a crouch, moving and stopping, changing direction to follow cloud-shadow, rain-mist and slight depressions in the sloping land, he moved toward the herd.

Nearly invisible in the dim light, the Kwahadi crept downward. Shifting wind brought the hot stench of massed cattle, the muffled lowing of animals moving from patch to patch of graze, the crunch of a shod hoof on stone. He flattened, a darker patch in darkness, his blanket nearly covering him. A horseman appeared in the gloom, almost over him, and he held his breath as he went by. A treading hoof fell inches from his ankle, but Chako lay still. As the rider passed, his horse caught the strange man-scent and whickered, shying aside, looking back. The rider peered into the gloom, brought his horse around a slow, full turn, then went on. Chako waited minutes before moving again. He reached and passed the first knot of dark cattle, moving around to pass downwind from them. The animals were not aware of him.

On he went, still angling downward, and a voice

came from upwind a few yards away. "Clete, what was that?"

Another voice, more distant, "What?"

"I don't know. Thought I saw something right over there."

"Wolves?"

"Dunno. I'll look."

The horse moved toward him and Chako could see the rider's outline against the dim sky. The man was searching. Chako found a small stone and flipped it out ahead. It thumped and clattered, near a small bunch of cattle, and the animals turned and raised horned heads. The rider looked that way, saw nothing out of place, and continued his surveillance of the ground ahead of him. But by that time Chako was gone. He huddled in ragged sedge a dozen feet from where the rider passed, and as the man rode by Chako passed so close behind him he could have reached out a hand and touched the horse's heels.

He was into the massed herd then, and crawled and dashed erratically, staying always just ahead of the rippling of dark bodies that marked his passage. His path described a wide arc, so that the shying of beasts from his scent would indicate no clear passage.

A rangy steer lowed and lowered its horns, threatening the low shadow that moved before it, but the shadow was gone then, among other grazing cattle.

Voices from behind indicated the herd riders there had noticed a skittishness in the herd and were curious, but Chako crouched low and moved on, carefully where the animals were spread out, fast where they massed together, and in the encroaching night no definite path could be seen in the movement of the beasts.

He was a wolf among the herd, and they cleared around him, but he geared his movements to seem no threat, to confuse the dull perceptions of the cattle, to seem to them no more than a passing shadow.

Dropping over a wash bank he rested in spiky thistle between the bank and a stand of prickly-pear. Cattle crowded about him there, so close that their odor was a warm, cloying presence. Staying beneath his trailing blanket, a turtle under its shell, he edged toward the spread of cactus and broke off several oval leaves, spiking his hands painfully in the darkness. With his knife he split the succulent leaves, avoiding their needles as much as possible. Then he rubbed himself with the moist interiors, face and shoulders, sides and belly, legs and feet. When he moved again, ever deeper into the great herd, the cattle noticed him less.

The river was a broad, open span of sand between low banks, winding and weaving through its valley. He worked far upstream to cross, and was completely exposed to view for several minutes as he ran across the sand, through and past fingers of tall grass on low shoals, and across the ice-rimmed stream itself, fifty yards wide and knee-deep at its center. Here he could pass for neither wolf nor cow, and he abandoned deception and ran. At the far bank he rolled deep beneath dark willows and lay still in pooled, freezing water while he listened to the darkness. The willow stand ran downstream several hundred yards. He followed it as far as it went, staying to its shadows.

From there the land sloped upward, climbing toward the valley's north rim, and was more broken than the south slope had been. Here the herds were scattered more, groups of cattle seeking better graze or shelter from the gamboling wind. Night riders worked among them, letting them drift but keeping them quiet.

Chako was halfway up the south slope when he paused crouching in a foot-deep runnel and heard a rider catch his breath yards away. He had been seen. He froze, motionless. There was silence, then the slither of a gun from leather and the stamping of a horse being turned. Chako dared not look toward the sound. He let his ears tell him. The rider had thought he saw something move, but was not sure. In these high plains the men were concerned about wolves, and on the lookout for them. He walked his horse directly toward Chako, straining his eyes. Did he see something there, or not? Only feet away, almost under his horse's nose, there was a darkness, and he leaned from his saddle to squint at it, seeking shape or movement.

The movement when it came was too fast for him to react. In a blur of motion Chako rose from his concealment and leapt at the rider. Hard hands closed on the man's neck and shoulder. A solid weight shifted past him and above him and bore him down, out of his saddle. He hit the ground and a knee pressed into his throat, crushing. He tried to raise his drawn gun and it was trapped, its hammer released, pin and primer separated by hard flesh between thumb and forefinger of a strong hand.

When Chako rose to his feet in the darkness the man's horse still stood where it had been, alert and nervous, but not stampeded by the silent, abrupt

286

scuffle that had ensued.

Chako's hand was bleeding where the gunman's firing pin had pierced the skin. He sucked at it, then wiped it on his britches. Then he rolled his blanket again, put on the fallen rider's coat and hat, and swung into the saddle of the standing horse. Turning the animal he walked it northward, up the slope. He rode hunched and casual, as the white men did, and he angled away from the nearing campfires, toward the cleft where the remuda was kept.

There was a guard there, but Chako came in quietly from the wind side and the man ignored him, satisfied with the vague silhouette he saw. Chako unsaddled the horse and turned it in with the rest. Then when the guard looked away he followed it, crouching as he came among the horses of the remuda, talking to them in the Indian way.

He worked through the herd, searching by touch and feel as much as by sight, until he found the animal he wanted. It was a paint gelding, strong and fresh, and he moved alongside it, a hand on its back, until he could grasp its jaw with firm fingers. He drew its head around, running his other hand up and over its ears, then held its muzzle firmly and blew into its nostrils. At first the horse tried to back away, but the strength of the man held it still. A moment later it stood mesmerized as he scratched its ears and stroked its mane. It was his horse.

With fingers in its mane and a hand on its muzzle he led it to the rope gap and retrieved the saddle he had removed from the other horse. Dimly he was aware of the night guard huddled a few yards away, turning to peer in the darkness. He bridled the paint, forcing the bit into its mouth as he blew into its nostrils again.

Someone else was approaching, a dark rider on a horse pale in the darkness. The rider was coming to the rope gap. Chako eased out of the stolen coat, let it drop to the ground, and swung into the paint's saddle just as the man came up to him. The man looked up, barely seeing him as Chako swung a heavy fist that knocked him from his saddle. Then with a whoop that was pure Comanche, Chako grabbed the reins of the pale horse, lashed at the paint with strident heels and ran straight past the shocked guard, around a limestone shoulder and up a steep incline to the canyon's lip.

For a moment the horses struggled, then the paint crested the rise and bolted over, the riderless white horse scurrying after, led by its reins.

Gunshots sounded behind him, and Chako leaned low in the saddle and drummed the paint's sides. Both horses lay into the run, thundering across dark prairie, veering around a low hill and up onto the flats. The sounds of the awakened valley receded into wind-whipped distance.

For a time he ran in darkness, then he reined in and angled to the west, toward the headwaters of Wolf Creek.

In a night black with low clouds and spitting sleet Chako made his way northwestward. There were men and cattle at Wolf Creek but he eluded them. On the high flats beyond he loped his horses through the night until a raggedness on the dark horizon told him he was approaching the Beaver.

He turned north then, following the Beaver's

course as it bent toward the east, and with the light of morning he entered the river's breaks, a wild Comanche on a painted horse and leading a saddled white, and crossed the rocky, cedar-lined bed of the Beaver somewhere in No Man's Land.

24

It was as though a battle line had been drawn across Seward County. As warming winds brought flurries of rain to melt the dirty snow that lingered in the hollows, as shallow water flowed over sand in the Cimarron Valley, freezing each night and flowing again each day, tempers flared among homesteader, drover and townsman alike.

Despite the efforts of Sheriff Guthrie and his officers, it became unsafe for people from Liberal to walk the streets of Springfield. Judge Will Tomlin's ruling, and the strange suit for dissolution of four counties, had had their effect. Already threatened by loss of their anticipated railroad, the Springfield town developers, business people and the settlers who depended upon the town for trade, blamed Frank Murdoch and his "stinking petition" for bringing greater calamity upon them. More than losing county seat status, it looked now as though they might in fact lose their county. Without an organized county there could be no law. And without law there could be no semblance of the kind of life most had come to western Kansas to find. To the cattlemen building herds of breed beef to feed the northern markets, it spelled disaster. The only thing that protected them from overrun by Texas herds was the herd law. One season without county organization—even a week without it if Texas cattle were en route—and they would be ruined. To the developers of Springfield, the townspeople who kept the businesses and did the trade, ruin was even more imminent. Lifetimes of saving had been invested in the structures, the stores, the business of the town, and Springfield stood to lose either way. If the county remained intact and Liberal won the county seat, Springfield would die the kind of slow death that its designation had forced upon old Fargo Springs years earlier. *If* the election were held. But if the county lost its franchise, there would be chaos. Texas herds would hit the railhead and all business—such as was left in a lawless territory—would shift there immediately.

To the homesteader the spectre of dissolution meant giving up his safety and his family's well-being. Some of the earlier settlers remembered clearly how it had been before the county had a government. The homesteader was by nature a farmer, and farmers could not exist in a battlefield.

People at Arkalon tended more and more to side with Liberal in the matter, and the story spread outward from Springfield that a Liberal group had made a deal with Arkalon merchants to move them to Liberal at no cost, to make them part of the new city. This, of course, would clinch any election that might be held. But the nagging fear was that there would be no election, nor any county to hold an election in.

On Trail Street in Liberal a Springfield businessman drew a pistol and fired three shots at Jim Henson. When Deputy Vince Cole disarmed the man he was weeping, babbling about how he would feed his family after "this mob here destroys everything I've worked for."

Henson, ashen-faced, came with Frank Murdoch and others to talk to the man, but he would not reason with them.

"I know what you're doing," he pointed a shaking finger at Murdoch. "You're out to wreck us all, just for your own profit. You were behind the suit, just like you were behind the petition. The rail's coming here and you stinking bigwigs think you have it made. You don't need a county!"

When they left Murdoch was as pale as Henson, and even in Liberal some were whispering similar comments.

The day Colonel Jason Self arrived in Springfield, to investigate Judge Tomlin's call for militia, there were three shooting incidents and a mob burned two buildings in Arkalon. Before Self returned to Topeka to make his report there had been a shooting on the streets of Springfield and reports of a mob retaliation being planned by Arkalon settlers with the support of Liberal. Springfield became an armed camp.

Three editors who had once been the best of friends now found themselves enemies. Judson MacNeill of the *Springfield Gazette* used his front page to accuse Liberal and all its citizens of murder, treason and a diabolical plot to overthrow civilization. That was too much for the usually whimsical Ben Post, present editor of the *Liberal Lyre*. Penning a diatribe as scathing as MacNeill's, Post went one step beyond.

He challenged MacNeill to a duel of honor to be consummated the "day that scoundrel chooses to set foot south of the Cimarron."

MacNeill filled suit against Post. Post counter-sued and Si Rutledge found himself sued by both of them when he suggested a truce. Never one to turn down a good fight, Rutledge filled the front page of the *Arkalon News* three days later with an explanation of the stupidity and ethical shortcomings of the other two editors, and suggested all three should call on the source of the problem, Judge Will Tomlin. The day after this edition appeared, Rutledge returned to his shop to find his windows broken and his type fonts scattered.

Twice each week the grim, silent Sturdevant mounted his tall sorrell and rode to Arkalon to visit the telegraph office. On this Thursday he collected a pouch full of messages and then walked across to Dillon's for coffee. He took his cup to a dim corner table and sat there, brooding and sipping, his Alexander Henry rifle on the table before him. On his way to Arkalon he had seen a pair of riders far behind him and he waited curiously now, watching the street through Dillon's streaked window. He had recognized one. When they appeared on the street outside he recognized them both. Colonel Jason Self of the Kansas Militia stepped down and tied his horse in front of the telegraph office, followed by the Springfield deputy, Henry Lattimer. They went into the office. Sturdevant picked up his cup and his rifle and moved closer to the window to watch. Long minutes passed, and Sturdevant noticed a buggy rolling into town from the west. It was the Liberal deputy, Vince Cole.

Cole stepped down in front of Dillon's, tied his reins and started across the street toward the telegraph office just as Self and Lattimer came out. They met there and stood in conversation for a time, then Self pulled his coat tighter around him and gestured across the street. They started toward Dillon's.

Sturdevant stepped back from the window, glancing at the little curtained alcove which would be opened for the dinner trade. At the moment Dillon was outside, tending his cookshed, and Sturdevant was alone. He parted the curtains, stepped into the alcove and let the curtains close behind him. Setting rifle and cup down carefully, he turned a chair and sat in it, silent in the semi-darkness. He heard Dillon come in from the back and a moment later the bell chimed as the front door opened and he heard men entering, their boots heavy on the plank floor.

"Still cold in the wind," Vince Cole remarked. Then, to Dillon, "Morning, Dill. Coffee hot?"

The restauranteur grunted and filled cups. The men carried them to a table.

"We got some bad news, Vince," Henry Lattimer said as they sat. "The colonel has been recalled by Topeka."

Cole gaped at him. "Recalled? You mean they won't send militia?"

"Afraid not, Deputy," the officer said. "The governor is withholding militia from these four counties because of that franchise suit."

"But why?"

Self shook his head. "Intervention from Washington. I gather someone has introduced a bill to make

294

the Neutral Strip a U.S. territory."

"But what's that got to do with us? This is Kansas."

"There's more to it. The bill calls for expansion of the new territory to annex unorganized portions of three adjoining states . . . Kansas, Colorado and Texas."

"But this county is organized," Lattimer protested.

"That, apparently, is in dispute because of the franchise suit."

"The one to dissolve the four counties? I haven't even heard who filed that."

"Neither have I," Cole said. "The state court hasn't released the names."

"It has to be someone in the counties, doesn't it?"

"Yeah, I'd think so. What are you going to do, Colonel?"

"What can I do? I'm ordered to return to Hays City, to take command of a contingent of two companies. We're going to patrol your northern boundary, boys, but we aren't coming in. It looks like the lawyers and politicians have things so screwed up we don't know whether this is Kansas soil or not."

"Hell," Cole said, "this sounds like two or three years ago when old Woods was making noises about a new state. But he was crazy."

"Was he?" Self asked drily. "Some pretty astute people in Topeka think that's what the Stevens County war was all about. Anyway, that didn't come to much in the end. Maybe this won't, either."

"Not come to much!" Cole was deeply disturbed. "My God, Colonel, have you been around Liberal the past few weeks? We've had shootings, near riots . . .

and now we have hardcases from No Man's Land crossing over every day to see what they can find. Hell, it's like the old cattle days again. The town council has hired Jim Henson as marshal and he has a half dozen deputies working around the clock. I haven't been able to get any funds from the sheriff . . ."

"He can't get the commissioners together to authorize any," Henry pointed out. "They're afraid to have a meeting."

". . . so I've got volunteers working as deputies." Cole ignored the interruption, intent on his point. "And I'm not the sheriff. I'm only a deputy. But I'm appointing deputies anyway. I've got Pearly and Cass and that highbinder Roddy Lewis working my territory right now, just so I can come in here to check the freight and get the messages."

"Why didn't you come to Sheriff Guthrie for help?" Henry asked, shocked.

"I did, Henry. He didn't know how to help me. By God, I wish Sam Dance were here!"

Henry Lattimer sipped his coffee and scowled, remembering the new sheriff's confusion . . . or maybe it was pure lack of awareness . . . about the differences between "sheriff" and "lawman." To no one but himself he muttered, "He still doesn't know."

They sat in silence for a time, then Cole turned to Henry. "I guess I have some bad news for you, too. The word is out down in the strip that By Stillwell is dead. Somebody killed him down in the Beaver breaks. I haven't heard much more than that, but I don't think it's just conjecture. I've heard talk like that before, and I have a feel for when it's founded. I think this story is true."

Henry sat frozen, staring at the other deputy. For a moment he was unable to accept what had been said. How could Stillwell be dead? A man like that . . . it didn't seem possible. But Cole seemed sure. "He's dead? Just like that? I don't see how . . ."

"It happens, Henry." Cole nodded in sympathy. "Yeah, he looked to me like he'd be hard to kill, too. But nobody is bulletproof. Somebody got him. At least that's the word. I know there were plenty who wanted to."

"It seems so . . . kind of unfair, Vince. First Sheriff Dance, now Mr. Stillwell . . ."

"He reminded you of Sam, too? That's the strangest thing. It took me a while to decide who he reminded me of, but it was Sam. Not the face, so much, but just something about him. I sort of liked him, too." He turned to the militiaman, who was listening curiously. "A drifter, Colonel. At least we thought he was, but he was something more than that. A complex man, I think. A real interesting type. We arrested him for the sheriff's murder, but it was circumstantial and he was set free. Then I had the feeling he was making a personal crusade out of finding out who killed the sheriff, and why. It was as though he had some very special, private reason for wanting to know."

"He did," Henry muttered, but offered no more.

"Anyway," Cole turned back to Henry, "that reminds me. Yesterday a bone hauler came up from the strip with an odd message. He said some Double-D cattle had been seen down in the Strip. He seemed to think that was real important."

Henry's elbow almost slipped off the table. He caught himself. "Double-D? But that's a hundred miles, Vince. That's where the . . ."

"Yeah. Little hard to believe they strayed that far, isn't it? And north? In winter? And that bone hauler isn't the kind I would expect to go out of his way to carry news. I wouldn't have thought he'd have thought much either way about whose cattle are in the Strip, much less come all the way up here to tell somebody about it. But I guess you know him. His name's Harper."

"No." Henry looked at him blankly. "I don't know him. Should I?"

Now it was Cole's turn to be puzzled. "Well, yeah. He was looking for you. Asked for you by name. He wanted to tell you about it, not me."

"I never heard of him. Not that I remember, anyway."

"Well, what reminded me," Cole went on, "was that this Lloyd Harper was the same one they brought in the day they brought in Byron Stillwell. They were together. And then to have him showing up at my office to tell you about cattle in the Strip . . . I don't know. I just wondered. Anyhow, he was nervous talking to a badge. He finally just told me what he had to say and then hightailed back across the line.

"But back to Stillwell," Cole continued, turning again to the colonel, "he was the one that raided Beer City. You've heard about that. The story is he put on a one-man raid down there. Killed at least one hardcase, injured another and burned out one of their gambling joints. There are people at Beer City who probably are very sorry he's dead. They wanted to kill

298

him themselves."

"I'm sorry I didn't know him," Self said. "Although that name certainly is familiar . . . is he the one Sheriff Guthrie told me about, the one who threatened to pay a personal visit to Judge Tomlin?"

"It wasn't any threat," Henry corrected. "He just said he intended to. But I don't guess he ever did."

"A lot of men have disappeared in No Man's Land," Self said. "A lot of them, like your friend . . ." he eyed the young deputy, "he was your friend, wasn't he? Yes. A lot like him have died there. No one will ever know how many unmarked graves there are down there. And no jurisdiction to raise the question. This talk of making it a territory . . . I hope they do!"

"Yes, but not if they take Seward County with it," Cole asserted. "That's crazy."

Self shook his head. "That's not crazy. That's politics."

"Could that really happen?" Henry wondered.

"Anything could happen. I'm no lawyer, but I know it has been talked about before. A lot of research—legal research—was done on that very question after the Stevens County thing, though I never understood how it took that turn or who brought it up. People were in Topeka from Ohio, Missouri, even Port Lavaca, Texas. I remember that one, particularly. Fellow named Wilson. Used to be a Congressman. He combed through the statutes like they were going out of style."

Vince Cole had glanced at Henry. Now he cocked an eyebrow at the younger deputy. "You all right, Henry? You look a little peaked."

"I'm all right. Look, Colonel, if it's all right with you, I need to get back to Springfield right away. We'd best get started."

When the three had gone, Sturdevant stepped from the curtained alcove. He crossed to the stove and poured more coffee in his cup, then stepped to the window. The colonel and the kid deputy had gone. As he watched, Vince Cole emerged from the telegraph office, climbed into his buggy and wheeled around in the street to set off up the west road.

Dillon came in again and Sturdevant tossed him a nickel, then hoisted his rifle across his arm and left. He crossed to where his sorrel stood, frisky in the crisp, bright morning, and mounted. Instead of the river road to Springfield he pointed the horse west until he was clear of the little town, then angled northwest, straight across the prairie. It was the shortest path toward Judge Tomlin's house.

Full night was closing on Beer City when the rider from the north came in. He was a seedy man, dark-coated and unshaven, a man who knew the paths that were not roads. With a furtiveness that was a part of him he tied his mount in a dark place away from the little sin-town's bustle and took shadowed ways toward the false-fronted plank building that housed Ace Pruitt's saloon.

Although mostly destroyed by storm a short time before, Beer City had risen again. Beer City always rose again. Keno Mora's half-burned building had been hastily repaired and though it showed its damages it was patched-in and open for business. Around the buildings a motley cluster of sheds, tents and quickly-framed buildings rang with music and drunken laughter, offering pleasures abundant to those who chose to visit.

Beer City was like Ace Pruitt's saloon. It had a false front. There was no substance to the town, yet as darkness fell it shone with lantern lights and seemed as substantial as any place else in the endless plains.

The seedy man's name was Twist, and he lived in a world whose substance was like Beer City's. Pulling his dark coat tighter around him to ward off the chill in the air he walked the shadows and came to Pruitt's place. He halted outside to listen, then eased through bat-winged doors and into the stale warmth of a crowded room.

Beer City was open for business and the men came. They filtered in through the lawless breaks of No Man's Land, they came up from the lonely plains of nearby Texas, but mostly they came from Seward County, hiding their faces as they crossed the line. They came for something Kansas—at least these far west counties—did not allow. They found it in Beer City.

A piano on a wagonbox tinkled out of tune, glasses clattered, voices were raised in slurred argument or raucous laughter, and the place stank of bad liquor. Hard-used women slipped through the crowd, cadging drinks, flirting, looking for scores.

Twist edged around the room until he spotted Calico, pacing a raised walkway along one side, his hard eyes surveying the crowd. Twist headed toward him. When he reached him, they conversed for a time, then Calico led Twist into the little wing room that was Ace Pruitt's office.

"You still puttin' up money for that Stillwell?" Twist asked the kingpin.

"He's dead," Pruitt glanced up at him, then went back to his accounting.

"I got word says he isn't," Twist pressed. "And I might know where he is."

Pruitt looked directly into the man's eyes now. "Stillwell is dead, Twist. Morgan Hayes killed him. There's no doubt about it."

"Well, I never knew . . . the person who told me . . . to be wrong. He says Hayes missed. Is there still a reward?"

Pruitt paused. Twist was a loser, a dark-sider all the way, but he remembered other times when Twist had "information" and it was right. "Who told you, Twist? Who sent you?"

"My own business." The man looked at his feet. " 'Cept I know what I'm talkin' about. I figured you'd be glad to hear it."

Pruitt glanced up at the big, scowling Calico. Calico shrugged, but his eyes gleamed and he fingered the double barreled shotgun he carried.

Pruitt looked back at Twist. "How far?"

"Not too far. A few hours. You'll pay?"

Pruitt considered it. Twist was seldom wrong, and Pruitt had experienced real disappointment when he heard that Byron Stillwell was dead. He had very much wanted to do that himself. He nodded now. "I'll pay. But you'd better be right." Then to Calico, "Keep him under wraps until we get shut down here. Then we'll see."

25

"I can't pay you men," Sheriff Sim Guthrie announced to the four he had called in. "The county auditor won't release any funds until the commissioners approve a budget, and I don't know when that will be. For the past three weeks I have run this office with contract money paid by the three towns for patrol service, but those funds are gone. Springfield has appointed one of our own," he paused and looked pointedly at Ted Mason, and the other deputies glanced at the man and shuffled their feet, ". . . as town marshal. Mayor Snell has advised me that the contract with the sheriff's department is rescinded."

"That's all three, then," Everett muttered, hunching his heavy shoulders down in the straight chair Guthrie had provided him. "Liberal's put a badge on Jim Henson, and Arkalon's hired him to put a deputy marshal there."

Ted Mason thrust his heads into his coat pocket and stared at the floor. He felt distinctly uncomfortable. "Look, sheriff," he mumbled, then spoke up defiantly, "they was going to hire somebody. You know that. If it wasn't me it would be somebody else.

And I need the money."

Guthrie shook his head. "Don't worry about it, Ted. You're doing what you think is right. But I wanted you to know there isn't any money here for back pay. I owe you for a week, and I guess you'll just have to wait, right along with everybody else. But Ted," he added, "you can't wear two badges."

"Oh," Mason nodded. He pulled a Seward County Deputy Sheriff star from his pocket and handed it across. "Yeah, I meant to give you this first thing. I just forgot."

The other men were silent as Guthrie gazed at Mason, waiting. Mason stared back a moment, then caught on. He was no longer a deputy. He wasn't needed here. With a shrug he turned and left the office.

"Good luck, Ted," Everett muttered sourly as the door closed.

"I can't keep the rest of you, either," Guthrie said.

"You got six prisoners in there," Everett pointed. "You going to tend to them all by yourself?"

"There were two barns burned last night," Barney Sands added.

Will Malloy chewed his lip. He was the newest of them all. He had only served as deputy for a week, and had never been paid. Still, he thought of his lonely claim shack, the wife and two kids waiting in Hays City for him to send for them, and how he would have nothing to bring them to if the law failed in Seward County. A man with a family couldn't survive without law. "I been ridin' circuit upriver, Sheriff. If I don't look in on those folks up there, who's going to?"

Everett nodded. Those were his sentiments, exactly. "Have you talked to Vince Cole? What does he say?" Of all those who wore the Seward County badge, Cole was most senior. Guthrie had already noted that, when a question arose, the rest of his men looked to the Liberal deputy. He grimaced. They were kind enough not to carry on about how they missed Sam Dance, but they did look to Vince Cole in his absence. Hell, they even looked to Henry Lattimer. For the thousandth time, Guthrie asked himself, what is a lawman? What is this thing that Sam Dance was and I don't seem able to be? Again, he had no answer.

"I haven't talked to him yet. I was planning to go down there this evening. But I can't ask any of you to stay on with no promise of pay, and unless there's someone here I can't leave the prisoners."

"Aw, crap, Sim," Everett came upright in his chair, wincing at the pain in healing wounds. "Why don't you just stop this holy-starched-collar business. So you can't pay us! So why now?" The big jailer glared at his sheriff, and the look was a challenge.

Guthrie stared back at him. "What do you mean, so what now? I can't pay you. That's all there is to it. Now it's your move. You saw Ted hand in his badge."

"Ted ain't a lawman," Will Malloy said, quietly.

All the frustrations of all the long days of his brief term burst loose in Sim Guthrie then, and he came out of his chair, glaring at the three. His fist hit the desktop and papers went flying. "Well, God damn it, neither am I! I never knew what this job would be like! I don't know the first damn thing about being a lawman! And I didn't even know I didn't until it was too late . . ." Suddenly he heard the tenor of his own voice, felt the hot moisture in his eyes and plopped back down in his chair, avoiding their eyes. "I'm sorry."

After a long silence Everett nodded. "I guess everybody has to start someplace. Now's as good a time as any. Go ahead, Sheriff. Say it all."

"Say what?"

"Say, 'Everett, and Will, and Barney, will you fellows stay on as volunteers so we can keep this county protected 'til somebody figures out what's going on?' Then say, 'somebody go find Henry Lattimer so I can talk to him and Vince Cole and figure out what we ought to do.' Say that."

Guthrie stared at the big deputy, blinking misted eyes. "Consider it said," he said.

Barney and Will looked at each other. "At least we don't have town patrol," Will said. "Ted is welcome to it."

Moving painfully, Everett stood and went around to the gun case. "I'll tend your flock for you, Sheriff. You and Henry need to get talkin' to Vince . . . my Lord, when's the last time anybody wiped grease on this shotgun? It's a mess." Loaded gun over his arm, he disappeared into the cell block, his voice trailing behind him. "Roll call, gents! Stand up and get counted! And if any of you's got trouble in mind, just remember that I don't know which one of you it was that shot me so I'm just assumin' all of you did and I'd like nothin' better than to get even."

With Henry Lattimer in tow a subdued and

thoughtful Sheriff Guthrie rode across the wide Cimarron Valley in the light of evening. In the past few hours he had done a great many things he barely understood. He had been giving orders, but the orders he gave were those suggested by his employees . . . his volunteers, he corrected himself. Instead of three deputies north of the river now, there were nine. That was Everett's idea. As long as he wasn't paying anybody, he might as well not pay a lot as not pay a few. Of the ten men he had selected—with his deputies' counsel—six had agreed to volunteer.

It was also Everett's idea that three of the new six were now on their determined ways to the homes of Seward County's three elected commissioners. The law stated that the county commissioners were required to meet to conduct the business of the county. The sheriff's office enforced the law. Commissioners Masters, Bennet and Brown were about to assemble in Springfield to conduct their required budget meeting, whether they wanted to or not.

"Sheriff Dance called it 'tight law,' " Henry Lattimer explained as they crossed the river flats and started up the rolling rise toward the south rim, following a beaten wagon path through the still-deep valley snow that had become crust ice. "He said he used it a couple of times in towns where there was trouble and it looked like bigger trouble might be coming. He said he just reviewed all the laws he had to work with, then tightened down those that would keep the system working so he could be ready. He said the local courts hollered about it, but courts don't have anything to do with keeping the law. They just sort it out afterward."

Though Guthrie found himself biting his tongue from time to time, taking lessons from a nineteen-year-old kid, he listened. There was a wisdom here that he needed. Henry Lattimer had learned from a lawman.

"Then there's the picket line principle," Henry continued. "That's when Sheriff Dance called what we're doing along the river . . . laying out patrol routes so our strength is concentrated there. Sheriff Dance used to say if you can contain your problems you can handle them, and it seems like most of the serious problems are south of the river. I don't mean stuff like Mrs. Watson losing her chickens and Mr. Philmont getting mad at Mr. Smalley over a bill of sale. I mean the hardcases coming in from No Man's Land, and the barn burnings, and the shootings we've had. That's been mostly in the south, so the first thing we do is keep it there . . ."

Wryly, Guthrie remembered Otis Kramer's cows. Because of Otis Kramer's missing cows he had almost lost a real felon from his jail, and had missed the opportunity to add two more. He had let himself be buried in trivia while the real job collapsed around him. He had not sorted out the differences. "Thank you, Henry," he said.

"What?" The youth turned shrewd eyes toward him.

"Thank you for teaching me. Keep it up. I'm listening."

"Oh, that's all right. And as far as using volunteers, that's a good idea. Vince Cole's been doing that for weeks now."

Now it was Guthrie who turned, wide eyed. "He's

done what?"

"Used volunteers. He's got a whole crew of men helping him out, and he can get more if he needs them. Oh, I know it isn't just by the book, but Mr. Dance always said the book's only good when a man has the leisure to read it."

Guthrie glowered. "He should have come to me."

"He did."

There was silence then, and Guthrie remembered. Cole had come, reporting on the problems in the Liberal section, asking for more help. He had told the deputy there was nothing he could do. "You're right," he admitted. "He did."

"The way Vince figures it is, one way or another, the job has to be done. I imagine he'd like it, though, if you would swear in all his deputies so they'd really be deputies. They'd probably feel better about it, too."

"I'm just surprised they haven't brought anyone in to jail, if they've been doing all that."

"Well," Henry said carefully, "Vince hasn't really told them how the book says things are supposed to be done. What they've been doing is just sort of taking care of things their own way, and Vince says he doesn't want to know too much about that as long as things stay under control."

Guthrie went pale at this news, but he held his tongue. Maybe this, too, was part of being a lawman.

Two miles past the road to Will Tomlin's house they met a group of more than a dozen men riding north. Approaching in the dusk Guthrie recognized Vince Cole in the lead, flanked by Frank Murdoch and Jubal Blasingame. Close behind them were Fred and

Ralph Simpson, brothers who held adjoining large cattle spreads, and another pair that Guthrie thought were Stanley Short and Bo Caraway. More men rode behind and around this group, and some of them wore red armbands.

"Those armbands, those are some of Vince's volunteers," Henry told him as they neared the group.

They met, hauled rein and gathered to talk.

"We were just coming up to see you, Sheriff," Vince Cole said. "These gentlemen think . . . *we* think we have an idea what's going on in Seward County. Hello, Henry."

Guthrie shook hands with some of the men, nodded to others. "We were just on our way to visit with you, Vince. We need to talk."

"We all need to talk," Murdoch said. "Did you get the report about the Double-D cattle over in the strip?"

"Henry told me, yes. He said a bone hauler spotted them. He said you were concerned about it, Vince."

"I think there's reason to be," Cole nodded. "That's why I've been talking with these gentlemen. Those cattle shouldn't be there, Sheriff. It just doesn't make sense."

"It does if they're being drifted," Stanley Short put in. "No other way."

Jubal Blasingame, white hair clipped and neat beneath his sturdy stockman's hat, nodded his agreement. Of them all, he was most expert in the ways of the cattle business. He had been the first to bring high grade breed stock to Seward County. His range, even larger than Murdoch's or the combined Simpson holdings, spread along almost seven miles of the south border. "Somebody has been cutting fences," he said. "All along the boundary. Every time I get my drift fences patched I find out they've been took down someplace else."

"Cass and Pearly caught a couple of gentlemen cutting fence on Mr. Short's place," Cole said. "They were drifters, low types from over in the Strip. They didn't get much out of them."

"We just took them a couple of miles over into No Man's Land and let them loose," Cass added.

"Dumped them in a cactus patch, is what we did," Pearly corrected. "We was hoping they'd say who put 'em up to it."

"I pay good wages to cowhands," Blasingame said sourly, "so they can put on armbands and go over and take care of Stanley's fences." He looked around at Short. "Oh, I know. We're all in this together." He shrugged. "Anyhow, Sheriff, if that Texas bunch is drifting a herd far enough to get into the Strip, and somebody is cutting our fences along the border, we figure that adds up to a drive."

Guthrie blinked at him, finding it difficult to grasp what he was saying. "There hasn't been a cattle drive from Texas into Kansas . . . not that I know about . . . for years, Mr. Blasingame. Not in years. The herd law . . ."

"The herd law only works if there's law, Sheriff. Unless it can be enforced, it ain't worth the paper it's written on."

"Well, certainly if someone plans a drive into Seward County, we will require the animals be inspected for tick, and properly quarantined. We can even require dip-tanks before they cross the line."

"What we think, Sheriff," Bo Caraway said flatly, "is that somebody down there thinks he's big enough to punch a herd right up through here and glut the railhead market, and whoever he is he doesn't plan to slow down for dip tanks or inspections or fence lines or anything else. I got a friend down there, works for the Rangers sometimes—'cept things are in such a mess in Texas right now the Rangers have their hands tied—and he tells me Double-D has just about took over everything west of the scarp. He says if Double-D moves cows, everybody else just better get out of the way."

"Double-D is a long way from here."

"Double-D *was* a long way from here," Vince said. "Those cows in the Strip didn't cross the Canadian on their own hook. They came from north of there. Maybe even Wolf Creek."

It was becoming dark, and the wind was chill. "Let's go to Liberal," Guthrie suggested. "We can talk there."

They turned south. Guthrie looked back to where Henry Lattimer and a pair of young punchers sat their horses, staring fixedly toward the northeast. "You fellows coming?"

"Coming, Sheriff," Henry said, and the three set out after the rest. "Did you see that?" Henry asked Cass.

"Yeah. Somebody up on a windmill tower, watching us."

"Little cold to be sittin' up in a windmill tower," Pearly allowed. "Man could catch his death that-away."

On the high prairie only patches of snow remained

312

now. The bright days of sunshine were doing their work, driving moisture deep into the sod below the thick, brittle winter grasses. In this arid land the roots went deep and matted. Little enough moisture fell here. None of it could be lost.

"Early spring," Blasingame commented to those near him as they rode. He removed his hat, combed back his white mane with strong fingers, and put his hat back on. The dark air was cold. "Early spring, I'd say, and dry. See how the snow is going."

Sim Guthrie edged his horse over to ride beside Vince Cole. He held his silence for a time, then turned to the deputy. "Vince, I think if you had run for sheriff you'd have had the job instead of me. Why haven't you ever run?"

Cole regarded him in the near darkness. "Politics," he said, finally. "I'm not interested. Besides . . ." he seemed to think better of what he was about to say and left it dangling there.

Guthrie pushed. "Besides, what?"

"Well, I don't think I could have beat Sam Dance, even if I'd wanted to. He was a fine lawman."

That word again. Guthrie nodded. "Still, I beat him. It was close, but I did. And I'm no lawman, Vince. I know that."

Cole shrugged. "I guess people wanted a change."

"They'd have been better off," Guthrie's voice had a bitter edge, "keeping what they had."

Cole looked at the sheriff again, squarely. "Possibly. But since when have people known what's good for them?"

* * *

313

Others were bound for Liberal that evening. A pair of buggies rolled westward from Arkalon. In the first was Judson MacNeill, editor of the *Springfield Gazette*. In the second were Si Rutledge and Patty Mills. The truce was Patty's idea. She had brought them together to talk things out, had pointed out that they were both at fault in widening the schisms that were cutting across the county. Her brother, aware of the vague threat to his county that lay in the accumulated papers of Sam Dance—and the real threat brought about by the rulings of Will Tomlin—was inclined to negotiate a treaty. Judson MacNeill was of a fiercer and more stubborn turn of mind. But though he was fat and fifty, he was not immune to Patty's blue eyes.

So, MacNeill and Rutledge had exchanged apologies. Now they were on their way to Liberal to see if they could persuade Ben Post of the *Lyre* to reason.

"You haven't looked at the mail I've been getting about Sheriff Dance," Patty chided her brother as they rode through darkening lands. "I am learning a great deal about him."

"I haven't had time," Rutledge admitted.

"For one thing, I learned that he did try to recover his son. You remember, the boy he sent off to relatives after his wife died?"

"Yes."

"Well, about three weeks later . . . in 1880 . . . he was employed as a marshal at a place called Palestine. He took a leave of absence and went to get his son. But he returned without him. I have a letter from a minister there who remembers it. He says Mr. Dance was very bitter after that."

"Odd," Rutledge admitted. "Where was the boy?"

"The minister didn't know or doesn't remember, except that it was someplace in South Texas."

"How long was he in Palestine?"

"That's another odd thing. Shortly after he returned someone tried to kill him. Two men. They waylaid him at a livery stable and shot him, but he survived it. The men were never found. But as soon as he was recovered he left Palestine. He resigned and just disappeared for a while."

"Sam never told me about any of that."

"Well, I don't suppose it's the kind of thing a person would want to talk about. It wasn't until a few years ago, 1885 I think, that he turned up in Joplin and became the sheriff there."

"And then came to Kansas from there," Rutledge nodded.

"Yes. I have also written to Darke County, Ohio, to see if I can learn anything from there. There is that strange thing, that murder he was tried for . . ."

"Three men."

"Yes. That was right after the war. He must have been very young. And he was acquitted."

"A lot of pretty hard things happened after that war."

"Yes."

A sliver of moon had risen in the east, just enough to add luster to the quilted patterns of snowcrust dotting the vast, flat plains. The lights of Liberal, still miles away, were plainly visible.

26

I was dying then, and the time of things in the real world collapsed into the times of things past. I was a child sometimes, traveling the country with my mother and her songs, always secure in the three of us—but sometimes puzzled as to where the third one could be, the man who was my father. Then sometimes I was feeling again the rocking blows of Boston Charley at Pueblo, hearing the laughter of men I did not know. Or riding, running, hiding up and down the Cimarron breaks, waiting for the chase to wear itself out.

I was lying on sunbaked sand at Tucson with a bullet hole in my leg, watching a young man cough up his life blood, seeing his eyes glitter with vengeance when he said others would come for me, then buying his gun from him. Then I leaned on a cedar pole and walked with wolves. I drove horses with Chako, and learned arts from him I hadn't known.

I strolled a chandeliered hall with a gowned girl at my side and listened to the works of Victor Hugo. I saw Mattie Stillwell's hair streaked with gray and knew I had been part of that, and heard her fierce words of denial . . . her pride in the son she had raised and the man whose son he was.

I sweated in the heat and stench of branding time on the Lazy Eight, and helped hunt down the men who ruined Bill Walsh by overburning to change Lazy Eight to Two Box. I saw them hang.

I faced again the drunken man in Fort Worth who would not be called off, and saw his gun rise from its holster. I ran again from the friends who vowed to avenge him. I splinted Chako's arms and fed him Double-D beef until he was strong, then with him I drove horses. And I read again the message from Virginia that sent me toward Seward County looking for the sheriff, looking for Sam Dance.

Fifteen miles of night prairie I rode, on a horse too proud to quit, then three miles angling across a river valley to reach him before . . . but it was too late. Again and again I tried to jump a high bank with a tired gray horse, and always failed, and always was too late.

Three shots. From a quarter-mile away I heard them, from where I topped the valley's rim. I knew what they were. Two shots close together, then one more. I didn't have to know how he died. I heard it from there. As dawn light flared I pulled aside, into a draw, to let a tall young man with a badge walk past along a descending road. Tears streaked his face and he walked as one blind.

My horse was tired and I could not catch them. They rode east and I followed. They turned north and I followed but then they were gone except for a pair of stragglers. I caught them there and they talked to me.

But they didn't know anything. Some men had paid them to come from the Strip, to make up a mob. One of them panicked then and brought out a gun. I dumped their bodies in the outhouse pit at the old Fargo Springs school, and scooped cold soil to bury them.

From Arkalon I sent a wire. It might have been kind not to, but Mattie Stillwell never liked not knowing. So I sent just a few words: *Mourn him proudly, Mother. He was everything you said.* Later, when I had them, I sent her the old theater poster he had kept and her old hymnbook, still marked. *Shall We Gather At The River* . . .

I was dying and I lived it all again and it wasn't enough. A debt was unpaid. A score was unsettled. There were Double-D cattle in No Man's Land and someone had to know. I lived again the blue eyes of Patty Mills, reading my mind by soft lamplight . . . and it just wasn't enough.

Lloyd Harper said it wasn't the bullets that did it, or even loss of blood. It was the fever. When I was dying it was of fever, and I very nearly did. Morgan Hayes came that close to killing me. The first bullet may have caught folds in a pair of blankets, and it may have flattened and bound in the heavy wool of my serape, tight woven as it was. That may have cost it some of its punch. As it was, it did enough damage. Lloyd dug it out from between two ribs and both of them were cracked. The second shot, in the back, had gone clear through, just to one side. That was the one I bled from.

Lloyd's dark little dugout was as good a place as any to come back to life. The long dreams became serrated, lost their continuity and a distant voice like breeze in summer cottonwoods said, *Go, Brother Wolf*. Then I was awake and hurting, staring up at dark sod. Lloyd came in a while later and fed me, but it was days before I could send him off with a message.

When he came back he grinned at me. "You know what, By? You're dead. I heard that in Beer City."

I wondered how they knew that. Morgan Hayes had been going south. Someone down there must have sent word, then, to someone up there.

"I didn't find the kid deputy, By. But I saw that other'n, Vince Cole. I told him. But I didn't say anything about you. Maybe you want to stay dead a spell."

"You didn't leave any tracks, did you, Lloyd?"

He looked down his nose at me, insulted. It was answer enough.

The days went by and it was warmer. Lloyd came and went, about his private business, and I tried moving around a little. I paid attention to staying out of sight, but once when I was out of the dugout I had a strong feeling that I was being watched. It raised the hackles on my neck, that feeling. Yet, as far as I could see, there was no one around. I decided my imagination was still stirred up from those fever dreams. But when Lloyd came in again I told him about it, and he went out and scouted pretty thoroughly. He found no trace of anyone.

The nights were cold, but the days were bright and water flowed in the streams. Lloyd was gone again for a time, and when he came back he paused at the doorway where I sat and sniffed the air. "Spring will

319

early this year," he said. "That blizzard may have been the last of winter. Don't usually see it like this, but it's sure all right with me. Before long, son, I'll show you a sight I bet you ain't never seen before."

"What's that, Lloyd?"

"Backfirin'. Snow ain't even all gone yet, an' already that old buffalo grass up on the flats is dry as tinder. An' don't you believe them squatters up across the line ain't watchin' it! There's some up there—old man Blasingame comes to mind—that knows what it is to be burned out by spring fire. So they don't take chances. Won't be long now every place up there is gonna be backfirin' around their 'steads, burnin' off enough pasture so's a prairie fire mightn't get to them. When they start that we'll haul up on that hill yonder an' watch. Prettiest thing you ever seen at night. Fifteen-twenty mile away, an' them fires is so bright you can read a newspaper by 'em. Fact. It looks like the edge of the world is just burnin' itself away."

I could only be up and around for an hour or so at a time. I was weak as a kitten, and slept a lot. Lloyd had laid a pallet for me over by the wall of the front room, where I could get air. The room had two windows and the only door. The windows had heavy shutters, and Lloyd would never use a lamp unless the shutters were secure. Living in No Man's Land had made him cautious. But after the lamp was out he would open both windows and let the breeze flow through.

One of those nights along in there I had that hackle-raising feeling again. It woke me up, and I came up with my gun in my hand, weak and wavering but alert. But after I was awake I couldn't find anything. The windows were open. Lloyd was snoring across the room, and cool breeze brought dim night sounds. Coyotes chorusing somewhere far away, the bay of a wolf on scent, nothing more.

I lay back down and my ears rang with weakness and exertion. It had been nothing. I rolled in and slept again. But then Lloyd was beside me, shaking my shoulder.

It was still dark, but now it was dark of morning, with the feel of that time just before dawn when things go hushed and wait to see what sort of day will present itself.

"By," he whispered, "I got a feelin' somebody's around. Can you stay awake for a little bit?"

"Sure," I told him, though I wasn't too certain.

"That's good. I'm goin' out an' scout around. You just lie here but keep your eyes open. Be light in a bit. Maybe if somebody's snoopin' out there I can blindside 'em."

I wanted to caution him, but he was gone in the darkness and I didn't even hear the door as he closed it. I was dizzy, and so weak I could hardly move. I had walked around a little during the previous day, and had almost collapsed. The fever that had waned for a time was not yet gone.

Time passed, slowly, and a faint gray light grew, outlining the stark branches of the cottonwood beyond the window above me. Suddenly there was no cottonwood, but the dark silhouette of a large man, right in the window, and I saw his eyes looking down a me, saw the glint of his teeth. He carried a shotgun and he started to raise it, then just seemed to freeze there where he stood. The shotgun lowered again, out of sight, and I heard something drop to the ground. The man stood there, staring. Then he sighed and crumpled forward to dangle across the windowsill. The hand that brushed my face was limp. His hat fell off and his hair smelled of filth. I was just raising up, trying to pull away, when a voice shouted, "Now, Calico!" and the door crashed open. The man who stood there had a gun in his hand and saw me immediately. He pointed it and I shot him through my blankets. It was a good hit, but not clean, and he pitched to the side to cling to the doorframe. "Stillwell!" he shrieked. "Stillwell, I'll . . ."

I shot him again.

Outside, in the distance, I heard a gunshot, then a moment later another, and Lloyd Harper was shouting. The shout stopped abruptly.

I got to my knees and backed into a corner, trying to watch all the openings at once. The world kept swimming redly. A shadow crossed the far sill and I triggered a shot that thudded into the cabin wall. Then I lost my gun. The fever had hit me again in the night, and the world kept going away.

Someone else was in the doorway, backed by morning light—a broad, sturdy figure carrying a man on one shoulder. I tried to find my gun, but he was there and he kicked it aside. He stepped across then and dropped Lloyd Harper onto his bed, then came back and picked me up as easily as if I had been a rag doll. I wanted to laugh because I was dreaming again, but at the same time I knew it was no dream.

The staring face of Ace Pruitt passed below me, a booted foot shoving it aside. There was bare ground, then brush parting and closing as he strode through it. His heels padded below my face, but they made no sound.

"I can walk," I said. He made no answer.

Up a hillside and Lloyd's dugout was below. A man's legs hung from a window there, awkward and still. Light and shadow and no sound but the rustling of brush. Then a ledge with a dead man below it, face down. Beyond him a little pasture, and three horses standing. Down a hidden path among cedars. Two more horses waited there, a white horse and a paint. He draped me across the white and played out a saddle rope, securing my wrists and ankles, with a loop at waist and saddle horn. His hands were square and strong, his bare arms thick and brown. I raised my head.

"Too many people know this place, Brother Wolf," he said. "I have found a better one."

In a deep, narrow canyon where a little stream ran beneath cottonwoods, the Kwahadi built a tiny hut of blankets and put me inside, stripped to the buff. He heated rocks and brought them, then doused water over them to make steam. He dug the roots of soapweed and cut the leaves of agave, and made a paste of these for plasters for my wounds. I had begun to sweat. He made a tea of bitter bark and made me drink it.

"Is Lloyd dead?" I asked him.

"Your friend would have killed me. I had to knock him out. He will be all right." He made more steam and the sweat poured from me.

"Were there others, Chako? Is Lloyd in danger there?"

He shook his head. Strong teeth glinted in a dark face. "Only three. He can bury them when his head stops hurting, and he can keep their horses."

After a time my head was clear and I could move around. Chako was gone for a time. When he returned, silently up the canyon, he carried a cowhide full of meat—backstrap and tenderloins, heart and tongue. He grinned as he turned the hide to show me its brand. It was Double-D.

"This one strayed," he said. "But soon there will be more of these than you can count. Double-D is at Wolf Creek. They will drive across the flats. I know places we can hide and watch. Maybe we'll kill a few of them as they pass." He grinned again, anticipating the sport.

"No one drives cattle to Kansas any more," I argued. "The herd law closed them out. It just isn't worth it. Why would they even try?"

"No herd law," he said. "They killed the law. Nobody left to stop them."

"They killed Sam Dance? Double-D?" I was trembling, and Chako wrapped more blankets around me.

"Sure," he said. "Who else would know how to stop them?"

"But there are plenty of people up there who know how to turn a herd."

"Not a herd," he said. "All of Double-D. Maybe fifty thousand, maybe more. Too many to count. And gunhands driving them. Nobody will stop them."

"But why? Why would they do that?"

He looked at me curiously. He had long since ceased to wonder at why white men did the things they did. But he knew the question mattered to me, and I could see him sorting things out. "There is a woman," he said, finally. "She listens to what they say. She says the young one wants to take the railhead for his beef. But the old man wants this land."

"This land? The Strip?"

"All of it. The Strip, some of Kansas, some of Texas, some Colorado, maybe. All one territory and all his. Lupita listens good. She says this."

The shivers I was feeling were more than fever weakness. What he said made sense, in the way a great insanity can make sense. Someone was playing a huge game for high stakes, double-dealing for a pat hand, wiping out anyone who held high cards. It wasn't the first time. History is full of such games, and the ones that succeed become the way of the world. Such things are too big to care about . . . unless you happen to be the one with the lonely high card, the one who is in the way. I cared. The longer I thought about it the more I cared, and I felt a rage begin that would not go away.

Chako saw it, and there was concern in those cruel Indian eyes. "You heal," he said. "Few more days, then we will go hunting. This is good land for hunting. Maybe Pony Bidell will come, and we can hunt Pony Bidell."

"And Morgan Hayes," I said, tasting the words. Chako's concept of war was tempting . . . a hunting game, one on one and don't stop 'til it's over. But it was not the game I had learned. Mattie Stillwell had told me of war, as she learned it from the man who loved her, and it was not a game to play. It was a thing to stop, to put an end to once and for all, at whatever the cost might be. Chako had his way, I had mine, and I knew I would not go hunting with him. Someone had killed a man I never knew, and though my mother had never married, that someone had made her a widow. An order had been given casually, thoughtlessly, because he was in the way.

Hunting—as Chako meant it—would not make that right. One thing might. The people who did it must fail. The reasons they did it must fail. Their ambitions must come to nothing. Sam Dance alive might not have stopped them, but Sam Dance dead must stop them cold or there was no justice in this world. I wanted more than to see a few Double-D hardcases across my gunsights. I wanted their plan—whatever it was—to fail absolutely and their ambitions to be dust in their mouths. Chako was Indian and thought in Indian ways. I was too much white for that. The rage growing in me was a white rage, a searing heat that I accepted gladly just as I accepted that it was beyond all reason.

When I slept the fever was gone, and I knew that Chako—simple, deadly Chako, wolf of the Kwahadi—watched over me and was puzzled. He, who lived for anger, lacked the European blood to fathom rage.

27

The snow was gone. Warm winds swept from the west and thunderheads like brooding mountains walked across the land on dazzling legs. There had been no further snows, but neither was there rain, and Jubal Blasingame looked with worried eyes across the miles of curing grass, silver-hued and crisp.

"Bad season," the old rancher allowed to those riding with him. "Too early, too soon. Feel that wind? It'll blow like that for a month or more before we have a calm."

Vince Cole gazed off across the plains, then turned in his saddle to look back the way they had come. The land was wide and open, seemingly endless and featureless except for the occasional soddies and claims that dotted it sparsely, miles apart. "It's a hard land, Mr. Blasingame. It makes its demands. But we can only tend one trouble at a time. Let's tend to this one first."

There were fourteen men in the group riding north. Frank Murdoch and Elmer Bell carried the warrant from the Liberal town council, and Jim Henson rode with them wearing his star. Cole, Cass and Pearly wore deputy badges. Commissioner Bennett sat his saddle nervously, but his mouth was tight with determination. Blasingame and Stanley Short were grim and worried. They rode apart from homesteaders Abel Selman and Jim Reece, and from the Liberal townsmen who clustered about Ben Post. All of them were armed.

Three miles south of the Cimarron where the high plains fell away toward the distant valley they found Si Rutledge waiting for them, backed by Commissioner Brown, Deputy Marshal Tommy Jones and three members of the Arkalon town council. These six also carried arms. Only Max Bernheim, who had brought them, had chosen not to.

To the north, just rounding a rise by the trail, they could see another party coming toward them, and as they neared they recognized faces. Sheriff Sim Guthrie rode with Commissioner Masters and Mayor Snell of Springfield. Two other city councilmen were there, along with editor Judson MacNeill, storekeepers Saul Bingham and Frank Farley, postmaster Pratt and several homesteaders from the north side of the county. Deputies Will Malloy and Henry Lattimer rode flank, both carrying rifles.

When they met, Cass and Pearly set stakes and strung line to tie the horses. There were thirty-eight men here now, assembled on the featureless prairie, hatbrims shading faces from the brilliant sun. A fresh wind rolling ahead of thunderclouds in the west whipped dust from the road beneath their feet.

When they were all gathered Sheriff Sim Guthrie stepped forth in the open center of the crowd. He clasped his hands behind him and turned slowly, looking at faces.

"You all know why we are here," he said. "It has been covered in meetings at Springfield, Liberal and Arkalon, and those meetings will be posted as extraordinary sessions of the respective city councils. Likewise Commissioners Masters, Brown and Bennett have met in executive session . . ." he smiled at the three, very much aware of what it had taken to bring them together, ". . . and have approved a series of actions recommended by Counsel Bernheim. Among these is a petition attesting to the legality in the organization of Seward County. It refutes, step by step, every claim enumerated in the suit that has been filed in Topeka, and it states . . ." he beamed as he said this, watching the faces ". . . the unequivocal faith of every signer of the legal structure of the county and the ability of its sheriff and his deputies to uphold the law."

"It's damned well written, too," Rutledge declared with no slight modesty.

Guthrie raised a hand and three men stepped into the circle. "Most of you don't know these gentlemen. May I present the honorable Justice Harmon Gayle of Topeka, Marshal Thomas McGee representing the Federal District Court at Leavenworth and Mr. Wendell Pitney representing the governor. These gentlemen have advised me that it was their understanding that there was a war going on in this county, and that the structure of law had broken down. I have assured them this is not the case. I believe this meeting, conducted here in the exact center of Seward County and attended by representatives of all portions and fractions, will verify that."

Judge Gayle looked around at them. He had never in his career attended quite such a meeting as this. "Sheriff Guthrie says you men are willing to provide affidavits that I can take back to Topeka. Is that correct?"

Around the circle, men nodded.

"And that the county government and the governments of the three major towns have prepared resolutions of accord?"

Mayor Snell opened his case and drew out a legal paper. Bell and Arkalon Mayor Osgood did the same. Gayle turned to his companions. "Marshal McGee, Mr. Pitney, will you please witness my receipt of these documents?"

Guthrie took the county petition from Masters and handed it to Blasingame. It was a sheaf of paper, already containing nearly a hundred names. "Jubal, sign this and pass it around. Everyone here who has not already signed is to sign it now."

At the edge of the crowd Vince Cole eased over to where Henry Lattimer stood. "Henry, have you been telling our sheriff about 'tight law'? This reminds me of how Sam would have handled this mess."

"He asked," Henry said. He looked very pleased.

When the petition of confidence was signed, Guthrie handed it back to Masters. The three commissioners signed it and initialed all the pages. Farley attested the document as county clerk and handed it to Gayle. McGee and Pitney affixed their witness seals.

"There has been a lot of question," Guthrie addressed the men again, "about that suit for dissolution of Seward County. It looks as if everybody in the county has tended to blame everybody else. However, Judge Gayle has brought a copy of the filing papers—an attested copy—and has agreed to release the names of the complainants. Judge?"

Around the circle, men looked at one another suspiciously. Most of them had pretty good ideas who the traitors in their midst were. It was just that no two of them had the same suspicions.

Gayle took a paper from McGee, holding it carefully, turning to shield it from the wind. "This was filed in state court by an attorney with a firm in Topeka. The complainants' names are as follows." He began reading.

With each name, the assembled men became more puzzled. When the judge finished reading Saul Bingham turned to Frank Murdoch. "I don't know any of them. Do you?"

Farley chewed on his mustache, then glanced at those around him. "I've never heard any of those names. I don't think there's a Seward County resident in the bunch."

Guthrie held up a hand. "They're residents, all right. Or were when the suit was filed. Marshall McGee was kind enough to visit the federal land patent office for me before these gentlemen boarded their train. There are sixteen names here. Each of these people filed on a quarter section between June and August of last year. They are listed jointly in county records, Max. They filed with you as The Lavaca Company. La vaca is Spanish. It means 'the cow,' for whatever that's worth."

Farley nodded. "We got a Lavaca Company listed

somewhere. I never knew it was homesteaders. Where are they?"

Guthrie licked his lips. "They filed on all the quarters of Sections One through Four of Range 33 west, Township 31 south." He saw lips moving, fingers ticking off numbers as the men calculated the location in the county of these sections.

Farley got it first. "Hell, that's nothin' but sandhills! Why would anybody claim up there?"

"That's right on the north edge of the county," Stan Short said. "I didn't know there were any 'steaders up there."

"I didn't know there was *anybody* up there," someone else added.

"There isn't now," Guthrie told them. "Deputies Lattimer and Malloy rode up that way yesterday. There isn't a sign of anyone. Whoever had those claims put stakes in the ground, camped there long enough to file suit, then moved out."

"Chiselers," Blasingame spat. "Nothin' but political chiselers. Probably some bunch from the Strip."

"Probably," Guthrie nodded. "Somebody put them up to it for a reason, though, and the reason was to dissolve this county—or make enough trouble that it wouldn't matter."

"Why?" MacNeill asked.

"We're working on that," Guthrie told him. "But in the meantime, the important thing is that we have just put the county back together. I think Justice Gayle can handle things in Topeka now. I want a committee of five volunteers," he looked around him and pointed, "You, Si, Commissioner Brown, Mayor Snell, Mr. Murdoch, and Fred Simpson. You'll do. I want you five to go back to Topeka with these gentlemen and do whatever is necessary to clear up this mess. The county will pay your travel expenses and a dollar a day for your time."

"Now come on, Sim," Brown started, then caught the sheriff's scowl and subsided. "Oh, all right. I guess Ruby can keep the store."

"I'll send two deputies along with the group," Guthrie told the judge. "Now, if you and your group would like to head for Arkalon, there's a train due out tonight. The rest of you can just about make it if you hurry." To the judge again, he said, "We have some other things to do today, that I'm sure don't concern you."

The look that passed between them, and among most of those present, said it was no secret what came next.

"No," Gayle said. "It may well be that I'll hear all about it in trial court or review at some future date. Right now I would just as soon know nothing about it." He tipped his hat, nodded to those around him and went to the horses.

Ten men left the group then, seven toward Arkalon and three who lived elsewhere hurrying home to pack their bags, to join them there. Malloy and Cass went with them, both grinning. Neither had ever been to Topeka.

When they were gone Guthrie turned to the remaining group. "That was the easy part," he sighed. "Boys, we have some things to do now, and at least one of them is going to be damned unpleasant. So for that one, the only people going along will be the ones I have officially deputized." He looked around, singling out faces. "You men will be acting under my orders now, as deputies. You will take no initiative, other than exactly what I order. God only knows what's to come of this, but whatever it is, let it rest squarely on me."

Cole tilted his head, studying the sheriff. In many ways, he was seeing the man for the first time. "You sure you want to go through with this, Sim? If we've guessed wrong, you're looking at big trouble. Serious big trouble."

Guthrie's face had a gray cast, but his chin was firm and his eyes were steady. "I ran for this office, Vince. I ran for it and I won it. I guess the voters didn't elect the best man for the job, but I'm the one they said they wanted. I may not be a lawman, but I knew one once. I'm going to do what Sam Dance would have done."

"All right, Sim." Cole stuck out his hand. "I guess you might be as big a man as he was. You want me to go along with you?"

"You have your own job to do, Vince." Guthrie's eyes misted slightly as he shook the senior deputy's hand. "But thanks. I have all the help I need. You take charge here now." He turned. "Henry, Pearly, come with me."

As the three rode off, heading north, Vince Cole got the attention of the rest. "There is not to be one word about these proceedings beyond this group. And I mean *not one word*! Not until Sheriff Guthrie says otherwise. There's trouble coming, and we don't know exactly what it is but we have some notions, and we're acting on them. You all know what we expect. Somebody is going to try to slip a cattle drive in without quarantine. Drives have been stopped before, and we'll stop this one. But right now we're starting a sweep. Fence cutters and barn burners have been running loose. You folks," he glanced at Henson and Jones, "pick up your warrants and sweep your towns clean. Get them out where we can see them. We'll run them out of the county."

Seward County was organized. More than organized, it was under what Sam Dance had called "tight law." Heading back toward Liberal, Vince Cole felt better than he had in a long time.

At the road atop the Cimarron rim Sheriff Sim Guthrie and his two deputies met Barney, who had been waiting there. "Nobody's gone in or out," he said, "so I guess he's up there."

Guthrie turned to the right and Lattimer and Pearly followed. Barney retrieved his horse, mounted and brought up the rear. They rode the mile to Tomlin's house and the deputies spread around the place while Guthrie dismounted and went to the door. He knocked.

Moments passed, then Judge Will Tomlin opened his door, ducking to clear the sill as he stepped out. "Sheriff Guthrie? I'm surprised to see you. What is this all about?"

Guthrie's attitude startled him, his stance bothered him, and he glanced around, noting the deputies still mounted, one beyond the gate, one thirty yards away watching the west corner of the house.

The sheriff cleared his throat. "Official business, your honor. On the eighth day of January you entered

335

a deposition that your life had been threatened by persons unknown. Is that correct?"

"Essentially," Tomlin frowned down at the smaller man. "You know all that, Sheriff. Why the question?"

"You alleged at the time . . ."

"Alleged?" the judge's brow lowered. "See here, Guthrie . . ."

"Alleged. You alleged that on the sixth day of January you found a death threat in writing in your coat pocket. Is that correct?"

Tomlin took a deep breath, his face flushed. Something was terribly wrong here. "You know it's correct. The note said I was to be killed the following Monday morning. And it was true. You were there when those men showed up. Former sheriff Dance died there that morning."

"Yes," Guthrie breathed. "Sam Dance died there. Your honor, where is that note?"

Tomlin glared at him. "You know very well. I told you I lost it. I so stated in my deposition, as well. Are you questioning my integrity?"

"Oh, no, sir. Not at all. I just want to be very clear about it. You are sure there was such a note? You verify now that there was?"

"Damn it, yes! Of course there was! Look, Guthrie, I am tired of this. Now state your business and go your way. I put that badge on you. Don't forget it!"

"The voters of Seward County put this badge on me, your honor. You said so. And my business is this: because of the verified threat to your life, I have decided to place you under protective custody until all the parties involved in that threat have been identified and dealt with. As of this moment, your honor, you are under arrest and in my custody. One of my deputies will accompany you into your house if there are things there you will need. Another is hitching your team for you. Five minutes from now we will escort you to a place of safety." He raised his hand and Henry Lattimer swung down, strode through the gate and nodded to the judge.

Tomlin's face had gone chalk white. He seemed to be in shock. Henry saw a curtain move at the window, and started to raise his rifle, but there was a thudding in the house and he heard a back door crash open. "Keep him here, Sheriff," he barked, and sprinted past the tall judge. The front door opened to his touch and he ran through two rooms and a kitchen. He heard a shout from outside, followed by a shot and the roar of a heavy rifle, then sudden, staccato drum of hooves running, receding.

The back door hung open. Henry ran through, saw a rider disappearing around the corner of the barn. He ran into the yard at an angle, saw the rider again and raised his rifle. Something tugged at his coat collar and another heavy boom rolled back at him. He dodged aside. When he looked again the man was out of range, going away.

Pearly came out from behind a woodpile, his face ashen. "He took my horse," he said. Then he walked to one side and picked up a cut log. It was six inches across and one end of it was a confusion of fresh splinters where a big chunk had been gouged away. "What in hell's name is that thing he's shooting?"

"I never saw another one like it," Henry said. "But

Byron Stillwell called it an Alexander Henry. It sure is some rifle."

Back at the dooryard Henry told Guthrie, "That was Sturdevant. I saw him. He shot at both of us and stole Pearly's horse. He went south. Do you want me to go after him?"

"Absolutely not!" Guthrie said, aghast at the idea. Against Sturdevant and his rifle, Henry wouldn't last five seconds. He turned then to the gaping Will Tomlin. "Better get your hat and coat, Judge. It looks like some questions are beginning to be answered."

It was late in the day when Sheriff Sim Guthrie and three deputies escorted Judge Will Tomlin to an invisible line on the prairie where four men waited. All four wore the shields of Stevens County law, and Sheriff Jack Mitchell rode forward to meet the arriving party. He grinned coldly at the tall jurist. "Hello, your honor. Welcome back." Then to Guthrie, "I sure didn't think you'd have the guts. I really didn't. But we'll take good care of him for you. I can't imagine a safer place for Will Tomlin to be than a nice secure room in the Stevens County jail. It'll be just like old home week."

28

"You said that country up there would split wide open!" Davy Dawes stood spread-legged before his grandfather, his eyes bulging, neck swollen with rage. "You said all we had to do was just push 'em in. You even had my own father killed to make sure of it . . ."

Peter Llewellyn Dawes sipped his tea and studied the large young man who was his grandson the way another man might study a balking horse. "You throw that up to me, do you, Davy? About Sam Dance? You know what he was."

"Of course I know what he was!" The young man shouted. Always, Dawes noted, when he was angry he turned red and shouted. "How could I not know what he was? You've been telling me all my life! He killed my mother. He killed her like he killed your brother after the war. Crap! What difference does it make? It's nothing to me. What I want to know is, do I push those cows through or not? I can't hold eighty thousand cattle on ten thousand acres of grass. They have to move!"

"We're waiting for word," the old man said. He found this oaf of a grandson more and more distasteful. "With their lawman gone, and our men stirring up trouble, it is natural that the people there become disorganized. They may be to that point now, they may not. It is best to know for sure."

"Well they don't sound disorganized." Davy turned away, pacing to expel his energies. "Damn near every fence-cutter we had up there got run out. And all in two days!"

"Fluke," the old man said. "Pure fluke. The sheriff they have now knows nothing about strategy, and that dimwit judge has done his job. The county is dissolving. But we will wait to be sure."

"Wait to be sure!" Davy chided. "Wait to be sure. You know what's wrong with you, Grandfather? You're too old. What can they do about us? A few farmers and ordinary cowhands against our men? I say we go now. Everything is ready."

"Ah, Davy." Dawes sipped his tea and set it aside. He pulled his shawl more closely around him. It was cold here, despite the constant fire in the big tent's stove. For nearly a week now they had camped here, on the rising prairie between Wolf Creek and the Kiowa. From here they could see the cattle . . . miles of them, dark masses of them as far as the eye could see, with riders working day and night to keep them bunched at the Wolf, ready to move.

"You said this was my operation," Davy swung around again, to challenge the old man. "Is it or isn't it?"

"The drive is your operation, of course, Davy. It

always has been. But do you think that is all we are here for? Yes, we'll make money. For a season we shall make a great deal of money. But, Davy, I already *have* money. What I want is . . ."

"Your own state. I know, Grandfather. I know. Christ, how long have I heard it! The state of Liberty! Liberty! You old hypocrite, you want the state of Dawes!"

The old man flinched slightly, but then his mild, cold eyes rested again on his grandson and he smiled. "It is, after all, your name too."

"The hell it is! That's another of your fictions. I've grown up Davy Dawes, so I'm comfortable as Davy Dawes. But my name, Grandfather, is Samuel David Dance!"

"Dance was nothing!" the old man's eyes sparked then, his hands shaking. "Sam Dance was always nothing! My brother and his sons would have been wealthy men. They would have owned half of Ohio by now. But he killed them. All three. He killed them. Over some petty thing . . . a couple of farm women . . . things happen in wartime! That's when fortunes are made! He should never have come back!"

Davy watched him, mercurial mood turning from anger to curiosity as he watched the feeble old hands writhe in the fringes of his shawl. Maybe he would die now, he thought. He watched and waited. The old man subsided, trembling.

Curiously, Davy pushed a little more. "But then you had Troy send for him. That was dumb, wasn't it?"

Old Dawes breathed deeply, regaining his composure.

"I thought I could use him, Davy. I could have used him for a time, then . . ." he moved a hand slightly, a chopping motion. "It would have been satisfying."

"Stupid," Davy said, bluntly. "You broke your own rules. Instead of playing your game he played his own, and wound up being my father."

"Your mother was always weak. I couldn't have known."

"Stupid," Davy repeated, enjoying it. Then he thought of his cows and his anger flared again. "I say we go now. To hell with it!"

The cold, ancient eyes of Peter Llewellyn Dawes looked up at him, hooded now, unreadable. "Do you think you are strong enough, Davy? Strong enough to go against me?"

"If I have to!"

"I doubt it. But it might be interesting to know. I'm telling you, there is something wrong. We need more information."

"And while we wait I'm losing beef and those people up there maybe get themselves another lawman. And we lose the element of surprise! Have you thought of that?"

"Yes." The old man's voice was reedy. He was cold and he was tired. "Very well, young stallion. You may take the lead. Take your railhead and make your profits. But hear me well, grandson of mine. I will have the state of Liberty, and if you or anyone else jeopardizes that goal . . ."

"What will you do? You're old."

"There is still a great deal I can do, Davy. Don't ever forget it."

* * *

At the little railway depot in Mobeetie Troy Wilson stepped down from his buggy, lifted his valise from the floor and pulled his hat more tightly on his head against the whipping wind. He glanced up at the driver and nodded. "That's all, Coke. You can return to Double-D."

Coke touched his hatbrim in mock salute. His pale eyes, startling in a too-lean, sundarkened face, held Wilson for a moment, then turned away. "Yes, sir," he said. He snapped the reins and turned the buggy around. Its narrow wheels lifted feathers of dust in the broad common and the wind caught them and whipped them away. Wilson walked across the depot's plank walk and went inside. At 61, Wilson was a striking man. Tall, well-proportioned and crowned with a mane of snow-white hair, he had a face that had become more handsome with the years, a benevolent, thoughtful face that had served him well in his time.

But now the eyes in that face were haunted and bitter.

At the agent's window he paused. "Will the eastbound leave on time?"

"Yes, sir." The man glanced up. "They're making up in the yards right now. She'll be in the station in about ten minutes . . ." he pulled a watch from his vest pocket, "and will depart at 5:20."

Wilson walked across to the row of varnished benches and sat, his valise in his lap. Five-twenty. At five-twenty he would be eastbound and he would not look back. Where had the years gone? And to what purpose? They had gone to serving Peter Llewellyn Dawes. Mostly, he admitted, they had been good. Because of Dawes, he had never wanted for the comforts. He had lived a sort of life men might dream of, in fact. He had served two terms in the Ohio state assembly before he was 28, thanks to the old man. Those had been lucrative years. Then during the war, still in his middle thirties, he had been appointed supply commissioner for a district. Later there were the remarkable years of transition from Ohio to Texas, doing things—some of them unpleasant but many of them heady—for Dawes, and the subsequent term in the Texas Senate followed by two terms as Congressman.

No, he had no cause to be disappointed in the years. But he was no longer happy. Now he felt betrayed and bitter, and he was washing his hands of it all. He had arranged many things for Dawes over the years, but never before had he felt the old man had used him. He had helped arrange the death of a sheriff in Kansas, though, and now he knew that sheriff had been Sam Dance.

If Dawes was capable of that, after all these years, he was capable of anything.

A whistle sounded, distant on the wind, and he knew the eastbound was leaving the yards.

He had known Dawes hated Sam Dance . . . back in the old days, after that Darke County business. Carl Dawes and his sons had tried to move too far, too fast, back there, and some people had died when they got in the way. With the war moving toward its end, the older Dawes and his sons were acquiring land by whatever means they could. It was just unfortunate

344

that the Dance woman and her daughter refused to sell out. More unfortunate, her son returned home and found their graves.

Ah, Sam, Wilson thought. You always were a detective.

A jury in Ohio had acquitted Sam of murder, but Peter Dawes never forgot.

And yet, Wilson had been so sure the old man had forgiven. It was his idea to invite Sam to Port Lavaca when a lawman was needed there, to support him and get him started in a bright career.

Then when Sam suddenly married the old man's daughter, and took her away to Tulia, Wilson had seen rage in his employer's eyes. And later, when she died there, he had wondered.

But little Davy had come to take her place. Little Davy, whose name became Dawes and who grew up hating the father he barely remembered.

Wilson sagged a bit, buttoned his coat and straightened his hat. He remembered too much. He would go back east, make a fresh start, forget all this.

The whistle sounded again, long and strident, and he felt the vibration of approaching engine and cars. Taking his valise, he left the depot and stood on the platform, watching the train approach. Steam billowed from the engine's undercarriage as it passed him, slowing to bring the pullman coaches to the platform. Other people came out to board, and bustled about him.

Someone jostled his arm then, startling him, and he turned to stare into the pale eyes of Coke. "What's the matter?" he asked. "I thought you had gone."

A strong hand gripped his forearm and strong

fingers pulled his valise from his hand. Then Coke smiled at him, his hand spread against Wilson's back, and he pushed.

A woman screamed. Startled people looked and then ran forward, to recoil at sight of the mess beneath the wheels.

Coke could still hear the excited voices, the clanging of the bell, as he climbed into his buggy and snapped the reins, heading for Double-D. The dust of his wheels was whipped away eastward by quarreling, rising winds.

Across a gray prairie where insistent winds made rolling waves of grass and shafts of sunlight slanted through thunderheads to glisten in their crests, Sturdevant held his horse to a steady trot and worried over what was to be done. On this mount he had no boot for his big, sleek rifle so he carried it across the saddle.

He had started for Arkalon, after they came and took the judge. But partway there he had seen a party of riders going east toward Arkalon and knew he must avoid them. So, cut off from the wire, he made his way south, grim and silent. The old man must know what had occurred.

He veered wide around the end-of-rail camp where crews were coming in to extend the rails to Liberal. He had not been there since the day he had followed Byron Stillwell and cleaned up the trail as he went. He remembered the stinking whiskey peddler in the little shack. The man had begged him not to kill him. It had been better at the dairy farm where Penny

Bassett died. Bassett had been asleep. He had never even known it.

Sturdevant fondled his rifle and urged the horse forward. He had tried to tell them. He had tried to make them understand, but they would not. The smug, devious bastards. They used Sturdevant. They relied on him to do their work. But they would never listen.

From the moment he had first seen Byron Stillwell he knew, and tried to tell them. The man was dangerous. He would spoil things if he lived. He had thought the judge understood, had seen him go into the jail to see for himself. But then they had turned the man loose and the judge had done nothing.

Sturdevant was a simple man. He had no subtlety and he had no humor. He saw things clearly, always in black and white. There were no shades of gray. He worked for Mr. Dawes and he guarded Judge Tomlin and he did the bidding of both. Yet he wondered how they could be so smart and see so little. One look at Byron Stillwell and he had known. Sturdevant knew a wolf when he saw one.

He had hoped, on that first day, that the man might run. That would have resolved it. No one ever outran Sturdevant's rifle, although some had tried. Later he knew they would try to kill him in the jail, and he was not surprised when they failed. They were no match for that one. So he had tried, himself. Three men had died in two days, men who might have made trouble because Stillwell had infected them. But he had lost Stillwell. And there had been no further chance. Maybe they were right. Maybe Morgan Hayes had killed him. They seemed certain of it. But Sturdevant wasn't sure. Things were going wrong just as he had tried to tell them things would go wrong, had told them about Stillwell. But they didn't listen.

Across featureless miles of wind and waving dry grass Sturdevant pushed on. The course he chose kept him far afield of most of the squatter places and away from the breed herds where men might be.

Sturdevant preferred to be alone. He had no love for people, no friendships, no need for women . . . in fact had never experienced any such feelings. He was a simple man. He saw things clearly, did as he was told and his rifle seldom missed.

He knew by the drift fences when he had crossed the Kansas line and entered No Man's Land. Many of the fences were down, but in the distance he saw men repairing one.

He needed to report what had happened. He needed for someone to tell him what to do. They had taken the judge, and without the judge he was without orders.

They should have listened to him, he thought. Although he didn't understand how, he knew that Byron Stillwell was the cause of all this.

Grim and steady, Sturdevant pushed forward, a hatchet-faced, hawk-nosed nemesis in dark wind-flared coat and deacon's hat.

On a rise above the breaks just into No Man's Land he paused, his eyes catching a speck of movement far ahead. Holding his horse steady he reached into a coat pocket and withdrew a telescope. It was Judge Tomlin's telescope. He had taken it when he ran.

Carefully then, with growing certainty, he scanned

348

the distant figure coming toward him. The rider wore a dark serape and rode a sleek white horse. The slits of Sturdevant's eyes tightened. He studied the flat-crowned hat, the slope of the shoulders, the easy, upright way he sat his saddle, and he knew.

He was not surprised. He had never believed Stillwell was dead. Even after he had sent Twist to Beer City to make sure, he had not believed it. They wouldn't kill the wolf so easily.

But he would.

He put the telescope away, studied the distant rider's direction, then touched heels to his horse. His hand tightened around the big rifle on his saddle. He knew now what he must do.

They had not listened, and because they had not the wolf was still alive . . . alive and returning now to stalk among them.

A mile beyond, Sturdevant found what he sought. It was a high bank, the gulch below it hidden by brush, and it faced upon a broad, climbing meadow rising from the breaks. He hid the horse, climbed the bank and settled himself into a little pocket where he could see the whole meadow. There was even a leaning stump there, a solid dead snag shoulder-high as he sat, and he rested the Alexander Henry rifle across it. From just below him to a ridge a quarter mile away, the meadow spread open and clear, all of it well within range of the big rifle.

At peace now, Sturdevant waited.

Cloud shadow scudded across the land, across the meadow, and foot-deep grasses rippled in the wind. Overhead a large hawk motionless, head into the wind, its head tilting one way and then the other, searching for game.

He did not hear the horse when it came. Its steps were muffled by the sod and muted by the wind. But he saw it, suddenly, topping out from a low swale almost in the center of the meadow. It was middle distance, and he blinked his eyes to clear them, then leaned into the stock of the Alexander Henry. Practiced fingers cupped the forestock, raising and lowering a fraction of an inch to align the sights on the dark serape. He would take no chances. He would shoot dead center. The white horse, seven hundred yards away, walked on, its shoulders rising above the intervening meadow, then its entire body in full view. The figure atop it sat straight, almost stiff, and Sturdevant found his target and squeezed the trigger.

The big rifle's boom resounded across the breaks. Above, the hawk swerved, quartered the wind and shot away. The gun's recoil thudded into his shoulder and its snout rose a foot above the resting snag. Sturdevant took a deep breath, blinked again and rested the rifle to look beyond it. The white horse had shied at the report, now stood quartered toward him, its head tossing. Atop it the hatted, seraped figure faced him squarely.

His eyes widening, Sturdevant wrestled the rifle into place again, buried his cheek in the stock, aligned the sights dead center, hesitated a second and fired again. The rifle bucked and he lowered it. The white horse had gone into a pitching fit, circling and bucking, head down and uncontrolled. In its saddle a serape flopped limply, and there were no legs below it. The horse pitched again and the figure crumpled, seemed to dissolve atop the saddle.

Sturdevant grasped his rifle again, then stopped. There was movement and his eyes flicked downward. There, not fifteen feet away and just below him, Byron Stillwell stood, hatless, in shirtsleeves, his gun in its holster and his hands hanging at his sides. "That sure is some . . ."

Sturdevant twisted, tried to bring the big rifle's bore down, half-raised where he sat as the snag stopped it and then settled back as fire blossomed from the revolver that had appeared in Stillwell's hand.

". . . rifle," Stillwell finished.

But Sturdevant didn't hear him. The officer of the court sat in a pocket on a high bank, his Alexander Henry rifle rested across a snag, his head back against the red clay, eyes staring upward.

Byron Stillwell left him there and went to get his horse.

29

"It isn't a drive," I told them. "It's a full-scale assault and I think by now it's on its way."

I sat in a tub in the kitchen of Frank Murdoch's hotel, making a spectacle of myself, and there were plenty of people there to witness. Vince Cole and a newspaperman by the name of Post were making notes as fast as they could. The sheriff, Sim Guthrie, kept pacing the length of the room with Henry Lattimer dogging his steps, and at least a dozen other men kept popping in and out of the room.

"I don't know how many cattle they have down there, but there are thousands. Tens of thousands. And every man on the drive brings down gun wages. Unless you have an army to call in, sheriff, you aren't going to stop them head-on."

"We have protested the boundary orders placed on the state guard," Guthrie said. "In a few weeks . . ."

"We don't have a few weeks, Sim," the white-haired old rancher told him. "You heard the man. If they're moving now we don't even have four days."

"Excuse me, Mr. Stillwell," the editor said, pawing

through his notes. "You said Mr. Sturdevant had died."

"Yes. In No Man's Land."

"Would you care to comment on how he died?"

"Vigorously, sir, and in the best of health. Would you hand me that soap, please? Thank you."

"We have word also that the population of Beer City has decreased again. Do you have any comments about that?"

"I don't frequent the place, myself," I told him. "Henry, have you been taking care of that dog?"

"Sure have, By," he grinned.

"Where do you think they'll come across?" Blasingame asked.

I thought about it. "If they bunch them, the head of that drive will be at least a mile wide. I saw a dozen places east of here where the drift fences are down for at least half that distance. I guess if there are holes they can hit, where they don't have to stop to cut fence, that's what they'll do. At any rate it will be the east half, I'd think. They'll be aiming at the railhead and they'll take the quickest route."

"That means crossing the Beaver below the willow bottoms, then right up across the flats." The old rancher's eyes were hard. "Through my place, then. And maybe Short's. That's likely. Nearest the river and nearest the rail. And if they once get in over there we can kiss this range goodbye."

"We can kiss Seward County goodbye," Max Bernheim added. "Our whole case in Topeka rests on stability and the structure of law. The herd law is the basis of it."

Outside the wind moaned, a warm, dry wind that

swept the land unhindered and rattled windows in the little kitchen. As gusts picked up, some of the men looked out, worried. Clouds banked high in the west, and lights flickered in the dark bases of them.

"Selman said he and the boys might try backfirin' their place today if the wind laid," Pearly said. "I hope they changed their minds about that."

"Too much wind," Blasingame nodded.

Henry Lattimer was scowling. "Pearly, what were you doing out at Selman's?"

"Patrol," the cowpoke answered blandly.

"Well, that isn't your area to patrol. You stay on your own ground, Pearly. I'll look after the Selmans. You just stay away from there."

Pearly turned, thrusting his chin forward. "Who says so, Deputy? You?"

"Yeah, me!"

Some of the older men were trying to control tight grins. Guthrie stabbed a finger at them, first one and then the other. "If you young studs want to fight, how about figuring a way to fight Double-D? Damn! Can't anybody pay attention long enough to get anything resolved here?"

I had shaved in the tub. Now I finished my bath and got out to towel off and most of them turned away politely. Most of them. "Christ, By," Pearly gaped. "How many times have you been shot at?"

"More than I've been hit," I told him. "And that's more than enough." I knew the scars were ugly, but I had come by most of them honestly. Pearly's curiosity, though, had given me more attention than I really wanted. There are all kinds of scars. Unfortunately the physical ones are always visible. I saw Guthrie staring at the scars, then glancing over to where my gunbelt lay on a chair. It was as though he were remembering some questions he had wanted to ask the first time I met him and hadn't ever got around to.

Vince Cole had noticed the same thing, and said, mildly, "This world ain't any picnic, Sim. If some of us get through without bad scars it's because others pick up more than their share."

Silently I thanked him for that. I got fresh longhandles on, and a pair of clean pants, and somebody had slicked and oiled my boots for me. With that, and a clean linen shirt and my hair trimmed a few licks, I felt human again. I noticed that Pearly and Henry had set aside their animosity long enough to be making a joint examination of my serape. Altogether, front and back, there were seven holes in it. "I wasn't in there when most of those were punched," I assured them.

"The word was that Morgan Hayes had killed you," Vince Cole said.

"Yeah, I imagine he thought he did. He was one of the men who killed Sam Dance, Sheriff. I know who some of the others were . . ."

"We have six of them in jail at Springfield," Guthrie said. "Henry brought them in."

"With help," Pearly added.

"Six?" I whistled. "You got all of them, then."

"Weren't there more than that?"

"I mean the six I was tracking before I took off after Hayes. Let me guess: you already had Ira Fox. So you picked up Slim Cavanaugh, and Larry Doyle, and Jack Little and Hobie Moore. They were all in it.

Who was the other one?"

"Name of Byers," Guthrie said. "Horace Byers. He said he shared a claim with Ira Fox, in Stevens County."

"Byers?" I looked at Henry. "By?"

He nodded. "That's whose name I heard, By. I mean, they called him 'By', out there."

"And that pair Johnson and Smith, that had checked out before, we think they were in it, too," Cole said.

"Johnson is Ed Johnson," I nodded. "But that was no Smith. Have you ever heard of Pony Bidell?"

Some of the faces paled at the name. Plenty of people had heard of Pony Bidell.

"The Texas killer?" someone asked. "I thought his territory was down in south Texas."

"He's with Double-D. Henry, you remember the man who fired the third shot. The one who came up on the rim and shot the sheriff after he was down. Can you describe him?"

He thought about it. "Sort of, I guess. He was about middle-sized, kind of slim . . . narrow-looking, I guess. I'm sorry, I just couldn't see very well."

"Did he walk with a slight limp?"

"Well, yeah. I guess he did."

"Pony Bidell. I figured as much. It's the kind of thing he'd do. It's funny, though. I had about decided he was 'Bi.' "

"No. That was Byers."

"And the big man you saw, with whiskers, was Morgan Hayes. We might not ever know for sure, but I expect he fired the first shot out there, and I just guess Key Begley fired the second one."

356

"Then we don't have any of the actual shooters in jail?" Guthrie asked.

"You have some deserving souls in your jail, Sheriff. Just make sure they stay there a long time. Take them to court, convict them, send them away, hang them, draw and quarter them, whatever's right. They've earned it. But, no, they didn't actually shoot Sam Dance. They just helped. Well, I guess in three or four days Hayes and Pony will be back up this way again, with Double-D's cows. I'm looking forward to that."

"You don't wear a badge, Stillwell."

"I don't need one, Sheriff."

"You didn't mention Key Begley," he fixed me with intelligent eyes. He wanted to know if I had killed the man in Bingham's shed.

"I'll give you Key Begley," I said.

"I think you already did."

Blasingame had had enough. "Sheriff, time is running out. If you don't have some ideas about that herd, then I guess the boys and me will have to come up with our own. I don't want to do that, but I'll tackle them if I have to. I don't want that herd on my land."

I looked at the fierce old man and he reminded me of another strong old man who had been left dead in a canyon above the Cimarron Valley. That other old man had stood up to men he did not know, and they had killed him. Watching the determined, weathered face of Jubal Blasingame I could picture him—and maybe others with him, out in the prairie above the drift line proudly standing their ground—trying to stand off Double-D.

I wondered how many minutes they would last. Would their grit be enough to even slow that giant herd? Probably not. They would see them there, a brave little line on the prairie, and they would send a few gunmen out ahead. Then when the herd crossed the line it would flow over the bodies and not leave enough of them in its wake to identify.

And there wasn't much I could do to help them. Not up here in Kansas. Here a sparse little sprinkling of decent people were working to civilize a sullen land, and they were using the only tool settlers have . . . the law.

But law can be an obstacle to a man with other ways in mind. I couldn't help them up here. But I wouldn't be here, anyway. They had their methods, I had my own. South was No Man's Land, and down there a man could do anything he set his mind to and was big enough to finish. There was no law in No Man's Land.

They were still arguing, still bickering, when I followed a few of them over to Vince Cole's office to write up a report on what I'd told them.

I saw something begin to happen there that I wouldn't have expected from past experience. I saw Sim Guthrie, who was no more a lawman than the druggist down the street, begin organizing a plan. Backed up by Vince Cole and that spunky kid Henry Lattimer, the sheriff took charge in a way that was impressive.

"We'll need every man in this county," he stated. "I want riders out within the hour, and I want every man who can carry a gun or drive a team to report to me at Stanley Short's place by tomorrow sundown.

Tell them to bring wagons, anything that can be used as barricades. Once we see the herd we'll know where to put them."

"Those are gunmen," Short said. "A *lot* of them. We're not gunmen."

The sheriff looked at me then. "Stillwell, will you stand with us?"

I shook my head. "I've got my own fish to fry."

That left a silence for a moment or two. I guess they had assumed, since I brought word, that I was joining up. Henry Lattimer stared at me and his eyes said I had betrayed him, but then the others started glaring and Henry turned to them. "He doesn't owe us anything. We haven't done anything for him. Besides, he came to tell us. That's all we could expect."

There was agreement with that, but from that moment I wasn't part of the group any more. I was just there. That suited me fine. What I had to do was best done alone.

"If we can hold them until the herd is close," Vince Cole told them, "we might figure out some way to stampede the cows. If the front ones were turned back . . ."

"Too many," Blasingame said glumly. "You can't stampede a herd that size. There's just too many of them to react. The front ones might turn, but they'd just run into those behind, and then more behind them, and pretty soon the whole herd is just pushing forward again. There isn't any way to get the attention of that many cows all at once."

Stan Short agreed with him. "Nothin' short of flood or fire will turn a herd that size."

I guess I was grinning, because I glanced up and Henry Lattimer was staring at me. Gradually, his face began to go white. But the others didn't notice. They went on talking and planning. I was out of it as far as they were concerned.

I had finished my report for Guthrie. I put the pen away, closed the inkwell and walked to the door. As I passed Henry I beckoned him to come outside with me.

The wind whipped along Second Street and threw tumbleweeds ahead of it in long, spiralling bounds. Dust and sand lifted in little sheets from every cleared piece of ground and gave a sullen, gray-brown cast to the filtering sunlight. I watched it for a time. The wind was straight out of the west.

Finally Henry couldn't stand it any more. "You're going to do something. What are you going to do?"

"You know, Deputy," I told him, "there are some elegant places back east where a lot of undesirable people get away with some pretty rotten behavior because it isn't the custom to object strenuously. Never. It just isn't done. And in some other places, like New Orleans, a man might crap all over you and get away with it. You might challenge him, or maybe get a lawyer and go after his holdings, but a gentleman there does not simply haul off and hit him in the face. It simply is not done.

"Every place that people get serious about law and order, or civilization, there are codes that evolve that are stronger than the law. There are things a decent person just will not do . . . wouldn't even consider, much less do. That's why people like me are valuable sometimes, Henry. I'm not a 'decent' person. I'll do those things and not think twice about it, if they're what it takes."

He was staring at me, hearing what I was saying but not understanding it. He was part of this land, part of this dry, volatile, windy land and it had molded him to its laws that were stronger than the laws of man.

"I'll see you around, Henry," I told him. "When you go back in there you tell them Sim Guthrie's ideas are good. Get every man you can find down on that line, out east of here. And have them bring their wagons. But you tell them to load those wagons with water and gunnysacks, and bring plows and moldboards and draft teams. I don't know if they'll need them or not." I studied the wind again. It was erratic, but strong. "But they just might."

I clapped him on the shoulder and went off up the street. I had seen a buggy go by, to stop in front of the hotel, and a trim, wind-whipped figure had gone in there. I followed.

She was in the foyer, fixing her hair before a fussy little oval mirror between the coatracks. I came up behind her and when she saw me in the mirror her blue eyes sparkled with gladness and I knew I had not been dreaming totally alone. "I have thought of you," I told her reflection. "There were times I thought of little else."

"They told us you were dead. I didn't believe it. I didn't want to. But I've had such odd dreams, By." Her mirror-eyes held mine, searching. "I keep dreaming of people . . . people I don't know, but they are very beautiful, and very sad. They . . . oh, that is so silly."

"A man and a woman." I felt a tingle at the nape of my neck, and wanted to look away. I didn't.

"Yes. As if long ago. People in a sweet, sad story. But it had no ending."

"It needs an ending. It is incomplete."

Her mirror-eyes went wide. "Yes. That is exactly what the . . . the voice says when I dream. And then I'm frightened, because it seems to be them talking, but the voice isn't theirs. it is someone . . . something . . . relentless. Something implacable." She turned then and we were very close and she looked up at me. With no mirror between us her eyes held something else. A wisdom grew there. "Will the ending come soon, By?"

"I told you once you could read my mind."

"I have learned a great deal since you went away. The things you left for us . . . about Sam Dance. Do you suppose people dream more than they know?"

"And know more than they see. Yes." On impulse I took her hand, and her fingers were warm in mine. "Patty, do you suppose . . . suppose there were a fine theater, and gaslights and strolling couples, and carriages arriving . . ."

"And the streets are wet from evening rain," she added.

"They glisten. Suppose there were music, and someone came to your house in Camden and brought flowers and said, "Ma'm, may I escort you?" Suppose all that. What would you say?"

"Would he promise sherbet after, at the China Sea?"

"I'm certain he would."

The smile that played at her lips brought dimples.

362

"Then I should say, 'Oh, sir, I thought you'd never ask.'"

Her fingers held tight to mine. She was very close. "When stories end," I whispered, "then others can begin."

No promises. Not now. Just something to remember. I leaned and she was there and her kiss was sweet and lingering. We would remember.

My gear was in the barn, and all the things I'd need. I saddled the white horse and rubbed his ears—ears now marked in the Comanche way. Leaving Liberal I rode east for a time, then swung south. Down there was No Man's Land.

Down there a man could do anything he was big enough to do.

30

Henry Lattimer stood aghast and watched the tall, lithe figure of Byron Stillwell, elegant in dark coat and flat-crowned hat, stride away along the street and then across it to enter the hotel.

The words had been casually said—so casually, so easily, that Henry doubted their meaning and tried to find other meanings for them. Shifting winds whipped and gusted around him, sheeting dust along the streets and hurling tumbleweeds through it and over it, and Henry wrestled with a realization that was almost unthinkable. Stillwell's face remained before him, a face almost Indian in its quiet, sardonic humor, its tempered nonchalance that could suddenly turn laughing or hard, the dark eyes that saw everything and said nothing unless he chose. The face remained and the casual words echoed. Water and gunnysacks. Plows and moldboards. And in the dark eyes had been a deep contentment, a cruel, cold laughter at a huge joke about to be played, a score abut to be settled.

Henry realized his mouth was open. He closed it. He knew what Byron Stillwell intended to do.

With a start he turned, hurried into the deputy's office and slammed the door behind him. Then he told the men there what Stillwell had said. And when they stared at him, trying to comprehend the unthinkable, he told them what it meant.

Jubal Blasingame was the first to react. "He's crazy," he said. Then he jumped to his feet and shouted it. "He's crazy!"

"I won't allow it!" Guthrie stated. "Where did he go, Henry?"

"To the hotel. He went inside."

"He can't do that," Blasingame spat. "Nobody would do such a thing."

Vince Cole, pulling thoughtfully at his lower lip, turned to wander over to where a map hung on the wall. He stared at it in wonder.

Stanley Short slumped in his chair, stunned. He looked from one to another of them.

Blasingame was at the window, staring out at the wind-whipped street. "He doesn't know what it's like. He doesn't know how it can be. God! My place is out there . . . everything I own."

"It might work," Cole muttered, staring at his map. "If they are coming through here, and he starts . . ." he traced an imaginary line, ". . . here. Lord knows it could work, Sim. Look . . ."

"That's enough, Vince." Guthrie crammed his hat on his head. "Come on, Henry."

Cole turned. "Where are you going?"

"I'm going to arrest Byron Stillwell. Henry! I said, come on."

Henry was looking at Cole's map. "I guess I could," he said. "But what if the wind shifts?"

Cole's eyes were haunted then, thinking of the possibility. "He wouldn't take that kind of chance, would he?"

"Why shouldn't he?" Short spoke from his chair. "Why should he care? What does he care about any of this, anyway? What's his stake in it?"

"He wants the men who killed Sheriff Dance," Henry said.

"But why? What difference does it make to him?"

Henry bristled at that, liking the dark stranger despite everything. "He has a good reason, Mr. Short. I guess he has a better reason than anybody in this county."

"Henry!" Guthrie ordered. "I said to come with me."

Henry shrugged. "Yes, sir."

He followed the sheriff across to the hotel and inside. Only the clerk was inside, in the lobby. Guthrie demanded, "Which room did Byron Stillwell take?"

The clerk studied his register. "He didn't take one, sir. He said he wasn't staying."

"He came in here. Where did he go?"

The clerk shrugged. He hadn't seen him.

The white horse was gone from the barn.

Back at the office, Guthrie said glumly, "We missed him. He's gone."

"Plows and moldboards," Cole said. "Water kegs and gunnysacks. And me. A lot of men. And shovels."

"Everything I own is in that place," Blasingame was still staring out the window. "My house, my barns, Eleanor's piano . . . everything. I've got nearly a thousand head of prime stock out there . . ."

"Stock can be moved," Short pointed out, staring at his boots. "If there's time."

"Well, crops can't be moved," Guthrie said, pacing. "Those people out there, the homesteaders, what they have can't be moved."

"They'll lose it anyway if that herd comes through," Cole said quietly. "We'll need men."

"There aren't enough men this side of the Cimarron to fend that line," Short had moved to the map, was looking at it. "We'll need the northside people, too."

Guthrie leaned both hands on Cole's desk, lowered his head between his shoulders and sighed. Then he straightened. "Then I guess what we had better do is go get them."

"Why should I help them down there?" Bingham demanded. "That other thing, that's a threat to the whole county. But not this. You know that herd won't go past the river, Sim. And neither will a prairie fire. It isn't our concern."

The store was full of people. Springfield townspeople. They glared at the dusty, grime-streaked sheriff.

"Saul's right," Ted Mason said. "That whole bunch over there—them and their petition to move the county seat—I say they can fight their own battles."

Guthrie glanced at the ex-deputy, then ignored him. He focused on Bingham. "Haven't you heard anything I've said? It *is* the whole county they're after. If that herd gets across that line, we won't have a county for there to be a seat of. Mr. Bingham, you told me yourself that you weren't afraid of a county seat election. You said Springfield could hold its own in a vote against Liberal. Have you changed your mind?"

"I have not."

"Then the only question is, will you men from Springfield show what kind of stuff you're made of? They need help down there. Wagons and casks and teams and plows . . . and men. They need all the men they can find. Are you going to help them? Or are you," he glanced at Mason with clear contempt, "going to run and hide?"

On the windy plains east of Liberal cattle were moving. Nearly a hundred horsemen worked the miles of rangeland, bunching and gathering, pointing and pushing the sullen livestock that were the beginnings of bred beef herds in Kansas. The cattle bore the marks of Blasingame, Caraway, Short, Murdoch, the Simpsons and a half-dozen others, and among them were the dairy stock of Adolph Cort and the farm cows of a dozen homesteads. The men pushing them were cowhands, settlers and not a few townsmen from Liberal and Arkalon. They headed them west, for the lands above Liberal. If necessary they would take them into Stevens County.

"This here is almost like the old days," May hollered across to Smitty as he reined hard about to cut off a belligerent dairy cow. "Not exactly the same, but a little."

"One main difference," Smitty shouted back.

"Soon as we stop drivin' these critters, somebody's goin' to have to get down and milk a lot of 'em."

Beef breeds, dairy stock, oxen, horses and mules, they pointed them west with the rising dry wind in their faces and pushed them as fast as they would move.

At Abel Selman's homestead Henry Lattimer and Pearly struggled to bring a heavy oaken hutch from the dugout house, one carrying each end, as Dora Selman fussed about them, worried for her furniture. Peggy Selman pushed past them, her arms loaded with household treasures, and said, "Excuse me."

"Yes'm," Pearly said. In order to remove his hat he had to drop his end of the hutch and Henry, below him on the shallow stairs, strained as the full weight of it rested on him.

"Pearly!" he shouted. "Doggone it, are you going to help or are you going to gawk?"

"Watch the glass," Dora pleaded, her hands to her mouth.

Pearly replaced his hat and resumed his share of the burden. "Sorry."

From the lot beyond the barn, where Abel Selman and his sons were working a pair of plows, turning sod and crops under in a widening strip west and south of the buildings, Abel saw them emerge with the hutch and wondered whether his wife had more help than she could stand. As soon as the hutch was safely aboard a wagon, he decided, he would have to go and chase the young homesteader-deputy and the young cowboy away. "I'll send them over to help

Adolf," he mused. "He needs muscle and he doesn't have a pretty daughter to attract it."

At the head of rails men from other places went about their work, rough-laying ties for temporary rails fanning across the prairie like branchs from a main stem. At the moment they were not extending the line. They were laying out a makeshift yard capable of shunting and assembling hundreds of cattle cars. Puzzled foremen shook their heads at the change in orders, and bolstered their crews, shifting graders to tie-handling and gandymen to drive spikes.

The orders had come down from Chicago, and the cars would arrive soon. There had to be a rail to hold them when they came. Somebody had pulled some big strings somewhere and the rail crews worked to prepare for the shipping of huge numbers of cattle.

From Hugoton and Woodsdale, along the dim wagon path called nine-mile road, grim men rode eastward. They moved in separate groups, men of differing views but with a common purpose now, and Stevens County lawmen rode among them, alert to trouble. Vince Cole led them eastward, and his eyes were on the knee-high, cured prairie grass that spread like an endless sea across these plains, and on the waves and currents there that told him the direction of the unrelenting wind.

In Beer City the clustered shacks and tents of

paradise were strangely still. A piano tinkled in a saloon tent, a few revelers staggered from place to place, but most of the usual crowd was absent. No one came over from Kansas on this day, and the drifters and hiders who were the denizens of No Man's Land listened to the wind and the words of others and hurriedly packed their saddlebags to retreat into the breaks. Big things were afoot, and the furtive populace of the land nobody wanted hurried to get clear, to find safe and remote holes in which to to wait out the storm.

From south and east a band of armed men assembled on the high prairie and rode in, hard eyes alert, guns ready in holster and sleeve, riding silent and sure as they spread among the hovels of Beer City. Morgan Hayes and those with him in the lead turned to look east, where blown grasses marched away under a burning sun. Out there was where they would be needed. They would be the spearhead that would pierce the Kansas line. They knew men would be waiting, squatters and fence-cattlemen, armed and ready to challenge them. Hayes smiled and fingered the heavy gun at his hip. Beside him Pony Bidell licked his lips. His pale eyes beneath his hatbrim picked up the glare from the gray-cured grass and glowed with a fierce, happy fire.

A few miles away, on a broad, plodding front, Texas cattle were crossing the Beaver.

31

"There is a fierceness about you, By," my mother had said. "Sometimes people are afraid of you. They don't know what kind of person you are."

She had never known, either. Mattie Stillwell had undertaken to raise her son by herself, the best way she knew how. And realizing that a boy needs a father, she had given me a father—not a flesh and blood one that I could see and touch, but one every bit as real because whatever else she was Mattie Stillwell was a communicator. She could communicate to audiences through music. She communicated to me through all the arts she knew, and the illusion of completeness was real.

She created an image and the image taught me pride, and strength, and reason. But in creating it she left herself open and I learned other sides of it, too. I knew the loneliness, the bravery that masked the sometimes fears.

By creating a companion from aloneness she taught me companionship . . . and I learned to act alone. By teaching me her gentleness couched in the form of

372

a loving father, she also showed me the hard strength that must lie beneath such gentleness for it to be real. She raised me and she taught me . . . much more than she knew.

She taught me to learn, and I learned in ways that satisfied what I had become.

Had he been with us all those years I would have learned from both of them, and learned the surface things each chose to teach. But I learned from her, and from her as him, and all the sides were clear.

People in their cultures have a thing in common with the dogs they keep. They are predictable. Reliable. They are trained or train themselves to do the right thing according to their understanding of the culture.

Mattie Stillwell had tended and cherished her son as surely as a mother dog tends and cherishes its pup. But that pup, in normal surroundings, grows up to be a dog. Mattie Stillwell, with all her strength and sweetness, had not raised a dog. She had raised a wolf.

"There is a fierceness about you, By," she had said, and was puzzled and worried by it. I was never puzzled. I always knew.

Thunderheads like standing mountains built and built in the west, and it was dark where their bases poised above the distant lands. Yet the wind that blew across the high prairies was warm and dry, and it sucked the moisture from the blades of silver grass and left them dry and cured.

Spring had come too early. The grass was tall and pale and tinder-dry, and there had been no rain. The sun quartered into the west and hid behind the towering clouds, to play hide-and-seek among their dark faces.

Astride a good white horse I rode easy, surveying the prairie that spread from the Cimarron to the Beaver without interruption. Twenty unbroken miles wide, the plain of bowing grass ran east and west a hundred miles or more and the wind was a constant, physical force, sweeping along it from the west. When Chako came, finding me unerringly, I saw him first as a spot of motion miles away across the grass.

He had been watching the herd, watching the men who tended it. "They come," he said, and swept an arm to the east where the miles of cattle now moved across the Beaver.

The wind was true from the west, a sustained dry gale of thirty-five or forty miles an hour. Cattle might move ten miles a day, fifteen if driven, and these would be pushed now, heading for the waiting Kansas line. They would reach there about nightfall. I turned and rode north and east, Chako beside me.

"The gunmen left the herd. They went toward that place." He indicated Beer City, several miles away.

"That figures," I said. "They'll go east from there, along the line, and take out the defenders one by one. Was Hayes with them?"

He nodded. "Hayes, Johnson, others. One was Pony Bidell."

We rode a mile, and then another, and I kept an eye northward. In a shallow depression we reined in, and soon I saw them, tiny in the distance. A dark knot of riders, they moved east at a steady pace, on their way to do their job. We waited until they had passed, then swung north to cross their trail. We were less than a mile now from the Kansas line. The wind still held true from the west.

"This is as good a place as any," I said.

Chako backed off and watched as I untied one of the heavy jugs slung from my saddle, uncapped it and began pouring its contents into the grass. Walking the horse, I poured steadily, letting the coal oil pour in a long line southward. When it was empty I cast the jug aside and got out a Lucifer match. I struck it and tossed it. The coal oil smoked for a moment, then flared, and suddenly a great sheet of roaring flame shot upward from the dry grass, carrying black smoke above and ahead of it as the wind caught it. The flames leaped and roared and the face of the blaze raced back along the fuel-doused line. I opened another jug and moved on. When I touched off the second one I looked back. Taken by the singing wind, the flames raced eastward, their front line a half-mile wide now and growing steadily, a swatch of white fire so bright it hurt the eyes, raging over the land, propelled by wind.

Chako watched all this with eyes impossible to read. Then he nodded, and moved his dancing mount beside me. "The gunmen," he pointed. "They will run aside, maybe get free. Then they will come back to see."

"I'm counting on it," I told him.

Already there was a head of dark smoke spreading over the miles, turning the land ahead of the fire night-dark. The fire grew and spread and raced away, adding fuel to itself as it went, its tremendous heat now creating winds of its own that dwarfed the wind of the prairies. The racing line of fire was a half-mile

375

across, a mile or more wide now and its flame sheeted into the air twenty-five feet or more, mingling with the rolling dark smoke.

I looked around and Chako was riding away, going his own way, not looking back.

"Go, Brother Wolf," I thought. "My war is not yours."

I reached for another jug, then glanced down. I had brought six. I had used two and only three remained.

Moving southward a mile then, I began again. The first fire now was a distant, giant thing, racing eastward through No Man's Land, engulfing mile after mile of rich, dry grass. South of its spreading course and further back, I started another one.

Great palls of smoke now rose above the wind, found high cross-currents and began spreading back to rain dark ash upon a vast land burned black by flames. I had not noticed the passing of time until I noticed it was growing darker. The sun had set behind the western clouds, and the prairie fire east of me was the brightest source of light. I rode along behind it, following, slowly catching up to its trailing edges, and it was a fierce great shield of light in gathering darkness, undimmed by a constant rain of ash that now curled high behind it, thrown aloft by its vortex forces and falling behind to race with the west wind back into the leaping fires.

I hoped those people over the line had made ready. I had given as much warning as I dared.

What I was doing was not a thing Sam Dance would have done. But it wasn't Sam Dance doing it. I had never known Sam Dance.

But I wasn't Sam Dance. In a way I was doing this for him, because he was dead now and I had never known him and this was the best I could do for him. And I was doing it for me, too.

"There is a fierceness in you, By," she had said.

A grass fire now four miles wide raged and roared and swept eastward toward the Double-D herd, and I followed it on an ash-darkened white horse as wild as the fire it followed, waiting for them to find a way around. I waited for them to come.

Two came first, and they came in frenzy, smoke-blackened and hysterical, riding at a gallop and firing as they came. They came from my left. I heard their bullets whine. I drew and fired, and one was gone from his saddle. The other wheeled, firing once more over his shoulder, and I took my time. He was fifty yards away when I put a bullet between his shoulders.

I thumbed the spent cases from the Colt, replaced them with live rounds and went on, a hundred yards behind the tail of raging fire but still so close its heat was like a furnace. Driving, pummeling ash drove from behind, occluding a landscape out of hell, black above and black underfoot but as bright as sunlight where I rode.

Another horseman appeared, just to my right, his coat afire and his horse rearing madly. He was a black shape against hellfire, but he raised a gun toward me and I shot him from his mount.

Then there were two more. They had seen me, had gotten through a break somewhere and seen me, and they came thundering from the right, their guns barking. I heard a slap and felt my horse falter below me, and snapped a shot at the left one that took him in the gut. For a moment he came on, then he slumped forward and yanked his reins and his horse skidded into a turn and leapt. In an instant rider and horse were gone, directly into the fire.

The white horse pitched, stumbled and went to its knees. Fire-blaze glistened on blood pumping from its neck. I half-jumped, half-fell from the saddle as the dying thing surged upward and then fell, its mouth open in a scream of madness. Before I could recover the second rider was on me, but his horse stumbled over mine and went down, throwing its rider to sprawl on the fire-hot black ground. A cloud of black ash erupted about him, completely hiding him for a moment before the wind took it away. In that moment he was on his knees and seeking me. His hat was gone and I could see his face. I knew him. It was Ed Johnson.

He brought his gun into line and I fired as he did, feeling the sting of a gash across my ribs. My shot took him in the face.

The fire was moving on and I ran to stay behind it, to be near it. I could feel my face and hands blistering from the heat, but I wanted to be near it, to keep pace. A pitching, riderless horse appeared in the brilliant blackness and I caught its reins and swung aboard, sawing at its bit.

Tumbleweeds caught by the pulling wind sailed high ahead, to hit the leaping flames and be vaulted upward, balls of bright fire in lunatic dances. A jackrabbit, its fur afire, leapt from a burrow ahead of me and went bounding off to fall and kick on the sparkling, roasting black ground.

Ahead now and slightly to my right a break appeared in the wall of flames as they crossed a widening, sandy blowout where there was little grass to burn. For long minutes the opening grew and I watched it, riding hard, the horse beneath me crazy with panic but still running. They came through the gap then and I counted two, then another, and one more. The last man was aflame from head to legs, and even as he appeared his horse went down with him.

For a moment they didn't see me, a black shape against darkness, their eyes still dazzled by the searing flames. I fired once, twice, and one man lurched from his saddle to fall in a cloud of ash as a second slumped forward and went weaving away, his horse in an all-out run.

The one remaining was Morgan Hayes, and I had saved him for the last.

He saw me, then, and turned, not knowing who he saw, and I rode directly to him and hit him in the mouth with my gunbarrel. The blow rocked him, but he stayed in his saddle, swinging his head like an injured bull, throwing blood spray about him. I backed off, waiting until he was recovered enough to see me again, to draw his gun, then he paused and his eyes bulged in black sockets above a nose and mouth bright with blood. He saw me close, as black as he, soot-streaked and ash covered, and he stared.

"Sam?" he shouted, his voice rising almost to a shriek. "Sam Dance?"

I let him stare for a moment, then I put two bullets into him, a pair of inches apart.

I started for the fire again, or thought I did, but I found I was lying on my back on burning ground, and there was ash in my mouth and it choked me. I had fallen from the horse, but I couldn't remember when.

When I got to my feet I was staggering and the world was weaving about me. All around was blackness. Nothing but blackness, except out there a few hundred yards away where a racing, receding wall of bright fire whipped in the wind, and its curving line of brightness seemed to go on forever, a belt of flame bisecting the earth, taking all that was before it.

I couldn't remember how many shots I had used, so I stopped to reload my gun. My hands were burned and blackened and I dropped the ejected shells, tried to find some more.

I am in good health, Mother, I thought. I am traveling and having a wonderful time.

I have a purpose, Mattie Stillwell. You gave me everything you could, even gave me all the father you knew how, but there was always something missing. I never had a reason, Mattie. Never a purpose.

But I found a purpose. A gang of men gave me one, and I needed that. Your blue soldier died, Mattie, in a cold, bare canyon in the Kansas plains. He died because he was old and slow and wouldn't give up, and he wouldn't give up because he had a purpose. He hated what he had seen people do, and when they started doing it again he got in their way so they killed him.

I never knew your soldier, Mattie. I wish I had. He had a purpose.

But when they killed him I found a purpose. Your wandering wolf found a trail, and it's the trail of those who killed him and of those they killed him for.

I got some loads into my gun. I couldn't tell how many. The fire was going, going away, and I tried to catch it.

After a while there was a man there, a narrow man on horseback, and he blocked my path and grinned at me. He was black and streaked with the fire beyond him, but his pale eyes burned like coals beneath his hatbrim.

"Stillwell," he said. "Byron Stillwell." Slowly, deliberately, he drew a gun and I tried to draw mine but I was dizzy. I fell to my knees.

I could see him, Mattie, just the way the kid deputy described him. Dark of morning and he walked to the rim, looked down at the gunshot old man sprawled on the slope, then pulled out a gun and took slow aim and fired one shot. From where I was I heard that shot, but I was too late. I was always just too late.

I tried to get to my feet, but I fell to my knees again and laughed. He raised his gun slowly, taking his time.

Then there was a thunder of hooves and a voice like burning ice called, "Pony Bidell!" and he turned and fired.

I saw the bullet hit Chako, saw it slap him in the chest and saw him lurch in his saddle at the shock of it. And I saw Pony Bidell's grin freeze on his face as Chako's gun appeared and thundered, two long tongues of bright fire that blended together. The sleeves of Bidell's shirt seemed to explode, one just below the elbow, the other above, and little mists of red spray showered there. Bidell pitched backward off his horse, hit the ground and lay still a moment, then he started screaming. He was still screaming when Chako knelt by him, picked him up and slung him across the rump of the paint horse. Chako was weaving and he climbed back into the saddle, and there was blood on his chest and on his back. Pony Bidell's arms were useless crimson things that flopped against the side of the paint horse.

Chako glanced back at me, weaving unsteadily in his saddle, then he touched heels to the paint and was gone in blackness and wind and clouds of blowing ash.

32

Across a blackened, hell-burnt land Chako rode, life draining from him with each mile, and a dimness crept into his vision. He coughed and blood sprayed before him, bright in the dusk and the blowing wind. The paint horse faltered beneath him and he kicked his heels, urging it to more miles. Behind his saddle Pony Bidell screamed sometimes, and sometimes was silent. When he became conscious he screamed and struggled, and when he struggled Chako smashed a fist into his back, stilling him again.

Riding, relentless, covering the miles, Chako reached the edge of the burnout where grasses still smoked and sputtered into flame, and beyond it was the Beaver breaks. He kicked the paint again, and they entered rough lands. A mile beyond there was another plain, rising from the Beaver to span the miles to Kiowa Creek.

The paint horse almost made it there before it balked.

Bleeding freely, his chest and back matted, Chako staggered to his feet and lifted the gunman, his shattered arms dangling, to carry him on his shoulder. With the other hand he caught the reins of the heaving, panting paint and tugged, forcing it to follow.

Weaving a crooked path, he climbed and walked on.

Last light was on the tall, windblown grass of the prairie as Chako reached the toplands there and dropped Pony Bidell to the ground. The gunman came awake and started screaming again.

Slumping, barely able to stand, the Kwahadi tied a rope to Bidell's ankle and looped its other end around the saddlehorn. Then he brought the jug of coal oil from his saddle, opened it and emptied its contents onto Pony Bidell, soaking his thoroughly.

With his last strength Chako climbed again into his saddle, flared a match, tossed it back onto Pony Bidell, then urged the horse forward.

The animal moved only at a walk, head down, but it was enough. The screams of the gunman died in sooty flame as he burst into fire and the grass around him smoldered, caught and danced tall flames before the constant wind.

Chako lasted nearly a mile before he fell from the saddle. By that time the thing he was dragging no longer burned, but a wide fire swept eastward behind him, cutting off retreat south of the Beaver breaks.

When the Kwahadi fell his hand released the loop of rope on the saddlehorn. An exhausted paint horse staggered on, head down, to finally stop and stand a hundred yards away.

* * *

First there were flights of birds, racing with the wind, then pronghorns and some deer, far out on the grass, with three stray horses running among and through them. Henry Lattimer watched, awed and frightened.

He had done all he could do for the Selmans and the Corts, and for two other families along the way. He tested the wind and it held steady from the west. He didn't know where the fire would come from, except that it would be west. He didn't know what to expect. He had never seen a prairie fire, but he had seen Jubal Blasingame's face when it was mentioned. That was enough. He waited now with other men, one of many groups spread out over a pair of miles on the prairie that was the south portion of Blasingame's pasture and a piece of Stanley Short's. Wagonloads of water casks stood at intervals, their beds piled high with rectangles of burlap. Long stretches of plowed earth, as many rows wide as time had allowed, separated them from the knocked-down drift fence just inside the Kansas line, two hundred yards away.

Across the prairie, riding hard, two horsemen raced toward them from the south. Pearly was waving his hat. A hundred yards to his left, Henry saw Sim Guthrie raise a telescope and peer through it, then Guthrie lifted his own hat and began waving it in long, slow arcs.

Henry squinted into the growing dusk. Out there, close now, the huge Double-D herd was approaching. Pearly and Chester Grady had gone to look, now they were racing back. Double-D was coming.

The sun had long since lost itself behind thunderheads in the west, and darkness would come soon.

But the Double-D riders apparently intended to be on Kansas soil before they stopped.

More deer, nearly a dozen of them, appeared from somewhere and ran eastward, one of them passing so close to the nose of Pearly's horse that is spooked and almost threw him. A herd of pronghorns ghosted across the prairie further away, bounding and racing, fleet shadows against the blowing, silver grass. The air had a muddy look to it, and a man standing near Henry's suddenly pointed. "My Lord! Look!"

There, to the west, a rising black cloud seemed to fill the lower sky and even as they watched it grew and grew, blacking out the last of the sunlight. A bounding jackrabbit hurtled crazily past the end of the drift fence, veered into the plowed strip and almost ran into Henry's legs as it sped by him. Behind it a pair of coyotes ran along the fenceline, oblivious to the men grouped there, and in the distance a prairie wolf appeared, head high, looking westward, then turned and loped away. Flocks of pigeons winged overhead.

The dark cloud grew, curling upward to spread inky tendrils atop the wind, and there was a smell of smoke in the air. A moment later it was raining gray ash, like a veil of dancing motes out on the prairie, less than a quarter mile away.

Pearly and Chester broke out of the veil, raced their horses the remaining distance to the fence and slowed them to cross the plowed strip. Further down the line east, men still worked the plows, frantically.

A thin line of brilliance appeared at the base of the smoke clouds and Henry gasped. The fire was enormous. It seemed to spread southward to the end of the world. "It's still south," someone said. "I don't think it's got beyond the Strip."

"Where's the wind?" someone else asked, and faces turned upward to look at the tendrils of smoke racing by, now overhead. The wind held from the west. Down the line, a few men had removed their hats and were praying.

"It'll still spread," Stanley Short said. "That's the problem, even if the wind holds true. It'll still get wider and wider."

"It looks like it goes all the way across to Texas, now," Henry said.

"It might not pass the breaks. Probably won't unless there's a strong shift."

Henry peered south again. There were more and more prairie animals passing out there, all of them going east. A buck mule deer with new antlers changed course a short way out and charged toward the line, scattering the men waiting there. Its head was high and its eyes were wild. As it passed Henry could see that it ran with its mouth open. He looked south again. He rubbed his eyes. The air seemed gritty. Far out on the flats there was a darkness, low to the ground, as though a great mass were filling the horizon. He blinked, trying to clear his vision. They were cattle. He wished he had Sim Guthrie's telescope.

Pearly was beside him. "We got a good look. Rode to the head of the herd, damn near, then they started shootin' at us, so we hightailed. Lordy, I never saw so many cows in one place in all my life. Chester thinks there's more than fifty thousand out there. Maybe a hundred thousand. I don't know. Can't see the other end of 'em."

The line of fire below the smoke cloud was wider now, and flames were clearly visible, shooting into the air, great tongues and gouts of bright fire that flared upward to lick the sky. The near end of the line of fire was a mile away, and just below the drift line, slowly creeping northward as it raced to the east on the wind. Now they could see flecks of brilliance dancing above and away from the fire . . . tumbleweeds alight, bounding in an inferno of swirling, shifting ground winds and updrafts.

The wall of fire was not straight across the strip. It angled sharply away from them, its leading edge the nearest point, like a gigantic bright scythe angling into stubble.

Miles still separated the fire from the great herd, but as Henry watched it looked as though the face of the herd, obscured by distance and the sooty air, began to dissolve, streaming slowly eastward, a ponderous mass melting before a flow. He squinted and glanced at Pearly, whose grimed face had gone pale.

"Stampede," was all Pearly said.

"They're breakin', all right." Henry hadn't even noticed May standing beside him until he spoke. He looked at him and there were tears in the old man's eyes. "God help the dusteaters out there. God help them."

"You care, Mr. May?"

May swallowed and drew a sleeve across his face. It left streaks of grime. "I drove cows most of my life, son. I've rode point an' brightside an' drag, an' I've eat dust more than a few times. I guess there isn't anything in the world I hate worse than a stinkin' cow herd, but there isn't anything I know more about, either. An' nobody who's ever saw a stampede has ever forgot it." He looked then toward the approaching fire, now growing by the minute. "God help 'em."

Up the line now, two miles away, men were working frantically to turn the spreading head of the fireline. Henry could barely see them, but he knew what they were doing and he prepared to do it, too. One by one, in approaching order, the groups of Kansas volunteers broke out water caskets and burlap and took up shovels. The plowed strip would hold the wall of fire on the ground. It was up to them to catch what jumped across.

Three hundred men in all, men from Liberal and Springfield and from Stevens County, townsmen, ranchers and settlers, they faced the inferno and prepared themselves to fight.

Peter Llewellyn Dawes, a wool blanket about his shoulders, sat in his ambulance atop a hill and watched as the Double-D cattle streamed up from the Beaver breaks and northward, across the flats toward Kansas. From here he could see—or could imagine he could see—the elements of what could one day be a new state . . . his state, the state of Liberty. He had done all he could. The legal machinery was in motion, all the manipulations done. Out there, lost in the vastness of horizon, was the lower tier of western Kansas. And, behind, not much further away, the upper tier of the Texas Panhandle. This No Man's Land between was the key, and he would control it.

He envisioned a rectangle of territory, a hundred miles by two hundred miles, and his cold eyes glinted.

He looked westward then, where tall thunderheads stood above a flat horizon. Out there . . .

"What is that, Coke?" he asked his driver, pointing.

Coke shaded his eyes. There was something wrong with the horizon. It seemed too close, and was smudgy. As he watched it seemed to move, to arise, to roll in the distance like a writhing thing. He squinted and looked again. "Smoke? I think it's smoke, Mr. Dawes."

Clasping his blanket tight around him Peter Llewellyn Dawes stood in the ambulance, trying to see more clearly . . . to think clearly. The wind was a physical force, buffeting him above the sides of the ambulance. Slowly the thing on the horizon took shape, a wall of smoke, growing.

He looked north again, across the breaks. Cattle still streamed upward out there, like a dark carpet being drawn across the broken land to flow smoothly on the plains above. Distantly he could make out some of the riders, the dusteaters on the downwind side of the herd, working to keep them moving, keep them tight. The cattle moved, but so slowly, and Kansas was still miles away.

He sat down again, and a gray hue spread across his cheeks as he understood. Those men over there, those squatters, they had done the unthinkable. They had fired the range.

He estimated distances and knew he had lost.

"It's movin' fast, Mr. Dawes," Coke said. "Do you want a rider to go for your grandson?"

Dawes shook his head. Davy was out there with the herd, probably at its point by now. They were so close, and Davy would want to be the first to cross the line. Dawes felt the weight of defeat settling upon him. He had been so sure . . . with Sam Dance gone, he had been certain the opposition would disperse, would simply dissolve.

Prairie fire. He saw his dreams dissolve.

"My grandson will have to look out for himself," he said quietly. "Turn us around, Coke, and waste no time about it. We are going back to Texas."

The wall of fire was nearly fifteen miles wide as it roared down on the fleeing remnants of Double-D. The cattle ran blindly, as ash rain deepened around them and flaming tumbleweeds bounded from the closing flames to burst among them, starting new fires in their midst.

Davy Dawes rode desperately through a searing, brilliant darkness. The world was flame and motion, hot winds that seared his back and sparks that set his shirt ablaze. He glimpsed other riders and tried to call to them, but the roar from behind overcame all sound. With a curse he angled his running mount in toward the solid stream of cattle that had thinned now as they ran, and others followed with him. Just beyond now were the breaks, and they could escape that way. He was among the cattle then, edging into them, through them, running with their flow. A tossing head bedside him, a horn pierced his hip and ground against bone. He screamed, he cursed, he kept going. Beyond him a rider went down. He was there and then he was gone, horse and all. Davy roared his anger and pushed further through the stream. Crests of fire were above him now, high above and leaning with the wind as new fires burst forth below them.

He tried to breathe and felt the heat sear his lungs. The horse trembled below him, lost its pace, then regained it. And suddenly he was beyond the stampede, running for his life in open, burning ground.

His horse ran, stumbled and plummeted over an embankment to crash to the ground below. Davy was thrown clear. He rolled in sparkling brush, got his feet under him and ran, down and down, away from the fire. There were cattle here, milling, snorting, and other men. He ran.

A rider passed him from behind, his shirt ablaze, and then fell from his saddle. Davy ran, jumped over the man and caught the reins of his horse. He vaulted into the saddle.

South through the breaks they ran, a dozen or more riders, skirting the clusters of cattle, coming together as they each chose the best of open courses. Davy found he could breathe now, and he slowed to look back. Past the breaks, everything was fire and smoke, a wall of flame that engulfed everything.

Others joined him and he headed south. The fire was edging down into the breaks now, blown burning debris exploding from it to set brushfires in the broken lands. They rode through a darkening hell, slowly drawing beyond the burning lands.

They crossed the Beaver, just a trickle now, and urged spent mounts up the far slopes. Finally Davy saw the rim, and they came out onto grasslands buffeted by cool wind.

But there, again, there was a brightness and the

smell of hot smoke. They looked to their right, and one of them croaked, "Ah, God, no!" From the west, roaring toward them, a wall of fire spread across the open lands and raced upon the wind.

At the drift line men worked and sweated, men blackened and ash-covered, stained and exhausted, but always working. The worst had been the head of the flames, roaring across the land, throwing flame high into the air, exploding outward to jump the backfire line in a hundred places as men ran to beat out the flames with shovels and wet sacking. It had seemed to go on and on, forever, but then it seemed the fire was less, and they worked in a black world, seeking out sparks, widened eyes turning to the ground and the sky, defending.

The raining ash covered them all, and the sounds of their coughing matched the ring of shovels, the slaps of wet burlap. Henry Lattimer looked up from his efforts, surprised by a silence about them. Distantly, the prairie fire lit the sky to the east, narrowing now as it funnelled southward, its edges encroaching on the Cimarron Valley there and spending themselves.

In the brush lands above, somewhere east in the Neutral Strip, it would play itself out and then be over. Slumping in his weariness, noticing the other men around him so blackened he could not identify them, Henry dragged his shovel behind him as he walked out across the plowed strip and stared at the lands beyond. Few features were visible there. It was a nightmare land, black and desolate in the gloom, and he knew the desolation would extend as far as the eye could see.

Someone came up beside him and he didn't know who it was until he spoke.

"We've kept our county," Sim Guthrie said. "At least, we haven't lost it." The sheriff took him by the shoulder and turned him. "My Lord, but you look awful."

From somewhere Guthrie pulled a kerchief, and with it he wiped the soot from Henry's badge, and then his own. They looked at each other then, and the laughter when it came was beyond control. They were blackened and stained beyond recognition, but on each of them a badge shone brightly.

33

I awoke to darkness and a smell of impending rain. I lay for a long time, letting the blessed cool air wash over me, drawing it into my lungs deeply, feeling it heal there.

The sky was clear to the east but black in the west to almost overhead, and in the clouds lightning danced, displaying bright contours in random orders. The wind had lessened and now there was a feel of rain.

I knew I had fainted from lack of oxygen, that and maybe the heat. I had burns on my hands, face and legs that would need tending, but they would heal. How long had I been out? I didn't know, but there was a trace of light in the east that might have been a distant fire or it might have been the promise of morning. Starlight showed me a black velvet land where nothing moved, a land that would be dead until the rains came and brought green grass to stand above the runneling ash and recover the prairie.

Finally I got to my feet, hurting everywhere but fully alive. What was left of my serape hung for a moment, then it fell away in tatters. Beneath it my garments were charred.

I didn't try to remember everything just then. There was too much. I would let it come in its own time. But there was a sense of completion that lingered above all else, and with it was a strange sense of peace that seemed to be a part of me now and had not been there for most of times past.

Wind gusted, blowing dark ash from me, and I stood and felt its coolness.

Then something moved.

Distantly it seemed, in the gloom, a spot of brightness moved in starlight and I walked toward it.

It was a painted horse, limping badly, its head down as it came, reins dragging. The saddle it carried was dark and stained. I took its reins and rubbed its head and neck, pressing my face to its cool hide. The memories came then, and I felt a wetness in my eyes I had not known for a very long time.

I looked back the way it had come, and a great, bittersweet hurt grew inside me.

"Go, Brother Wolf," I whispered. The cool winds gusted and carried the sound away.

Author's Note:

This book is a work of fiction. Although based loosely upon an actual incident in Seward County, Kansas, in 1892, this does not purport to be a factual account. The names of towns, counties and places, and the descriptions of these, are as they may have been in the early 1890s. But all persons and events herein are fictitious, and no resemblance is intended or implied between these and any real persons or events, with one exception: an early sheriff of Seward County was killed in a canyon above the Cimarron River on January 5, 1892. He was shot three times and the wounds were as described here.

THE NEWEST ADVENTURES AND ESCAPADES OF BOLT
by Cort Martin

*Available wherever paperbacks are sold, or order direct from the
Publisher. Send cover price plus 50¢ per copy for mailing and
handling to Zebra Books, Dept. 1728, 475 Park Avenue South,
New York, N.Y. 10016. DO NOT SEND CASH.*

THE WORLD-AT-WAR SERIES
by Lawrence Cortesi

COUNTDOWN TO PARIS   (1548, $3.25)
Having stormed the beaches of Normandy, every GI had one
dream: to liberate Paris from the Nazis. Trapping the enemy in
the Falaise Pocket, the Allies would shatter the powerful German
7th Army Group, opening the way for the . . . COUNTDOWN
TO PARIS.

GATEWAY TO VICTORY   (1496, $3.25)
After Leyte, the U.S. Navy was at the threshold of Japan's Pacific
Empire. With his legendary cunning, Admiral Halsey devised a
brilliant plan to deal a crippling blow in the South China Sea to
Japan's military might.

ROMMEL'S LAST STAND   (1415, $3.25)
In April of 1943 the Nazis attempted a daring airlift of supplies
to a desperate Rommel in North Africa. But the Allies were lying
in wait for one of the most astonishing and bloody air victories of
the war.

LAST BRIDGE TO VICTORY   (1393, $3.25)
Nazi troops had blown every bridge on the Rhine, stalling
Eisenhower's drive for victory. In one final blood-soaked battle,
the fanatic resistance of the Nazis would test the courage of every
American soldier.

PACIFIC SIEGE   (1363, $3.25)
If the Allies failed to hold New Guinea, the entire Pacific would
fall to the Japanese juggernaut. For six brutal months they
drenched the New Guinea jungles with their blood, hoping to live
to see the end of the . . . PACIFIC SIEGE.

THE BATTLE FOR MANILA   (1334, $3.25)
A Japanese commander's decision—against orders—to defend
Manila to the death led to the most brutal combat of the entire
Pacific campaign. A living hell that was . . . THE BATTLE FOR
MANILA.

*Available wherever paperbacks are sold, or order direct from the
Publisher. Send cover price plus 50¢ per copy for mailing and
handling to Zebra Books, Dept. 1728, 475 Park Avenue South,
New York, N.Y. 10016. DO NOT SEND CASH.*

THRILLERS & CHILLERS
from Zebra Books

DADDY'S LITTLE GIRL   (1606, $3.50)
by Daniel Ransom

Sweet, innocent Deirde was missing. But no one in the small quiet town of Burton wanted to find her. They had waited a long time for the perfect sacrifice. And now they had found it . . .

THE CHILDREN'S WARD   (1585, $3.50)
by Patricia Wallace

Abigail felt a sense of terror form the moment she was admitted to the hospital. And as her eyes took on the glow of those possessed and her frail body strengthened with the powers of evil, little Abigail—so sweet, so pure, so innocent—was ready to wreak a bloody revenge in the sterile corridors of THE CHILDREN'S WARD.

SWEET DREAMS   (1553, $3.50)
by William W. Johnstone

Innocent ten-year-old Heather sensed the chill of darkness in her schoolmates' vacant stares, the evil festering in their hearts. But no one listened to Heather's terrified screams as it was her turn to feed the hungry spirit—with her very soul!

THE NURSERY   (1566, $3.50)
by William W. Johnstone

Their fate had been planned, their master chosen. Sixty-six infants awaited birth to live forever under the rule of darkness—if all went according to plan in THE NURSERY.

SOUL-EATER   (1656, $3.50)
by Dana Brookins

The great old house stood empty, the rafter beams seemed to sigh, and the moon beamed eerily off the white paint. It seemed to reach out to Bobbie, wanting to get inside his mind as if to tell him something he didn't want to hear.

Available wherever paperbacks are sold, or order direct from the Publisher. Send cover price plus 50¢ per copy for mailing and handling to Zebra Books, Dept. 1728, 475 Park Avenue South, New York, N.Y. 10016. DO NOT SEND CASH.